TOOTH FOR TOOTH

Book 2 of the Talion Series

J.K. FRANKO

TALION PUBLISHING

Published in the United States and the rest of the world by
Talion Publishing

Cambridge, UK

A catalogue record for this book is available from the British Library

ISBN   978–1–9993188–1–9

Printed and bound in Great Britain by
Clays Ltd, Elcograf S.p.A.

This book is dedicated to my children, Pi, Coco, and Jay. When your grandkids are old enough to read this book, tell them how much I loved you.

What three things can never be done?
Forget.   Keep silent.   Stand alone.

The Book of the Dead
Muriel Rukeyser

PROLOGUE

Before meeting Susie and Roy, I had never met a murderer. But then, I had also never lied to the police or destroyed evidence. I had never seen the inside of a jail cell. And I had most certainly never been complicit in a homicide.

I have to reluctantly admit that I am a better person for the experience. I now appreciate that murderers really are just regular people like you and me. Indeed, I have come to consider Susie and Roy more than mere patients... they are friends. And I think back on our time together with nostalgia—fondness, even.

This did not happen overnight. It was a process.

What would you do if you found out that your neighbor was a murderer? Would you double-check that you'd locked your doors every night? Keep an eye out for strange comings and goings? Would you ultimately put your house up for sale, not disclosing what you knew about the folks next door to potential buyers?

For most people, being in the proximity of a killer is neither pleasant nor desirable.

Imagine how I felt about having not one but two as-yet-undetected murderers as my patients. Sitting with each of them for hours every week. Trying to guide them toward more moderate conflict resolution techniques. And failing.

Well, I'm here to tell you that despite the complexities inherent in that situation, I found my path to inner peace and happiness.

I know. I may have said elsewhere that, as a psychologist, I'm not a big believer in "happily ever after." But my thinking has evolved.

I've come to believe more in choices—in the power of decision. This is the key nugget of wisdom I have taken away from this whole mess: We are not what happens to us. *We are what we choose.*

And I am pleased to report, for the first time in years, that I can finally say *I am happy.*

You have to understand that my unhappiness was not due to lack of trying. Chalk it up to naiveté—but, at first, it was difficult to process everything Susie and Roy told me and still be happy.

It's hard to put a positive spin on murder.

Selfishly, I was overwhelmed by the fear that they might turn on me. They had shared everything about their crimes with me in meticulous detail. It was manifestly apparent that I was the weak link. The one person who could bring them down.

I was not just *a* loose end.

I was *the* loose end.

And, though I tried, I could not initially find peace under these circumstances. But, as I said earlier, happiness is a choice. And it was a choice that *I made* which finally ended my torment and brought me to a place where I could be at peace—even though everything ended tragically: my relationship with Susie and Roy, their marriage, the whole mess.

For you to understand the rest of my journey with Susie and Roy, I must share with you something that happened years ago at an ostensibly happy event. I say 'ostensibly' because it was a wonderful night for *almost* everyone concerned.

There were two people at that event who figure in this story—in my story.

The first is Sandra Bissette. For her, the night in question was the beginning of what would become a successful career in politics and law.

For the other, Billy Applegate, the night would end in tragedy.

PART ONE

Billy Applegate
1974

Everybody loves a party.

And there's nothing quite like an election night party.

What makes an election night celebration different? The guest of honor. You see, all parties—birthdays, anniversaries, wakes—feature a guest of honor. But an election night party is a completely different animal because it isn't about any one person or couple. It's not even about the candidates.

At an election night party, the guests of honor are the attendees.

The people who gather to watch election results together are all of one mind. Of one spirit. They are like pack animals, all focused on the same outcome. They all share the same heroes and the same enemies.

If their candidates win, they all win. And a "win" means real-world changes for them—tax breaks, preferential government spending, judicial appointments—and money in their pockets.

Now, *that's* a party.

This particular election night party took place in Maryland in 1974. To be precise—because I can be—this party was held on the night of the 1974 midterm elections, on Tuesday, November 5th.

It was a good year for Democrats.

This was the first national election after Watergate. Nixon's resignation had severely damaged the Republicans' chances in the election. Gerald Ford was just three months into his presidency, having taken over from Richard Nixon a few months earlier. And, of course, having pardoned Nixon in September, Ford had destroyed his own hopes for re-election and added to the national animus against Republicans.

This election night party took place in a spacious colonial-style home decorated in red, white, and blue, with American flags hanging from the windows and banisters. It featured a spacious living and dining area. The kitchen was large and well-equipped. There was a generous backyard with a comfortable deck and a terrace around the pool. All four bedrooms—aside from one guest bedroom—were upstairs.

There was even a "pin the tail on the donkey" game set up near the bar, for those with a sense of humor. No one actually played.

This house belonged to Dan and Annette Applegate, two proud and active members of the Democratic party in Maryland.

Dan's family had always been active in politics. His grandfather had been a state representative. His father had served as a county judge for most of his career. Dan—born Daniel Parsons Applegate IV—was the fourth generation of Applegates admitted to the Maryland bar. While he would never actually serve in public office, he understood the value of political contacts and actively cultivated them.

This party was part of that effort.

Dan was dressed in a three-piece, tan wool suit, a white Brooks Brothers shirt, and a burgundy silk tie. The lapels and tie were wide, and the shirt collar oversized—all very fashionable at the time. Annette wore a slim, gold-belted, navy blue flare-leg pantsuit with a pale blue silk blouse and a pair of simple gold earrings. Apropos for the gathering, and it went quite nicely with all the flags, she'd decided.

Their twelve-year-old son, Billy Applegate, was in dark green overalls with a white shirt and blue Keds. A handsome boy, Billy had inherited his mother's cornflower blue eyes and his father's thick sandy blond hair, which he wore in a neatly trimmed surfer cut.

Billy was an only child. His parents doted on him, as did his grandparents since he was the only grandchild in both families. Even so, Billy was a good boy and knew to stay out of the way when his parents had guests, though he stayed close enough to be in the mix and see what was going on. He was at the age where he still enjoyed watching the grown-ups. Spying on them. In fact, he was familiar with many of the faces that night from other events of this kind. It was a small community.

Tonight, Tuesday night, the guests were arriving early, many coming over straight after work before polling places even closed.

It was going to be a long night.

The band played. Alcohol flowed. Anticipation and excitement were in the air at the prospect of big Democrat wins. And, after everything Nixon had put the nation through, how could voters not want a change?

In the living room, a handsome mahogany console TV with a big twenty-five-inch-diagonal color screen announced results as they came in. Dan was loitering by the avocado green Trimline rotary phone, mounted on the kitchen wall, that rang periodically with live information. The spring-coiled, twelve-foot receiver cord allowed him to pace anxiously as he fielded calls from the few Democrats charged with providing up-to-the-minute results from county polling.

Remember, this was back in the days before computerized voting machines. Back then, voters travelled to their precinct's designated polling station and used a machine to punch holes in their ballot. These were then collected and transported to a central counting center where the ballots were put through a counting machine which tabulated the results that were then released to the public.

Dan relayed results to his guests, with each ring of the phone bringing more good news. More cheering and more drinking.

It was a good year to be a Democrat.

At the peak of festivities, there were over 250 guests in and around the property, to the point where the party overflowed onto the street, which was not a problem. No one was going to complain, as most of the neighbors were in attendance. And these were all good white folk. The police were kind enough to block off both ends of the street and make sure that those who'd had too much to drink made it home safely.

Inside, the house was a political orgy. Supporters rubbed elbows with candidates. Candidates rubbed elbows with incumbents. Incumbents rubbed elbows with donors. And lobbyists rubbed elbows with everyone except each other.

There were a number of judges in attendance. Several city council members hovered by the buffet, and a few state representatives were sprinkled through the crowd.

It was into this whirlwind of excitement that Sandra Bissette arrived.

At a time when men still ran everything in politics, Sandra hoped to make a name for herself. The fact that she was a Yale-graduated lawyer didn't hurt, nor did the fact that she had both the figure and the looks of Jackie Kennedy.

Sandra was the daughter of lifelong Democrats, and her father happened to be the county sheriff. Although Sandra was not part of the elite set in Maryland, she was making her way. She was two years into working as an associate at a top law firm after having done a couple of high-level summer internships in D.C.

That night, Sandra was primarily interested in meeting two people: one was Annette Applegate. Although Sandra knew that both Dan and Annette were active in the Maryland Democratic party, Dan was known to be a snob—his career consisted of riding on his family's coattails. Annette was universally recognized as the nicer of the two. Annette knew everyone, and everyone loved Annette. It was with her that Sandra was hoping to build a connection.

The second person who Sandra had added to her charm offensive for the evening was Harrison Kraft—another young Yale lawyer who, unlike her, was connected in all the right ways. Having graduated a few years ahead of her from law school, Harrison was running for state representative. He checked all the right boxes—family pedigree, education, professional credentials. There was no doubt the man was going places. Sandra had heard good things about him as a person and was interested in seeing for herself.

It was a little after 9:00 p.m.—Dan had just announced the results from Precinct Four in Montgomery County when Sandra saw an opening. Annette was by the buffet chatting with Howard Patrick, an older lobbyist—handsy, and a bit of a bore. Sandra straightened her back, raised her chin, and approached.

"Hello Howard," she said with a big smile.

"Sandra! Hello, my dear. Don't you look beautiful tonight?"

"Why, thank you, Howard. Ever the charmer," she said, allowing him to kiss her hand.

"Have you met our hostess, Annette Applegate?"

As Sandra turned to greet Annette, she noticed that the woman was looking past her, over her shoulder.

"Um, excuse me, young man!" Annette said, eyebrows raised and pearly white teeth dazzling.

Sandra turned and followed Annette's gaze to a young boy in green overalls filching shrimp from the buffet. She guessed he was just shy of being a teenager.

"Aw, crap," said Billy as he chewed.

"Come here, you," Annette said, narrowing her eyes in mock disapproval.

The boy hesitated as he took in the young woman, the fat old man, and his mother, who stood waiting for him expectantly with her hands on her hips. He'd never seen the young woman before. She was new.

Unconsciously, he slowly moved to return the three shrimp in his sticky hand to the platter.

"With the shrimp, silly," his mother said, shaking her head.

Billy moved toward her, chewing rapidly so he could stuff the other shrimp into his mouth.

Howard put his hand against the small of Sandra's back, a little too low, and harrumphed to her under his breath, "Better seen, not heard. That's how it used to be."

Sandra tried to smile and fought the instinct to pull away. Howard's breath smelled of scotch and cigarettes.

Annette overheard, but ignored the old lobbyist's comment.

"I suppose I don't need to ask if you've had dinner? I left meatloaf for you in the kitchen."

"I know. But, Mom, these shrimp are amazing."

"And the meatballs?" asked Annette, looking over Billy toward the platter on the buffet.

Billy blushed. "Those, too."

"Well, it's getting a bit late for you," Annette said, ruffling her son's fair hair and then kissing him on the forehead, making him squirm. "Finish up the shrimp and get to bed."

"What about Dad?" Billy asked, looking around.

Annette's face darkened, and she sighed. "I'll send him up for a goodnight kiss. But you come along now, young man." She put her hands on her son's shoulders and steered him towards the stairs. "Excuse me for a moment," she said over her shoulder.

Shit, thought Sandra as she twisted politely away, getting the old lobbyist's hand off her lower back as he struck up a conversation. While she tried to focus on what he was saying, it was all she could do not to stare at the green thing wedged in between the man's tar-stained teeth.

It took her ten minutes to extricate herself from Howard, thanks to Alan Watts—a wiry man who was only modestly more interesting. His family ran a small chain of grocery stores. Alan had asked her out a while back, and though she'd declined, he still had hopes—she could tell.

After a few more minutes of polite conversation, Sandra fell back on "old reliable" with a forced smile. "Excuse me, gentlemen… ladies' room."

Once she was sure she had escaped, she continued to work the room. About half an hour later, as she accepted another glass of white wine from a passing waiter, she felt a hand pressing low on the small of her back.

Oh fuck, not again.

"Yes, Howard?" She turned, fake smile firmly in place, to find Annette Applegate standing behind her.

"Gotcha!" laughed Annette.

Sandra laughed, both from relief and from delight at the

inside joke made by the woman to whom she'd hoped to ingratiate herself.

This is going to be a great night.

While Sandra and Annette chatted amiably, many other members of the party were well beyond civility.

The drinking had begun five hours earlier, but there was more than just alcohol flowing. Other substances were being abused. It was all very discreet, of course. Most were partaking solely for recreational purposes, but a few were ingesting more heavily. Beyond alcohol and drugs—and most hazardous of all, given that it was infecting everyone to some degree and was in ample supply—was the potent and dangerous combination of two psychological stimulants, victory and power.

You see, politics doesn't attract only "normal" people. As in every part of society, there is a spectrum. And politics, too, has its outliers. The smug and the superior. The arrogant and the snide. And the sociopaths.

Victory and power are dangerous to all, but more so to the sociopath.

Do not consume alcohol or operate heavy machinery while taking...

For these select few, the alcohol, drugs, and victory combined with power was toxic. It created a euphoria that knew no rules.

No limits.

No fear.

* * *

Upstairs, Billy had fallen asleep with the soothing press of his mother's goodnight kiss still fresh on his cheek.

A small nightlight plugged into a wall socket illuminated his bedroom, casting a warm glow on a baseball snuggled in a catcher's mitt that lay in a corner next to a wooden Adirondack baseball bat.

On one end of his small dresser sat a model airplane—a Douglas A-20 Havoc that he'd built with his grandfather. It was a replica of the plane Gramps had flown during World War II. The model was flanked by a teddy bear that Billy claimed he'd outgrown but refused to give away. The other end of the dresser was reserved for the little boy's current prized possession—Rock'em Sock'em Robots. A gift from his parents for his birthday.

The room was quiet, the party sounds muffled.

Suddenly, the door opened, spilling light into the little boy's room along with the blare of music and the chaotic chatter of voices. Then, just as quickly, the door shut, returning the room to calm semi-darkness.

Billy was groggy and didn't try to open his eyes. Instead, he just spoke out loud. "Dad?"

He felt the bed sag as his father sat next to him in a cloud smelling of alcohol and cigars.

Then he felt dry lips on his forehead. The kiss made him smile sleepily.

A hand stroked his head and his hair as Billy snuggled into his pillow and drifted back to sleep.

Suddenly, the same hand that had been stroking his hair gently clamped over his mouth. It was a man's hand, but it was soft. Clammy. It was not his father's....

Billy tried to sit up, but the hand squeezed harder, the man leaning into him, pushing him down and pinning him to the bed as a second hand groped at him, pulling away his sheets.

Billy didn't know what to do. He was terrified. He opened his eyes, but with just the little nightlight on, he couldn't see anything other than the vague shape of the form pressing down on him. He could smell booze and food on the man's warm breath.

Tears came as the vise over Billy's mouth forced him to suck air noisily through his nose as the groping continued—searching, finding, fondling, stroking, then reaching, penetrating, sending a hot shard of searing pain through his body. Inside.

He tried to fight, but couldn't. The hands were too strong. The body too heavy. He felt sick. The stench of cigars, food, and alcohol on fetid breath was nauseating. And he was scared. Terrified. In pain.

Bile rose in Billy's throat. But the hand over his mouth prevented him from vomiting. He gagged, then swallowed everything back down.

His body began to convulse.

To thrash.

As it did, the second hand stopped.

The man's weight eased on top of his body, no longer pinning him down. The hand over his mouth loosened slightly, and Billy felt the other stroking his hair. He wanted to move, but he was paralyzed with fear.

The whole ordeal lasted minutes, but it felt like hours.

Then the presence leaned over and whispered, "Sleep. Sleep. You were dreaming. Go back to sleep."

The weight lifted from the bed, and as it did, the hand fell away from Billy's mouth, leaving him shivering in the aftermath.

The door opened, first slightly. Through the crack, the man looked out into the hall as the babble of music and voices invaded the bedroom. Then the door swung fully open, and as it did, Billy saw the man clearly in the light from the hallway. The image burned itself into his memory. The image of a stranger whose identity he would eventually learn.

The door closed and the crowd cheered as the band started playing—"You Ain't Seen Nothing Yet."

And Billy Applegate cried himself into a fitful sleep.

CHAPTER ONE

Sunday
January 7, 2018
Beaver Creek Village

Winter had come to Beaver Creek Village. And a beautiful winter it was. Only three days earlier, Susie and Roy Cruise had sat on their balcony having that fateful discussion about life, death, and revenge that set everything in motion against Joe Harlan Junior.

Now, only three hundred yards away from that balcony as a crow flies, another conversation took shape that would unknowingly set Bethany Rosen and Kristy Wise on a collision course with Susie and Roy.

The Beaver Creek Village plaza and its surrounding buildings were gaily decorated with holiday lights while the un-melting, sharp-edged features of giant ice sculptures attested to the below-freezing temperature. Spread out at intervals, large fire pits gave off a welcoming glow around which small groups gathered to eat, drink, and partake in friendly conversation. Light poured out of large store-front windows and glass retail doors as patrons entered and exited, adding to the warm glow. In the center of the plaza, a large ice-skating rink hosted children, amateurs, and a few competent skaters, some gliding and twirling, but most shuffling cautiously along the railing, and more than a few falling—mainly from lack of skill, only a couple from light intoxication. The village bustled with holiday-clad visitors and locals who were merrily attired, all in après ski mode.

Bethany Rosen and Kristy Wise had been friends for over

six years—nearly a quarter of their lives. But they had been through far more together than many women who were much older. What neither could imagine, as they sat sipping chilled prosecco despite the cold, were the twists and turns that fate still held in store for them.

The two were on the terrace of a restaurant called Hooked, seated at a high table and huddled close to a tall, mushroom-style heat lamp. They were dressed for the weather, wearing several layers of clothes along with snow beanies and boots. Their table was just far enough from the epicenter of activity that they didn't need to struggle to hear one another over the cacophony of music and laughter. The other tables were out of earshot, and both girls were comfortable believing that they could speak freely without being overheard.

They were on their third prosecco each. While Kristy generally didn't drink much, Bethany had no issue with enjoying alcohol... or other substances. Bethany partook equally in chemical and non-chemical diversions. She took after her father, who was a trial lawyer, an avid skier and hunter, a scotch-lover, and an all-around liver-of-life.

As the oldest of two children—Bethany's sister Sophia was four years younger and just starting high school—she had evolved into the young adult version of a tomboy. She was *that* girl... the one at the party who could armchair quarterback your fantasy football choices, explain in detail the best way to gut a deer, match you tequila shot for tequila shot, and still get up to run a 5K the next morning.

The Rosens loved the mountains. For a number of years, they had owned a condo in Beaver Creek where Bethany and her family had spent the holidays. They were all skiers and lovers of the outdoors.

While Tom Wise loved the mountains, his wife Deb was a beach and cruise ship aficionado. Having grown up on a ranch, Deb had fond memories of her annual escapes to the coast with her mother's sister, Aunt Jenny. Cruise ships meant sun, fun, and sand. The mountains reminded Deb too much of the ranch, of work and responsibilities.

For that reason, Kristy Wise had been surprised when her

mother had proposed that they forgo their annual Christmas cruise and "mix things up." They had finally taken the Rosens up on their standing offer to spend the holidays in Colorado. Although Kristy did not snowboard or ski, she loved the mountains, the cold, and the snow. There was a certain magic to spending the holidays in a winter climate—getting a truly white Christmas.

And she was excited about reconnecting with Bethany. Since Joe Harlan Junior's trial, Kristy and Bethany had drifted apart. The two had been inseparable through high school and into college. They got along marvelously, in general. Where Kristy was rational and analytical, Bethany was intuitive and impulsive. Yin and yang.

But, just as the rape and subsequent trial had affected Kristy in many ways, it had opened an unexpected rift in her relationship with Bethany.

Bethany felt guilt. She felt guilty about having encouraged Kristy to go out that Halloween night. But for her insistence, Kristy would have stayed home studying, and nothing would likely have happened. And Bethany felt guilt that, despite her testimony at the trial as the sole eyewitness, Harlan had been acquitted.

Kristy felt resentment. While she hated the fact that she had been taken advantage of by Harlan, a part of her wondered what would have happened if Bethany hadn't stumbled upon the scene. If it all simply "hadn't happened."

Kristy wasn't sure if she would have preferred that the whole incident go undetected, with the bastard getting away scot-free. But she resented that she'd had no choice about making the matter public and going to the police. And for better or worse, her friend being the sole eyewitness, Kristy blamed Bethany for that.

Bethany's sense of guilt and Kristy's misplaced but understandable resentment had taken a toll on the relationship. What added tension to their friendship and had ultimately resulted in the two drifting apart for a time was a more fundamental incompatibility.

Kristy was the more stable of the two. She generally acted in moderation. She was slightly more introverted and did not take great pleasure from social activity, much less from large gatherings. More so since Harlan's acquittal. In this, Bethany was her polar opposite. Bethany thrived on interaction and indulgence. Yet, as a result of her sense of guilt during and leading up to Harlan's trial, Bethany had curtailed her social activity. Instead, she'd doted on Kristy. Out of guilt, she'd stayed in with her when she would rather have been out being social and partying.

At first, Kristy had appreciated the company. But when she'd realized why Bethany was staying in, and particularly as she'd begun to notice small signs that Bethany in fact missed going out, Kristy had added Bethany's sin of pity to the resentment she'd felt against her. She'd come to loathe the fact that Bethany felt obligated to stay in with her.

Slowly, Bethany had begun to reconnect with friends for social engagements, dinners, and parties. Kristy had insisted that she do so—without her. The two young women had thus begun to see less and less of each other.

Kristy suspected that this trip to the mountains was her mother Deb's way of cajoling her and Bethany back together. And, frankly, she didn't mind. It had been a little over two years since the trial, and probably six months since Kristy had spent any real quality time with Bethany. Now, they were making up for lost time. The two had spent several days snowshoeing, sightseeing, and shopping in Vail and Beaver Creek. They'd caught up on everything. The one thing that they had both studiously avoided was talking about *it*.

As they both sat at Hooked, despite the cold, dry air and the altitude, Bethany was smoking—a lot. She was on edge. The elephant in the room had a name, and it needed to be addressed.

"So, how are you holding up?" asked Bethany nonchalantly.

Kristy had known this moment was coming, and had decided that she would not hesitate, opting to address the issue head-on.

"Good days and bad, I guess. Sometimes it feels like it didn't even happen—like another life, or a *lifetime ago* anyway. I just want to put it in the past. And it was. I thought the whole thing was finally over, until Dad went and pounded on the son-of-a-bitch. So, now we're dealing with *that*," Kristy replied.

After Harlan's acquittal on the charge of date-raping Kristy, things had quieted down and almost returned to normal for her. Until, one day, her father Tom had run into Harlan in a Whole Foods parking lot. His anger had gotten the better of him and Tom had attacked Harlan. Although the two had quickly been separated by security guards, Harlan had filed a civil lawsuit against Tom over the attack. There were criminal charges pending, as well.

"So, no hope of settling?"

"Doubtful." Kristy shook her head. "I overheard them earlier, my folks, talking to Riviera, Dad's lawyer. Apparently, Harlan's refusing to settle, so it's all going to trial. We'll see." She shrugged.

"Well, the fact that he won't settle sucks. But, hey, my old man thinks there's not a jury in Texas that'll convict your dad. All things considered, no way," she said. "Hell, he should get a medal for *just* kicking Harlan's ass and not doing worse."

"That's what Riviera says." Kristy hated the idea that her family and their plight was a topic for discussion, especially among people who knew them well.

"Well, he's right. My dad knows his shit. This isn't the first-ever case of a father stepping in to avenge his daughter. It's happened before. And us Texans, well, let's just say there's still a pretty strong vein of frontier justice that runs in our blood, you know?"

Kristy nodded, smiling ruefully. While Bethany was brash and quick tempered, she also had a high emotional IQ.

"What is it?" Bethany asked, studying her friend's face. "It's not the lawsuit...."

Both were silent for a few moments, and then Bethany reached out and took Kristy's hand, asking, "You just want it all to fuckin' end, don't you?"

Kristy looked up, eyes watering slightly despite her repeated commitments to herself that she wasn't going to cry about it all with Bethany, and nodded. "I'm just fuckin' *drained*. I want.... I *need* for the whole thing to just fade into the past. And it was. And now, here we are *again*. In the news *again*. I fucking hate it. It feels like, ever since Harlan got acquitted, I've been on the defensive. The 'girl who cried wolf.' I'm sick of it. It's like I have no control over my life."

Bethany nodded. She was about to reply to Kristy when a woman's voice rose in volume—"Well, it should be a no-smoking area. It's unhealthy."

Kristy looked over her shoulder and saw a thirty-something-ish couple sitting at the only other occupied table on the terrace. The woman had been speaking to her other half, but the remark had clearly been intended to be heard by Kristy and Bethany.

No one else appeared to be within earshot.

Kristy turned and saw that Bethany was already on her feet. *Oh shit*, thought Kristy. She knew her friend well. And Bethany was not one to join in passive aggressive games. She always went for the throat.

"Take no prisoners" was her motto.

"Beth..." She reached out to grasp at Bethany's arm and attempt to stop what she saw coming, but she was too late.

Bethany took a deep drag on her cigarette as she walked toward the couple. She didn't weave, but Kristy could tell that whatever she was about to say had the weight of three proseccos behind it.

Bethany exhaled smoke in the direction of the two. Her body language itself was not aggressive. A bystander, viewing from a distance, would have thought that she was perhaps commenting on the weather, asking where they were from or making small talk.

What the couple and Kristy heard Bethany actually say was, "Smoking *is* allowed out here, actually. But I *am* pretty sure this is a no fat cunts zone. So, why don't you head inside—there's a trough at the far end of the bar where I know you'd be more comfortable."

The woman's face fell. It was clear that she'd been unprepared for such an aggressive response. Bethany stood there, hands on hips, waiting.

The woman looked to her significant other and then back at Bethany, expecting him to say something. His face betrayed that he was torn between defending his woman on the one hand and attacking another, younger woman whom he didn't know and who might be in the right. About the smoking, at least.

Finally, the man suggested to the air in between Bethany and his date, "Why don't we just go inside? That'd probably be best."

CHAPTER TWO

As Bethany returned to her and Kristy's table and sat down, the couple spoke in hushed voices, then retreated into the restaurant with the woman glaring at them and shaking her head as she went.

"Way. Too. Much. Beth." Kristy shook her head with true remorse and pushed her half-empty prosecco glass toward the middle of the table.

"Shock and awe, Kris," Bethany said, opening her palms and raising her shoulders in some sort of faux-gangsta gesture. "Where does she get off—?"

"But this *is* a 'no-smoking' zone, Beth. All of this area is..." Kristy replied, indicating the entire plaza with her hand.

Bethany looked down at the cigarette. Then she raised her glass and cocked her head to the side, smiling and communicating, *Too much of this, I guess.*

Kristy shook her head.

"Oh, alright... sorry," Bethany moaned. "I *am sorry*, Kris. Maybe too much," she said, shrugging and putting a hand over her heart. She studied her friend and seemed genuinely concerned. She sighed, suddenly appearing sober. "You want me to go and fuckin' apologize?"

Kristy shook her head. "No. That'll make it worse. Just let it go." Kristy looked down at her watch. "It's getting late, anyway."

Bethany took a deep drag off her cigarette—not even half-smoked—exhaled, and dropped it to the ground, crushing it with the toe of her boot. It was the next best thing in her mind to asking forgiveness. She picked up her phone to check the time, then tried to pick up on the conversation where they'd left off.

"It's barely eight, Kris. And it's our last night. One more?" she asked, fluttering her eyelashes coquettishly.

Kristy looked at her friend with a flat face, then rolled her eyes and smirked, agreeing. "Just one."

"Cool. And look, I hear what you're saying about Harlan and all." Bethany paused. Kristy studied her face, and could tell that she was deliberating, struggling with what to say next.

"Out with it. Since when do you hold back?" Kristy asked, cocking her head toward the table which the couple had just abandoned.

Bethany chuckled. Then, she looked hard at Kristy, organizing her thoughts. "It's just... I feel like..." She shook her head. Her eyes narrowed. She reached out and picked up Kristy's half-empty glass and took a big swallow, draining it, and then said, "I just feel like, after the trial, you just sort of gave up. And, don't get me wrong," she rushed to add, holding a hand out toward her friend, "I know, it's horrible. It *sucks*. What you went through is a nightmare I can't even begin to imagine. But *it happened*. It's in the past. And, you know, sometimes you've just got to say 'fuck it' and move on. You know?"

"I have moved on," Kristy said, her eyes and voice colder than the icy air around them.

"I know. Martial arts and guns and all that. What? Are you carrying right now?"

"Maybe," Kristy replied, unconsciously putting her hand on her purse.

Two months after the rape, she'd obtained her concealed carry permit. Since then, Kristy had made it a habit of going to the gun range weekly. She carried a handgun with her everywhere the law permitted, and often where it didn't. For daily carry, she favored a 0.22 caliber Smith & Wesson J-frame Model 317. It was tiny, weighed only 11 ounces, and she could consistently hit a bullseye at ten yards with the eight rounds it held.

"Well, that's cool and all. I know you've been dealing with it *in your way*," Bethany added air quotes. "But you've got to rejoin the living, man."

"What does that mean, exactly?"

"Well..." Bethany pondered for a moment, "look, Harlan's back at his company, his start-up. He's living like nothing happened...."

"You're *really* using *him* as an example of how I should live my fucking life, Beth?"

Bethany shook her head vigorously, holding her hands up. "No. No. No. No." She attempted to collect her thoughts. "My point..." Bethany hesitated.

"Your point is that you're drunk, Beth!" Kristy hissed. "You just insulted two people for calling you out on smoking in a no-smoking zone, and now you're telling me I should aspire to live my life like the motherfucker who raped me? Brilliant fucking advice." Kristy's voice rose. "Well, hey, here's a thought... I've got some advice for you. Go fuck yourself!"

Kristy had moved to stand up and leave when Bethany looked over Kristy's shoulder and made a *someone's coming* gesture with her eyes wide.

At first, Kristy thought it was just a ploy to keep her in her chair, but as she turned to look, she felt the presence—someone was approaching. Kristy immediately went on alert, into defense mode; she reached out casually and grabbed her prosecco glass, prepared to use it as a weapon if necessary as she continued to turn to face the person.

"Sorry, ladies," said the young man, hesitantly approaching. From his shirt, he appeared to be a staff member, just a bit younger than the two women. He was tall, with casually wavy brown hair and several days' growth of beard.

Bethany rolled her eyes and turned to face him, smiling.

"I hate to interrupt," he continued as he stood shifting from foot to foot, hands in his back pockets, "but I got a complaint..."

"What's your name, sweetie?" asked Bethany, all smiles and big brown eyes. Her jet-black hair hung in two braids dropping from each side of a festive white snow beanie with red snowflakes, and her cheeks were rosy from the cold and the booze.

The young man seemed confused, and slightly intimidated

by the two attractive young women. "Todd. I'm Todd," he replied.

She reached out and gently tapped his arm, saying, "I'm Beth." She smiled brightly. "And this is Kris."

"Hi. Uh, well... it's just that... these folks," Todd gestured with his head back toward the restaurant, "they said you guys were rude to them? And asked me to step in."

"Which folks exactly? You mean the lady that said her guy was staring at us?" Bethany looked at Kristy with pursed lips, shaking her head. "I told you she'd had too much to drink."

"No doubt," Kristy said as she nodded in agreement, her voice an octave higher than normal.

Todd seemed confused. Bethany plowed on, explaining to him how alcohol brought out the nasty side of certain women. Then she added, "You might want to cut her off. I'm sure she's normally a very nice lady, but I think she's one of those that gets jealous when she's had a few, you know? Starts seeing things that aren't there? I mean, we were just sitting here minding our own business. Didn't even notice them until she started in on him. Right, Kris? I guess that's why she wanted to move inside? I think she just got pissed at him, and wants to take it out on us...."

In spite of herself, Kristy marveled at Bethany. She'd forgotten how, when she turned on the charm, she was unstoppable. After a bit more chatter and light flirting, Todd walked away smiling—convinced that the whole thing had been a misunderstanding—having taken Beth's order for another round of drinks.

Kristy turned back toward her friend, but Bethany pointed urgently towards Todd.

"Not yet, Kris. You're missing the best part."

Kristy turned.

"Check out that ass!"

Kristy smiled and scoffed, turning back to Bethany while shaking her head. "You're fucking nuts, you know that?"

As soon as the door to the restaurant closed behind him, Bethany lit up a cigarette, sucked in deeply, and then replied through her teeth, words coming before the smoke, "It's what you love about me, man. Admit it. Takin' the bull," she said, rocking her head from side to side, "by the horns...."

Kristy laughed, and facetiously made a "Hook 'em" sign with her hand.

A waiter brought their fourth round, and as he put them down, said, "These are on the house." Bethany thanked him reservedly while making googly eyes at Kristy behind the waiter's back.

"I think momma's getting her some 'hot Todd-y' tonight," said Bethany in a low voice to Kristy as the waiter walked away. She raised her glass to Kristy and sipped. "Now, where were we?" Bethany saw a dark cloud passing over Kristy's face and quickly pointed to her friend with her cigarette. "Look. Forget everything I said before. You know I'm not the best when it comes to talking about feelings and shit.

"I can only tell you what I see. And I see a fantastic woman in front of me that had something bad happen to her *one night*. Fifteen minutes of one night. Probably less, knowing that limp-dicked motherfucker. And it seems to me like she's letting that moment define her."

Bethany paused, not satisfied with the point she was trying to make.

"You know what?" she added. "This whole situation here is a great case in point… that bitch and her boyfriend. I know—" she held up both hands, "it pales in comparison, but the lesson holds. You can't let *people* affect you. You've gotta stand up for what you think is right... even if you're wrong. Especially if you *know* you're wrong. Fuck 'em! All of 'em! Sure, this whole lawsuit thing, your whole situation, *is* fucked up. You know it and I know it. Hell, everybody that knows anything about it knows it."

Bethany took a sip from her glass, savoring the bubbly wine.

"But," she said, lowering her voice and nodding, "I think your dad had the right idea. He just didn't think it through. Look, the system failed you." Bethany breathed in deep on the cigarette, blowing out smoke, and her eyes watered a bit.

The emotion in Bethany's face hit Kristy hard. In that moment, she felt that Bethany really cared, and in her way, she wanted to help.

"I say... we *do something* about it—about *both of them*—Joe Harlan and Frank Stern. Me and you. Vigilante style."

"I get Joe, but Frank, too?"

Bethany looked down at her hands. "Those two were thick as thieves.... They came to the party together...." She shook her head. "Regardless. Let's focus. Joe for sure deserves punishing, and *we could do it*. I mean, who would ever suspect two pretty, helpless little things like us?" she asked in a faux Texas drawl. She studied Kristy, then added, "If we're smart. If we're careful, we could pull it off. And if... *if*... we got caught, no one would hold it against us. Not you, anyway. No fucking way. And me... fuck it... I can fend for myself."

"You're nuts," Kristy replied, wide-eyed. "Fuckin' nuts...." But it was not the first time the idea of revenge had entered Kristy's mind.

"You're repeating yourself now, girl. Too much bubbly?" Bethany asked, raising her glass toward Kristy. She held it aloft, waiting and insisting until Kristy responded by clinking and they both took a sip.

The two sat in silence for several moments, Bethany smoking and waiting for Kristy to react in some way. She could tell that her friend was processing the idea.

Kristy reached out and picked up the cigarette pack Bethany had left on the table. As she did, a tiny heart tattoo on her left wrist peeked out. Bethany smiled—she had given Kristy the tattoo herself. She had the same one.

Kristy removed a cigarette from the pack and ran it under her nose, unlit, breathing in the smell of raw tobacco.

"Tobacco and coffee," Kristy said. "Man. They smell so good before. Un-lit. Un-brewed. You know?"

Kristy looked at the cigarette for a few moments, then at Bethany. She toyed with the lighter. Then she carefully lit the cigarette. As she drew in air, the tip turned into a bright orange ember. She exhaled her first, deep drag and asked, "How exactly would we do it?"

Bethany smiled, leaned in conspiratorially, and said, "I have some ideas."

CHAPTER THREE

Bethany was just about to share her thoughts with Kristy when they were interrupted again.

"Beth!" a tall young man called out from a few feet away.

"Jack!" exclaimed Bethany. She rose and gave him a big hug, then introduced Kristy to Jack Sparks. Bethany and Jack had learned to ski together as kids, and had been hanging out on the mountain during holidays for years. Jack and his family lived in Denver.

"Is this why you've been ghosting us this year?" Jack joked, smiling at Kristy.

The two young women didn't laugh, and Jack realized he'd somehow stepped in it. He quickly recovered. "Hey, you guys have plans? I'm heading over to hang with some friends at Villa Montane." Jack was referring to a condo unit one street away from the plaza. "You remember Victoria?" he asked Bethany, who shook her head indicating that she did not. "She's from San Diego. Having a few of us over. You wanna come? Alfie will be there," he said to Bethany. "He's been asking about you. And Steph's maybe coming by, too, after something she's got with her dad and the new step-monster...."

Bethany seemed tentative. She looked at Kristy, who as expected seemed to shrink from the idea.

"Maybe later," Bethany replied.

Jack didn't press, but texted Bethany the unit number. He gave Bethany a hug and kiss goodbye, and raised a hand in a peace sign to Kristy.

As he walked away, Kristy watched him and noticed that he looked back at them several times as he went, all while Bethany told her a bit more about how they had met and began to explain who the others were.

Alfie was Alfredo Kruger. His family was involved in cattle ranching in Argentina, although Alfie had gone to boarding school in England and college in the States. They'd been coming to Beaver Creek for a number of years and owned a house up on the mountain. According to Bethany, he was a "sweetheart."

Stephanie was from New York, an only child. Her father was a hedge fund manager and collected sports cars and wives—his own as well as other men's. Stephanie was a little hard to take, until you got to know her. But she was "good people." They'd only met Stephanie a few years ago. She was a newcomer to the group, as was Victoria, who Bethany seemed to only vaguely remember.

"He mentioned ghosting?" Kristy said. "Have you been avoiding them to hang out with me?"

Bethany quickly replied, "No. No. Not avoiding. I just wanted to spend time one-on-one with you, you know? It's been a long time."

"But, if you want, why don't you go hang out with them? It's late anyway. And I'm wiped out."

Bethany saw Kristy was again taking the opportunity to call it a night. She tried to convince Kristy to stay and have another drink, but when that failed, she asked if she would at least walk with her to Villa Montane and meet some of her friends. "What if someone tries to kidnap me or something?" Bethany joked. "I need you to protect me. You can whip out that magnum you're hiding and take out the bad guys."

"It's not a magnum, but fine. Let's do it."

They called for the check, and Bethany giggled as she showed Kristy the receipt, upon which was written, *Thanks and come again! Todd 971-345-1765.*

The plaza was still crowded as they made their way over to Villa Montane, and a light snowfall accompanied them.

They entered the main building and were greeted by a beautiful, mountain-style lobby with a giant Christmas tree and a roaring fireplace. Several people were seated near the fire drinking from mugs and a few children sat in a corner working on a puzzle. A large table in the middle of the room held a wooden bowl that was full of apples. It was a very homey holiday scene.

The two made their way to unit 227, where Bethany rang the doorbell. A tall blond man—mid-twenties—opened the door, and he immediately recognized and greeted Bethany. It was Alfie. He led them up the stairs to where everyone was congregated.

It was apparent that the condo they were in had been recently renovated. Everything had a new look and feel to it. The group was hanging out on the main floor, which combined an open kitchen with a dining room and a living area facing a TV and a fireplace.

Jack came over and greeted Kristy and Bethany. "I'm so glad you guys came." This time he gave Kristy a hug, as well.

"I was just walking Beth over. I really should get going," Kristy told them both.

Alfie overheard and interrupted, "At least stay for one drink. What would you like? We have everything. Beer? Champagne? A glass of wine?" He spoke English with a slight accent suggesting both Spanish and British background, and as Kristy got a better look at him, she saw that he was drop-dead gorgeous in a European aristocracy kind of way.

Kristy hesitated, though she seemed a bit less reluctant than earlier. Bethany noted the change and jumped in, "Champagne for us both, please. We'll stay for one, but then we *both* have to go."

While Alfie served the drinks, the balcony door opened and another young man named Bennett entered with his goatee and a young woman in tow, who turned out to be Victoria. They came in from the cold, bringing chilled air and the scent of marijuana with them.

Kristy sat at the kitchen island and slowly sipped champagne while making small talk with Alfie and watching as Bethany caught up with her friends.

Alfie, it turned out, had been born and raised in Buenos Aires. His family had moved there from Germany at the beginning of the Second World War. His great-grandfather had sold everything early, before the persecution of the Jews had begun in earnest. He'd re-invested in land and cattle in Argentina at that point. They'd been lucky to get out.

Alfie spoke some German, Hebrew, Spanish, and English. And, he was getting his MBA at UT Austin. Kristy experienced a slight moment of panic, wondering whether he might have heard about her and Joe Harlan Junior, but he was in his first year of the program and showed no signs of recognizing her or her name. They chatted about travel, and he got a bit carried away explaining to Kristy the differences between skiing Beaver Creek and Bariloche.

He had just asked her about what she did in Austin and why they had never met when the two were interrupted by Bethany and Victoria laughing hysterically. They were seated on the sofa, while Jack and Bennett sat across from them on the ledge in front of the fireplace.

"Kris," said Bethany, almost in tears, "you gotta hear this. Tell her," she said to Jack, "Tell her!"

Jack stood and said, "Well, we were just talking about revenge and stuff, and I was telling Beth and Victoria that I stopped seeing this chick like a month ago. Melynda with a 'y' was her name. She was kinda nuts." Jack swirled his index finger at his temple. "Which is why I ended it. But she saw it coming, I guess...." Jack shrugged. "So, to get back at me, turns out at some point she managed to get into my underwear drawer. And she rubbed raw habanero peppers on all of my briefs.

"I figured it out the hard way."

Victoria was still laughing uncontrollably on the sofa.

"Thought I had some sort of STD from the burning." Jack did a little dance on his toes with his legs spread apart. "Went to the doctor and everything. He figured it out pretty quick. I had to buy all new underwear."

The whole group was laughing good-naturedly along with Jack. Kristy found herself smiling, though she wondered to herself exactly what "revenge stuff" the four had been chatting about.

CHAPTER FOUR

Bethany drained her champagne glass and held it up in the air—to which Alfie reacted, quickly taking the glass from her and re-filling it.

"Okay. That *was* funny, Jack!" Bethany said. She looked at Kristy and her eyes sparkled. "But, that's very mild. When I say *revenge*—" Bethany drew the word out as she said it, "I'm talking about real revenge for a legit evil act. Like, what if, for example," Bethany looked at Alfie as he handed her back a full glass, "some guy took advantage of your sister. What would *you* do as revenge?"

"Death." Alfie hadn't hesitated. "No question."

"Word, dude," agreed Bennett.

"Isn't that kind of extreme?" Victoria asked, sitting up on the sofa, folding her legs under her and hugging a pillow. "I mean, don't get me wrong. Rape—I guess that's what we're talking about?" Victoria looked at Bethany, who nodded. "Rape is horrible. But isn't death a little too much as a punishment?"

"That's what they do in a lot of cultures," said Bethany. "The death penalty."

"Really?" Victoria asked, biting her lip skeptically. "I somehow doubt that—"

"Hold on. Listen," Bennett said, holding up his mobile phone and reading. "Punishments for rape: India—life imprisonment to death sentence; China—death sentence or castration; Saudi Arabia—beheading; North Korea—death by firing squad; Egypt—death by hanging—"

"Yeah," interrupted Victoria, "sure. But those are all backwards-ass countries. Pick somewhere civilized."

Bennett scrolled down on his phone, then continued, "France—fifteen years to life; Israel—sixteen years to life…"

"See? I get imprisonment, but death? It seems extreme."

"Whoa! The Supreme Court agrees with you, Victoria," continued Bennett. "Says here that the death penalty for rape in the U.S. is actually illegal."

"Really?" asked Jack, surprised.

"Dude. It's unconstitutional. It's considered 'cruel and unusual punishment'—"

"Well, that's a crock," Bethany said.

"What do you think, Kristy?" Alfie asked.

Kristy had been listening to the entire conversation with cool detachment. She could tell from the flow of the discussion that no one here—aside from Bethany—had any idea what she had been through. And that knowledge helped her to separate herself from it all, as well. For the first time in a long while—in a group setting—she felt the way she had felt before everything with Harlan had happened.

It felt good. She felt a fondness for these people due to the simple fact that they knew nothing about her.

Kristy indulged the pretense, and went along with the discussion, "Death does seem extreme. But I guess part of the problem is that there really isn't an equivalent punishment that can be imposed, you know?"

"That's a good point," agreed Alfie. "If you get caught stealing, you have to return what you stole and you get jail time. Restitution and punishment. But how do you undo a rape?"

"Castration," said Bethany.

Jack cringed. "That's so… permanent."

"But it's a great deterrent," chuckled Bennett.

"I think that's a critical distinction," added Victoria. "As far as a deterrent, the more extreme the better. But like Alfie said, as far as restitution and punishment—"

"But we're not talking punishment!" Bethany interrupted, almost shouting. "I asked about *revenge,* people! Punishment is what the legal system would do. That's all about restitution and deterrence and so forth. I'm talking more personal here. What would *you* do to a person who did *that*," she paused, looking at them all one by one, "to someone you love?"

To Kristy, it seemed that the words hung in the air. She thought for certain that Bethany was being too obvious. Too passionate. The group was going to figure out that there was something more underlying the conversation. Kristy felt certain that she was going to be found out.

She was wrong.

Jack looked at Kristy and made his eyes wide, communicating, *There goes Beth again...*

And the group continued the discussion as an abstract hypothetical.

"Well, for *revenge*," Victoria said, drawing the word out the way Bethany had, and several of the group laughed—including Bethany. "I don't like death. It's just *done*. It's over. I like the idea of castration better." She smiled at Jack, making snipping motions at his crotch with her fingers. "Oooh! Or, wait..." she interrupted herself, "what about, like, what was that book where the girl tattooed 'pig' or something on her molester?"

"Oh yeah," added Jack. "I read that one."

"*The Girl with the Dragon Tattoo*," Alfie put in.

"Bingo!" Jack replied.

"Really?" Bethany asked. "I don't remember that part..."

"Yeah, it's in there. And it wasn't short, like 'pig,'" Alfie replied.

"Since when do you read, Beth?" asked Bennett.

"Touché, asshole." Bethany smiled sarcastically at Bennett. "But I saw the movie."

Kristy chimed in, "She tattooed, 'I am a pervert, a sadistic pig, and a rapist' on his chest and belly." Everyone looked at her, surprised at the direct quote. "It's in the book," she added.

"Yes!" exclaimed Victoria. "Something like that is better. Something that the fucker has to live with..."

"That's so long, though," said Jack. "Lots of words for not

a lot of space." He looked down at his own belly and chest, as if measuring.

Alfie shook his head. He didn't seem convinced, and Kristy saw that he was about to speak when Bennett said, "Dudes, this is getting way too heavy for me. Anyone want some more weed?"

Victoria clapped girlishly in approval, and Bennett and Victoria headed back out onto the balcony. This time, Jack joined them and Bethany rose to follow.

"You guys want a little?" Bennett asked Kristy and Alfie as he opened the door. "It's really mild stuff. Sativa. Got it here locally."

"Not for me," said Kristy. "I think I'm gonna call it a night."

"Oh, come on, Kris. Just one little hit. So we sleep better? Then we can go," Bethany pleaded.

"You go ahead," said Kristy. "I'll wait."

"Two seconds," said Bethany. "I'll be right back."

Kristy and Alfie were suddenly alone inside.

CHAPTER FIVE

Kristy stood and began to explore the room slowly, champagne glass in hand, while Alfie watched her. As she looked at family photos on a shelf, he asked, "Did you read them all?"

She paused for a moment, and was about to ask what he meant when it clicked. "Larsson, you mean? The Millennium series?" She looked over her shoulder at him.

He nodded.

"Nah. The first one was great. *Uh-mazing*... didn't finish number two."

The sound of laughter from out on the balcony was somewhat muted by the door and windows, but could still be heard inside.

Kristy turned to him and leaned back on the wall next to the fireplace. The pose felt somewhat flirty to her. She prodded, "You were going to say something. About revenge. Before Bennett interrupted."

"Oh. Yeah. It was nothing."

"Nothing? Really?"

"Well..." he shook his head, "it's a very dark subject."

Kristy found his accent mysterious in some way, which seemed silly to her. He was just a business student, after all—nothing mysterious about that. But still... "What was it? I'm curious."

"Well, it's just that if you're going to step outside the system, I think it's a mistake to take baby steps. Once you cross that line, you're on your own. The system isn't going to protect you. That's why, when Bethany first asked me the question, I said 'death.'"

He paused, looking up at the ceiling as if trying to summon a memory.

"'If an injury must be done to someone, it should be so great that their vengeance should not be feared.' Machiavelli said it, I think—something like that."

Kristy nodded.

"See—" Alfie stood, and began to walk toward her, "if you castrate a guy, or tattoo a bunch of stuff on his chest, he's not going to be happy about it. And if he knows it was you, he will probably seek revenge. You'll have to watch your back, you know?"

"But," Kristy continued Alfie's thought, pointing at him with her champagne glass as he approached, "there's no such problem if you simply kill him."

Alfie stopped a few feet from Kristy—not quite in her personal space, but hovering tantalizingly on the edge. "Exactly. Unless, of course, he doesn't know who you are. But vengeance *is* hard to do anonymously. I mean, part of revenge is for the guy to know that it's you doing it, isn't it?"

Kristy nodded.

"So, if that's the case, then your best bet is murder. A dead guy—he won't ever bother you again, will he?"

Alfie took a small step forward. Kristy felt her neck and face flushing from the heat coming off the fireplace. Or maybe from something else. She removed her snow beanie, and her long blonde hair tumbled out and over her shoulders. "Makes sense," Kristy whispered.

A blast of cold air and laughter cut into Kristy and Alfie's conversation as the rest of the group came back in from the balcony. Bethany was holding her phone and chatting and giggling with Victoria as they came in.

The doorbell sounded. Victoria screamed with delight and then she and Bethany broke into raucous laughter.

"That was fast!" exclaimed Victoria, and both she and Bethany burst into a new round of laughter.

Alfie winked at Kristy, then headed downstairs to get the

door. As he did, Bethany came over to Kristy and mischievously held out her phone.

> Bethany: Wanna join us and some friends for a nightcap?
> Todd: Sure. Where?
> Bethany: VM 227
> Todd: See you in 15

Kristy smiled. *Typical Bethany.* "Okay. Now I really do have to go. I'm beat," Kristy said.

It wasn't Todd after all. Alfie returned with a young woman who was introduced as Stephanie. As she integrated herself into the group, Alfie and Bethany tried to convince Kristy to stay a bit longer. Despite their pleas, Kristy was adamant this time.

"Well, let me at least walk you back," Bethany said.

After a bit of argument, they agreed that Alfie and Bethany would walk Kristy home. It was a short walk, only one building over. Alfie claimed that he needed some fresh air, and Kristy found that she liked the fact that he insisted on accompanying them.

On the way, Bethany hung back, messaging on her phone. Though, Kristy wondered if she was simply trying to give her and Alfie some space.

"How much longer are you here?" he asked.

"Heading back tomorrow."

"That's a shame. I enjoyed our talk."

"Me, too."

"Maybe we can get together back in Austin? For coffee or something?"

Kristy shrugged, smiling a yes. "That would be nice."

As they said their goodbyes, they exchanged contact info. Bethany insisted that the three of them also take a selfie, which she then texted to them both.

There was a part of Kristy that wanted to spend more time getting to know him.

Some other time, she thought.

As she walked upstairs, Kristy wondered at the workings of fate. She was the responsible one. The cautious one. While Bethany was... well, reckless. She'd probably end up hooking up with Todd, a guy she hardly knew. Yet, for all her caution, Kristy was the one who'd ended up getting raped.

Life ain't fair was what Kristy's mother Deb would say to that.

But then, Deb also liked to say, *What goes around, comes around.*

CHAPTER SIX

Saturday
March 10, 2018
Austin, Texas

Despite having reconnected in Beaver Creek, when Kristy and Bethany returned to Austin after Christmas break, they saw little of each other. Bethany was in her final year of college at UT while Kristy had fallen a semester behind due to the rape and the trial. Regardless, the two had no classes together since Bethany was studying marketing while Kristy was finishing her BA in psychology.

Kristy did hear from Alfie. But while she was interested in getting to know him better, being back in Austin made her feel less inclined to connect with him. In Austin, the whole Harlan mess was very present for her. She worried that he would somehow find out, and she preferred to avoid him rather than to have to deal with all of that.

About two months after the Beaver Creek trip, at 2:30 a.m., Kristy's mobile phone rang, waking her from a deep sleep.

She looked at the screen. *Sophia Rosen*

"Soph?"

"Kristy," a panicked voice replied, "there's been an accident."

Forty minutes later, Kristy arrived at St. David's Hospital and tracked down Mr. and Mrs. Rosen, Sophia, and several young women whom she didn't know, all of whom were crammed into a waiting room. Mrs. Rosen was near hysterical, and Mr. Rosen was trying to calm her.

Sophia came over and hugged her.

"How is she?"

"We're still waiting," Sophia replied. "Apparently, she was going out to party and took what she thought was X. Best they can tell, it was PMA cut with Ketamine or something. She started having seizures and overheating."

"PMA?"

"Dr. Death? It's like X, only way more toxic." Sophia sighed, then added, "Same kind of high—only it takes longer to kick in—so you think maybe you got watered down X and take more. That's what happened to Beth."

"Oh fuck," Kristy said, shaking her head.

"Alfie was there. He called 911." Sophia looked over to a corner of the waiting room where Alfie sat staring blankly at a wall. He didn't appear to have noticed Kristy's arrival.

Kristy felt something odd in her belly at seeing him, but that was quickly replaced by anger. Her blood boiled. She turned from Sophia and headed over to Alfie.

"What the hell happened?" she spat.

Alfie looked up and stood to greet her, but she put a hand out against his chest, keeping him at arm's length.

"What the fuck did you do to her?"

"What? Me? Nothing. I got there, saw how she looked, and called an ambulance."

Kristy caught herself. She'd jumped to a conclusion that may have been erroneous.

She softened a little, and arms crossed over her chest, asked, "Well then, what exactly happened?"

"I was hanging with some guys downtown when Bethany texted me. She was with some friends at a condo on Fifth Street and we hadn't seen each other since Colorado. So, we agreed to meet. It took me a while to get there 'cuz the guys I was with bailed on me. When I finally did get there, they—" he indicated the other girls in the waiting room, "had her laid out in the bedroom. She was shivering and looked like hell. So, I called 911."

"So, you weren't there when she took the drugs?"

"No. Not my thing. You know that," he replied.

Kristy recalled that she and Alfie were the only two who'd passed on the pot at Beaver Creek. "Where'd she get it, then? The X?"

"The police asked, but nobody seems to know anything." He shrugged at the girls. "But," he added, "one of them claimed to have 'found' what Beth took, and gave it to the doctors. I think that's how they're figuring out how to treat her."

Kristy looked over at the girls, who were in various states of dishevelment and confusion. She marched over to them and, keeping her voice low enough so as not to disturb the Rosens, asked, "Which one of you bitches will tell me what the fuck happened?"

The three looked at one another blankly. Finally, the red-haired girl stood up and signaled that they should walk.

Her name was Ellie Grant. She was about Kristy's height even though she was wearing high heels and Kristy was in running shoes. Ellie had grey eyes, freckles, and a tiny doll nose. She looked to Kristy like an Irish sprite.

"We all thought it was X, I swear," Ellie explained. "I mean, it looked like X. And... we were all gonna take some...." She hugged herself, clearly thinking of what could have happened if they had.

"Where'd the drugs come from?"

"It was Pippa. Pippa Warren. She brought the drugs. She thought it was X."

"Where'd she get them?"

Ellie shook her head.

"Fine, I'll ask her. Which one is she?" asked Kristy, looking back at the remaining women.

"Not here," replied Ellie. "Went home. Her dad's a judge up in Beaumont. She—" Ellie imitated a high-pitched nasal voice, "*can't be involved in this.*" Her face revealed her disgust. "I got the drugs from her before she split. Gave them to the paramedics."

"So, no one else took any? Why is only Beth in there?"

"No one. We were all going to take some before we went out. After a few drinks at my place. But..." she shrugged. "Well, you know Beth... she started early. And after a while, she said it was weak-assed crap and took two more."

"Where is she now? Pippa. Address?"

Ellie seemed reluctant at first, but upon seeing the look on Kristy's face, she shrugged again and pointed with her head back toward the other two girls. "The blonde, Kate. She's her roommate."

As Kristy got into her car, she heard, "Wait up!"

She turned to see Alfie.

"Where are you going?"

Kristy explained, and Alfie insisted on going with her.

As they drove, Alfie tried to calm Kristy down. "Shouldn't we just call the police?"

"Bethany's an adult, Alfie. No one forced her to take the drugs. The cops won't care where the drugs came from unless there's a big fish there—a dealer or someone they can go after."

They arrived at Pippa's address at 3:15 a.m. It was an apartment complex. The two climbed stairs and found the unit number. Lights were on.

Alfie rang the doorbell.

After a few moments, they heard movement behind the front door. It opened with the security chain still in place. A young woman peeked through the door crack. Her face was stained with mascara, and her eyes betrayed that she was either drunk or high. "Oh, you... Whadda you want?" she slurred.

Kristy gently pushed Alfie to the side and stepped in front of the door. "I want to know what you gave Beth and why you're hiding here like a sorry little coward."

"I dunno what you're talkin' about." She wiped her nose with the back of her hand. "Beth was the one that brought 'em. They were her drugs, man."

"That's bullshit, and you know it!"

Pippa shrugged. "Look, man. It's late. I gotta go." The door began to close.

"At least tell me where you got the fucking drugs!"

Kristy heard a voice say, "Close the fucking door!"

As Pippa pushed the door toward her, Kristy looked up behind Pippa, and just visible in the living room, she saw the source of the command.

It was Frank Stern.

CHAPTER SEVEN

In many ways, revenge is much like an extramarital affair. It never just "happens." Nobody cheats without having fantasized about it in advance, without having savored the idea.

Revenge, like seduction, is a process. It is a game of inches.

First, the idea presents itself with its three key elements: the target, the reason why vengeance is warranted, and the final critical ingredient—the *desire* to see the deed done. As with all human acts, desire lies at the root.

Once the flame of desire is lit, then comes the *creep*. The slow evolution from a vague thought, an ill-formed cloudy blur of a thing, to a specifically imagined act. Something concrete enough that it can be verbalized.

That is the critical juncture.

Crossing from thought to spoken word—to the verbalization that it could actually happen—that is where we cross the line from fantasy into reality. More so if those words are spoken to another.

From those verbalizations sprout the green leaves of action— generally nothing drastic in the beginning—not the purchase of a gun or the hiring of an assassin. Little things. Carefully re-reading a news article about a homicide, an article that one previously would have glossed over, in order to understand how it was done. Delaying watching the latest episode of *Modern Family* to watch an old episode of *Dexter* because it might be somehow instructive. Furtively, perhaps without consciously realizing what it does, the mind seeks clues, instruction from the universe.

This is the path on which Bethany and Kristy found themselves in the succeeding months. Their discussion in Colorado had opened the door. Their belief that Frank Stern sold the drugs that had caused Bethany's overdose sealed the deal for the two: Joe Harlan Junior, the "acquitted" rapist, and Frank Stern, drug-dealing slime-ball.

Bethany did all she could to fan the flames.

"He's a creep, Kris. Everyone knows it. Your roofies had to come from somewhere. And *everyone* knows, or everyone I talk to, at least: weed, X, coke, even the really hard stuff... Frank is the go-to guy on campus. No one wants to drive into east Austin and buy God knows what kind of garbage off a street corner if they can avoid it.

"What Joe did to you would never have happened without Frank. And look what he did to me."

Kristy and Bethany enjoyed fantasizing about how to exact revenge. The idea became a regular topic of conversation between the two young women.

And they took action. They started a file. Addresses. Phone numbers. Friends. They began to investigate what Joe and Frank did. Where they went. What kind of schedules they kept. They slowly made progress. They even purchased a pre-paid mobile phone—a burner.

Their planning complete, they were in the midst of agreeing on when to exact their revenge—starting with Joe—when fate intervened.

A penis appeared on Senator Harlan's front door.

A few days later, the police confirmed that Joe had gone missing in Miami.

It was real. The bastard was dead.

In a strange way, Kristy felt that Harlan's death validated her plan for revenge. The universe was listening. And it was on her side.

With Harlan gone, Bethany and Kristy's planning shifted focus to Frank Stern.

The plan for Frank was simpler than Joe's. And, there was a certain poetic justice built into it, as well.

While Bethany was all for acting as soon as possible, Kristy had other obligations to meet. She had taken time off from college after the rape and would be graduating a semester late—in about eighteen months. She didn't want to risk anything interfering with her classes and pushing her graduation date out even further.

"Revenge is a dish best served cold," Kristy would say, claiming the quote was from *The Godfather*. To which Bethany would always argue facetiously that the quote's origins were in fact Klingon, citing *Kill Bill*.

In the end, they agreed to lay the groundwork slowly and methodically. That would give Kristy time to finish all her coursework and ensure that school was not distracting her when the time came to deliver the final blow against Stern.

"That's not your only distraction, sweet pea," said Bethany, trying to get a rise out of her friend.

"What are you talking about?" Kristy looked up from her textbook. They were in her bedroom. Kristy was at her desk, reading for class.

Bethany held up Kristy's mobile phone.

"Hey, bitch," said Kristy, reaching out, "give me that!"

"How about lunch tomorrow?" Bethany asked in a faux British accent.

"Now!" Kristy bolted from her chair and grabbed her phone.

"Most men would be discouraged by now," continued Bethany with the accent, laughing, "but I am not most men!"

"Not. Funny. Beth." Kristy pouted and went back to her desk. "Fuckin' Pepe le Pew..." she said under her breath.

"Oh, come on, Kris!" Bethany replied, now in her normal voice. "You guys are amazing together! Stop with all the 'coffee at Starbucks' one week, a 'quick lunch, gotta run' the next. Go on a proper date and just fuck him already!"

"It's not like that, Beth. We're taking it slow. He's cool with it, and so am I."

Alfie and Kristy had been "getting together" regularly— she refused to call it dating—since returning to Austin from Beaver Creek. He now "knew" about her; it had been inevitable once the news had hit about Harlan's penis and death, as Kristy had been all over the news as part of the backstory.

Alfie didn't care.

"I had the measles *and* the chickenpox when I was young. So, we've both survived nasty attacks by vermin," he'd said.

Little by little, Alfie was consuming more and more of Kristy's bandwidth—mental and emotional. There was a part of her that wanted to tell him about everything. About Bethany. About the plan for revenge against Frank. But she wasn't sure.

Kristy's thinking was: finish college, get Frank Stern, and then get serious with Alfie. What she didn't count on was getting exactly what she wished for. You see, Kristy was right about the universe. It does listen. It listens to all of us. She would get what she wanted. Everything would fall nicely into place.

She would work hard and finish college as planned.

And then, she would get her wishes—regarding Frank Stern and Alfie, too. But, in exchange, the universe would rain tragedy on Kristy Wise.

CHAPTER EIGHT

Wednesday
May 1, 2019
Austin, Texas

Fourteen months later, near the end of the spring semester of 2019, Frank Stern was sitting at the kitchen table in his condo, doing his best to ignore Pippa Warren.

"Come on, bae! You promised!"

Frank gritted his teeth. Pippa's combination of nasal whine and vocal fry made nails on a chalkboard seem soothing. "I can't tonight, babe. Business," he replied as he reviewed his list of deliveries for the evening.

"Fuck business! What's the point of working so hard if you don't play hard, too?" Pippa was wearing a short black skirt and a black lace top. No bra as far as Frank could tell. She was standing barefoot with her hands on her hips, glaring at her boyfriend.

Frank Stern and Pippa Warren had been dating for almost eighteen months. Seventeen months too long in Frank's opinion. But, after Bethany Rosen's overdose, Pippa had saved his ass. Actually, her father had.

Her dad—Judge Bill Warren—had gotten a lawyer friend to represent him and Pippa. *And* he'd pulled some strings, calling in a few favors. The whole mess had gone away. In reality, it had all been Pippa's fault. She'd stolen the PMA from Frank's drug safe thinking it was ecstasy. He'd been stupid not to be more careful about the combination to the safe. That problem, he'd solved. But he was still stuck with Pippa.

Judge Warren didn't like Frank—not one bit. And he'd made that clear. He had "fixed" the problem for his daughter. Frank had just gotten lucky—a free pass. Still, Frank owed Pippa, and she didn't let him forget it. So, partly out of a twisted sense of obligation, Frank was still fucking her—which was precisely what her old man didn't want.

Ain't life strange?

The other reason Frank didn't break it off with Pippa was to spite her father. He couldn't understand why Judge Warren didn't like him.

Frank Stern had a lot going for him. He was good looking—with dark, wavy hair that he kept long, though not quite long enough to pull into a man-bun. He had unusual pale brown eyes with a slight eastern tilt that was just enough to give him an exotic look. He was slightly above average in height, which, living in Texas, he could add to by wearing boots that put him at just over six feet tall.

At only 26 years old, Frank was also the CEO of an early stage company that had raised over ten million dollars in funding. The fact that the venture was built largely on technology stolen from Frank and Joe's ex-partner Marty McCall was beside the point. Frank had built relationships with movers and shakers in the Austin start-up community, many of whom had told him, "You're not really an entrepreneur until you get sued."

Frank understood that the line between perception and reality is not just thin, but sometimes non-existent. So, he had sued his ex-partner first in a move that had been met with kudos by the local founderati. More kudos had rained down on him when the case had settled. As the settlement terms were confidential, the fact that Frank and his company had taken a big hit to resolve the lawsuit would never be made public.

Frank was touted widely in local start-up circles as a "golden boy." The closest Frank had come to a blemish on his resume was Joe Harlan Junior. Being besties with an accused date-rapist was a big no-no. But, even there, Frank had lucked out.

First, Joe's acquittal had softened the negative impact of the rape claims. Of course, it had also meant that Frank had to let Joe come back to work at the company. Fortunately, as a good friend should, Joe had been decent enough to get himself killed, thus eliminating the only dark cloud that had ever cast a negative shadow on Frank's otherwise charmed life.

As icing on the cake, Senator Harlan had inherited Joe Junior's stake in the company, meaning that the senator was motivated to help with the business wherever and whenever possible. Given Joe Junior's role in starting the business, Senator Harlan felt that helping Frank was keeping Joe's legacy alive in a way.

But it was his "other business" that was keeping Frank from partying that evening. You see, in addition to working as a start-up founder and CEO, Frank Stern also sold stuff on the side. Drugs. Nothing terrible, and never to minors. It was something he'd started in college and had kept doing once he'd graduated.

Sure, in part, he did it for the money. He had built up a pretty solid white-collar clientele. And Frank loved to be the go-to guy when the "rich and famous" in Austin needed a fix. The contacts he had made were invaluable. The money was good. And, there was a certain category of chick that would do anything—*anything*— for a fix. This was something Pippa suspected but couldn't prove. One of those chicks, Angela—a forty-ish mom who lived up in the Hills—was on his delivery list that night. He started getting hard just thinking about her.

"Wait here," he said. "I gotta get some stuff."

As Frank walked into the large closet next to the kitchen, Pippa replied, "I'm not gonna peek, you dick! You need to start trusting me again! If it wasn't for me, you'd be in fucking jail..."

Frank pulled a string hanging from a bulb in the ceiling to turn on the light and closed the closet door. Though he could still hear Pippa ranting, he tuned her out as he opened the safe. The top two shelves were carefully stocked with different types of drugs. The third shelf was stacked with bundles and bundles of cash.

So much moolah.

Frank loved seeing the stacks of money every time he opened the safe, even though most of it wasn't his to keep. In a moment of monumental stupidity, he had decided to expand his business and committed to taking on more drugs from his supplier, Jerry. Frank had vastly overestimated how much product he could move. He was steadily burning through the inventory, but still digging himself out of a hole that was about eighty thousand dollars deep.

Frank carefully removed enough cocaine, molly, oxy, and weed to fill his orders for the evening. He added a "plus one" to each order, because when delivery time came, customers often decided they wanted "a little more."

Just as Frank was closing the safe, his phone vibrated. He didn't hear or feel it so much as he saw the screen light up. A text message from a phone number he didn't recognize.

| Unknown: | Got any R2? |

Unusual, but not unprecedented. Sometimes, even though he demanded that they not do so, clients would share his number with friends. It was a pain in the ass, as he had to vet these new clients to make sure he wasn't getting bogied by the cops.

Frank:	Don't know what that is.
Unknown:	Circle. Mexican valium.
Frank:	Who is this?
Unknown:	An old friend.
Frank:	No idea what you're talking about. You must have wrong number.
Unknown:	Pretty sure I don't. It's me.
Frank:	?
Unknown:	Your partner... Ex-
Frank:	Fuck you, Marty.
Unknown:	Nope. Try again...
Frank:	???
Unknown:	It's Joe, man.

Frank stared skeptically at the phone for almost a minute. He began to type, then deleted, shaking his head. Then he typed again in reply.

| Frank: | *Who is this? This is sick.* |
| Unknown: | ☺ *No worries. Been a while. Who's the babe?* |

Frank sat heavily on the floor. He could still hear Pippa through the door, explaining why he should take her with him on his delivery run.

"...and swing by my place. Then we can meet everyone down at Kung-Fu. Ginny and Matt are gonna be there. And..."

Unknown:	*???*
Unknown:	*She's hot*
Frank:	*Joe?*

Frank waited almost five minutes, but there was no reply.

CHAPTER NINE

Thursday
August 29, 2019
Austin, Texas

Katie Roberts sat in a chair facing Senator Joe Harlan Senior. The two were sitting in Senator Harlan's Congress Avenue law office in Austin. A bright blue, cloudless Texas sky shone through the fifteenth story window, reflecting off the high shine on the senator's black American Alligator skin boots. At just over sixty years old, and having reached a certain level of success, there were very few mundane things the man still did for himself. But one of those few things was shining his own shoes—his boots. A proper spit shine.

You see, Senator Joe Harlan liked to shine.

It was apparent on his person. He wore a navy blue silk and wool suit with a blindingly white Egyptian cotton shirt accented with gold Texas Senate cuff links and a blazing red tie. A bright gold Rolex sparkled on his wrist.

It was also readily apparent in his office. The floors were a rich oak parquet waxed to incandescence. No rugs. His impeccably clean, glass-topped desk rested on highly polished chrome risers. On the desk sat only a black cordless telephone, his silver laptop, and select trophies in the form of crystal paperweights. Several for IPOs. A lifetime achievement award from a chamber of commerce.

On his wall of fame—directly behind the desk—hung his diplomas and his law license, but they were afterthoughts, ancient prizes long since overshadowed by other successes that were evidenced by almost fifty shiny framed photos of Harlan with presidents, prime ministers, royalty, sheiks, and dignitaries.

But, his favorite photo—and one which he'd pointed out to Katie just as he did for all of his guests—was a picture of him with Elizabeth Warren in 1985, back when she'd been a research associate at the University of Texas at Austin.

"Back then, Lizzie was about as staunch as you can get," he'd laughed. "A Sunday school teacher—literally. More Republican than me!" Then he would pause for effect, before a quick dagger thrust! "Of course, that was back before she went 'off the reservation.'" He'd guffaw jovially. It wasn't conversation. It was scripted, as most of Harlan's life was, these days.

Harlan's eyes shimmered as he talked Katie through his wall of fame. He furtively admired her curves, attempting to glimpse what lay beneath her blouse and lingering over her thick lips. But the senator was careful, extremely cautious.

He was living in the #MeToo era. One misstep could destroy his career. He was in campaign mode, too, running for re-election. While Katie was appealing in many ways, for Harlan she was merely a means to an end—a way to get the word out, "his" word, to connect with the lemmings and convince them to elect him yet gain. And she, though young and new to the game, appeared to be a willing dance partner.

But youth and inexperience sometimes go down unexpected paths.

She leaned in and said, "I'd like to ask you something a bit personal—and I know it must be hard for you—about your son, Joe. If you don't mind?"

The shine never left Harlan's eyes, but his face perceptibly hardened, shifting from open joviality to a steely stare. He glanced briefly at the recording device Katie had placed on his desk at the beginning of the interview.

Is this a fucking set-up?

"Of course," he said, his rich southern drawl imbued with enough poison that a seasoned journalist, or indeed any rational adult, should have sensed the chill in his words. Katie was either oblivious or had another agenda.

"Let me begin by saying how truly sorry I am for your loss. It's been over a year now since the tragic disappearance of your son. Can you, not as a senator, but as a father, tell our readers, your constituents, how you feel?"

Harlan had been asked many questions about Joe Junior's disappearance. By the press. By the police. In fact, he questioned himself almost daily about the events leading to his son's disappearance and presumed death.

Is Joe really dead?

Why did he go to Florida?

Could I have done something different? Something to save him?

Did I miss something? Some clue as to what was in store for him?

Who fucking did this to him?

To us?

Senator Joe Harlan sat deathly still, fingers steepled and pressed against his lips in contemplation of the question on the table.... *As a father, how do I feel?*

The only sound in the office was the faint creak of his chair as it rocked ever so slightly with the rhythm of his breathing. Katie began to shift uncomfortably in her own chair, thinking maybe she had crossed a line she hadn't seen. She swallowed hard.

Harlan abruptly inhaled and spoke.

"There's a young man," he said, "who reminds me a lot of Joe. Not looks so much, but his spirit. A kind spirit. A loving soul.

"I saw him—this fellow, he's an actor—the other night on TV. He's one of these action guys. All guns and stunts and such. And I was struck by him. You see, he was on one of these late-night TV shows. The interview shows. Like Leno, you know? And he was asked a very similar question by the host—a question like the one you just asked me. The host asked, 'What happens after we die?'

"It's a question that, when you hear it, it makes you think about the hereafter, you know? About our mortality or immortality.

Do we just end? Or, do we continue? Do we transition? Is there life after death? Heaven? Hell? Nothing?

"That's the way I took it, anyhow.

"And this young man—wise beyond his years, Katie, so very wise. He didn't hesitate, not even a second. 'What happens after we die?' asked the host. "And the young man answered, 'Those who love us will miss us.'"

Harlan paused. He wiped a tear from his eye and cleared his throat.

"We can't know what comes next," he continued. "What happens after we die. But, when you ask me how I feel about Joe—as a father. Katie? That I can answer with scientific certainty. I miss my son every day."

CHAPTER TEN

After the interview ended, Senator Harlan went for a walk. He picked up a cappuccino to-go from Austin Java on Second Street and headed south toward Town Lake. He was out for a walk because he had an important decision to make, and he liked walking. It helped him clear his head. Get perspective.

Harlan is of average height, though most days his cowboy boots—standard attire for the Texas state senator—make him three inches taller, putting him at about six feet tall. His skin is leathery, with deep crow's feet around his eyes. He wears his wrinkles well, his face framed by a receding hairline, but he still has enough hair to avoid whispers about combing-over.

It is his physique that beguiles. Harlan is a swimmer. He is religious about it. This keeps him fit, lean, and his posture erect. He walks with a spring in his step—athletically. Most would judge him to be about fifty years old, if a hard-lived fifty judging from his wrinkles. The reality is that Harlan's features belie his years. He's actually just past sixty.

Some have told him he looks like the actor Robert Patrick, a comparison which he revels in since he loves the character Patrick played in *Terminator 2*. But when Harlan smiles, the similarity ends, as the senator has a very wide, toothy mouth—a velociraptor lurking just beneath the surface.

As he walked the trail on Town Lake that morning, Senator Harlan was not smiling. The velociraptor was ruminating, but it wasn't a government issue he was contemplating, nor a legal one.

This was personal.

That goddammed reporter.

Joggers passed the senator going in both directions. The sky was clear. The air was cool for August, though as he walked the trail that wove along the lakeshore, the rancid smell of the lake grew strong. It was a smell that brought back memories.

El Salvador.

1981.

Harlan was twenty-two years old at the time. Army Special Forces. Intelligence and logistics.

Officially, there was only a small group of advisors in the country training the El Salvadoran military; unofficially, the CIA was providing additional support. Harlan knew that there was more going on than training, but he initially didn't know how much. He learned the truth from an ex-Marine-turned-mercenary nicknamed Slipknot.

Slipknot was an odd-looking man, just barely five feet tall and completely bald. His face was craggy with what appeared to be acne scars. It was apparent to Harlan that the man lacked formal education and attempted to compensate for that in many ways, including an almost obsessive fascination with vocabulary—highfalutin' words, Harlan would call them in his folksy way.

Slipknot had come up through the ranks during Vietnam. He'd done three tours and earned a number of commendations, including two purple hearts. In the end, he had left the military with an honorable discharge—at least he claimed he had, though Harlan later learned that was not the case.

Harlan had just graduated West Point, was new to the military and to El Salvador, and looked younger than his twenty-two years. Slipknot alternated between calling him *Cherry* and FNG—*fucking new guy*—though not in front of the enlisted men. Harlan learned a great deal about how things worked "on the ground" from Slipknot. For a good six months, they were in regular contact in El Salvador.

Drinking buddies.

At one point, Slipknot explained to Harlan how he'd earned

his nickname. It was the knot he favored when he interrogated his Vietcong prisoners—his calling card. He would leave his dead with a slipknot tied to their bruised, swollen genitals.

It was a fuckin' war, man. There was dead gooks everywhere. But mine stood out, you know? Mine were gift-wrapped—with panache. That knot sent a message. The gooks knew that the same guy was fucking them over—again and again.

Psychological warfare, Cherry. More powerful than bullets.

When Harlan left the country, Slipknot was away on "business," as he liked to call it. Harlan later learned that the timing of that particular business trip coincided with the massacre at *El Mozote*.

Harlan never did manage to bid farewell to his erstwhile mentor. In fact, he never thought they would meet again. They'd lost touch. Harlan completed his military service and went on to political life. At one point, he looked into Slipknot via a friend— Congresswoman Anne Hertig, who served on the House Armed Services Committee. He didn't learn much other than that the man he had once considered a mentor had been *dishonorably* discharged, and that his last known address was that of his family home in Georgia.

Years had passed, and the mercenary had faded from Harlan's mind until recently.

Two weeks before this walk, Harlan had boarded a Delta flight from D.C. to Austin, going through Atlanta. He'd been seated and already reading, as he liked to do on flights, when someone had stopped in the aisle.

"Hello, Senator."

Harlan looked up to see Slipknot standing in the aisle.

"It appears we're traveling together," the man said, taking a seat.

Harlan smiled. He was pleased to see his old friend—it was sentimental, in the way passing by your old high school is nostalgic. You remember the good ol' days. All the good times.

They re-hashed those old times over a couple of scotches. Harlan caught Slipknot up on his career and life in general. Slipknot nodded with interest and made all the right noises at the appropriate places. But Harlan could tell he was just being polite, which was soon confirmed.

"I've been keeping up with you, Joe," Slipknot confessed, nodding. "Not a lot of Joe Harlans in politics out there. You're one of a kind. What you've been doing for America, it's great. No," he said with emphasis, "it's *patriotic*. You're a real patriot, Joe." He paused. "And I was sorry to hear about your son."

"Thanks." Harlan pursed his lips, looking down at the plastic cup on his tray table that was half-filled with Johnny Walker Red. "Yeah. That was a bad time."

"They ever find out what happened?"

Harlan shook his head.

"Joe, you know," continued Slipknot, "my gig now, it's mainly security work. But I do some investigative stuff, too. I'd be happy to look into it a bit if you like—your situation. As a favor. I can pursue avenues the cops probably didn't... or couldn't, if you know what I mean?"

"I appreciate it," said Harlan, and was about to decline outright, but instead he said, "...let me think about it."

They sat quietly for a bit, sipping from their cups. Then Slipknot spoke.

"You know, funny thing about the word *patriotic*. Did you know that it comes from an ancient Greek word?" Slipknot had apparently not lost his fixation on words and their origins. "It actually comes from the Greek noun, *patér*, which means 'father.' In Roman times, it came to be associated with the *patria,* which meant 'fatherland, country, city, a place.' But a special place, familiar." Slipknot adjusted himself in his seat and turned to face Harlan. "See, *familia* and *patria* are tied together linguistically, like family and father. You see the connection, don't you?

"Patriot. *Patria? Pater?* Father?

"What you're doing, Joe, Mr. Senator, is like acting as a father to your state. To Texas. And a father's got responsibilities, you know? To his family." Slipknot looked into Harlan's eyes, which were welling with tears. After a long moment, he gently patted the politician's arm. The intimacy of the touch made Harlan slightly uncomfortable.

Slipknot shifted back into his seat, picking up his cup. "You know I always had a thing for words, Joe." He chuckled and downed the rest of his drink. "Words are mightier than weapons. But then, you already know that."

CHAPTER ELEVEN

At the end of the flight, Senator Harlan and Slipknot exchanged contact information, business cards, and promises to keep in touch.

Per his business card, Slipknot's real name was Ronald Clayton. He was based in southern Georgia. Harlan laughed out loud later in his Uber on the way home as he added the man's contact information to his mobile phone. He had long ago forgotten the man's real name—somehow, it had never felt right.

As the days passed, Harlan thought long and hard about Slipknot's proposal and what he'd said about being a father. The senator was no fool. He understood exactly what Slipknot meant about pursuing other "avenues."

Slipknot didn't need search warrants. He didn't need to follow due process. He could rough someone up a bit if need be, to get information.

The idea resonated with Harlan. He'd been frustrated by the failure of the police to make any significant progress toward solving his son's murder case. It had been over a year now, with no leads of significance.

Truth be told, Harlan was more than frustrated. He was pissed off.

Joe Junior was the only family he'd had left. After his son had disappeared, for the first time in his life, the senator had felt completely alone in the world.

Being alone was something he could adjust to. He had his work to keep him busy. But, not knowing what had happened to his son grated on him. He had his suspicions, but they only made things worse. Believing that someone had done this to him—to them both—and was still out there, unpunished, getting the last laugh… that kept him awake at night.

It was a question of pride—which Senator Harlan had in abundance.

He had a decision to make. Should he reach out to Slipknot for help? His political instincts told him to let it lie. Nonetheless, one night on the way home from a dinner after a few too many scotches, he'd picked up a pre-paid phone at a gas station.

Still, he'd put it off, delayed. But, the reporter's questions earlier had been like rubbing salt in an open wound.

How do you feel?

Fucking stupid question! Angry? Cheated? Violated?

The thing is, this wasn't just about feeling. He had to play it smart. And as he walked along Town Lake, he tried to do just that—to think through the pros and cons of reaching out to Slipknot. He tried to analyze the situation rationally.

Yet, try as he might, emotion kept taking over.

No one fucks Joe Harlan over.

He was a father. He owed it to his son to set things right.

He dialed Slipknot's number.

"Hello."

"Hello…" Harlan was about to say "Ronald," but his tongue tied. The name just didn't seem to work. "Slipknot."

"Mr. Senator. You took your sweet time calling, didn't you?"

Harlan heard that familiar chuckle, and asked, "How are things?"

"Good. Things are good. But I'm intrigued, Senator. This ain't your cell phone. And it ain't your office phone. I put 'em both in my contacts after we reconnected." Slipknot's lips smacked. "You're calling me from a burner phone, aren't ya?"

The senator could almost hear the man's smile. "Mm-hmph. Seemed like the smart way to go," he responded with his own smug smile. He was no amateur, and he was glad Slipknot had noticed.

"So, I take it you're calling to do bidness?" Slipknot asked, using the southern perversion of the word *business*.

"That, I am."

"Very good. Well, as I said before, I am happy to oblige. So." Harlan heard a creak over the phone line. He imagined Slipknot leaning back in an office chair. "The best way for me to get started is for you to send me as much info as you can on what the cops have already done. You know, save me some time. You think you can get a copy of the case file for me?"

"Yep. I have it. Back when Travers—Art Travers, the detective on the case here in Austin—back when he called me to let me know they were closing the file, I asked him for a copy. He probably shouldn't have given it to me, but I *am* in the state senate, after all."

"Membership has its privileges," Slipknot laughed. "Perfect. Well, you send me that. Regular mail is fine—not traceable. We're not in a hurry at this point. My methods aren't really affected much by timing, if you know what I mean?"

Harlan did. But he felt uncomfortable. He didn't want to get into any details about how Slipknot would go about his work. He could imagine, but he didn't want to know.

Plausible deniability, he thought.

"I'll drop you a copy of my entire file in the mail. There's some related information from a lawsuit that my son was involved in, with an ex-business partner named McCall. There's also..." Harlan stopped himself. He was excited. But there was no point in giving the man a list. "Well, I'll send you everything I got," he said.

"Send it all, Joe. You never know what I might find in there. Where a tiny thread may lead. Anything you have that has anything to do with your son disappearing or with that rape—alleged rape."

"That's fine, but before I take too much of your time, I'd like to know what I owe you for this. I mean, what's your rate?"

Harlan hoped to keep things on the cheap.

Slipknot laughed. "Consider it a favor."

"Come on, now. I insist. I don't wanna take advantage of your generosity," Harlan said disingenuously.

"Well, then...." Slipknot paused. "How about I only get

paid if I get you results? A success fee. I'm thinking ten thousand dollars. That's fair, don't you think?"

Harlan paused. He liked that idea. After all, the police had found nothing. This was really a Hail Mary. Odds were, Slipknot would hit a dead-end just like the authorities had before him. No point in paying if he had nothing to show for it.

"That sounds fair," Harlan replied. "I'll send you copies of everything I have today."

"Perfect." Slipknot hung up without saying goodbye.

Harlan continued along the lake, sipping the last of his cappuccino, which was now almost cold. He recalled walking along the same path with Joe. They'd walked Town Lake often, as it was close to their home. Walked and talked. Quality time. It was at moments like these that Harlan most missed his son, when he did things that he'd once done with Joe Junior, but now did without him.

All in all, he was a good kid.

Harlan felt nostalgic again. Sentimental. Just as he had when he'd run into Slipknot on the airplane.

The funny thing about nostalgia is, we only tend to remember the good things about the good ol' days. It's only when we stop, and actually walk back into that old high school building, that all the bad shit comes rushing back.

CHAPTER TWELVE

Thursday
September 12, 2019
Austin, Texas

A couple of weeks after Senator Harlan's walk on the lake, Deb Wise was found dead in her Jaguar in the parking lot of the Austin Animal Shelter.

She was still in the driver's seat.

Well, most of her was.

Both of the car's front windows were open. There was a light breeze blowing, which made its way into and through the car, though it didn't seem to bother the flies that were congregating on what remained of the right side of Deb's head.

Her car keys were still in a cup holder on the console. The car was one of the fancy modern ones with a push-button ignition.

After being shot, Deb's body had fallen to the right, toward the passenger's seat of the vehicle. Her upper body was twisted at an odd angle, such that her head was almost facing the seat next to her.

Looking in from the driver's side window, the back of her head was visible. No wounds. It looked as if she were reaching for something in the passenger seat, but her progress had been stopped by the seatbelt that held protectively to her left upper arm. She'd been shot once in the left side of the head.

At close range, once was enough.

After the police ran the license plate and identified the car's owner, Detective Art Travers got the call. Normally, someone more junior would have handled things and Travers would have been brought up to speed the following day, once the evidence was collected and preliminary information had been gathered and organized. But the connection to Joe Harlan Junior was clear, and Natalie Bates—the crime scene investigator who had been called to the scene—knew that Travers would want to see things himself, in person.

Travers arrived at the crime scene just before 3:00 a.m. He stood next to the Jaguar, looking through the driver's window at what was left of Deb Wise.

Crime scenes are never pretty. It's worse when you actually knew the person. The change from living human being to corpse is dramatic. The difference—the contrast—stays with you. Having known the person and then seeing the transformation makes the crime very real. Very personal.

Though Travers had seen a lot of corpses, this one hit home.

He felt sick.

Thankfully, the night was cool. The light breeze helped, as did the fact that the body didn't smell yet. Otherwise, he might have lost it.

As he stepped away from the vehicle, he spotted Natalie and walked toward her. "What have we got?" he asked.

She shrugged, raising her glasses with one hand and letting them rest on top of her head. She was holding her mobile phone in her other hand. She'd been dictating into it when Travers had approached. Natalie usually wore her hair up, but it was late and several stray strands were blowing in the breeze about her face. She looked nice—pretty—a little ray of hope shining in an otherwise bleak setting.

Travers and Natalie stood just on the edge of the murder scene, surrounded by a sea of darkness. It felt as though they were alone, castaways stranded on a small island of light created by LED balloon lights, with the car and the corpse at its center.

"Officer called it in about an hour and a half ago. Just on routine patrol. Thought it was weird that the car was sitting here in an empty lot after business hours. Figured he'd find some kids making out in dad's car. Instead," she nodded at the Jag, "he found her. We ran the plates, and I thought of you." She smiled.

Travers only half-returned the gesture. "Any shell casings? Or a slug? Looks like it went in and out."

Natalie dropped the smile and put on her business face. "Yep, in and out," she replied, moving toward the vehicle. "Best we can tell, the shooter was standing outside her window." She moved to where the killer would have stood, pointing her hand like a gun. "Right about here. He was in pretty close—there's very slight stippling on the side of her face. Maybe three feet away... max. The gun was definitely more than two feet away or we'd see more tattooing. He shot through the open window, hitting the left side of the head. The bullet exited her skull and apparently went on out through the passenger side window."

Travers looked beyond the car at the likely trajectory. There were a few trees, then a small field he had passed driving onto the property, beyond which lay a string of roads including Levander Loop, Airport Boulevard, and Highway 183.

He could see more balloon lighting in the field.

Natalie looked in the same direction and continued, "The guys are searching for the slug over there. But shit, it could have gone any which way. And from the looks of the exit wound, it was probably a hollow point. May have come out in pieces. Some of it may still be in there. In her head, I mean."

Travers nodded.

"Her purse," Natalie pointed into the vehicle, "was on the floor on the passenger's side."

Travers looked, but it was gone. Already bagged as evidence.

"Mostly empty," Natalie added. "We found a matching coin purse—Louis Vuitton—over there." She pointed toward the parking lot exit. "No cash, credit cards, ID. We'll have it fingerprinted. See what shows."

Travers nodded, pondering. *Robbery? Or misdirection?*

"Time of death?" he asked.

"Body was somewhat warm, but rigor setting in. Significant

lividity. I'd guess somewhere between five and six hours before we got the call. So, between eight and nine p.m.?"

"Anything indicating what she was doing out here?"

"Not a clue, Art. The shelter closes at seven, so assuming I'm on target as to time of death, she was here after-hours. Or at least she was shot after hours. I suppose she could've gotten here earlier?"

"That would be strange. Hang around an hour after closing time, then get shot," Travers said, as much to himself as to Natalie. "No weapon, I suppose."

Natalie paused. "Yeah, sure, Art. We found the weapon. Did I not mention that? Along with a note with the name and address of the killer."

Travers squinted inquisitively at her. Natalie glared back. "Whoa, Nat," he said, raising his hands defensively. "Sorry, I asked."

Her expression softened. Then she shook her head and laughed. "Sorry, Art. Three fucking a.m." She inhaled deeply, then sighed. "And I'm quitting smoking. Again. I'm not even supposed to be on call."

"Good on you on the smoking. My bad, though. You're right, it *was* a stupid question. If you'd found anything, you—"

"I wouldn't have buried the lead, yeah. No problem. Forget it." She looked at him. "So, you gonna make the call?"

"Yeah, I'm meeting Glo at Magnolia Café. They live in Tarrytown."

Glo was Gloria Spoor, a victims' advocate with the Austin Police Department. Death notification procedures called for notification in person and, when possible, in pairs.

"You think this has anything to do with the Harlan mess? With the kid, I mean?" Natalie asked.

"No idea at this point, Nat, but I suppose we'll find out."

Art puttered around a bit longer, took a look at Deb Wise's coin purse, then thanked Natalie for calling him before leaving.

As Travers drove toward Tarrytown, he thought through the mess of connections between the Wises and the Harlans: Kristy Wise's alleged rape, Tom's attack of Joe Junior at Whole Foods, and then

Joe Junior's unresolved disappearance—well, partial disappearance. His penis had made it home, after all.

The last contact Travers had had with any of them had been at Joe Junior's funeral, almost a year and a half ago.

As Harlan's body had never been found, his casket had contained nothing but his penis. Travers thought, at the time, that cremation would have been a better option, but he later learned that the Joe's father, Senator Harlan, opposed cremation for religious reasons.

Still, it *was* a bit odd, standing there in the church looking at Harlan's casket. A full-sized casket—full human sized—with only a dick in it. How did that even work? Did they place the penis on a pillow where his head should have been? Or did they place it where the penis should have gone, mid-casket, with empty space all around? Did they put it inside pants? A full suit? Who knew?

The mortician's problem, Art had thought.

It had been a closed casket funeral. Obviously.

And though it had seemed strange at the time, it had been oddly *apropos*. One not-too-sorrowful mourner who Travers overheard had summed it up nicely, saying, "The guy *was* a dick."

Dark humor. Very.

Harlan's funeral had been well-attended not because Joe Junior would be missed, but out of respect for his father. The senator had spoken briefly, eulogizing his son. But the whole thing had felt more like a state ceremony than a funeral—very few tears.

There would be another funeral shortly—for Deb Wise.

Travers sighed, pulled out his mobile phone, and called Glo. He was approaching Tarrytown. It was just past 4:00 a.m., and he decided he'd rather have her meet him at the Wises' house than make another stop.

Travers hated this part of the job.

CHAPTER THIRTEEN

Sunday
September 15, 2019
Coral Gables, Florida

Liz Bareto closed her laptop and put it gently on the coffee table in front of her. To the left of the laptop was a glass of Syrah that she'd started on when she'd initially sat down to check email. To the right lay a Glock G42 380 ACP Sub-Compact 6-Round Pistol—fresh out of its factory box, which still contained one magazine, a carry case, a bore brush, a rod, and the owner's manual. A small open box of Federal Ammunition 0.380 caliber bullets was on the table, and a second box and a receipt were still inside the plastic bag they'd put them in at Stone Hart's Gun Club when she'd picked everything up earlier that day.

She was at her home, a mid-sized Mediterranean style house on Blue Road in the picturesque Italian Village of Coral Gables, Florida.

Coral Gables dates back to the 1920s. As part of an early marketing campaign for the community, the developer George Merrick set aside certain areas for the construction of homes featuring internationally distinctive architecture. There are a number of such "villages" featuring different types of architecture—French, Chinese, and Greek, among others.

The house was "comfortable." Not what Liz was accustomed to, not by any stretch, but good enough for a newly single woman. *A divorcée,* she reminded herself, looking about the place. And with the alimony she was receiving from her ex-husband, a very happy *divorcée.*

It was 7:03 p.m. Liz had just emailed Detective Eddie Garza.

After her son Liam's death, she'd kept in touch with Garza. She'd never known a police officer before, not personally. Eddie was a bit crude sometimes, but the positive spin on crude was down-to-earth. That, he was. Down-to-earth *and* compassionate. He'd been understanding and helpful throughout the investigation of Liam's death. She felt like everyone, including her husband—*now ex*, she thought happily—believed that she was deluded.

Eddie was different.

He agreed that there was something more to Liam's death than her boy simply succumbing to injuries. Of course, part of that could be the fact that Eddie was sweet on her. Yes, she had noticed, although she played it cool, secretly relishing the fact that she still had *it.*

But she'd kept in regular contact with Eddie because she wanted to keep her son's case alive. She knew in her heart of hearts that her son, her baby, had been murdered. She just couldn't prove it—yet.

Eddie, despite his crassness, was a professional, and had given her much food for thought.

Liz picked up the Glock and pulled the slide, confirming that a round was chambered. She glanced briefly at the owner's manual, verifying that she had properly loaded the gun. The gun was heavier than she'd expected for such a small weapon. The slide and barrel were cold to the touch, and the thing smelled mechanical, metallic, like oil.

Liz used her free hand to take a swallow of Syrah, then got up off the sofa and began to pace the living room, holding the handgun in one hand while thinking and sipping her wine. She was barefoot, and the cool wood floors felt fantastic against her skin.

When Liam had died in the hospital, the news had devastated her. Yes, her son had been in a head-on collision, but she had also been told that the prognosis was good. Solid.

What happened just didn't make any sense.

Still, he was gone.

And so was Camilla Cruise, the girl in the other car who'd been killed instantly. As a mother, Liz had mourned for her and her parents. But when she'd lost Liam, everything had changed.

After Liam's second autopsy, the one *she'd* paid for, she'd immediately suspected Camilla Cruise's parents—Roy Cruise and Susie Font.

It wasn't just what the autopsy had uncovered. It was her intuition, as well.

Detective Eddie Garza was there for her then. He brought the couple in for questioning. But that interview yielded nothing except for the fact that the two had been in South Carolina when Liam died. A clear-cut, verifiable alibi.

At the time, as painful as it was, that had been enough for Liz. She'd convinced herself that her intuition was wrong and that those two couldn't possibly have hurt her son.

You should have known better, Liz.

But since then, she had received new information.

Some time back, Eddie had confided to her that Roy Cruise had been questioned in connection with another murder investigation. Over a year ago, a young man named Joe Harlan Junior had traveled to Miami to meet with one of Cruise's partners, apparently for business. The boy had disappeared while in Miami. A week later, his penis had been found nailed to his father's front door—a Texas State Senator, Joe Harlan Senior.

The case went nowhere. There was no body. No crime scene. Just that one thing nailed to the father's door. It was horrifying, and yet, to Liz, revealing.

According to Eddie, Cruise was questioned, but it turned out that, conveniently, he wasn't in Miami when the young man disappeared. He was out of the country. He had an alibi.

Eddie had shared all of this with Liz shortly after the case file closed, just over a year ago. He'd thought it interesting that Cruise was verifiably out of town *again*. Eddie had been clear, while he suspected foul play, he didn't want Liz to get her hopes up because ultimately the only thing that would ever make a difference was evidence. She needed to understand that.

"In the scheme of things, it's probably nothing, Liz. Probably just coincidence. But, statistically, it's weird. Statistically, the odds of your average joe schmo being associated with not one, but two homicides in their lifetime are low. Very low. And it's even weirder for that person to have an ironclad out-of-town alibi in each case. Just sayin'."

Liz thought it was weird, too.

This revelation had made her question—indeed, regret— that she had so quickly discounted the possibility that Roy Cruise or his wife had been involved in Liam's death simply because they had an alibi.

It had been after that conversation with Eddie that she'd made up her mind; if she wanted justice for Liam's murder, it was up to her.

Liz had done some research and, after a number of interviews and meeting a lot of hacks, she'd narrowed her search pool to one. One private investigator who she trusted enough to look into Liam's death—or, more specifically, into Roy Cruise and Susie Font.

There's more to those two than meets the eye.

The private investigator's name was Maximiliano Ureña. His friends called him "M." He was an ex-police officer, as most private detectives are. She'd hired M over a year ago.

Unfortunately, within days of hiring M, her husband had served her with papers. *Irreconcilable differences* was what the divorce petition said. *Inability to deal with the loss of Liam* was what he told her. He'd claimed that she was obsessed, and that it was her obsession which was stopping *him* from moving on and had destroyed *them.*

That son-of-a-bitch didn't bat an eye. He didn't care that Liam was murdered. He abandoned his son's memory just like he tried to leave me swinging in the wind!

The divorce had been long, drawn out, and nasty. She'd brought a lot to the marriage, and they'd done well together. But they'd married before prenuptial agreements had become *de rigueur.* So, they'd had to fight it out.

Liz was okay with that. She was a fighter. And she'd held her own, although it irked her that the proceedings had temporarily frozen her ability to use funds for purposes beyond "normal maintenance and support." The private investigator had, much to her displeasure, been put on hold.

But just days ago, through mediation, they reached an agreement on how to divide their assets. At last, it was over. She could once again use her money as she wished.

Her first order of business had been to buy the gun and to contact M and resume the investigation.

The first payoff came almost immediately. M had telephoned her that evening—while she was checking email—to confirm that he'd received her wire transfer and to touch base. He'd wanted to let her know that, curiously, Debra Wise—the mother of the girl who had allegedly been raped by the Harlan kid—had been found dead of a gunshot wound in Austin, Texas just a few days earlier.

M considered it an odd coincidence and thought she should know.

Liz agreed.

Yet another death connected, even if incidentally, to that couple. First Liam, then Harlan, now Wise.

What are the odds of that, statistically...?

Liz had Googled Debra Wise and found a couple of news articles relating to her death, along with the obituary. She'd emailed all of it to Detective Eddie Garza.

Eddie,

You said you thought it was odd that Cruise has been connected with two murders. 'Statistically odd', you said. Well, how about three murders?!

There is something going on here, Eddie. More than meets the eye.

See links below.
Deb Wise murder
Deb Wise obit
Liz

Liz stopped pacing and paused to look at herself in the mirror. An attractive, forty-ish woman looked back at her. Pixie-short jet-black hair, pale brown eyes, full lips.

She raised her eyebrows. Well, she tried. They moved slightly—she was three days into her first Botox treatment, and just as Doctor Castrillon had predicted, she could still move them a bit. The effect was natural, just as he'd promised.

Damn, he is good.

She smiled at herself. That smile. Suddenly, Liam was looking back at her in the mirror. He'd had the same smile. Everybody had told her that. Her smile. Her nose. His father's grey eyes and sandy brown hair.

"This isn't over, Lee-Lee," she said aloud, using the pet name she'd given him when he was a baby. How he'd hated it when he'd become a teen. She smiled again.

"Those motherfuckers are going down. I promise you," she said, looking in the mirror as Liam's face morphed back into her own. She raised the gun up beside her head, James Bond style, with the business end pointing up at the ceiling. A smile crept across her mouth as she looked in the mirror at herself and the weapon, liking what she saw.

Then, she drew in a deep breath and raised her wine glass to the reflection in the mirror. "Cheers, girl. Here we go," she said, clinking the glass against the frame before downing the contents and then returning to the kitchen for a refill, the Glock hanging loosely in her right hand.

CHAPTER FOURTEEN

I am going to tell you more about Billy Applegate shortly. But, in order for Billy's story and mine to completely make sense, you need to understand more about my thinking as far as Susie and Roy were concerned.

You will recall that Joe Harlan Junior was last seen—intact—leaving the Intercontinental Hotel in Miami on May 2, 2018.

And you know that Deb Wise was found dead in her car on September 12, 2019.

Sixteen months passed between those two deaths.

What were Susie and Roy up to during those intervening months?

Nothing special, really. After killing Joe Harlan Junior, they returned to normal life—as if nothing had happened. Roy continued chasing deals at Cruise Capital. Susie took a job as a commentator at a local TV station.

My world, however, was turned upside down. I was treating them, two murderers, one of whom—Susie—had actually been under my care when the two killed Joe Junior. Not long after Harlan's death, Roy became a patient of mine, as well.

Of course, through our psychotherapy sessions, I did what I could to help them with their issues. I carefully studied Susie and Roy, and their decision-making and problem-solving processes. I took inventory of and analyzed their emotional and cognitive responses. While this was done as a part of their treatment, I also used the information to try to answer another—in my opinion, more pressing—question: would they kill again?

Megalomania—more commonly referred to as "delusions

of grandeur"—is a psychological condition characterized by *irrational* beliefs that one is wealthy, exceptional, above the law, and omnipotent.

Emphasis, you will note, on "irrational" beliefs.

You've probably met one. They're very similar in behavior to narcissists. I personally can't stand them. They're my least favorite psychopathology. I agree with Erich Fromm that this pathology is "the quintessence of evil." Megalomaniacs are dangerous because they take actions based upon a mistaken belief in their omnipotence.

I did not believe Susie and Roy suffered from clinical megalomania. Their issue was deeper, more troubling, and more dangerous.

Consider Susie and Roy's situation immediately after Joe Harlan's murder.

They were wealthy. Roy had been very successful in his business, and Susie's career in journalism didn't hurt. Financially, they were very well off. In addition to this security, they were both well-educated. Both studied law at a top U.S. law school—UT Austin. Both had successful careers. In many ways, they were exceptional.

They'd also gotten away with murder. And I'm not talking about an accidental hit-and-run kind of murder. I'm talking a premeditated, carefully planned murder. They knew the risks. They faced them. They killed. And they got away with it.

What's worse is that, including Harlan's death, Susie had in fact been involved in three murders—little Joan Diaz, Liam Bareto, and Joe Harlan Junior—without suffering any legal repercussions.

So, you see, Susie and Roy did not suffer from megalomania because their beliefs were not irrational.

Their wealth was not an *illusion*. It was real.

They did not *imagine* themselves to be exceptional individuals. They were exceptional.

They did not have *delusions* of being above the law. They had proof.

All the things that a megalomaniac irrationally believes of himself, and which he uses to justify actions the rest of us would find reprehensible... all those things were actually *true* of Susie and Roy.

But, unlike a megalomaniac, whose actions are based on fantasies— and who typically overestimates their capabilities—Susie and Roy were very aware of their strengths and weaknesses.

They were not handicapped by a false sense of their omnipotence.

Susie and Roy's true problem was that there was nothing clinically wrong with them, yet they had within them the potential— which they had already proven by their actions—to commit murder.

My conclusion, my expert opinion, was that Susie and Roy would kill again, given the right circumstances.

And, if they did, they would get away with it.

CHAPTER FIFTEEN

On April 18, 2019, the Thursday before Easter, Susie confessed to me that she and Roy had killed Joe Harlan Junior. When Susie left after that session, I felt sick to my stomach. I knew that I had failed to properly diagnose my patient. She wasn't harmless. She was a cold-blooded killer. Thankfully, she was my last appointment for the day.

It was late afternoon, and a very bright day in Miami. Birds were chirping in the trees. I closed the blinds, lowered the AC temperature, turned down the lights, and sat in my office for quite some time, thinking.

I had a family dinner later that evening, one I had been looking forward to. My kids were in town from college for the holiday. But I had lost all motivation.

It was the same week that Notre Dame Cathedral burned. That event was destabilizing for me. It brought home to me how impermanent *everything* is. Even something *that big* and ancient and treasured could be destroyed in a blink.

I recognized in myself the beginning signs of depression. I felt conflicted and helpless. Useless.

Months before that session, Susie had told me about the murder of Liam Bareto. But I'd thought then that it was a one-off crime. As I sat there in the semi-dark, the gravity of what I had just learned weighed on me. My client had confessed that she was not only a murderer, but a serial killer. Perhaps not for pleasure, not like Dahmer or Gacy, but a serial killer nonetheless.

What *could* I do?

My first thought was to go to the authorities.

However, as I have mentioned before, when Susie told me about Bareto, she made sure to point out my legal obligations. Everything she shared with me was in regard to things she had done in the past. And it was all shared in the course of seeking mental health treatment. As such, it was protected by physician-patient confidentiality.

That said, given Susie's most recent revelation and that she had committed Harlan's murder with her husband Roy, I now felt strongly that they were a danger to others. In light of this new information, surely I had a duty to report them. No?

I needed to understand the full extent of my obligations vis-à-vis my patients, given these new circumstances.

I called my lawyer, who told me that the situation was outside his bailiwick. He referred me to a top criminal defense attorney named Melissa Losilla. We met at her law office.

When Melissa entered the conference room where her receptionist deposited me, she was not at all what I'd expected. On the phone, her voice was deep and raspy, like a smoker's. I'd expected a large woman for some reason. A bull in a china shop. Melissa was all that personality-wise, but she was physically tiny. Maybe five-foot-two in very expensive high heels. She had long dark hair, streaked with grey, which she wore loose, almost carelessly. She was dressed in an elegant, navy-colored skirt and a cerulean blouse that made her eyes seem more blue than grey. They were lively eyes, and moved quickly in sizing me up, studying my face, analyzing me.

As she reached out to shake my hand, I noticed that she had fine, elegant fingers with perfectly manicured French nails that held the gold Mont Blanc which she used to take notes during our meeting. She was calm, which had a soothing effect on me. But she gave off an aura of pent-up energy, like a tightly-wound dynamo waiting for an excuse to explode.

Without naming names, I explained my situation in detail. I had even prepared several pages of notes for her, which she quietly reviewed after scrawling 'Notes for legal counsel. Attorney-client privileged.' across the top of each page.

After laying out all the details, I summed up: "I want to understand if I have any obligation—or if at this point I'm at least allowed to report what they've done. I've become privy to all these crimes—no, not just crimes, murders... the victims, details, and literally where the bodies are buried. But it's all in the past. It's all already happened, and it was all disclosed to me during therapy sessions with my patients."

Melissa took her own notes. She asked a few questions, and then told me she'd like to meet again in a few days.

"The law on this is pretty straightforward," she said. "But, given the..." she searched for the right word, "complexity of your situation, I'd like to refresh myself on the legal nuances and dig into the cases a bit."

The next time we met, a week later, I noted that she was tanned, her nose slightly sunburnt. "Boating," she explained, but she kept the small talk to a minimum.

"It's pretty much as I thought. The short of it is that Florida is *not* a 'duty to warn' state. The Florida Supreme Court has ruled that imposing on therapists like you a duty to 'predict' whether a patient will harm another person would place an *unfair burden* on therapists. You shouldn't have to guess what your patients may or may not do. That's not your job. So, the law does you a favor by not obligating you to predict when a patient may do something illegal. And the law doesn't hold you liable if they do.

"Bottom line, legally, you have no obligation to say or do anything." She paused, then rephrased, "Not only do you *not* have to do anything, you can't even be compelled by law to reveal what your patients have told you."

Melissa looked at me, waiting for me to absorb this information. "My advice to you?" she began, pausing again before continuing, "Do nothing. If you go to the cops, your clients can sue you. And they'll win. And you'll probably lose your license. On top of that, they won't even see the inside of a jail cell because nothing they told you can be used to convict them of any of their past crimes. They probably won't even be arrested. It's all confidential—no court will allow it into evidence."

I must have looked as sick as I felt because she sat still, only watching me.

I sighed. I wanted to cry, both from my predicament and the sheer frustration of it all. "Should I continue treating them?" I asked.

Melissa thought, tapping her Mont Blanc on the legal pad in front of her. "Have they said they want to stop?"

"No."

Her face changed slightly, softening. She put down her pen and leaned forward. For a moment, I felt she was addressing me as a fellow human being rather than as a client.

"Look, you're in a fucked-up situation. I'm not your conscience. I can't tell you what's moral or the right thing to do, or any of that bullshit. And I can't tell you what is best as far as your own…" her eyes searched the corners of the room for the right word, "…peace of mind? I can tell you what the law says. But I can also tell you what… *I think*, at least… the practical reality is."

I nodded, wanting to hear more.

"Right now, you're of value to them. As long as you're treating them, that doesn't change. But, if you stop being of use to them, you stop being of value." She looked down, pursing her lips. "And it doesn't sound like that's a good place to be."

We both sat for a moment in silence.

"But," she began addressing her client again, picking up her pen, "if they tell you that they're going after someone in particular, a specific person, call me. Or if they threaten you. Then things change." She ended the sentence with a shrug and half-smile.

To me, it seemed that the law on this issue was very badly written. But then, those who'd written it probably hadn't contemplated this kind of situation.

So, at that point, it was clear to me that I was stuck with them.

Susie confessed Harlan's murder to me on April 18, 2019. When I spoke with my lawyer as I've just described, it was about five months before Deb Wise was found dead in her car. While Susie and Roy were living life as if nothing had happened, I was a wreck.

However, not too long after I talked to my lawyer, something strange happened. Things began to align themselves in such a way that my relationship with Susie and Roy evolved in a very unexpected direction. I experienced hope—a light at the end of the tunnel.

Little did I know that while I was pursuing that possibility, the universe was setting us up for catastrophe. Deb Wise's death set into motion a chain of events none of us could have anticipated. Her death changed things for all of us. Surprisingly, the one person without whom things might have ended very differently for me, and Roy and Susie, was Kristy Wise.

I have no doubt that the things she did were well-intentioned and probably even saved lives in the short-term. But, ultimately, Kristy led us all to disaster.

CHAPTER SiXTEEN

Wednesday
September 18, 2019
Austin, Texas

Kristy had come to despise funerals—particularly wakes. As she put it, "*Wakes fucking suck!*" Really, the whole funereal process sucks, because among other things, it's way too long. Apparently, this is especially true if you're Catholic.

First, there's the Rosary a night or two before the funeral. It's a short ceremony, maybe thirty minutes, of prayers for the deceased. Everyone offers the family their condolences.

Then, there's the actual funeral ceremony, usually accompanied by a mass. The saying goodbye—the eulogy. And everyone offers the family their condolences.

Then there's the burial. After a long, slow drive from the church to the cemetery, you have more prayers and more holy water sprinkles. Body into the ground. And everyone offers the family their condolences.

Then, finally, the wake. After the burial, everyone goes back to the family's house to eat and drink. This was the worst part, according to Kristy, because a wake is really a party. But it's a different kind of party. A party where the guest of honor is the only person not in attendance. This type of party is usually conducted in whispers—it starts that way, at least, until the alcohol gets flowing. Then it's like any other party, except when the next of kin are close by. Then, the mood changes, becomes more somber, and...

...everyone offers the family their condolences. *Again.*

For Tom and Kristy Wise, it was all finally over. The wake lasted a bit longer than Kristy would have liked, but at 7:23 p.m., the ordeal had ended.

And Kristy was fried.

After the last guest left, she changed out of her funeral clothes into sweats and a t-shirt. She did a few stretches, just to loosen some tightness, and then made herself tea.

She was sitting at the kitchen island in her parents'—now her father's—house with Bethany Rosen, who was usually perky and energetic, but this evening was understandably subdued. Kristy's father was snoring in the living room. She stared blankly at the oven, reflecting, watching as the digital clock announced the time, advancing one minute at a time. Each change of number was a part of the countdown, reminding her that one minute less remained in her life.

The whole ordeal had been draining. If it hadn't been for Bethany, Kristy didn't know if she'd have made it through.

Everything had started six days before. Her father had called her on her iPhone—slurring slightly, which hadn't surprised Kristy. His drinking had been a problem for some time now.

"Hi sweetie. I need to see you. Will you be home soon?"

"I'm here, Dad. Upstairs. In bed."

"Oh. Okay. Can you come down?"

Kristy had glanced at the time on her phone. It was almost 5:30 a.m.

He'd sounded drunk, but she'd thought nothing of it. He'd do that sometimes. Get wasted and then text her. Sometimes, he'd call. He'd get sentimental. Morose. And he would often lose track of where she was.

Kristy had come downstairs to find her father sitting at the same island where she now sat. He'd been entertaining three guests—Art Travers, Glo Spoor, and Johnny Walker Black.

No sooner had she walked into the kitchen than he'd unloaded a rambling slur of an explanation. The gist of it was that her mother had been found shot dead. He hadn't even given Kristy the chance to sit down before he'd dumped it all on her.

The news had been devastating, made worse by the callous way in which it was delivered.

Though he'd tried, Tom Wise had been unable to articulate what had happened, or what he'd been told had happened. Kristy had received most of the details, or at least all that was known at that point, from Detective Travers. Not that any of it mattered anyway.

Her mother was gone. That's all she'd heard.

Practically speaking, so was her father.

Since that day, he'd sunken into a depression marinated in whiskey. When he'd gone on benders in the past, Kristy's mom had usually been able to straighten him out. But for the last week, with Deb gone and his having to deal with her death, he'd not stopped drinking except when he'd passed out. Like now.

Kristy had to take time off from school to handle all the funeral preparations because her dad could barely tie his shoelaces. She was the one who'd contacted the funeral home and dealt with everything—the Rosary, the clothes for her mother's body, the mass, the burial, the eulogy... she'd even written her father's words for him. Thankfully, Bethany had come around to help without even being asked—a real life saver. That's just the kind of friend she was.

The only time Bethany hadn't been with Kristy during the past six days was when Kristy and her father had gone to see the lawyers to deal with the estate issues. That was a private matter, after all. Deb's last will was simple enough; aside from her jewelry and some odds and ends, she'd left everything to her husband.

But Deb had also left three envelopes in her attorney's custody, to be delivered upon her death. One for Tom, one for Kristy, and one for a woman named Susie Font.

Kristy had been given hers.

Tom had been given his.

And the attorney had said that he would mail out the envelope for Susie Font.

"I'd like to see her letter," Tom had said.

"I'm afraid that isn't what Deb wanted, what she provided for in her will," George Pringle, the estate lawyer, had replied.

"Fuck that, George! I'm her executor. She's gone, and I want to see it," Tom had shot back angrily.

Kristy had been surprised at the intensity of her father's reaction.

Pringle then paused, and Kristy could see the calculus running in his head—honor the wishes of "dead client" or maintain the business relationship with "living client." As he'd mulled over his decision, Kristy looked at the envelope, and although his hand covered most of the address, she could see that the destination was in Florida. Pringle opted for a pragmatic, Solomon-like solution.

"Let me have Teri make you a copy. I'm obligated to mail out the original. Teri..." he called out.

Kristy drove her father home from the meeting. He'd put the copy of the Font letter in his laptop bag along with his own letter. Kristy was curious about the letter, and she asked her father about Susie Font. She wanted to know who she was and why her mother would see fit to leave her an envelope of her own. He ignored the question, asking instead whether or not Kristy had confirmed the priest for the ceremony.

With everything she'd had going on in terms of funeral preparations, she'd taken the bait and forgotten about the letters.

Until now.

CHAPTER SEVENTEEN

From across the kitchen island, Kristy heard, "Whatcha thinking?"

Bethany was smiling gently, probing.

"Those letters. The ones from my mom...."

Kristy rose quietly and padded into the living room. Tom was asleep, passed out on the sofa. He was snoring deeply. Kristy knew the sound. From the depth and timbre of the snoring, she was sure that he wouldn't wake for a while.

Bethany came up quietly next to her.

"Can you watch him, Beth? Let me know if he wakes up?" Kristy asked.

Bethany nodded rapidly, conspiratorially, folding her arms across her chest and leaning against the doorframe.

Kristy went into her father's office. His computer bag was on his chair. Both his letter and the copy of the letter to Susie Font were there. The seals on both envelopes had been torn. Tom had apparently read them.

Kristy read her father's letter first.

July 12, 2018

Dearest Tommy,

Well babe, I guess it's over. And, if you're reading this, it's because I went first.

So, that means I need you to buck up for Kristy. Losing a parent is tough. She'll need you now more than ever, and you need to be there for her.

You know how I feel about that.

You know what I was willing to do for her, and damn the consequences. You also know that I would have been willing to do the same for you. I need you thinking that way now. You're not going to have me around anymore to push you when you need it.

Tommy, I don't want my goodbye to be a Debbie-downer, but as much as I hate to say it, when it most mattered, you weren't there for Kristy. Not the way I was. Not the way Susie was. I know how you feel about her, but you have to admit that she really came through for us. She did what needed to be done. You can't blame her for how it went down, or for your small part in it. If anything, blame me. Susie would never do anything to hurt us. You need to believe that.

I've asked our lawyer to send her a letter from me. Please don't interfere with that.

It's all up to you now, babe. Stay away from the drink. Be the man I know you can be.

You know I love you, so I won't get into all of that.

It was a fun ride, babe.

See you on the other side.

Love,

Deb

Kristy's stomach tightened. Her mouth dried. She read the letter again.

Tears welled in her eyes.

Then she started, and listened carefully.

Silence.

Had Tom stopped snoring? She heard someone clear their throat in the next room, as well as some hushed words.

Was that Bethany warning her?

Kristy folded the letter and carefully placed it back in her father's computer bag next to the other. As she did, she heard her father grunt. He was getting up off the sofa!

She tiptoed over to the bookshelf and grabbed a novel, then turned to leave the office just as her father was coming in.

"Oh, hey, Dad."

"Hey. I thought I'd left the light on," he mumbled.

"Nope, just me. Looking for something to read. I need a distraction." They stood for a moment looking at each other until Kristy spoke, "Well, good night." She kissed him lightly on the cheek as she passed him and headed up the stairs.

Tom watched his daughter walk away. He was feeling nauseous.

Back up in Kristy's room, Bethany spoke first. "Sorry about that. He just woke up all of a sudden. Did you find them? The letters?"

Kristy raised a hand and said, "Hold on, before I forget," and sat down at her desk, scribbling everything she could remember from the letter she'd just read onto a sheet of paper. She spoke the words out loud as she did so, for Bethany's benefit.

"What do you think she's talking about, Kris?" Bethany reached for the notes.

"*...you weren't there for her.*"

"*Not the way I was.*"

"*Not the way Susie was. ...she gets things done.*"

"Any ideas?"

"Beth, you know how my mom was. She could be tough. A real... you know."

"I remember," Bethany said tenderly.

"But there's only one time she ever accused Dad of not being there for me."

Bethany nodded, looking down at the paper in her hands, and whispered, "Harlan?"

Kristy nodded.

"It's been a long day, Kris. How about we sleep on this? Scarlett O'Hara style?"

Kristy nodded, smiling. "I'll think about it tomorrow."

Before turning out the light, Kristy opened her desk drawer to put away the notes. As she did, she removed and re-read the letter her mother had left for her only daughter.

July 12, 2018

> *My darling Kristy,*
> *One burden we must all bear as children, in the natural order of things, is laying our parents to rest. If you are reading this, it's because life has followed its natural order, and I am thankful that it has.*
> *You are an amazing young woman. I have so many hopes for you. The greatest and most important is happiness. Find people you love in this world, and who love you, and do everything you can to keep them close. Remember, what matters in life is not what happens. Shit happens every day—and we can't control any of it.*
> *What matters in life is what you DO. And you have complete control over that.*
> *Take care of Dad. I know he's been having a hard time. We've been dealing with issues, but we always are one way or another. That's life—especially married life. And, you know, I'm probably not the easiest person in the world to be married to!*
> *Be tough, little munchkin.*
> *I'll always love you, no matter where I am.*
> *Much, much love,*
> *Mom XOX*

Kristy swallowed the lump in her throat as her eyes began to burn. She wasn't sure if it was her emotions or fatigue, but either way, she didn't feel like changing into pajamas. She climbed under the sheets, slid down in the bed, and put her head on the pillow.

But she couldn't stop thinking about the letters and what her mother had written to her father. As she drifted into a fitful sleep, Kristy kept hearing those words in her mother's voice.

> *"…you weren't there for her."*
> *"Not the way I was."*
> *"Not the way Susie was…"*
> *Oh God, Mom. What the fuck did you do?*

CHAPTER EIGHTEEN

After the rape and Harlan's acquittal, Kristy learned what it was like to be truly alone. The guys on campus ignored her. She was the girl who had cried wolf.

The girls were of two mindsets. One set wanted her as their poster child, to tell her story, to warn others. #MeToo. The other set tried to treat her as if nothing had happened, but Kristy could feel it—just below the surface, a tension that hadn't been there before.

Faced with all that, she preferred to simply be alone.

Her mother had helped her through it. She knew when to give her space and when she needed a gentle push to slowly inch her way back to the life she'd once had. Her mother had always been there for her, and now she was gone. That sad realization brought Kristy's thoughts back to her current predicament.

Kristy was in the zone.

If you're a runner, you've been there. You enter a state that's almost like meditation, where your physical self is flowing, but it feels like it's not a part of you, and you are one hundred percent in your head. Thinking becomes clear. Ideas come fast. Solutions appear out of nowhere.

She was completing mile seven of her ten-mile run for the week and hadn't felt her feet touch the ground for two miles. Her running watch showed her at a seven-minute-mile pace. Not that she was looking at it. She was in her head. At peace. Muscles firing, heart and lungs pumping, sweat dripping, dopamine flowing.

She was analyzing what she'd learned from the two letters her mother had left behind. The two she had managed to get her hands on, at least, and she was trying to decide what to do next.

She'd talked it through with Bethany again that morning. Bethany had very clear opinions about the situation.

It seemed to Kristy that, in the letter to her father, her mother had been referring to something to do with Joe Harlan Junior. She knew her mother as well as any twenty-two-year-old woman did. She had some sense of what she was capable of. But her mother having had anything to do with Harlan's disappearance seemed—on its face—extreme, even for Deb. It was the reference to this Susie woman which gave her pause. Harlan had disappeared in Miami, and the woman's address was in Florida.

Kristy thought back to the time around Harlan's disappearance. The whole thing had come as a shock to her. To her parents, as well—at least, it had seemed that way to her. As she thought more about it, however, she realized that it was right around that time when her father had started hitting the booze again, and heavily.

Interestingly, he'd held up well when Harlan had been under trial for raping her. He'd also held up well during his own trial for assaulting Harlan. It had only been after Harlan's disappearance that things had deteriorated. Kristy had previously attributed it to the pressure. That the whole series of events had all been too much, and that something had finally had to give.

She began to rethink that analysis. Maybe there'd been something else going on.

Bethany had reminded her that, although he was generally a "mellow guy," her father was capable of violence. After all, he had attacked Harlan at Whole Foods.

"Maybe he went further, Kris," Bethany had suggested.

As Kristy gamed different scenarios, she kept coming up against the same brick wall of impossibility. Until she finally had to ask herself: was her father capable—and she still hesitated to think it—of murder? Was her mother?

She didn't think so. She didn't want to believe it.

Kristy pulled up, breaking her pace while shaking her head, and slowed her running to a jog, then a walk.

She began to laugh out loud at the absurdity of it all.

Come on. This is fucking ridiculous!

This isn't The Sopranos. *My parents aren't killers. Tom and Deb Wise are not murderers.*

Okay. Sure, there's something weird going on here. But what you really need is more data. More information.

Kristy realized that she knew practically nothing about Susie Font.

Only what she'd gleaned from Deb's letter to her father.

I know how you feel about her...

Susie would never do anything to hurt us.

Clearly, her father didn't trust Susie. Why? And why would her mother emphasize that Susie *wouldn't* hurt them?

Kristy thought back to the principle her psychology prof harped on: *Excusatio non petita accusatio manifesta.* Or, as Bethany had summarized it, quoting Shakespeare, "The lady doth protest too much, methinks."

Was Susie dangerous? Had her parents discussed that possibility? Or did her father know something her mother hadn't?

Her mother's death weighed on Kristy. Losing a parent is bad. Losing a parent young—and due to violent crime—is worse.

Kristy's greatest fear was that her mother's death might, in some way, be attributable to something her mother had done *for her.* If that was the case, she wanted to know. She needed to find out. And if this whole Harlan mess had somehow cost her mother her life, she planned to do something about it. Whoever was involved would pay, and pay dearly.

She resumed her run, and as her shoes pounded the pavement on Veteran's Drive heading toward her car, she decided that Bethany's suggestions made sense. Kristy needed to see what she could find out about this Susie woman—a bit of online sleuthing was bound to get her some information.

CHAPTER NINETEEN

Monday
September 23, 2019
Miami, Florida

Eddie Garza had been swamped at work. He'd read Liz Bareto's email and he'd followed and read the links she'd sent about Deb Wise's death. He'd even done some of his own research, but found nothing new. Liz was right, though. Deb Wise's death marked a third killing that was at least tangentially connected to Roy Cruise.

Eddie decided to give Art Travers a call to see if he had any additional information. At the very least, it would give him an excuse to call Liz back.

Shit.

A picture of his wife and little girl stared at him from the corner of his desk. Life was good. Why the hell was he even thinking about Liz Bareto?

He had no idea.

What he did know was that there was something about her. It was probably her vulnerability. He knew he had a bit of a weak spot for women in distress. And Liz, a mother who'd lost her child in somewhat questionable circumstances, certainly qualified.

She was attractive in a natural, no-makeup kind of way. Not a Barbie doll. She was elegant and refined. And she was sensitive, her pain tangible. She was so far removed from the people in the dog-eat-dog world that Eddie inhabited daily that he felt she needed his help all the more. Liz knew nothing about killers. She'd never dealt with them, but Eddie did on a daily basis. They were part of his world, and it was a dark place full of very nasty people. It was something he wanted to protect her from. And while he understood—admired, even—her desire to get justice for her son, he believed in his heart of hearts that the kid had in fact died from the injuries sustained in the car accident and nothing else.

Still, he wanted to help her. He couldn't stand to think that he hadn't done everything he could for her, and that included chasing down every possible lead.

"Hello, Eddie," Travers said, answering his mobile phone.

"Howdy, Tex. How are things?"

It had been a while since they had spoken, and the two detectives bantered for a minute before Eddie came to the crux.

"So, I got an email from Liz Bareto. Tipped me off that Deb Wise ate a bullet?"

"If you eat with the side of your head, then yeah. Nasty. You get the basics online?"

"Yep. I was calling to see if you could color it in for me."

"Yeah, sure. We found her in the parking lot of an animal shelter here. The scene was spotless. One bullet to the head through an open driver's side window. Time of death around 9:00 p.m. Autopsy was clean. Just the one wound. Lab results, same. No drugs or alcohol. Nothing. No security cameras. No witnesses. Officer patrolling the area found the body around 1:30 a.m. Not late enough for the family to have even missed her."

"Really? At 1:30 in the morning?" Eddie asked.

"Well, when I got there, the daughter was in bed asleep and the husband was pretty drunk. I'm guessing he was out of it."

"Robbery?"

"Maybe. We found her coin purse about twenty feet from the car. Cash gone. No prints."

"Any idea why she'd be at an animal shelter that late?"

"No clue." Travers paused. "I made the visit to the house—"

"How'd the husband take it?" Eddie interrupted. Spouses were always good first picks for suspects.

Travers sighed. "Not good. But like I said, he was pretty

drunk when I got there. He's been 'not good' for a while. Been to rehab."

"Shit. Those folks can't catch a break, can they?" Eddie asked. "Was he okay for an alibi?"

"Yep. Said he was at home. He was asleep on the sofa when I rang the bell. The daughter, Kristy, went to bed around ten. Said he was home all night. I swabbed him for gunpowder. Nothing. Then, I talked to Kristy. She said they were doing fine. Her parents' marriage, I mean. Ups and downs like any couple, but better than they'd been. And they've been through a lot, so that's saying something."

"What about motive? Him—I mean Tom?" Eddie asked.

"Nothing I can find. No financial windfall. Community property—they owned everything fifty-fifty. There's life insurance, but it's a last-to-die policy, so he gets nothing. Daughter collects when he goes."

"So, you buying the robbery angle, then?" Eddie asked.

"Nothing else for sale right now," Travers answered. "How is it Bareto knew about this before you did?"

"She hired a private dick, man. Can't let the thing with her son go. The PI told her; she told me. She treats me better than you do, Art!" Eddie laughed. "You could keep me in the loop, you know? For old time's sake."

"It's only been a week, Eddie. I was going to call you. But it didn't seem that pressing."

"Yeah, yeah. You don't call. You don't write. You don't send flowers."

"Ah, now that you mention it. I'll tell you who did send flowers to the funeral. Senator Joe Harlan—he sent a big-ass bouquet. One of those round deals. But he didn't attend."

"Classy, I guess. You think he might have been involved? Sending flowers 'cuz he feels guilty?" Eddie asked.

"No. Checked him out. Discreetly, of course. At dinner with another senator and two lobbyists in San Antonio. Spent the night down there. He couldn't have—at least, he couldn't have pulled the trigger."

They were quiet for a few moments.

"What about Roy Cruise?" Eddie asked.

There was another pause.

Travers harrumphed. "How the fuck do you connect him to this, Eddie?"

"I don't know. Just a thought."

"And?"

Eddie sighed. "There's no 'and.' It was just a thought. Never mind."

"You still got a hard-on for that guy?" Travers asked.

"It's just odd. People seem to die around him."

"Seems like a bit of a stretch to me, Eddie."

"I guess you're right."

CHAPTER TWENTY

On its face, connecting Roy Cruise to Deb's murder was a stretch. But there are two kinds of cops: the by-the-book, follow-the-leads breed to which Art Travers belonged, and the seat-of-your-pants, go-with-your-gut variety, of which Eddie Garza was a quintessential example.

Eddie decided to go with his gut, and he knew that if anyone could help him find the connection he was looking for, it was Spencer Shaw.

Shaw was an up and coming prosecutor who had earned a reputation for aggressive tactics and brilliant analysis in his five years with the Miami-Dade State Attorney's Office. His nickname—one that he relished—was "Shock-and-Awe."

Shock-and-Awe had bought into the idea of the trial lawyer as a warrior-scholar, and he carefully cultivated his reputation. He had completed an Iron Man Triathlon every year since coming to Miami right out of a one-year judicial clerkship after graduating from law school at Gonzaga. He also made sure everyone knew that he was a brown belt in Jiu-Jitsu. And, every year, he published an annotated case-law update to the Florida Rules of Criminal Procedure.

Shaw was extremely protective of his trial record. Part of his "wow" factor was based on the fact that he knew which cases to plead out and which to take to trial. He *only* tried winners, and he was always looking for new and interesting cases. Shaw loved getting into cases early, before—he liked to joke—"the cops fucked them up."

"Shock-and-Awe! How you doin', man?"

Shaw looked up from his computer and took in Detective Eddie Garza in all his sordid splendor: baggy grey pants, blue button-down shirt with a white t-shirt peeking out at the neck, comfortable shoes, and his very Cuban Canotier hat. Much of the lawyer was concealed from Eddie's view by his desk and laptop screen, but the detective could see that he was wearing a white shirt and a blue tie, and that his blue-green eyes popped in contrast. He smiled amicably at Eddie with brilliant white teeth.

"Hola, Eduardo." Though Shaw was not Cuban or Hispanic, he'd made an overwhelming effort to learn Spanish and had succeeded, though he spoke with that odd American accent which sounded to a Spanish-speaker like a robot doing Shakespeare.

"You look... different," Shaw added, swiveling his desk chair toward his guest. He cocked his head to the side, studying Garza, and then asked, deadpan, "Have you gained more weight?"

Eddie roared with laughter as he sat down heavily in a chair next to Shaw's desk. "That's just like you, man. Always on the offensive."

"Oh, I get it. Because I'm a prosecutor, not a defense lawyer." Shaw sighed. "Oh Eddie, always so unoriginal. Please, take a seat," he said as he folded down the screen on his laptop.

"A little late for that," said Eddie, indicating that he was already seated. "You're looking good, *compa*. Things busy around here?"

"*Como siempre*. It's the way of the world. There're always more bad guys doing more bad things and not enough of us good guys."

"Tell me about it," Eddie replied, drumming his fingers on Shaw's desk.

"So, what do you need?" Shaw took a sip from a white mug that bore the letters MIT in cardinal red. His undergraduate *alma mater*.

Eddie dove right in and explained his recent call with Detective Travers, giving Shaw an overview of the "Roy Cruise has been near a lot of killings" hypothesis. During the explanation, Shaw sat back with his head resting against his chair and his eyes barely open. Eddie had worked with him before and knew he was in concentration mode.

"So, what do you think?" Eddie asked when he finished.

Shaw sat motionless while Eddie patiently waited for him to process what he'd heard. After about thirty seconds of silence, his blue-green eyes opened and he said, "So, Eddie, it's not so unusual for one person to have a connection to multiple homicides. I mean, we see it all the time in gang-related stuff, drugs, that kind of thing. But in those cases, there is a predicate offense driving the behavior."

Eddie's brows knitted and he pursed his lips.

"For example, imagine that a guy's a dealer, right? Let's say he pushes *negrita* in Little Haiti. That's his business. And as time goes by, people close to him begin to die of questionable causes. Lots of them. Well, that's not unusual or unexpected because he's got the underlying behavior—drug-dealing—that's putting him in situations where his associates may meet untimely ends."

Eddie smiled. "Gotcha. I see."

"So, you, Eddie," Shaw pointed at the detective, "may be on to something. You see, your guy doesn't seem to fit any of those patterns. Gangs, drugs, gaming, whatever. There is no predicate offense... that we know of. And, what intrigues me even more about your case is that," Shaw raised his index finger, "one—there are four deaths, including Mrs. Debra Wise, and," he raised the middle finger next to it, "two—the first three—the sister, Bareto, and Harlan—are completely unrelated, and in different geographies." He lowered his hand and ended, "*That* is unusual."

"The sister. You think there's something there? We kinda thought she was irrelevant the first time around, so long ago and all. But when Deb Wise died, that seemed odd."

"You need to re-think your analysis. Your intuition tells you that Bareto and Harlan, and now Wise, are relevant because they are connected to Cruise *and* close in time. While the sister is connected to Cruise *and...*"

After a pause, Eddie asked, "And what?"

"That's precisely the point. Just because you haven't answered the *and what* doesn't mean that it doesn't exist. It just means that you haven't found it yet."

Eddie had no idea what Shaw meant, but he pursed his lips, head nodding gently and eyes looking into the near distance.

"This is interesting, Eddie. I can give it a whirl. Do a little digging for you. But these are cold cases. I can't give them priority. Let me think on them a bit and see what I can come up with. A week or two?"

"That'd be great. *Gracias, Shaw!* I owe you a big one."

"A little one is fine. I'm sure that's all you can manage." Shaw smirked, and Eddie guffawed all the way down the hall to the elevator.

CHAPTER TWENTY-ONE

Friday
September 27, 2019
Miami, Florida

Recollections of a loved one often trigger feelings of nostalgia. But, sometimes, the loss is just too raw. The pain too bitter. And recollection triggers nothing but heartache and despair. A pain that burns the soul.

The summer of 2019 had overstayed its welcome in Florida, lingering well into September. As if to make a point about global warming, the rabid sun scorched the waters of Biscayne Bay for weeks, generating a haze of humidity that blurred the line between the windless sea and the sky above. Not to be accused of playing favorites, the sun's rays beat down on the land with equal spite, pummeling grass, palms, and bushes into limp submission. The heat weaponized asphalt roads and cement sidewalks, the shimmery mirages above them a clear warning to all living things to stay away or burn.

Even the rainstorms that normally provided some relief from the heat seemed to rain down hot, adding fuel to the cauldron. The combination of heat and humidity suffocated Miami, squeezing hope and life out of everything, including Susie Font.

Susie was not dressed for the weather. She wore white Chanel and black patent leather Louboutin heels, and in the crook of her right arm hung a black Hermès Birkin bag. And she was wearing her diamonds. All of them.

Given her druthers, she'd have been in shorts, a boat shirt, and flip-flops. But this was not pleasure. For her, this was a battle, and one she needed to win. Hence, the body armor.

As she walked the fifty paces from her air-conditioned Tesla, weaving through other parked cars to reach the front door of Patti Gallardo's house, the heat and humidity easily flushed a glow from her face and arms. By the time she had climbed the last step up the front porch to the landing and approached the door, her feet were sweating, and she could already feel the premonition of a blister on the heel of her left foot.

This fucking heat!

She poked irritably at the doorbell with her right hand and heard a faint *dong dooong* through the front door. In her other hand, she held a gift bag from *Boy Meets Girl*. She waited, noting with annoyance a trickle of sweat running from the nape of her neck down her back.

Nothing.

She hit the doorbell again and waited three beats. No one came to the door. Susie turned the knob—the door was unlocked.

Okay, girl. Think happy thoughts. Positive energy. Happiness. Be the joy!

She breathed in deeply, forced a broad toothy smile at no one, and then opened the door and crossed the threshold into cool air conditioning where Elton John singing "Daniel" welcomed her briefly before a wave of women's voices—laughing, chatting, praising, fawning—repulsed her in equal measure.

She felt queasy, but she kept smiling as she nudged the door shut behind her and took in her surroundings.

High ceilings. Marble floors. A circular Persian rug in the foyer, upon which sat a round glass table with a small Botero sculpture as its centerpiece. The house continued to the left and right off the entrance. Directly in front of her, on the other end of the expansive foyer and facing the front door, was a floor-to-second-story-ceiling window through which she could see the backyard, the terrace and pool, and, beyond both, a mid-sized yacht docked on the canal. Susie turned to the right, walking toward the chatter of multiple conversations overlapping.

"I just looove your shoes. Wherever did you find that color..."

"Next time you go, try the lamb..."

"So, now we've got him taking SAT prep classes three days a week..."

"That's exactly what I said. If he's sending you flowers for no apparent reason..."

Everywhere she looked, she saw pale blue bunting and white flowers. On a far wall, a white banner with pastel blue letters read, "*Congrats, Veronica!*"

It was a typical Miami baby shower, and the hostesses had clearly done right by the expectant mother, Veronica Rios. Had it not been for their close friendship, though, Susie would never have come. Veronica had personally delivered the invitation to Susie over coffee, and delicately given her an "out" if she didn't feel up to attending.

"It's just going to be a little get-together. No big deal. It feels kind of silly even doing it at all for a third baby. If you have other plans, I totally understand..."

"Don't be ridiculous, Roni. I appreciate what you're saying... what you're trying to do, but life goes on. And I'm so happy for you! There's no way I would miss it!"

Susie felt none of that positive energy now as she passed through the foyer and stepped down into the first of several contiguous living areas. She scanned the small groups of women, already spotting a number of familiar faces rapt in conversation. She also spotted a few women here and there who were taking note of the fact that she had arrived, and discretely pointing her out.

After placing her gift on a side table next to all the others, she began to make the rounds, chatting and catching up on bits of gossip.

A wide range of ages was represented. Susie knew a number of the women well, and knew almost all of them by name. Roni's mother was in the dining room holding court over a gaggle of older ladies sipping Cuban coffee and munching on *pastelitos*. At the other end of the spectrum, the youngest women at the party hovered around the champagne bar, nibbling guiltily at hors d'oeuvres, mentally tabulating their own and each other's caloric intake like golfers—the one with the lowest score would know she had won.

The majority of the attendees, however, were Susie's age, and these had congregated in several small groups in the living room.

Susie sat with a group of four other ladies, fanning conversation and counting the minutes before she could gracefully exit. She needed to greet and congratulate Veronica, who was being held hostage in the dining room. Then, she could make her excuses.

Susie felt completely alien in this environment because, although the women had organized themselves into groups by age, from Susie's perspective, she had walked into a gathering of two categories of women: mothers and mothers-to-be. And she was keenly aware that she was the lone member of a third category. She knew it, and so did everyone present.

She was an ex-mother... a mother whose child was dead.

It had been over four years since Camilla had died, and Susie had fought to recover from that tragic blow. To re-take control of her life and her marriage. God knew she had done *everything* imaginable to end the heartache—she'd run the entire gamut from denial to medication to therapy to murder.

Still she fought the demon, though less and less lately. She was a survivor.

But there were cracks where the pain shone through.

That was where her armor came in. While many of the women wore more casual attire, Susie's outfit served to remind everyone—most importantly herself—that there was more to her than just what had "happened" to her, that one event did not define her. She was many other things, including a professional woman. She worked in television. And although she had taken time out of her busy day for this little frivolity, she had important places to be. Important people to meet. Important things to do.

Yet, all armor—from a lobster's shell to a Navy SEAL's flak jacket—ultimately reveals the same truth. All armor highlights vulnerability. It trumpets the fact that below that hard exterior lies an interior that is soft, fragile, and in need of protection.

"Oh my God! Susie Font! It's been ages!"

Gabi Rivas, the wife of a commercial real estate developer, plopped down on the sofa beside Susie.

It *had* been a while, and Susie was surprised at how the woman had changed. Her forehead was frozen in place—from Botox, no doubt. She had odd wrinkles around her nose and mouth from what Susie speculated were excessive Restylane injections. She was obviously wearing hair extensions, as the back of her hair was full and voluminous, but the top and front were overly teased to add volume. Her bosom was spilling out of a dress that was one or two sizes too small and far too short. Though she was of average height, she wore very high heels to compensate because everything about her was simply bigger and better.

As they chatted, Susie's stomach turned. Gabi told her about her perfect husband—though she'd cheated on him with his boss and everybody in town knew it. Her perfect children—her oldest, a girl, was fourteen going on forty, and her son had been expelled from school for possession of cocaine and was now in a home-schooling program. Her perfect life—they'd been in litigation fighting to keep their six-million-dollar home out of foreclosure for over three years. Everyone knew it, and yet the woman was about as oblivious as they come.

"It is so good to see you! And how is Roy?"

At the mention of Roy's name, Susie sensed the demon's familiar, icy claw beginning to tighten around the base of her neck.

Her mouth became dry.

Her throat began to close.

Oh fuck. Keep it together. Ignore it! Let it go....

She shrugged her shoulders, willing it away, trying to ignore it, and smiling all the harder. But as she did, she felt the room begin to close in on her. The beginnings of tunnel vision. She raised her glass to sip water, but noted a slight tremor in her hand and tension in her neck that made her think better of the move. She carefully put the glass down, spilling just a bit.

She tried to focus on the conversation around her. But the sense of impending doom grew stronger, bit by bit, slowly invading her space until it came rushing down and hit her.

Hard.

Her ears burned. Her face and chest flushed. Her heart constricted.

The claw had her in its grasp. Strangling her. Sucking her breath away.

CHAPTER TWENTY-TWO

"Excuse me," Susie almost whispered as she peeled away from Gabi and the living room, walking calmly but rapidly to the powder room. She closed the door with trembling hands, locked it, and then turned and looked at herself in the mirror.

On the outside, it was barely noticeable. She could see in the mirror that she looked fine, calm, placid.

On the inside, she was a wreck. Wave after wave of emotion crashing against her, stifling her breathing, making her heart race. She turned on the faucet and ran her hands under the cool water, running it across her wrists. She reached for a hand towel, and as she dried her shaking hands, she looked in the mirror again.

But all she could see, everywhere she looked, was Camilla. Her beautiful daughter.

Dead.

Susie fought against the tears, dabbing carefully with toilet paper and trying to save her makeup. But it was a losing battle. She left the faucet running and quickly turned on the ventilation fan to make noise that would camouflage what she knew was coming. And then it hit her—a giant wave of sorrow that exploded into sobs that wracked her body.

She gave in utterly, sinking downward as her lips silently mouthed *Camilla.*

Tok Tok Tok.

Someone knocked gently at the door.

Susie looked up, realizing that she'd somehow slid down to the floor. She was lying in a heap on the bathroom tile, her back up against the vanity in a semi-fetal position.

Oh shit! How long have I been here? Fuck. Fuck. Fuck!

"Just a sec," she said out loud, in as normal a voice as she could muster. She carefully stood then, straightening her dress and inspecting her face in the mirror.

Tok Tok Tok.

Another knock, and then, "Are you okay? Can you open up? It's me, Roni."

Susie pulled a lipstick and mascara from her purse to put herself back together, saying "Hold on" before she unlocked the door. As she leaned forward, pretending to be simply touching up her makeup, Roni came into the powder room, leaving the door barely ajar.

"Just touching up," Susie said, looking at Veronica in the mirror.

Her friend put her hand on her shoulder. Susie paused her lipstick application, then turned and hugged Veronica. After a few moments, Susie pulled away, a broad smile back on her face as she sniffled and wiped away what remained of her tears. "Good God, woman! You're huge!" she exclaimed.

Veronica held onto Susie's upper arms, not letting her go. Looking her in the eye. "Thank you so much for coming," she said, then pursed her lips.

Susie fought back tears, smiling. She swallowed hard.

Oh, for fuck's sake, Susie! Man up!

She looked down and placed her hand on Veronica's belly, which was tight and round. "What does your doctor say?"

Veronica looked down, moving her right hand to her belly and placing it on top of Susie's. "He's ready to come out. Any day now. Technically due in a week. I don't know," Veronica answered rapid-fire. "Sometimes I feel like it's going to happen any second, and I start to freak out. Then, other times, I feel like it's never going to happen and I just want to get it over with." She paused briefly for a breath, then plowed on, "I'm peeing constantly. I haven't slept a full night in months. It's like carrying an oven around, you know? And it's so damned hot this year... so uncomfortable. I don't know....

When you were..." Veronica paused, realizing what she was saying. "I mean..." she stammered.

Susie jumped in, "Camilla was the same. She came a week early. By then, I was ready to be done with it, too. You know what did it for me? Three things."

Susie separated herself from Veronica and turned back to the mirror to finish her repair work, but continued talking.

"First, castor oil. A spoonful. Tastes like shit, but it works!

"Second, chili peppers. Had some for dinner on my pizza—which I recommend with caution, because all that came back up later. But the spice supposedly works.

"And number three, a little... extracurricular activity." Susie smiled at Veronica in the mirror and winked.

"Sex? Really?"

"Of course," Susie replied, turning to her friend. "Why do you look so surprised?"

"Joe hasn't touched me in like four months." Veronica blushed, her face and chest turning deep red. "He's afraid to... hurt me, or the baby."

"Oh, sweetie!" Susie laughed out loud. "If his dick is that big, you're a very lucky girl!"

Veronica squealed from surprise at the vulgarity of Susie's comment, then quickly covered her mouth with both hands. She shook her head and whispered to Susie, "Not *that* big..."

As Susie and Veronica walked back into the party, Susie sensed eyes on her. The conversation flowed, but she was being watched, assessed. There was some pity in the air. And some envy. As well as some genuine concern.

Susie, for her part, took comfort in one fact. No one present, not even Veronica, really knew Susie Font. They didn't know what she was capable of. They didn't know what she'd done. They didn't know her secrets.

No one, not even Roy, knew all of her secrets. Like the little thing that was keeping her sane. A tiny yellow pill—2.5 milligrams of salvation in a tablet.

CHAPTER TWENTY-THREE

That evening, Susie sat at a table at one of her favorite restaurants—The Bazaar by José Andrés, on Collins Avenue in Miami Beach.

News of Deb Wise's death had not yet reached her, though it would do so shortly by mail. Deb's letter was making its way through the United States Postal Service Processing Center in Coppell, Texas.

That the news had not pinged on Susie's radar wasn't surprising. A shooting in Austin, Texas is not big news in Miami. And although Susie is a newsie (I know, it rhymes), she was also cautious about creating any digital, traceable connections between herself and Deb for obvious reasons, so the last thing she would ever do was create any "Debra Wise" alerts in Google.

As you know, Susie and Roy love boating. They love the water. But they've spent most of their time on the water in the Bahamas and the Gulf of Mexico, and so, as a surprise for Susie, Roy had been planning a little trip to mix things up a bit. A new experience.

That is why he'd asked his wife to meet him at the Bazaar and promised to be there by 7:00 p.m., as soon as he was done with work.

When Susie arrived at 6:56 p.m., Mauricio escorted her to their usual table. While she waited, Susie pulled her phone out of her purse and started reading a book on her Kindle App.

At 7:00 p.m., there was no Roy.

Miami traffic, she thought.

At 7:15 p.m.—still no Roy.

Odd. Not like him to be late.

A few moments later, a waiter she didn't recognize approached her with a plate covered by a silver dome and began to place it on the table.

"Sorry, I didn't order anything," Susie said.

The waiter smiled and responded, "From the gentleman."

Susie looked over and saw her husband walking toward her from the bar with a martini glass. He was wearing a navy blue suit, a windowpane-patterned dress shirt, and no tie. He still had a bit of his summer tan, which made his green eyes pop. Susie felt a flutter in her belly. He still had that effect on her.

The waiter placed the plate on the table in front of her. "May I?"

"Please."

With a flourish, he removed the dome. On the plate was a medium-sized box, maybe a foot long by eight inches wide and another eight inches in height. Susie was admiring the box as Roy stooped to plant a kiss on her cheek. She turned and kissed him full on the lips.

"Surprise!" he said, sliding into the chair across from her.

The box was made of wood, with an inlay of what appeared to be mother of pearl in triangular shapes forming geometric patterns.

"Okay. Let me guess. I know the box is from Spain, right?"

Roy smiled. "Very good."

"Do I need to get more specific, or...?"

He shook his head. "The box just indicates a country. Open it."

Susie smiled and carefully lifted the small metal latch before raising the lid. Inside were several items.

The largest item was a small clay figurine. It appeared to be a man, standing upright. He was wearing a hat and holding a staff. The little statue was mostly white, its features painted with pastel pink and green. The eyes and mouth were painted with little pink dots. It had green eyebrows and little ellipses of green and pink decorating the hat and body.

Susie smiled. "Oh, babe. It's really cute, but I have no idea."

She removed the figurine from the box and placed it on the table. Next, she picked up a small glass vial with a cork stopper and held it up to the light. The liquid was clear and offered no clues. She unstopped the cork and wafted the bottle under her nose.

"Almost no scent."

She held the vial in one hand, thumb on the bottom, index finger on top covering the opening, and then turned it upside down, wetting her index finger. She held her finger close to her lips and said, "Dare I?"

Roy smiled and nodded.

She placed the finger in her mouth and then removed it slowly—playfully, seductively. As she did, she rolled her eyes, feigning analysis. "Bitter, with a very light finish. I taste salt?" she asked. "Sea water? The ocean, perhaps?"

"Very good."

The last item in the box was a keychain attached to what looked like a miniature sandal. It was rubber-soled with leather uppers, open-toed, and had a small heel strap. On the upper that covered the arch of the foot was a small lizard design.

This, Susie had seen before.

"Mallorca?" she asked, laughing. "Mallorca!"

"You got it." Roy smiled.

Susie jumped up from her chair, threw her arms around him, and kissed him.

"This is amazing! When do we go?"

"We leave in about two weeks. I've got the whole trip planned..." Roy paused as he noticed that Susie's face fell.

"What's wrong?"

"Well, I've got to see... I've got to arrange time off, Roy. I mean..." It was Susie's turn to pause as Roy manipulated his phone and handed it to her.

"You devil!" she said in a mock whisper. On the screen was an email to Roy, from Susie's boss and a good friend of theirs—Manny Calvo—confirming Susie's time off and wishing Roy luck with his "surprise vacation."

"Is there anything you didn't think of?"

"You know me. I've planned it all out. A few days in Madrid and Barcelona, and then we keep heading east to Mallorca, where we charter a yacht for a week. So, we'll have some time on land. Eat good food. Do a bit of shopping. Then there's a lot of great diving up on the northeast coast, near a place called Pollença—an old Roman village. That's the plan, anyway."

Roy held up both hands, wanting to appear flexible. "But we can do whatever. We can circumnavigate the island or go to Menorca, Ibiza. Whatever you want. Just the two of us and a lot of ocean!"

"I *love* your plans. And I shall do as you bid," she teased.

Roy laughed.

"So," she said, picking up the figurine, "what *is* this thing?"

"It's called a *siurell de fang*—they're made of baked clay. I don't know the literal translation. I know that *fango* is mud in Spanish. *Fang*—*fango*, maybe? I guess the rest of it is the local dialect. They're typical to Mallorca. They've been making them for centuries."

"Does it have any kind of significance? Fertility, maybe?" she asked, coyly.

"I think that may be the case, actually. I guess we'll just have to see."

"Well, this is amazing! I can't wait!" She squealed.

Roy signaled to Mauricio, who came over and took their order.

Over dinner, he laid out the details of the vacation he had planned for the two of them—he had even downloaded photos of some of the dive sites he'd found online and prepared a dossier of his proposed itinerary.

He shared everything with her.

Well, almost everything.

Roy had another surprise in store for his wife—one that he'd been preparing very carefully, and that he would only reveal once they were in Spain.

CHAPTER TWENTY-FOUR

The next morning, Slipknot was sitting in his office chair, which was an old brown leather monster he'd picked up at a flea market—perfectly functional, lots of character, and only thirty dollars. He'd probably spent half his day every day for the past five years working in this chair.

Slipknot had inherited his home from his father, a professional drunk who had abused him through most of his childhood after his mother had left them. His office was actually set up in the master bedroom, as Slipknot saw no point in using the large master for sleeping. Instead, he bunked in a smaller bedroom that contained only a narrow cot. The third bedroom in the house was set up as a gym that he used religiously—three times a day.

Work first, then play.

Ronald Clayton was not a big man. Never had been, even as a child. He'd been plagued all his life by nicknames. His father had called him "shithead" on good days, "fuckhole" when he'd been upset. At school, he'd been known as "Scrawny Ronnie," though only behind his back after Jimmy Lange had called him that to his face in seventh grade and lost two teeth for it.

Clayton's size and terrible acne had relegated him to a group called "the freaks" throughout high school. Hunting and weed had gotten him through those years.

Upon graduation, he'd joined the Marines, where he'd been nicknamed "Pizza-face" by his drill sergeant due to his cavernous acne scars. But Pizza-face had surprised everyone by performing exceptionally well in Basic Training, save for one small hitch.

By the end of Basic, he'd lost all his hair. Every hair on his body—head, pubic, nose—gone. The military doctor had diagnosed it as alopecia areata universalis—very rare. The additional downside of this disease, over time, was a terrible itching and burning sensation all over his skin, such that, whenever he could, Slipknot did not wear any clothes.

Thus, he was sitting completely naked in his office, reviewing his *Joe Harlan Junior List*.

Slipknot had been through all of the materials Senator Harlan had sent him, conducted some background checks as well as research into all of the major players, and built a timeline of the different events. But, in the end, everything came down to a list:

> Joe Harlan Junior (victim)
> Joe Harlan Senior
> Frank Stern
> Kristy Wise
> Tom Wise
> David Kim
> Roy Cruise
> Debra Wise (deceased)
> Marty McCall

There was a method to everything Slipknot did. He was obsessive in his need for order. His list began with the victim, and then he'd included those significant persons who'd had contact with the victim in decreasing order of familiarity or proximity.

The victim. Then the father. Then the business partner and "best friend." Then the woman the victim had had sex with. Her father, the man who'd attacked the victim. The man who'd contacted the victim about coming to Miami. And then Cruise and Debra Wise, the latter of whom he'd included for the sake of completeness. She was dead, but she may have been involved, and may even have been the killer. Last, Marty McCall.

Slipknot stood and began to pace. As he did, he spoke to the people on his list. He had gotten to know them all very well. But one of them was keeping a secret from him.

"One of you motherfuckers killed him. But why?" He thought better when he paced, as the light touch of the air on his flesh relieved the incessant burning.

"Mr. Senator, sir," he chuckled. "My little Cherry. You, sir, are no genius. But there's no way in hell you'd get little Ronnie Clayton involved in this mess if you'd done it, would you now? No siree... this all comes down to the kid's dick," he said, looking at the wall to the left of his desk.

He had downloaded photos of everyone on his list and taped them up on the wall.

"It wasn't enough to simply kill him," he added as he looked from person to person on the wall. "You needed to send a message, didn't you?

"I get it," he chuckled. "I appreciate *your* panache. But, are you fuckin' with me?" he asked slowly, looking from photo to photo as if expecting a reply. "With that *4 Kristy* bullshit? Just a wild goose chase?" He looked at Marty McCall's photo for a moment, then at Roy Cruise and David Kim.

Slipknot found it interesting that Cruise Capital had invested in Procurex—Marty McCall's start-up company. About nine months after Harlan Junior had disappeared, the lawsuit between his company and TrueData had settled. But before settling, the lawyers for TrueData had managed to get their hands on a list of McCall's investors through pre-trial discovery. And there on the list had been Cruise Capital, in for $200,000.

McCall, of course, lived in Seattle and had an ironclad alibi. Cruise had been out of the country. Another ironclad alibi. David Kim had been in Miami on the day Harlan had disappeared. His alibi was the weakest.

Slipknot reached out and tapped David Kim on the chin.

Then he shook his head and turned to study Tom and Deb Wise's faces on the wall. "Wild goose chase," he repeated, "ooor," he drew out the word, "was this *really* all about Kristy?"

He shook his head again, looking down, and then spun and slammed a backhanded fist into David Kim's face, and laughed.

"Hoo! Hoo! Hoo! Gotcha, Gook! You may fool Scrawny Ronnie, but you ain't fuckin' fooling Slipknot, motha-fuckaaa!"

It was becoming clear to Slipknot. Kim's alibi was the weakest. He'd been in Miami when Junior had disappeared. He'd actually been the one to call him and lure him to Florida. And he was a 'gook'.

Slipknot returned to his desk and booked a flight to Miami.

Satisfied with his afternoon's work, Slipknot returned to the wall and studied Kim's crumpled photo. He reached up and gently touched it with the back of his hand.

"See you soon, asshole..."

Then he stepped back and looked at Kristy's face. He frowned, shaking his head. He studied her closely. It was an image he'd found amongst the media coverage of the rape trial. A photo of Kristy from her high school yearbook. He had others in the file, but this was his favorite.

So pure. So innocent. Before she'd been defiled by Joe Junior.

"My, my, my, little princess..." he whispered, reaching down and cupping his balls and his dick in his hand. "I can see why you fucked her, Junior."

He licked his lips.

"Appreciate your taste in whores, little man..."

Slipknot clutched gently at the weight in his hand and felt his genitals stirring. He looked at the clock on his desk. Almost 3:00 p.m., and time for his afternoon workout.

He walked down the hall to his home gym—a room filled with weights and dumbbells. From a peg on the wall, he took down a small length of rope which was about two feet long. He expertly formed it into a slipknot, which he tied around his genitals.

He then began his weight routine, the whole time thinking of Kristy Wise's face. He felt himself swelling as he worked out, the fire in his crotch increasing. The rope tightening. The pain increasing.

"Work first, then play," he repeated rhythmically, basking in the pain while completing his third workout of the day. Once he was done with the weights, he would be free to play for the third time that day, as well.

PART TWO

Billy Applegate
1981

It is odd how the confluence of two completely disconnected circumstances can create a "moment."

On one side of New York, a disc jockey sits in a booth. He's just come back from a break, maybe smoked some weed in the alley. He's a bit bored with all the pop music he's playing and feeling nostalgic. He starts flipping through the catalogue for something a little older to play, a throwback.

Six miles away, a college sophomore is at his girlfriend's apartment working on a research paper—one that's due the next day.

The college student is Billy Applegate.

You remember Billy. He's grown—nineteen years old. It's six years on from that election night party I told you about. Billy is now in his second year at Columbia University.

He's sitting at a tiny kitchen table in a small apartment. A half-finished burger sits in its wax paper wrapper on the table in front of him, next to wilted fries and a half-finished beer. The radio is on—"Bettie Davis Eyes" is playing, but Billy doesn't hear it. He's concentrating on a project. Literature. Poetry.

Billy is an English major. When he was younger, he hated reading. His mother, Annette, stressed out over that fact. With time, however, Billy came to love books. He discovered that they were a refuge. Reading allowed him to explore the world from the safety of a controlled environment—his bedroom, his home, a coffee shop, a library cubicle.

However, it's one thing to read for pleasure, but quite another to analyze literature. And Billy was learning that the hard way. He did okay his first year at Columbia, but not great. He explained it away to his parents as an "adjustment" year. The reality was that the last-minute cramming skills which had been good enough for him in high school were not holding up so well in college. Billy was still struggling to keep up a year later.

Now, while his girlfriend Emma was out with friends, he'd come to her place to get out of the dorm and away from distractions.

The project for his twentieth century poetry class was based on T.S. Elliot's *The Waste Land*. His assignment was to do a short analysis of the Fisher King as a metaphor in the poem.

The poem began innocently enough.

> *April is the cruellest month, breeding*
> *Lilacs out of the dead land, mixing*
> *Memory and desire, stirring*
> *Dull roots with spring rain.*

Billy ate and drank as he read. It was when he reached Part III that he stopped eating. He took a swig of beer and continued, even as his face flushed and sweat began to break out on his neck.

> *He, the young man carbuncular, arrives...*
> *The time is now propitious, as he guesses...*
> *Flushed and decided, he assaults at once...*
> *Exploring hands encounter no defence...*
> *His vanity requires no response,*
> *And makes a welcome of indifference....*
> *Bestows one final patronising kiss...*
> *And gropes his way, finding the stairs unlit...*

Perhaps these words alone would not have been enough to push Billy over the edge, but just as he was finishing reading the passage, the DJ introduced a track that he described as a *golden oldie*. A song that—to Billy—was so much more.

B-b-b-baby, you ain't seen n-n-n-nothin' yet...

The grind of Bachman Turner's electric guitar combined with T.S. Eliot's words to conjure images that Billy had fought for years to suppress. Suddenly, he was back in his room on election night, alone and helpless. The clammy hands, the fetid stench of cigar and alcohol, the vomit he'd swallowed, the groping. Billy felt dizzy, nauseous, and was paralyzed as waves of shivers washed over him. His hands shook and his palms turned sweaty.

Billy was older now. He knew he was safe. But his anger had no external target. It focused inward, against himself. He hated himself for the fear that he felt, and even more so for the fact that he'd not fought back harder that night so many years ago. But he could fight now. In an instant, paralysis turned to rage coursing through his body like an electrical current.

Breaking the spell, he jumped up from the table and stalked across to the room to change the radio station. But as he reached for the dial, his hand was shaking so much that he couldn't get a hold of the knob. So, he made a fist and slammed it down onto the power button, but the track continued: "*...you ain't seen n-n-n-nothing yet...*"

"Fuuuuuck!" he screamed as he grabbed the radio with both hands, yanking the power cable out of the wall as he hurled it across the room.

* * *

Billy squinted at the sunlight that was shooting white needles into his eyes and through his brain into the back of his head. He rolled upright. As he did, his leg bumped against something cool and hard, and then the *tonk tonk tonk* sound of glass bouncing on the tile floor echoed through the room.

It was an empty bottle. A big one.

"Ah, you're awake," Emma said. "Hellooo?"

Billy pulled himself into a leaning position against... the wall.

Did I sleep on the floor?

"Here you go."

Billy squinted and Emma came into focus. She was holding out a large glass of water. She was sitting on the floor cross-legged in front of him, nursing her own cup of tea.

Emma was British. A pixie of a girl—rail thin, blonde, blue-eyed. She wore cut-off Levi's and a white NYU sweatshirt today. She was gorgeous. They'd met the first week of class and hit it off immediately. For Billy, she was his first. Sure, he'd messed around in high school, but he had never had a *formal* girlfriend. Not until now.

Billy took the cup and sipped while slowly peeling his eyelids open. As his eyes adjusted to the light, his head felt thick, swollen, as if it were about to explode. He was cold. His mouth was dry, and the water burned as it went down his throat. The water tasted... acrid. Then he recognized the taste. Vomit.

Fuck.

His cheeks flushed. He looked around, but either he'd made it to the bathroom or—he cringed—Emma had cleaned it all up.

"Oh shit," he said, remembering his project. "What time is it?"

"It's almost two."

"P.M.?" His stomach churned. "Fuck! I missed class? Why didn't you wake me up?"

"I tried. You were passed out. And what's the point? You didn't write your paper."

He closed his eyes and groaned as he remembered the poem, the song, the radio, and the mess he'd made. He drank some more water and wiped his brow with the back of his arm. He was sweating, which reminded him of how he'd felt the night before, but the rage was gone now.

All he felt was shame.

He stole glances around the room and saw that the radio, or what was left of it, had been picked up, the floor swept clean.

Emma moved to the sofa and sat down with a big sigh. "Look, petal," she began. "I don't think this is going to work."

It took him a few seconds to register what she was saying through the fog in his head.

"I don't know what exactly your problem is darling, but this is the fourth time I've come home to find you passed out, drunk on the floor, alone."

"Emma..." Just speaking the word made him feel queasy. He wanted to say more, but he didn't have the strength.

"No, baby. I mean, you're an amazing guy and everything, and I really care about you, but I just can't do this anymore, Billy. I don't know if you're an alcoholic or what, but this is not what I expect from a boyfriend."

With that, she stood, walked over and kissed him on the forehead, and then made her way to the door.

Billy knew that he had to say something. He knew that if he spoke, he could stop her. He could fix this. That's exactly what he wanted to do. But something inside him gave up.

I don't deserve her. I'm not worth shit. I don't deserve a woman like her.

"You need to get your stuff together and go, please," she said. Then, with one hand on the doorknob, she stood waiting.

Say something!

But he couldn't. Instead, after several seconds, he slowly hauled himself to his feet and made for the door. He paused when he reached her and opened his mouth to speak, but no words would come to him.

Emma shook her head hopelessly and watched the man she had fantasized about marrying walk out the door.

CHAPTER TWENTY-FIVE

Tuesday
October 8, 2019
Austin, Texas

In between classes, schoolwork, and normal life, Kristy invested a significant amount of time into scouring the web for everything she could find about Susie Font. She had also done research on Harlan's disappearance to see if anything popped up that would give her a clue as to how her parents and Font might be connected with it. There wasn't much online about Harlan's disappearance that she didn't already know.

But she had learned quite a bit about Susie—her career in journalism, her advocacy work, and her blog. She learned all about Camilla and Liam Bareto, as well.

In addition to the online research, Kristy had searched her own house for information. She'd paid particular attention to her father's office, where she'd used the results of previous snooping to open the family safe. She'd even checked the gun safe in the garage, though she'd found nothing there but guns and ammo.

The only item she'd been unable to access was a small lockbox that her father kept in the family safe. Despite searching the house from top to bottom, she hadn't been able to find a key that fit it.

Reviewing what she had learned left her frustrated, bordering on angry. All the information she'd found failed to shed any light on what her mother had been referring to in her letters.

And she hadn't found *them*, the two letters her father had brought home in his computer bag. They'd disappeared.

She had found the transcript of her father's deposition in the lawsuit over him attacking Harlan at Whole Foods. And although there wasn't much of use there, it had triggered a memory.

Kristy recalled that around the time of Harlan's disappearance, her father had been questioned by the police. She clearly remembered overhearing an argument her father had had with her mother, during which Deb had told him that he was free to do as he wished, but that neither she nor her daughter would submit to questioning of any kind without a warrant. Where was the transcript of that interview?

So, although she knew a bit more about Cruise and Font, she still had more questions than answers. She'd talked over next steps with Bethany, who was always a great sounding board.

"Why don't you just call her?" Bethany had asked. "Just fucking call Susie Font, and tell her who you are, and see what she says?"

"I don't know." Kristy was pacing in her bedroom. "I don't know her—at all. If she had something to do with killing Mom, she'll just lie. And by phone, I won't even be able to see her, her body language, to look for tells. No," she sighed, "when I talk to Susie, it's going to have to be in person."

"Okay, then do that! Just show up at her front door!" Bethany always went for the drama. "The surprise factor alone should tell you a lot. Watch how she reacts. Curiosity? Pleasant surprise? Shock? Fear? Anger?" She clapped her hands together. "Hell yeah, you'll learn a ton just from seeing how she takes it."

Kristy loved the way Bethany approached life. So much like her mother. *Just go do it. Take no prisoners.* Kristy had more of her father in her—more cautious, more of a planner. It was that planner in her that replied to Bethany.

"Okay, and then what? All I have are questions. Sure, I could bluff. But that'll only get me so far. Right now, I know so little that, if she clams up, I've got nothing to say. Nothing to accuse her of." She looked at Bethany, shaking her head. "No, when I go see Susie Font, I need to be ready, well-prepared, and armed with as much information as possible."

"Well then, that means exhausting all other possible sources of information first. You've already exhausted fucking Google. But, dude, your dad is right downstairs." Bethany paused, smirking. "And he drinks," she said, pretending to slur, feigning drinking from her hand and making a drunken face.

Kristy laughed.

But Bethany was right.

CHAPTER TWENTY-SIX

Kristy waited until Saturday, the one day of the week when she always had lunch with her father. It was also a good time of day, still early. Tom should be relatively sober, more like the father she'd once known.

Lunch that Saturday was grilled cheese sandwiches and salad, served in the kitchen. He'd gotten an early start that day—which could be good or bad—so by the time they were seated and eating, Tom was already sipping on his fourth beer. He seemed to be in a good, mellow mood.

"So, Dad," she began, "nothing new from the police on Mom's case?"

Her father shook his head slowly while he chewed, then swallowed and added, "Nothing new. Apparently, they don't have much to go on."

"I know that they said it looked like a robbery, but do you think that maybe it was someone who knew her? I mean, that there was another reason?"

Tom stopped and stared at his daughter before wiping his mouth with his napkin. Then, he took a long swig from his beer before replying, "I don't know, sweetie. What are you thinking, exactly?"

"Well," Kristy continued, "with everything that's happened—I mean, Harlan's disappearance and then them finding what they did on his father's door..."

"Why on earth would you think Mom's shooting has anything to do with that?" Tom interrupted her.

Her response was immediate. She and Bethany had role-played the conversation, and this was a question they had anticipated. "It's just... I read the letter she wrote to you. And the one to Susie Font," she lied, hoping that if her father believed that she already knew what the letter said, he'd be more inclined to open up about its contents.

Tom pursed his lips and shook his head. "Sweetie. There are some things that it's just best to let lie. Your mom... it's....." He sat back in his chair heavily. "That woman, Susie, those people... they're bad news."

"What did they do?" she asked in a whisper, as if she didn't actually want to hear the answer.

Tom sighed and then gathered his thoughts while slowly draining his beer. "Look, Kristy, there are things you don't—and shouldn't—know.... Susie and Roy..." he paused as the memories came back to him. Then, he looked away from his daughter.

The gesture wasn't lost on her, and she prompted, "Susie and Roy *what*, Dad?"

Tom left his seat and went to the refrigerator for another beer. As he fumbled in the drawer for the bottle opener, Kristy followed him to the other side of the room. "Look, Dad. You know I love you. You've always been there for me and you've never given me reason to think differently. But Mom, though... in the letter, she said otherwise. Why? She only ever said *that* about that asshole. That's the only time she ever said that you'd let me down, Dad. How?"

Tom turned to face her, but said nothing. The only sound was the pop and fizz of the beer bottle as he opened it.

"Dad!" Kristy pressed him. "What did Susie and Roy do? Was Mom involved somehow?" She hesitated. "Were you?"

There. It was all on the table. Out in the open. She watched her father carefully.

With his left hand, he groomed a non-existent moustache, stroking the skin above his lip. His right hand raised the beer bottle to his mouth as he looked at her. Then he paused, looked away, and took a long swallow from the bottle.

He's not going to tell me.

"Kristy, there are things in life that are best forgotten. People best avoided because... I can tell you that man, that Roy.... Well, you have no idea what he's capable of. I fucking knew it the moment I looked into his eyes." Tom had spoken the last phrase almost to himself, and with an ever-so-slight slur.

She was losing him to the alcohol.

"But, Dad, that's my point," she said reassuringly, attempting to get him to engage, to trust. "If he's capable of anything, maybe he... maybe *they* had something to do with Mom...?"

"Kristy, that's...." Tears welled in Tom's eyes and he moved away from his daughter. Then he composed himself and said, "Just leave it be. Leave them be."

He sat back down at the table. Kristy joined him and placed a hand on his arm. "Dad? You have to tell me," she said, her voice trembling. "What happened—"

"Enough! Goddammit! Just let it go!" he snapped, slamming his fist on the table. Then, immediately, and clearly regretting his reaction, he repeated softly, "Just let it go, Kristy. Please."

Kristy was taken aback by her father's outburst. He'd never raised his voice to her. Ever. Even when he drank.

She pulled away from him and left the kitchen.

"Kristy! I'm begging you... stay out of it!" Tom called after her, but she was gone.

Tom Wise sat in the kitchen, staring at the dirty plates. Only half his beer remained.

I need something stronger, he thought, chugging the rest of the bottle down. He rose and went to his office and poured himself four fingers of Glenfiddich. He sat down heavily in the desk chair and took a swallow.

How did things go so fucking wrong?

He knew the answer. He was living with it every day.

Just a little over two weeks earlier, Deb had walked into the same office where he was now sitting.

"Guess who just called me?" she'd asked him, closing the door behind her. Not waiting for an answer, she'd whispered, "Roy Cruise."

Tom had gone into high-alert mode. It had been over a year

since the whole Harlan mess. After they'd been questioned by the police, things had died down. They'd all gotten away with it. Why would Cruise want to stir the pot now?

"He wants to meet. Says it's about Susie," Deb had added.

"Do you think that's wise, Deb? You know how I feel about this whole mess. It's bad enough that we're involved with these people at all. Making contact with them just creates more loose ends. I mean, what could he want that isn't bad news?"

"I agree with you about the loose ends, Tom. I'm not sure what to think."

They'd discussed scenarios. Options. In the end, she'd convinced Tom. Between the two of them, they'd come up with a plan for how best to meet safely. It had been ill-fated from the start, and ended in disaster. And now she was gone.

Tom sat staring at the bottle of scotch on his desk.

What they had done—all of them—weighed on Tom.

Since Deb had died, he'd been trying to work up the courage to go to the police. He felt that was his one remaining chance for redemption. The old Tom wouldn't have hesitated. Of course, the old Tom would have done a lot of things differently. But the new Tom, the Tom who had been through Kristy's train wreck of a trial and Harlan's acquittal… that Tom no longer trusted the system.

And he had to think of Kristy. If he went to the police, everything would unravel. So, instead of doing what he knew was right, he'd avoided the issue, drowning himself in alcohol. Hoping it would all just go away.

But now Kristy was asking questions. The one person he'd wanted to protect in all this mess was her. And he was failing, miserably.

"This can't go on forever. You need to get sober, Tom. Gotta man up," he said aloud. He sat looking at the three fingers of golden nectar remaining in his glass. He sighed and drained the scotch. It burned down his throat, warming his belly and promising him peace.

He paused for a moment, staring at the half-full bottle of Glenfiddich. From behind the bottle peeked a family photo. He nudged the bottle to the side and gazed at it. It was a photo from two years back—Tom, Deb, and Kristy—up at Beaver Creek, against a snowy background.

Tom picked up the photo. He studied Deb's face. The smile. The eyes. That was *the trip*. The one when he'd approached Cruise at the bar about Harlan.

"How could I have been so naïve, Debbie?" he almost sobbed.

He put the photo down on his desk and looked back to the bottle of scotch.

After what seemed to him like ten minutes, he stood and took the bottle with him to the kitchen, where he uncorked it and poured it into the sink.

CHAPTER TWENTY-SEVEN

That same Saturday afternoon, Susie was sitting cross-legged on the sofa in Roy's home office, looking pensively at the diamond ring that she held in the palm of her hand.

This is when everything started getting complicated. Maybe I just should have said no?

She sighed heavily, then shouted, "Awww, fuuuuck!" The sound reverberated through the empty house.

Friday evening, she'd gotten home late for a dinner they'd organized at their house with David Kim and Rosa Peréz—just the two couples. Neither Susie nor Roy was crazy about the idea of having a homicide detective over, and they avoided socializing with the other couple as much as possible. But it would have seemed strange for them not to spend any time with the two, given how close David and Roy were.

When Susie had gotten home for the dinner, she'd made the mistake of flipping through the mail before joining everyone in the kitchen. There, in the day's correspondence, she'd found Deb's letter to her from the grave. She'd managed to make it through the evening without giving away how she was feeling or raising any suspicions, she believed.

Thankfully, at the end of the night, the "boys" had agreed to meet for lunch the following day before going over to Dinner Key Marina in order to take a look at a mechanical issue with David's boat.

So, now, at 2:00 p.m. on Saturday, Roy was at the marina and Susie was dressed for yoga. She would have to have left home at 1:00 p.m. to make her one-thirty class at the Equinox

Gym in Merrick Park, but she hadn't. She'd wanted to be alone. To think.

To re-read Deb's letter.

A lukewarm cup of tea sat on the side table next to her. On her lap was a lockbox the size of a loaf of bread. It contained several items that she held dear. One of those items lay in the palm of her hand: the engagement ring that Roy had proposed with.

It was an antique, rose-cut diamond—Victorian, according to the dealer—just over a carat with a domed top and twenty-four facets, no pavilion, and the flat bottom typical of rose-cut stones. Although the rose cut didn't have the fire of a brilliant cut, there was something beautiful about it.

Susie loved its simplicity.

She'd not worn it much since Roy had "upgraded" her for their twentieth anniversary, giving her a three-carat Van Cleef. Still, the original meant much more to her.

She carefully replaced the ring in its little box and then put it back in the lockbox.

Next to the ring box was a small cloth bag she'd had made out of linen; it contained a lock of Camilla's hair from her first haircut. Then there was a box containing Camilla's baby teeth and a baby's hospital ID bracelet. All of these were resting on top of a longer, sharper object—a twelve-and-a-half-inch fish knife in a Ziploc bag. Dried blood caked the inside of the bag.

It was the knife she'd used to sever Harlan's penis. She'd kept it as insurance. That had been Deb's idea.

"Don't clean it. Leave his blood on it," she'd advised her. "If the police get too close, you plant it somewhere. Implicate someone else. Throw the cops off the scent."

She could almost hear Deb's voice.

About time to toss that in the canal.

Susie carefully lifted the lockbox from her lap and placed it to the right, next to her on the sofa. She then turned to her left and picked up the manila envelope that she'd removed from the lockbox first, before she'd gotten distracted with reminiscing. Inside was the letter she had received in the mail the day before from Deb, by way of her attorney, which she'd wanted to re-read while free from distractions.

> *Dearest Susie,*
>
> *I'm dead.*
>
> *If you are holding this letter, it's because that's what's happened. I asked my lawyer to send it to you as a part of my last wishes. I asked that it be sent unopened, but you can't trust anyone these days. So, I can't tell you everything I'd like, but I think you'll understand, all the same.*
>
> *I hope that this letter finds you happy. You deserve to be.*
>
> *I have to say that I've enjoyed my life. I've been fortunate to have found love, and to have been loved in return. You know what I mean. There are obviously things that I would change about my life— things I did early on that probably kept me from enjoying your love and friendship as much as I could have. But that's all water under the bridge.*
>
> *I just wanted to send you a note to tell you that I love you. That I will always love you, no matter where I am. I'm glad that I was able to help you out when you needed it. And I thank you from the bottom of my heart for returning the favor. You and Roy both. I can't imagine all that it took. But it's made a big difference in all our lives.*
>
> *If you can, keep an eye on Kristy for me. She's not like us. She's fragile. And on Tom. He means well, and he tries hard. But he's no Roy.*
>
> *Well, that's it. I've never been much of a writer. You know that.*
>
> *Big kiss, girl. Be good. And sorry for all the headaches.*
>
> *I hope I went in my sleep. I always thought that's how I would want to go. Not that I deserve to. But it would be nice, you know?*
>
> *Love always,*
>
> *Deb*

She still couldn't believe that Deb was gone. But the fact that Deb was dead wasn't her main concern at the moment. She was more worried about whether or not Roy had killed Deb, and if so, whether she was next on his list.

CHAPTER TWENTY-EIGHT

Call it paranoia, but Susie had seen enough strange things in her life to take nothing for granted. As she sat on the sofa, she thought through the circumstances surrounding Deb's death, or what little she knew of it. And she worried.

Roy had been in Austin the day that Deb had been killed.

Roy's gun, their gun, was not in the safe.

Deb had been shot, once, in the head.

It was all circumstantial, but still.

I should never have let her convince me to send her that little fucker's dick!

Harlan's killing had been well-planned. A risky but nearly flawless murder. Had it not been for Harlan's penis being found on his father's door, there would have been nothing to prove the young man had been killed.

They'd still be wondering if he ran off to Mexico on a bender or something. He just would have been another missing person. People disappear all the time. But that wasn't good enough for you, was it, Deb? Fuck....

"There's a big difference, Susie," Deb had insisted. "Camilla's gone. And you know that bastard that killed her is gone, too, and you know how. But Kristy is alive. My baby girl is living with this shit every day, knowing that this Harlan fuck screwed her and got away with it. And the whole world knows—*AQUITTED*. They're making her out to be a liar. That ain't right."

Susie understood the logic. She'd reluctantly agreed to Deb's request. But Roy was no fool. He'd known immediately that the only way for that penis to have gotten to Austin was with help from Susie, and he'd confronted her. She'd come clean about it, too. Partially.

Susie had been very careful about what she had and had not told her husband. Her mind wandered back to Roy.

Shit.

Did you fucking kill Deb?

She knew that he was more than capable. Harlan's murder proved that.

But from what she knew of Deb's death, it seemed... sloppy. Not like Roy. But that was her perspective. It was based on her knowledge of how they had killed together.

Then again, though the murder seemed messy from everything she had read about it, the bottom line was that the police seemed to have no leads. And no one had called to ask questions—at least not yet. No cops poking their noses around this time.

So, if Roy had in fact done it, it fit his style in that it was clean forensically.

Moreover, as far as the cops were concerned, Roy didn't know and had never met Deb or Tom Wise. As far as the cops were concerned, there was no motive.

The fact that he'd been in Austin might raise a small red flag. But then, that was just a question of wait-and-see.

But why would Roy hurt Deb?

If he did kill her, did she tell him anything?

And if she talked, what did she say?

How much does he know?

As Susie ran through the list of secrets she still had from Roy, she realized it was relatively short, which made her suddenly nauseous.

Does he know about... Joan?

But even Deb doesn't know that Joan was Roy's sister. That is, as far as you know, Susie girl. Maybe she does. Did. Fuck...

Maybe he was just tying up a loose end? But if it was about loose ends, does he think there are others?

Me?

Her thoughts were interrupted by the sound of a car pulling up in the drive. She looked out the window.

Roy.

Susie carefully put the document back in the manila envelope, then put the envelope in the lockbox. She was just securing everything in the safe when she heard the door open and Roy shout out as he did when he was in good humor, "Lucy! I'm hooome!"

Susie put on a happy face and exited the home office to cheerily greet her husband with a kiss, leaving her worries and her little lockbox of singing bones in the cold metal confines of their safe—for the time being.

CHAPTER TWENTY-NINE

Saturday
October 12, 2019
Austin, Texas

Senator Harlan's phone rang.

The phone. The burner.

It was about 6:30 p.m. He was in his home office at his house in Westlake—a suburb of Austin, Texas. He was catching up on email.

It had been about six weeks since he'd sent the files on his son's case to Slipknot. He'd heard nothing from the man—not even confirmation that everything had been received in good order.

"Hello, Mr. Senator."

"Hello, stranger." There was silence on the line, so the senator added, "Am I to assume you received the files okay?"

"If I hadn't, you would have heard by now. Been through it all in depth. And been doing some digging into all of the parties in question. Lots of research. Lots of digging. Something stinks, alright. I don't know if it's the guys in Florida or the girl's parents, but something ain't right."

Harlan smiled. "Okay. what's next?"

"Well, I am calling you from sunny Miami. Gonna do a little bit of face-to-face reconnaissance here. See what I can find out from that. Take it from there."

"Alright. But please be careful."

"Of course. None of this comes back to you. You have my word."

"That isn't what I meant."

"No?"

"No. I'm just saying that if one or both of those two had anything to do with what happened to Joe, then they're obviously dangerous." Harlan heard a chuckle on the line.

"Don't worry. I know how to take care of myself. But I do appreciate your concern for me and my well-bein', Senator."

"You'll keep me updated?"

"Sure will. This is a team effort. Everything I learn, I'll pass on to you. But I need some autonomy, if you know what I mean, to get it done right. You understand?"

"Of course."

"I'll be in touch," Slipknot said, and the line went dead.

Harlan returned to his work. About ten minutes later, going through email, he came to a message from EBareto624@gmail.com

Subject: Mutual Friend

Dear Mr. Senator,

Forgive my being so forward, but I was hopeful you could make some time to meet with me. I am writing to you as a fellow grieving parent. I obtained your email address from a mutual friend, Congresswoman Anne Hertig. Anne and I go way back, and when I spoke to her about my situation, she felt certain you would want to speak with me. I am aware of the tragic loss of your son. I am so very sorry.

A few years ago, I too lost a son. His name was Liam. Like your son, he died under suspicious circumstances. And, also like your son, one of the people questioned by police as a person of interest was one Roy Cruise of Miami, Florida.

I would very much like to share with you some information that I have recently uncovered and which I believe you may find of interest regarding

your son's case. I will be in Austin this coming
week. If you could please find the time in your
schedule to meet with me, I can assure you that it
will be worth your while.
Regards,
Liz Bareto

Harlan picked up his phone and dialed Anne Hertig's
mobile phone.

"Hello?" Anne whispered.

"Hello, Anne."

"Joe. Listen, I'm in a meeting. Are you calling me about Liz
Bareto?"

"Yes, ma'am."

"She's a good woman, Joe. I've known her for years. She's
no kook, I promise."

"Uh huh."

"Look, I'd be happy to give you more information later, but
please meet with her, okay? Consider it a favor."

"Okay, Anne. I got it."

"Great. Thank you. I've got to go. Take care, Joe. Talk soon."

"You, too. Be good. Bye."

Harlan clicked "reply" and began to compose a response
to Liz Bareto. He was somewhat curious about what she could
have to say. And he was always happy to bank a favor with a U.S.
Congresswoman.

CHAPTER THIRTY

Liz Bareto had waited several weeks for her private investigator to do his work. She'd grown impatient. It had taken longer than she would have liked. But once she received and reviewed M's investigative report on Roy Cruise and Susie Font, she felt like the investigation into her son's death was finally under her control.

In the report, there was a lot of information that she already knew. The detective had done background checks on Susie and Roy. She now had all past addresses, cars owned, boats, corporate entities owned, board seats, license information—Cruise had a motorcycle license in addition to his Class E—even credit report information. The report was thorough, and long.

But, there were a few items that jumped off the page at her.

First, Liz learned that Roy Cruise was actually born Roy Diaz. He'd changed his name in his early twenties to take his maternal grandmother's maiden name, Cruise.

Liz also learned that Roy had a sister named Joan, a twin sister. Joan had died while attending camp in Texas at the age of eleven. A copy of a news article about the incident was included in the report. Apparently, the girl had been wandering around the camp site at night, lost her way, and fell off a cliff to her death.

Another death.

Liz also found it interesting that both Susie and Roy had concealed handgun licenses.

The last tidbit that Liz learned made her heart rate accelerate. M apparently had a friend at Homeland Security. He had been able to cajole out of him a summary of all of Roy Cruise's and Susie Font's travel records for the last few years.

Just as had been previously confirmed by Detective Garza, both Cruise and Font had flown out of Miami two days before Liam's death, and were in South Carolina at the time—they'd flown Miami to Columbia on American Airlines. This Liz already knew, and was not surprised to see.

No, what made her heart race was another flight that M pointed out in his report. On September 11, 2019, Roy Cruise flew from Miami to Austin, Texas. He returned on September 13.

Roy Cruise was in Austin on September 12, 2019—the day Deb Wise was killed.

Coincidence. Possibly. But, Liz intended to look further into that coincidence. She had made travel arrangements to go to Austin, Texas.

The evening before her trip, she was both pleased and disappointed in equal measure. She'd believed that it would be difficult to get a meeting with Senator Harlan, but it turned out that not only was the man happy to meet with her, he was looking forward to it.

Tom Wise, on the other hand, had proven more problematic. When she'd emailed him, she'd instantly received an "out of office" reply. Then she'd telephoned his office, only to learn that he was on personal leave. Understandable, given his recent loss. Not so understandable when the receptionist went on to tell her that his leave was indefinite. Wise's home phone number was unlisted, and she'd been unable to cajole a mobile number out of his receptionist.

So, she'd turned to M for help, and, once again, he'd come through.

In her living room, she sat on the sofa with a bulleted list of items she wanted to cover with Wise. She figured that, by calling on a Sunday evening, she'd be most likely to get the man on the phone. And, while she was hoping, and angling, to set up a face-to-face meeting in Austin, she had her list ready just in case he refused to meet with her—to try to find out what she could by phone. She was prepared.

Liz picked up the phone, took a deep breath, and dialed.

* * *

Kristy had been at the library studying, but she decided to wrap up early and go home.

As she entered the house, she heard her father's mobile phone ringing. It was almost 7 p.m. He was normally passed out in his office or on the couch by this time.

She expected the call to go to voicemail, so she ignored it and headed to the kitchen to get herself something to eat. As she passed her father's office door, which was ajar, she was surprised to hear the ringing end abruptly, followed by her father's sleepy voice. "Hello?"

She stopped to listen to what ended up being a short conversation.

"This is Tom Wise."

Silence.

"Thank you. Yes, it's been very difficult for us."

There was a long pause.

"Oh, I'm very sorry for your loss. That's... that's just terrible."

More silence. Then she heard the sound of Tom Wise's chair squeaking, closely followed by footsteps. Kristy could hear that he was pacing.

"Um, I'm sorry. I really have no idea what you're talking about."

Kristy heard creaking floorboards as he moved back and forth across the room.

"That's true, yes. But that's the whole point. I didn't know them or who they were. I don't know why the police even wanted to talk to me."

More silence.

"Look Mrs..." Tom paused, "Ms. Bareto. I feel for you. I really do. And I wish I could help you. But I'd never heard of Cruise or Font before that."

Another pause.

"I understand. And I'm sorry, but as I've said, I really can't help you.... No, I don't.... I'm sorry, but... I'm sorry, but best of luck—"

Silence.

"I don't think a meeting is possible. I'm... *we're* mourning a terrible loss here. I'm sure you understand?"

Silence.

"You, too. Thank you. Goodbye."

Kristy crept away from the door and hurried into the kitchen, where she quickly made herself a tomato and spinach salad. She slammed a few cabinet doors and made other obvious noises, then sat down to eat expectantly. Despite her efforts to alert him to her presence, her father did not appear.

So, she ate alone at the kitchen table. When she finished, she cleaned up and went back to her father's office.

He was asleep in his chair.

Kristy walked over and kissed him on the head. "Good night, Dad," she said warmly, in a normal speaking voice, but he didn't even stir.

She picked up his mobile phone and navigated to the call log.

Ms. Bareto was calling from a Florida area code, and Kristy took down the number.

CHAPTER THIRTY-ONE

Monday
October 14, 2019
Miami, Florida

Roy Cruise felt the alarm from the timer on his phone vibrate in his coat pocket. It was time to leave the Starbucks on Coral Way and 27ᵗʰ Avenue. Roy casually closed his burner laptop and headed for his Range Rover. He'd been on the Wi-Fi at the Starbucks for exactly fifty-eight minutes and felt comfortable that he now had everything he needed.

For the last few months, Roy had been researching overseas law enforcement practices. Europe's, specifically. He was interested in how to get away with murder in Spain, and if or how it might be different from what he and Susie had learned about killing in the United States.

He'd learned quite a bit.

All of the elements he'd learned from the *PHI* and Roy's Rules for Murder applied overseas. But there were some that were even more important in that context.

First and foremost, Roy had concluded that the amount of time between the murder and the time the authorities became involved was critical. Borrowing from a concept in economics, he called this *recognition lag-time*.

In almost every murder, even in the case of a perfect murder, someone will miss the victim. A missing person will be reported. The police will become involved. The longer that process takes, the better—in terms of witnesses' memories going stale, clues disappearing, and so on. In an overseas murder, recognition lag-time is even more important because it allows time for the killer to leave, to escape the jurisdiction of the country in which he has killed.

Bribery was another interesting distinction. In many developed countries, bribery was still a relatively acceptable practice—more so than in the United States. Thus, it made sense to carry sufficient cash to make payoffs.

These two points focused on the authorities.

In terms of witnesses, other elements applied overseas that weren't as obvious at home. A new rule was to assimilate culturally. Roy had laughed out loud when he'd come up with this rule. This was a part of the process that he enjoyed. He often found dark humor in applying concepts from other disciplines to murder. But the point was valid.

In terms of witnesses' memories, *not* standing out was important. And this was a function of culture. Knowing how to blend in with the locals was very important—it was a matter of being forgettable. Of course, another option was to operate in areas where there were many tourists.

Roy had also come across a pertinent CIA memo—this one thanks to WikiLeaks. The document provided advice to operatives on passing through immigration, and in particular gave advice on how to survive secondary screening by authorities without blowing your cover. The document self-described its contents as follows:

> This is a secret document produced by the CIA's CHECKPOINT Identity and Travel Intelligence Program to explain and advise CIA operatives on how to deal with secondary screening at airports, as they travel to and from covert CIA operations using false ID, including into and out of Europe.

The report had been enlightening, as it tied into his thinking on recognition lag-time and added useful tips for getting out of countries—in this case, countries in Europe—which was right on point.

There were other factors Roy had come across that were equally interesting, albeit not very helpful. For example, most European countries had abolished the death penalty. Thus, killing in Europe inherently carried a lower risk than killing in the U.S.

I suppose that's a plus, he'd chuckled.

Roy now felt comfortable that he had found everything available online in terms of understanding how to get away with murder in Europe. For his specific plan, however, he still needed to nail down some details. There were many variables to consider, including the fact that he'd never been to Mallorca. But he still had time to tie up those loose ends.

Roy made an effort to change gears mentally and focus on his next meeting.

As he pulled into the parking garage at his office, he checked the time. He was meeting David Kim for lunch, and he was right on schedule.

CHAPTER THIRTY-TWO

Since Roy was leaving for Spain the following day, he'd decided to take his business partner, David, to lunch at one of David's favorite restaurants, La Petite Maison. Roy had the *daurade au citron* with *haricots verts* on the side. David selected the *gnocchi à la tomate fraiche*, and between them, they easily finished a bottle of Domaines Ott, Château Romassan.

In the time since Harlan's disappearance, the two had grown closer—or so Roy believed. He was very pleased with how David had stepped up after making partner. And Roy was particularly excited by the fact that one of David's early picks, a company called NatureBalm, was in the final stages of acquisition talks. If the deal closed at the currently agreed upon price, Cruise Capital stood to pull in almost twenty million dollars—and under their partnership structure, David's bonus would come to almost two million.

David had some mixed feelings about their partnership. Before joining Cruise Capital, he'd never been questioned by the police, and certainly not in the context of murder. That had unnerved him. Particularly when, just after the police interrogation, their firm had gone ahead and invested in Marty McCall's company, TrueData.

Roy's approach to that investment had been unconventional, to say the least—especially the part where he'd traveled to Seattle to meet with TrueData's CEO without talking to David about it. They always collaborated on their approach to investments... but not that time.

Ultimately, the investment had turned out to be a sound one, and Marty McCall was turning out to be a pretty competent CEO. Although the unorthodox way the whole deal had been made had rattled David, especially given the Harlan disappearance, he'd ultimately chalked his doubts up to his pervasive paranoia, which was a personal trait that he readily recognized and, in fact, sought to foster since he considered it more of an asset than a liability.

All in all, the whole Harlan mess had ended up being a nasty bump in the road. And, in the end, it had actually been a good thing because that had been how David had met Rosa. They'd been dating for over a year now, and things were going very well.

As they walked back to the office, David said, "So, make sure you talk to Susie about Halloween. You guys'll have a blast. You know how Rosa is? Well, her sister is *even more* fun—she's super open and friendly."

Roy smiled. "I heard you, man. I'll talk to her. I just don't know if we'll be up for a party the night we get back from Europe. Jetlag after those long-haul flights is a bitch." Roy, like Susie, thought that the less time they hung out with David's girlfriend/homicide detective, the better.

"Roy, come on. You travel for a living. It's in your blood. You'll be fine. So, really, I want you guys to start thinking costumes now. In fact, you know what, I'll tell Rosa to email Susie. I know how you guys are—once you get into it, not just any old thing will do."

They were approaching their office building and Roy laughed. But, suddenly, he felt exposed, vulnerable. The hair on the back of his neck stood on end.

The heebie jeebies.

He glanced around—discreetly, so as not to spook David.

Nothing.

"I tell you what," he said, trying to focus on the conversation, "have Rosa talk to Susie and we'll take it from there. Okay?"

They entered the building and waited for their respective elevators—David's back to the office and Roy's to the garage. As they did, in the coffee shop across the street, Slipknot sipped on a cappuccino and watched the two men. They had been at lunch for precisely one hour and forty-seven minutes.

Must be nice...

Once inside his Range Rover and on his way home, Roy slipped on his sunglasses and checked repeatedly in his rearview mirror for anyone who might be following him.

Nobody.

Still, he couldn't shake that feeling.

Roy started complaining about what he called the *heebie jeebies* several months after I began working with him. I tried to explain to him that it was likely a derivative of his feelings of guilt over Harlan's murder. That it was his sub-conscience speaking to him.

Bullshit, Doc...

He agreed that it had to do with Harlan, but he attributed the sensation to his *survival instincts*. He believed that it was his lizard brain intuition—it knew that killing those of another tribe might result in retaliation, and as a result, it was extra-sensitive, often kicking into high alert—though this usually resulted in *false positives*. He went on to tell me that he welcomed the feeling because it kept him *sharp*.

He admitted that it also fostered feelings of self-doubt. As Roy drove home on this afternoon, those feelings took on verbal form.

"Can I really do this again without making a mistake? Before someone figures it out and comes after me? The police? The FBI? Interpol?"

Roy's *heebie jeebies* would come and go. He learned to live with them, but he also became more cautious. On this particular day, he took an indirect route home in order to give himself more time to spot any potential *tails*.

The longer he drove without seeing anything unusual, the better he felt. Paranoid thoughts dissipated, leaving room for others. Eventually, his mind turned to Susie and their imminent trip, and also to his sister, Joan.

CHAPTER THIRTY-THREE

As Roy drove home from the office, he once again felt pangs of guilt. Were it not for the few photos he had of his sister, he knew that, by now, he probably would have forgotten her face completely. The remorse was overwhelming—how could anybody forget the face of a loved one? And yet, the little he could remember about the last time they'd been together brought tears to his eyes.

* * *

June, 1988

"Cheer up, bro! It's only for two weeks," Joan said, way too cheerily for her brother's liking.

Her suitcase was open on the bed, both sides full. Too full. Little Roy wondered if they'd be able to get it shut, but he tried not to let the thought distract him from his moping. He wanted his twin sister to feel bad.

"It's not fair. What am I gonna do here all alone?"

"Don't be such a baby," Joan replied as she clambered up onto her bed and carefully sat on the contents of one side of her case. "Come on. Help me."

Roy reluctantly climbed onto his sister's bed and sat on the other side of the suitcase, compressing the contents. Once he was settled, Joan put her thin arm around him.

"It's gonna be weird," she said. "I mean, this is the first time we're gonna be separated for so long."

"Ever." Roy rubbed his eyes, fighting back tears.

Joan noticed, but pretended not to for fear of making the situation worse and crying herself.

"Okay, let's bounce," she said with a big grin, and then quickly added, "but not too hard."

The twins slowly bounced up and down on the suitcase in an attempt to squish the contents further. The bed made a squeaking noise beneath them. As it did, they began to laugh.

"What are you two sillies doing?" their mother asked, suddenly appearing in the doorway.

"Squishing!" they cried in unison with breathless excitement.

"Well, you're going to break it if you carry on like that. Come on. Off you get. Let's see if it'll close."

Reluctantly, the twins climbed off while their mother pushed down and zipped the interior closures to the suitcase, then closed and snapped the plastic latches shut.

"There we go. Good job. Why don't you go outside and play a bit? There's still some time before dinner."

They left the bedroom and ran out into the backyard. Roy idly kicked a waterlogged nerf football.

"Whaddya wanna do?" Joan asked.

Roy shrugged.

"Hey," she half-whispered, looking at the house and then back at him conspiratorially. "Come on." Joan skipped deeper into the yard.

Curiosity piqued, Roy followed his sister to the big tree with the rope swing. The circular seat that had hung at the bottom had broken the previous summer. But the kids had added another knot that was big enough to sit on if you crotched it and locked your legs. Joan did just that.

"Push me!" she said.

Roy grabbed the end of the rope that hung under her bottom and pulled her back as far as he could.

"As high as you can! High!" Joan ordered excitedly. She was the daredevil of the two. Roy hated heights.

"Ready?" he asked. "Three, two, one—"

"Grandma's coming!" Joan said as her brother released the rope.

"What?"

Roy watched his sister, who was laughing hysterically, and couldn't help but smile along with her. She leaned back on the rope to get maximum height and distance, then leaned hard to the side, turning her body and starting to spin.

"Helicopter! Helicopter! Helicopter!" she screamed.

As she swung back down, her legs came straight at Roy, who had to drop flat to the ground to avoid getting mowed down. After she passed over him, he rolled onto his back and waited. As gravity brought Joan back down, he reached up and grabbed the tail end of the rope as his sister attempted to sail by. The momentum yanked at his arms and dragged him for a short distance before she stopped amid her squeals of laughter.

"Grandma's coming?" Roy asked, eyes wide with anticipation as he hauled himself to his feet.

"It was supposed to be a surprise," Joan said through panting breaths. "I think Dad was worried she might change her mind. But I heard them talking this morning. She's coming, *and* she's taking you to the beach house!"

"Yes!" Roy shouted, hopping and bouncing as he performed a happy dance.

Grandma arrived less than an hour later in her sky-blue Cadillac Fleetwood Brougham.

It was a bittersweet time for Roy, who, the next day, waved goodbye to Joan and his parents before boarding the Caddy to Galveston— though he didn't know it at the time, never to return.

That was the last time he'd seen his sister alive.

It was so clear in his mind. She was wearing khaki shorts, a white short-sleeved polo shirt, and blue Keds.

But he couldn't remember her face.

* * *

When Roy was older, about nineteen, he'd driven up to Camp Willow and placed flowers at the overlook from which Joan had fallen. From there, he'd hiked the circuitous route to the riverbed at the bottom and placed a single white rose on the rocky shore.

Looking up, he'd calculated an approximate forty-foot drop. That was how far she had fallen to her death.

Later, research had told him that, from that height, his sister would have been traveling at about sixty miles per hour when her little body smashed into the jagged rocks.

Forty feet up.

Sixty miles per hour.

Impossible to survive.

* * *

Roy wiped tears from his eyes. He had arrived home and was sitting in the driveway, engine idling. He looked up. The garage door was open and waiting for him, beckoning him in.

He didn't want Susie to see that he'd been crying.

He hadn't told her that he knew about Joan. He hadn't shared what Deb Wise had told him on the night she'd died because he felt that, if he didn't say it, it wasn't real. If he didn't say it, it could stay buried in the past. But he also knew about burying things in the past, and about singing bones. He knew he couldn't keep this quiet forever. He had to confront Susie.

Just not yet.

After so many years spent believing that Joan had died by accident, he was still processing this new scenario—this new truth. And what to do about it.

The thing was, when Deb had spoken those words, when she'd admitted to killing his sister, it had been like the last tumbler in a lock clicking home and releasing the mechanism.

Everything had fallen into place.

He'd finally understood how it had all happened. The bond between Susie and Deb. Why Deb had agreed to kill Liam Bareto. And how Susie had suckered him into killing Harlan.

Susie knew that Joan's death had left a hole in him. A hole that he had tried vainly to fill—with success, with wealth, with Susie... and, thanks to Susie's manipulation, with vengeance.

The child is indeed the father of the man.

Roy sighed and tapped the accelerator, gently parking the Range Rover in the garage. He hadn't finished packing, and there was still so much to do for the trip to Mallorca.

So much to prepare.

So many details.

CHAPTER THIRTY-FOUR

Saturday
October 19, 2019
Miami, Florida

David Kim woke up in pain. He was stiff. Sore.

As he looked around, he realized that he could only see out of his right eye, and when he moved his left hand to check his other eye, he felt a tug. He looked with his good eye and saw an intravenous drip attached to his arm. He attempted to sit up, but froze when a sharp pain stabbed him between the ribs.

What the...

He sank back into the pillow. His mind raced as he attempted to get his bearings.

Where the hell am I?

He had no idea, but it smelled and looked like a hospital room.

He searched his memory for clues, but all that returned was fuzzy static. That's when spider legs of anxiety crawled up his balls and into the pit of his stomach.

Okay. Calm down. Relax. Losing it isn't going to help.

He tried to take slow, deep breaths, but the pain in his chest was excruciating. Instead, he tried holding short, shallow breaths to reduce his heart rate and the panic.

Get a grip, Kim. Relax. What happened? What's the last thing you remember?

He latched onto the most recent memory he could summon through the haze...

Lunch with Roy at La Petite Maison before he left for Spain. That was Monday.

Then...

Oh crap. That was days ago. I was working on the Avalon Ventures deal. Late nights.

Then...

Thursday! Yes, I had dinner with Rosa. Spent the night at her place. Nice.

Then...

Shit. Friday. Another late night at work.

David's belly pulsed, his palms and feet began to sweat, and his face flushed...

The guy in the green leather jacket!

He'd been waiting for him in the parking garage. David had been working late and had gone home to his condo at about 1:00 a.m. Downtown Miami, Brickell. It was a class-A building. A very safe area. The guy had surprised him. A little fellow. Bald. Creepy looking.

At first, David had thought he just needed help. Directions or something. But then he'd seen the gun. David thought he was getting robbed, and he'd offered the guy his wallet, his watch, his car keys…. But the man hadn't reacted. He'd just stood there holding the gun. Staring. A freaky, empty fucking stare...

Joe Harlan. He asked about that kid!

There was nothing to say. David had told him everything he knew. Told him everything he'd told the police.

Then there'd been electricity, or so he'd thought. He hadn't seen the first blow coming. It had hit him on the neck and sent shockwaves down his spine. As he'd tried to protect himself and crawl away, he'd seen what the guy was hitting him with—some sort of collapsible metal baton.

David tried to tilt his head; the pain was still there. His neck was swollen. Bruised, no doubt. He cringed at the memory of the subsequent blows. The bastard had wanted to know about the meeting they'd had scheduled with the Harlan kid. Was it true that the kid had been a no-show?

Yes! Yes, it was!

But the guy hadn't been listening. David remembered peeing himself from pain or fear.

Asshole!

He felt a swell of anger as things started to make sense. He was definitely in the hospital, with a large window to his left. It was dark outside.

No clock in the room, and his watch was gone.

Anger started to take hold. David was hurt physically, but more so, he felt shame and anger for allowing himself to be caught off-guard and for not fighting back. But, then again, the guy had a gun, and he'd put that gun in David's mouth.

Tears sprang to his eyes as he explored the inside of his mouth with his tongue. He thought he could still taste metal and oil.

With the gun in David's mouth, the guy had questioned him about Roy. *Where was he? What was he doing in Europe? When did he leave? When was he coming back?*

Then, there'd been more questions about Harlan and Miami. No, not more questions. The same questions, but worded differently.

Finally, the guy told him to shut up and he'd crouched down, his hot, coffee-tinged breath blowing against David's face with flecks of spittle as he hissed a warning.

No police. Or I'll come back for you and your little friend Rosa...

Then, the guy stood up and the last thing David heard before everything went black was that damned metal baton slicing through the air.

Gingerly, David hoisted himself into a sitting position, straining to reach the call button and pushing it to summon a nurse.

No police. Fine. But he didn't say shit about calling Roy.

The guy knew that Roy was in Spain. David needed to warn him.

CHAPTER THIRTY-FIVE

Spencer Shaw's fingers danced across the keyboard like an extension of his mind, his eyes never leaving the computer screen. His concentration was such that the room around him had long ago ceased to exist. He absorbed information from the screen, processed it, and milliseconds after his brain reacted, his fingers were executing commands, translating his wishes into bits and bytes that shot off into cyberspace to faraway servers.

He was fully immersed in another world—a world of colors and magic and sorcery. It was wrong, he knew. But he was hooked. Spencer Shaw loved online video games. It was Saturday, and he was at home. So, it was okay. He still felt guilty. Like he should be working. Or out running. Something. He could hear his mother's voice in the background of his memory, yelling at him for wasting his time and money on those shitty games....

Guilt got the better of him, and he turned at his desk and popped open his work laptop to check email. As he scanned through new emails, one caught his eye. It was from CBP—Customs and Border Protection; some data he'd requested. He opened the attachment and skimmed through the file, and, just at the end, saw something that piqued his interest.

Shaw opened his notes on the research he was doing for Eddie Garza, just to double-check, then composed a quick email.

To: Eddie Garza

From: Spencer Shaw
Re: Cruise

Hi Eddie,

I haven't forgotten you. Just got some data today
that I'd been waiting on. Going to dig in and
analyze in greater depth this week, but wanted
to give you a heads up. Your guy Cruise was in
Austin, Texas the day that Debra Wise was killed.
He flew in September 11 and out September 13.
And, he's currently out of the country—Spain.

More soon.
SS

CHAPTER THIRTY-SIX

Monday
October 21, 2019
Austin, Texas

After Tom received the call from Liz Bareto, Kristy found what she could about the woman online. Most of it, she'd already seen in connection with her research into Susie Font and her daughter's death. The only new bit of information she discovered was that Bareto had recently gotten divorced.

"So, you're sure that this Bareto lady that called is the same one, the mother of the guy that killed Font's daughter?" Bethany asked.

"I checked her out online, Beth. There's stuff about her son killing Camilla Cruise. A few pics of her. There was a YouTube recording of a radio show where she called in and tried to ask this Font chick about her son. I'm as sure as I can be that it's the same person. I mean, it's the same fucking name. And Bareto's a pretty uncommon name. And she called my dad from a fucking Miami area code!" Kristy was getting worked up. She took a breath. "So, yeah, I'd be willing to bet it's her."

"Dude, chill. Don't get all pissed off at *me*. I'm just tryin' to help."

"I know," Kristy said, taking some of the zing out of her tone. "I'm just really frustrated, you know? I mean, my fucking dad won't even talk straight with me about this crap," she said, stifling tears.

"Well, what's really interesting is that he told you to stay the fuck away from Cruise and his wife, but he told *her* that he didn't know them, right? That they'd never met."

Kristy nodded. "He's hiding something."

Bethany smiled and continued, "The way I see it, next steps, you've got two choices—the devil you know or the devil you don't. If you call this Liz chick, it's like what you said about Susie. You're at a disadvantage. You don't know anything about her except what you found out online. But," Bethany raised a finger, "she's calling your dad for a reason, with an agenda. It's *just like Font*. She holds all the cards. You need to at least find out as much as you can before you face her."

"And..." Kristy prompted Bethany to continue.

"So, you start with the devil you know."

The devil Kristy knew was Detective Art Travers. Kristy had gotten to know him before, during, and after Harlan's trial, along with her father's, and, more recently, he had worked on her mother's case. He'd even attended her mother's funeral. She felt she had built up some rapport with him. That, and he was the kind of guy to "tell it like it is." No sugar-coating. Just the cold, hard truth. And she needed some of that certainty right now.

The plan was simple. She would ask Detective Travers for an update on her mother's case and try to get him to open up enough that she could ask him about Bareto and find out what she could about the woman. She would also try to find out what the police knew about her parents' connection to Susie and Roy.

If need be, she would show him the letter from her mother and see if he could shed any light on Font and Cruise.

Could they have been involved in her mother's death? That was all she was interested in, and she was determined to get answers.

Kristy called Detective Travers and set up the meeting for that afternoon—at Jo's Coffee on Second Street.

She had never been the nervous type, and yet, as she waited for Travers, she noticed her leg bouncing under the table. The knowledge that her parents may have had something to do with Harlan's disappearance sat in her gut like a rock. She was starting to feel like a trapped animal. Maybe this hadn't been such a good idea. She needed a run. Now.

She fought the urge to call off the meeting, climb into her car, and get the hell out of there. Instead, she checked her watch. Travers was late.

Just as she felt frustration begin to rise in her belly at being made to wait, she saw him coming up the street. She made an effort to look unfazed by his tardiness and to stop her leg from moving. She assumed a closed defensive position by crossing one leg over the over, and then she pretended to check messages on her phone.

CHAPTER THIRTY-SEVEN

"Kristy. Hi. Sorry I'm late," Detective Travers said as he signaled to the waitress, who smiled and nodded.

"Oh, hello, Detective," Kristy said, feigning that she hadn't even noticed. "That's okay. Is everything all right?" she asked.

"Sure, sure. The usual. Always fires to put out. You know," Travers said, settling into his seat opposite her. "How are you doing, Kristy? How are you holding up?"

"Me? Oh, I'm fine. You know, it's everybody else that isn't." She forced a laugh.

They sat for a few awkward seconds, Travers wondering what she had called him for and waiting for her to share while she gathered her courage to start the conversation.

"It really was a nice ceremony, Kristy," Travers helped her along. "I think your mom would have been pleased with the turnout." He followed the statement with a sniff.

Odd, thought Kristy.

"Thanks, Detective. You're right. I think she would have."

"Please, call me Art. How's your dad doing?"

Kristy saw this as a good segue from the obligatory small-talk, condolence-offering bullshit—to getting to what she was after. She decided to shift the conversation to matters of relevance more rapidly than protocol demanded.

"Well, actually…" She trailed off here as the waitress approached with a cup and the coffee pot.

"Hey, Sarah, how's it going?" the detective asked, looking up at the thirty-something woman with a bulbous nose and peroxide-blonde hair.

"Oh, you know, Art. One foot in front of the other."

"Kids good?"

"Good isn't the word I'd use," the waitress said, finishing her pour. "You don't fancy a couple of three-year-old twins, do ya?"

"Can't say I do, Sarah," Travers said with a chuckle.

"Oh well, I tried. Can I top you up there?" the waitress asked Kristy.

"No, I'm good, thanks," Kristy said, automatically putting a hand over her cup.

The waitress shrugged. Then, with a "Y'all have a good one," she was off to serve an elderly couple.

"Anyway, you were saying, Kristy."

"Um, yeah. Detective, my dad. He's okay, considering. That's kind of what I wanted to talk to you about." She paused for effect and turned to look at the traffic on the street outside. She could feel the man's eyes on her. She wanted to believe that it was some kind of paternal interest, but wondered if it might be more. After all, she was wearing workout clothes. Tight. Form-fitting.

Art had always seemed like a good man to Kristy.

But she could hear her mother's words. *Even a good man is still a man.*

She turned back to him. "We're taking it day-by-day, you know. But anything more we could find out about what happened to my mom would help. Have there been any breaks in the case?"

"Um, we're chasing a few leads. And we're optimistic that something will shake out," Travers said, sniffing again.

You're lying. Kristy knew they had nothing. She let his words hang in the air between them for a few seconds.

He maintained a poker face—something he had no doubt refined during his many years on the police force. His eyebrows remained relaxed. But, as he moved to take a sip from his coffee, she noticed that his body shifted slightly away from her. It was something she interpreted as defensive.

She sat forward and placed her hands, which had been on her lap, on the table in front of her, palms facing in and upwards. Then she looked the man in the eyes.

"I wanted to meet with you because... well, maybe there's something... it's probably nothing. But, the other night, my dad got a call from a lady named Liz Bareto. It seemed kind of... his voice seemed, I dunno, odd. Strained. And, well, I was wondering if you might know anything about her? If, maybe, she might have something to do with Mom's case? I say that because she was asking after some other people—Roy Cruise and his wife?"

Kristy noticed Travers' rapid eyeblink at the mention of Roy Cruise's name.

Gotcha.

"Hmph." Travers shrugged, feigning disinterest. "Do you know what they discussed? Specifically, I mean."

"Nothing much, really. It was a short call. I only heard the tail end, and only Dad's side of it. But she, well, she just seemed really pushy, and I wanted to know if, maybe, she might be dangerous?"

Kristy noticed Travers hesitate. He was clearly considering how to respond. How much to tell her. She leaned further forward to coax him into intimacy. And, as he began to speak, she noticed that his shoulders relaxed.

Come on, Art. Talk to me. Trust me. I need your help.

"There's really not a lot to tell. I doubt she's dangerous. Just persistent. This lady lost her son in a car accident a while back. He caused a collision, and it killed the Cruises' daughter."

"Oh my God. That's terrible," Kristy replied with a gasp. She inserted a deliberate pause. "But, what does that have to do with my dad? Why would she call him? And why now, right after my mom died?"

Travers took another sip from his cup. Then it was his turn to lean forward and interlock his fingers before resting his arms on the table.

"Look, Kristy. High level—and none of what I am about to tell you here is top secret or anything," he said, glancing at his hands. Then, looking back at her, he explained, "This lady thinks that someone killed her kid—that he didn't die of his injuries from the car accident. She's hurting. And, like any grieving parent, she's looking for answers, for someone to blame. And these Cruise folks fall into that category."

"She thinks they killed her son?"

Travers nodded.

"But, didn't the police investigate that? Follow the lead or whatever?"

"They did. They were out of town—the Cruises were—when the boy died. So, it's a dead-end. I guess she won't accept that. And, when Joe disappeared, he'd gone to meet with a company down in Miami called Cruise Capital, founded by Roy Cruise. Cruise was also questioned about Joe. He was out of the country when that happened, as well."

"I see."

"So, I guess she's just following threads. Connecting dots. Trying to see what your dad might know about Cruise."

Kristy nodded.

Travers pursed his lips, then looked Kristy in the eye and added, "You know, we interviewed your dad back then, too." Travers paused. "About Joe's disappearance, and about Cruise. You know, how they knew each other...." He let the words hang, waiting.

He sniffed again.

Kristy's spidey-sense went off.

You lying sack of shit, she thought. *You're trying to get me to tie my dad to Cruise.*

She knit her brow and put on her best ingenue puppy eyes. "That is *so strange*, because Dad told this Bareto lady that he'd never met these people," she said. "He told me the same thing." She could feel Travers deflate from across the table.

Nice try, asshole.

"Of course, yes," Travers added. "You misunderstood me. I mean, we asked your dad about *how* they knew each other. But he confirmed they didn't. They'd never met, I mean—your dad and the folks from Florida." Travers looked over Kristy's shoulder and signaled for a refill.

"Do you think I could get a copy of Dad's interview? I just

wanted to read it and see if there's anything there that jumps out at me."

Travers looked at her, considering. "Doesn't he have a copy? He should."

"He did," she said, "but he can't remember where he put it. Misplaced. He suggested I call Harold Riviera, his lawyer, and have him request a copy from you. But I figured I'd just ask you directly. That way I'd save on fees. You know lawyers..."

Travers nodded, studying Kristy, and then replied, "Sure. I'll have my office mail you a copy."

"Or I can just swing by and pick it up. I'll call ahead and let them know I'm coming." She paused. "So, this Bareto woman...." Kristy exhaled, hoping to get Travers to tell her more.

Travers thought for a moment, then replied, "That's really all there is, I'm afraid."

After a few minutes of additional small-talk, Kristy ended the meeting and left Travers to his coffee. She was disappointed in the detective, but not surprised. The system—once again—was working against her. This time, trying to use her against her father.

At least she had added another small piece to the puzzle— Liz Bareto wanted to talk to her father because she thought these Cruise people had killed her son. But, if the police had found nothing, what evidence was she relying on?

As Kristy walked down Second Street to the parking garage, she realized that Bethany was right. If she was going to resolve anything regarding her mother, it would need to be on her own. And she knew who she needed to talk to next.

CHAPTER THIRTY-EIGHT

The Monday after receiving Shaw's email, Eddie Garza followed up with a call to Cruise Capital to check up on his two favorite suspects. He confirmed Shaw's information that Roy Cruise was out of the country and not returning for another week. He also learned that David Kim was out sick. He'd been in an accident. Eddie asked where he could send flowers and was told Mercy Hospital.

Eddie stopped by the hospital gift shop before finding his way to David Kim's room.

He arrived just as a nurse was leaving and smiled at her, holding up a small vase of flowers. The nurse looked at the vase and then at him, and half-smiled back, then pointed at her watch and said, "Don't stay too long now. He needs rest."

Eddie's smile vanished the moment he turned to knock on the door.

"Come in."

David was lying in bed, his face bruised and one eye swollen.

"Holy shit, Kim. What the fuck did you step in front of?" Eddie asked without any preamble.

David looked up and replied, "Detective. So nice to see you."

Eddie placed his little vase of flowers next to a small garden of get-well plants on a nearby cabinet. "What the hell happened to you?"

"Hit and run. I think," he said through a grimace as he moved gingerly into a more comfortable sitting position.

"What, you don't remember?"

David shook his head. "Last thing I remember is using my

key card to get into the parking garage at home. Next thing I know, I wake up here."

"Yeah. I checked the police report on my way in. No witnesses. No security footage. *Nada*." Eddie paused, seeming genuinely concerned. "What's the prognosis?"

"All good. Nothing permanent." David smiled. "I have a hard head."

Eddie nodded. Pensive.

"So, to what do I owe the pleasure of your visit?"

Eddie took a couple of steps towards David and said, "Deb Wise is dead. Did you know that?" He studied David's expression. There was no change.

"Remind me?" David raised his eyebrows.

"The mother of the girl that got raped. In Austin. She was shot in the head."

"Wow. That sucks. I didn't know. But I've been kind of out of it the last few days," David said.

"Been longer than that. A month. Since she got shot, I mean."

"I had no idea."

"You know, Mr. Kim, people are creatures of habit. Big part of my job is identifying patterns. You find the pattern, lots of times you find the bad guy."

David looked at Eddie, eyebrows raised again, waiting for him to continue.

"Your buddy Cruise—out of town alibi when Liam Bareto dies. Out of town alibi when Harlan disappears. Out of town alibi when his business partner almost gets killed." Eddie paused. "That's a pattern."

Eddie noted that although David Kim maintained a poker face, after a few moments, he swallowed hard. "Roy travels a lot, man."

Eddie nodded, and asked, "Has he called you? Since this happened?"

David feigned disinterest and forced a smile. "Roy's on vacation, man. I don't know if he even knows what happened."

"In the Bahamas, right?"

"Did I say that?" David asked, feigning confusion, and then he continued sarcastically, "No, wait, are you trying to pump me for information? That's very clever. I almost didn't notice. Must be that advanced police training."

Eddie chuckled.

"Detective. You should have pretended to care for at least a couple more minutes before starting the interrogation. You know... build rapport, lower my defenses."

The cop shrugged, but said nothing. There was silence for a several moments, punctured by a distant squawk asking a Doctor Harper to report to the ER.

"You been to Austin lately?" Eddie asked.

"Thanks for the flowers, Detective. Really nice of you. You can direct all further communication to my lawyer. Now, I gotta rest."

David tilted his head back and closed his eyes. After a few moments, he opened one eye. Eddie was still standing there smiling at him.

He sighed. "Don't make me call the nurse, man. Trust me, you're no match for her."

Eddie nodded. "Look, David—you may be a great negotiator when it comes to stock deals or whatever it is you do for Cruise, but you reacted just now—Cruise is out of town and you're in a 'hit and run.'" Eddie made bunny ears as he said "hit and run." "I don't know what you're hiding or covering up. I may never find out. But you be careful. This buddy of yours... your partner... he's bad news. I'm just here to try and help. So, if you have anything you want to tell me..."

"Lawyer. Lawyer. Lawyer," David began repeating in monotone. "Lawyer. Lawy—"

"Okay, okay," Eddie said, holding up his hands and taking two steps backwards toward the door before pointing and adding, "but, if you change your mind, call me."

"Shouldn't you leave me a business card? Like in the movies?"

"You can fuckin' Google me." Eddie smiled.

"Goodbye, Detective. Have a great day."

Eddie saluted David, then pursed his lips and pointed at him, adding, "*Dime con quien andas, y te diré quien eres.*"

"Sorry, Detective, English only."

Eddie looked up, pondering, and then said, "Kinda like, 'If you lie down with dogs, you get up with fleas.'" Then he shook his head and raised a hand, index finger pointing up, and corrected himself, "No, hold on, better... 'You can judge a man by the company he keeps.'" Eddie chuckled, shaking his head. "That's closer, but not quite. That shit just doesn't translate."

The detective exited, leaving the door open. As the minutes ticked by and David was sure he was gone, his hands and feet began to sweat.

Deb Wise shot dead. Then, I get the crap beat out of me by that son-of-a-bitch asking about Harlan. Now, the police sniffing around again.

Wasn't Roy in Austin a couple of weeks ago?

David's paranoia kicked into high gear.

* * *

Eddie called Shaw as he drove back to his office and explained what he'd learned from David Kim.

"It's interesting, Eddie. Unusual. But I don't think it's enough to justify setting up surveillance. It's close, but I think—"

"But it fits Cruise's MO. He's out of the country and his business associate is magically almost killed in a hit and run!"

"It doesn't sound like he was exactly on his death bed."

"What about the cameras—I checked the police report. All the security cameras on the floor where the accident happened were dead. And *only* on that floor."

Shaw sighed. "Eddie, surveillance isn't cheap. I'm sorry, but I need something more."

"Okay." Eddie sighed. "I'll keep working it."

PART THREE

Billy Applegate
1986

The first stainless steel revolver ever manufactured was the Smith & Wesson model 60, which debuted in 1965. The handgun weighed almost one and a half pounds and held five bullets—either 0.380 special or 0.357 magnum, depending on the model.

The model that sat on the desk in front of Billy Applegate was a 0.380 special. Next to it were a half-empty bottle of vodka and an ashtray.

Billy sat in his father's study. The window was cracked open to keep him from stinking up the house with the smell of the cigarettes. The frost from his breath was indistinguishable from the smoke he exhaled into the frigid November air that filled the room.

Four years back, Billy had come home a disappointment. He'd dropped out of Columbia University and returned to live with his parents after failing most of his classes his second year. It had been difficult.

His mother had been supportive. His father had not, as he'd reached the end of his patience with "the boy" and wanted to know what exactly was wrong with him. Billy had overheard them arguing after returning from an interview for a part-time job.

His parents were in the living room, and they obviously hadn't heard him come in through the back door.

Dan's voice was raised, agitated. "You coddled him, Annette. You treated him like a baby all those years, and now this is what we get."

"Stop it, Dan! This isn't the 1960s. Try to be more enlightened, more compassionate. Can't you see he's suffering? It's killing him to disappoint us. Especially you. There's something else going on with him."

"You bet there is. Chasing skirts instead of books."

"It's not that simple and you know it."

"It is that simple. That English girl was a mistake. A music major, for Christ's sake! I told him so. I told him to watch out. Make a schedule. Stick to it. But he doesn't listen to me. He *never* listens to me, and that's because he was never disciplined. And that's on you. Whatever *Mommy* says, goes. Well, how is that working out for you now, huh?"

"Hello, parental units," Billy said sarcastically, walking into the living room. "Arguing over the princeling?"

"See?" Mr. Applegate said to his wife, raising his eyebrows. "I rest my case. The boy has absolutely no respect. And the worst part is, he doesn't even recognize it." He turned to his son and almost shouted his next words in staccato: "He. Is. A. Failure!"

"Dan!"

"How'd the interview go at the paper?" Applegate plowed on, ignoring his wife. "And don't lie to me, son. Walter's a friend. I'll find out one way or the other."

Billy stared at his father for several seconds before turning and climbing the stairs.

"Hey! I'm talking to you! Don't you walk away from me, young man!" Dan said, following him to the foot of the staircase.

But Billy didn't stop or turn to face his father.

"There you have it! No goddam respect!" Dan flared. "If I'd behaved that way, my father..."

Billy closed the door so that he couldn't hear his parents.

But it turned out that the interview had gone well. Billy was offered a job at the *Baltimore News-American*. Initially, part-time. Later full-time, as a copyeditor.

And, much to his surprise, he enjoyed it. It earned him some spending money and kept his drinking under control. He wasn't sober by any stretch of the imagination, but there was a considerable improvement, which in turn led to a much more harmonious relationship with his parents. Even his father.

But then fate decided to start smacking Billy Applegate around. Again.

In March of 1986, Dan Applegate died. It was a Thursday. His secretary stepped into his office to see if he needed anything before she left for the day and found him on the floor behind his desk. Dead from a massive heart attack.

The days after Dan Applegate's death seemed like a dream to Billy. Reality bit particularly hard when he saw his mother dressed in black, weeping next to the coffin as it was lowered into the ground.

It was then that a sense of responsibility settled on Billy Applegate. This was undoubtedly brought on by a combination of guilt over having been unproductive for many years and at having failed out of college, a disappointment. A burden. Now, he wanted—no, he needed—to feel that he was of value in some way to his mother. So, he threw himself into his career with renewed determination and ditched the booze in favor of complete sobriety.

Then fate struck Billy another blow. Shortly after his father's death, the job, the focus that he had come to rely on, evaporated.

So Long, Baltimore, was the headline in the May 27, 1986 edition, the last edition, of the *Baltimore News-American*.

With his father dead and his job gone, Billy's mother pushed him to go back to college. It was important to her that he earn a degree. Billy agreed, provided that he could study journalism. It wasn't law—which was what his father had wanted for him. But Billy enjoyed the work. The camaraderie. The excitement when a big story broke. His mother could appreciate that.

So, he enrolled at the University of Maryland for the fall semester, majoring in journalism. He was doing well. He'd even made some good friends. There was light at the end of this new dark tunnel.

Things had been improving... until that November afternoon when he found himself sitting in his father's study with a 0.380 special on the desk in front of him.

* * *

Billy had come home to an empty house that day. His mother was visiting his Aunt Brenda on the coast, preparing for Thanksgiving. Billy had stayed back to finish his classes, which he'd completed that day. He just needed to pick up some clothes and then drive out to join them for a long weekend.

He was ready. Packed and everything. He had even called his mother to let her know that he would be leaving shortly.

However, it was as he'd started his father's Lincoln that he'd remembered he hadn't brought in the mail as his mother had ask him to do. He emptied the mailbox, flipping quickly through its contents to sort the junk from the useful mail. He was heading back to the car when he saw it. Right there, in a newsletter, just under the fold. A black and white photograph.

It was him.

The monster from the party.

And he was back, in Maryland. For one night only...

Billy didn't know how long he stood in the driveway, behind the Lincoln with its engine running, staring at that image. He didn't recall killing the engine and going back into the house. He did remember finding the alcohol in his father's drawer. The bottom one. Where, for some reason, he'd also kept his revolver. Billy also remembered opening the window.

And, there he sat. At his father's desk.

Alcohol and the gun on the desk before him. The freezing cold of autumn filling the room.

Billy contemplated his next move.

In every life, there is one significant crossroads where a choice must be made that completely changes one's destiny. For many, that fork in the road is only obvious in hindsight. A fortunate few see the crossroads for what it is as they stand before it.

That night, in 1986, Billy Applegate was one of those fortunate few. There were two clear options. Two choices.

Drink the booze and use the gun on himself.

Or rid the earth of the motherfucker.

CHAPTER THIRTY-NINE

Tuesday
October 22, 2019
Austin, Texas

For the second time in as many days, Kristy was sitting nervously at a table and waiting for a man. She was casually dressed—though not in what she had planned. Kristy had been ready to leave home in black jeans and a black silk blouse with black ankle boots. She'd been shooting for elegant. But Bethany had seen what she hadn't.

"Jeez, Kris. No offense, but—wow—that's pretty fuckin' *Zorba the Greek.* All you're missing is a veil."

Kristy had looked at herself in the mirror. *How did I not see that?*

"I mean, I know your mom died and all, but... fuck...."

She'd gone back upstairs and, with Bethany's input, opted for blue jeans instead of black, a pair of cute red heels with a matching purse, and a white silk top with a black leather jacket.

"Much better," Bethany had said, nodding her approval.

She'd arrived at the restaurant early and was taking a sip of wine when she saw Alfie enter and head toward her. She hadn't seen him since her mother's funeral, though he'd called a number of times and gently prodded to get her to go out.

She felt warmth around her neck as he approached—she'd forgotten how just looking at him made her feel. Then, she almost choked... he was wearing black jeans with a black shirt.

Thank God I changed!

She stood and kissed him on the cheek.

"You look lovely, Kristy."

"You, too," she replied. "But who died?" Even as she'd said the words, she immediately regretted them.

"I... um...." Alfie blushed. "This is a great table," he stammered.

"*Forget* I said that," Kristy said, blushing. "Do over." She paused. "You look great. And it's *so* nice to see you."

Alfie smiled—his eyes sparkled. Kristy felt a flutter in her belly.

They sat and, as they perused the menu in silence, he still seemed a bit flustered. Kristy kicked herself. She decided to diffuse her *faux pas* the only way she knew how. Directly.

"Okay. That was probably one of the awkwardest starts to a date I've ever had—and it was totally my fault."

"Don't worry, Kristy." Alfie put down the menu. "I'm just glad to get to spend some time with you. And I'm glad that—" he paused, and leaned forward slightly, "this is 'a date.'"

Kristy smiled. They'd been "getting together" as friends for a while now. Neither had referred to any of their outings as a date before.

"How is your semester progressing?" he asked.

Yes! Kristy was ecstatic. Alfie had elegantly skipped the "How are you holding up?" "How is your dad?" questions while still asking about her life. Kristy wasn't sure if it was a cultural thing or if it was just him, but he had the ability to make her feel at ease and make conversation while avoiding uncomfortable subjects.

Kristy told him about ups and downs at school, her classes, and an upcoming term paper. Normal conversation. With no talk of her dead mother or her drunk father. She felt as though she were back in Colorado on the night she'd met Alfie. Just a girl having fun—with no baggage, no history, no worries.

Alfie caught her up on his job hunting. He'd finished his MBA in May and landed an analyst position at an Austin venture capital firm. So, he'd be in Austin for the foreseeable future.

After a wonderful meal, they were splitting a crème brûlée

when he reached across the table and gently took her hand. Kristy's heart raced.

"I've missed you, Kristy," he said, looking into her eyes. "I don't think you understand what you mean to me."

She squeezed his hand and smiled.

"I'd like to spend more time with you," he added. "I know it's been a complicated period. And I understand that you need time for... other things. But it would make me very happy to—how do you say, *compartir?*"

"Share?"

"Yes, but more. To be a part of these things with you. To share the burden, so to speak."

"I really appreciate that," she replied. She fought to keep from tearing up. "You can't know how much. But—"

Alfie put his right hand on top of hers, such that he was holding her hand in both of his. She did the same. His eyes were light brown with flecks of green and caught the candlelight.

Kristy didn't want to talk anymore. She just wanted to stare into his eyes and hold his warm hands—to feel his flesh. She could feel heat creeping out from her belly—up to her chest and neck, and downward, as well.

"I don't want to lose *this*," she said. "But I have to get some things taken care of first."

Alfie nodded. "I don't want to hurry you. I know you have a lot on your plate. But I do want you to know that I am not going anywhere." Then he laughed, releasing her hand. "Well, actually, I am going somewhere—back to Argentina for a few weeks before I start work."

"You sure know how to kill a moment," Kristy laughed.

"But, when I get back, we will go on many more dates. And... it would make me very happy if you would consider going back to Colorado. With me. For New Year's? I don't mention Christmas because I assume you will spend it with your father."

Kristy smiled ruefully, remembering Beaver Creek. "We could pick up where we left off. Our discussion about revenge. What was it you said then? The quote from Machiavelli?" she asked.

Alfie smiled. "If an injury must be done to someone, it should be so great that their vengeance should not be feared."

"That's it! I remember now. But you had another angle—that defeated Machiavelli's argument. Anonymous revenge, remember that?"

Alfie nodded. "Of course. If they don't know you did it to them, they can't come after you."

"Exactly. I've thought about that a lot." Kristy picked up her wine glass and leaned forward. "Tell me. Do you really think that revenge can't be satisfying if it's anonymous?"

Alfie's face became animated as he replied. Kristy felt herself drawn in, drawn to him. She watched his mouth as he spoke, his strong shoulders moving under his shirt as he gestured.

She had so much to do. So much to resolve.

School. Her mother. Frank Stern.

But, as she listened, she decided that she needed to add New Year's in Colorado with Alfie to her list.

CHAPTER FORTY

The first week of Susie and Roy's trip to Spain was uneventful—three days in Madrid, then a high-speed train ride and three more days in Barcelona. Roy later told me that it was pleasant, but melancholy. They had been to Europe several times with Camilla. This was their first trip to Europe without her.

Roy and Susie saw the sights. Shopped a bit. Walked. Held hands. They laughed. It was nice, but there was no passion. Roy described it like a weekend date when the couple knows that they've overextended their relationship and it's time to break up.

Of course, the cause of that gloom was two-fold, though each of them only knew half the story.

Roy had to confront Susie about Joan's death. Losing his sister was probably the signal event in his life, and finding out that Susie was involved… that had to be dealt with. And Roy planned to.

On the other hand, Susie had good reason to believe that Roy had killed her best friend, Deb. She was unsure whether she could trust her husband. She had been studying him, watching for clues. He seemed subdued, in one of his funks. But she didn't detect anything more.

When the day arrived for the two to leave the urban throngs and move on to Mallorca, they were enthused. Getting away from people, from the crowds, the pollution, and out onto the water appealed to them both. They looked forward to getting closer to nature and the sea.

They flew out of Barcelona and arrived in Mallorca just before lunch, then drove north to their hotel.

Mallorca is only a thirty-minute flight from the coast of

Spain. It is the largest of the Balearic Islands—about two and a half times the size of Oahu, it boasts two forty-mile-long mountain ranges to the north and some of the most beautiful beaches in all of Europe.

As always, Roy had done his research, and knew where they should go and what to do on the island.

They landed at the airport in the capital, Palma de Mallorca, which is a typical small European town—a large cathedral and an old city center surrounded by a lot of ugly, multi-family buildings. It is congested, and almost everywhere, there is a smell of sewage that many small European towns share and which, after long-term exposure, the locals no longer seem to notice.

Susie and Roy picked up their rental car and drove out and away from Palma.

The beauty of Mallorca lies outside the sprawl—in its beaches and mountains. The best-known tourist spots are to the south and west. For example, to the south, Puerto Portals has a beautiful marina and high-end restaurants, where people like Bill Gates, Jim Carey, and Rod Stewart have been spotted. Another popular destination for the top one percent lies to the west in the mountains near Valldemosa, where Michael Douglas owned a home for some time.

Roy and Susie, however, drove north. Roy's planning had focused on hidden gems off the beaten path. This is what he told Susie. And it was true, partially. Though, there was more to it than that.

He had booked them at a hotel called Son Brüll near the village of Pollença. What began as a monastery in the 1100s is now a farm, vineyard, restaurant, and hotel nestled in the northern foothills of the island. The property has been updated to top standards, the service is impeccable, and the food is amazing.

"My God, Roy, look at that view." Susie was on the terrace outside their suite, which overlooked the valley. A cool breeze smelling faintly of the sea played with her hair.

"Amazing, no?" He smiled as he came up to her and gave her a hug from behind, resting his head on her shoulder.

"Are you okay?" she asked. "You seem a bit, I don't know, distracted?"

"All good. Better now. It's... it was shitty re-visiting places we went with Camilla, you know? I mean, home is one thing. We have so much history there, everything blurs. But all the memories I have of Europe include her, you know?"

Susie put her arms on top of Roy's, hugging herself. "Remember the first time we visited Madrid with Camilla? We stayed at the..."

While Susie reminisced, Roy held her, but his mind was elsewhere. He took in the view. The far-off horizon. Closer in—the hills, the pine trees. So peaceful.

Slowly, from the distance, his focus returned to the surrounding area. And to the grounds of Son Brüll. To the courtyard below. There were tables from the restaurant on the terrace, arranged on the coralina stone pavers. A few were still occupied from lunch. Roy estimated that the balcony where they stood was at least forty feet above the courtyard.

Forty feet up.

Sixty miles per hour.

Impossible to survive.

CHAPTER FORTY-ONE

Wednesday
October 23, 2019
Mallorca, Spain

"Take a right at the next roundabout," Susie said.

Roy was driving a Fiat, heading to the port of Alcúdia. The boat Roy had chartered was docked there and he wanted to have a look at her. He had also made dinner reservations at Bistro Mar—a popular restaurant on the marina.

Their boat was a 2006 Rodman 41 motor yacht with a flybridge, named *Altamira*. Rodman is one of the top boat manufacturers in the world, and well-known internationally for their naval and industrial shipbuilding. Their leisure craft line is very popular in Europe, and Roy was excited to spend time getting to know the brand.

At the marina, the broker gave Roy and Susie a very quick tour of the *Altamira*. Well-kept. Clean. Everything in order. They received keys and final instructions, and then the broker rushed off to another meeting.

After viewing the boat, Susie and Roy had dinner—mussels and a typical Mallorcan lobster stew.

Susie was quiet. Pensive. But she appeared to be making the most of their time.

The food tasted flat to Roy. He was feeling the wine, though. He was drinking more rapidly than normal, and Susie noticed. He was preoccupied, thinking about his plan. The more he thought about it, the more he was sure.

Tonight's the night.

After dinner, they returned to their room at Son Brüll, where Roy suggested they sit and have drinks out on the balcony.

Roy mixed two gin and tonics at the minibar—with gin produced on the property. He gulped down half of his glass and then refilled it before joining his wife out on the terrace. He handed Susie her glass. As he did, he noticed that her eyes were glistening as if she had been fighting back tears.

What is this about?

She placed her drink on the small teak coffee table between them, untouched.

"Listen, Roy," Susie said, turning to look at him. "You know I love you. I love you more than anything." She paused.

"Of course, Suze. I know that."

She took in a deep breath. "I need to ask you about something, and I want you to tell me the truth. I'll love you no matter what, but I need you to be honest with me, okay?"

"Of course. You know I would never lie to you, babe," Roy said, taking a seat opposite her and sipping from his glass.

"Okay. Um. So…" Susie took a deep breath, "I know what happened to Deb. I saw it all online." Susie paused and looked at her husband. His expression did not change. It was as if she had just told him that she preferred still to sparkling water.

"Deb… Deb Wise? What happened?" he asked, casually shrugging and shaking his head inquisitively.

Susie sat back, distancing herself from him. The sudden move upset the coffee table, knocking Susie's drink over. Gin and tonic sluiced across the table and dribbled onto the tiled floor. Neither Susie nor Roy made a move to do anything about it.

Susie looked long and hard at her husband, and he held her gaze—still, expressionless.

"You know what I mean!" she spat. "Don't *fucking* lie to me."

Roy carefully put his drink down. As he did, he righted his wife's glass and then looked her straight in the eyes. "Susie," he said, calmly. "*What* are you talking about?"

"Your last trip to Austin. That's what I'm talking about!"

He raised his eyebrows. He held his hands out and shrugged again, gesturing for her to continue. "My last trip to Austin...?"

"Okay, then.... Where's the fucking Glock, Roy? Answer me that! Because it's not in the safe. And Deb, my best friend, just happened to get shot in the head while you were in Austin."

Roy hesitated, his eyes darting sideways, mouth partially open. "She's... Deb's dead? And you think I killed her?"

Susie sat forward and seethed, pointing at him. "You're a fucking liar." She stood and moved away from him, walking over to the balcony railing. "I told you, I just fucking told you not to lie to me!"

Roy stood and followed her. His approach was slow and cautious. "Susie, babe, I really don't know what you're talking about. I didn't know she was dead, I swear."

"Then where's the gun, Roy?"

He took another step toward her and scratched his head. "The Glock's at the shop, at Stone Hart's. I *told* you. I'm having the grip backstrap reduced and they're gonna add forward cocking serrations."

She glared at him, but even in the low light, he could see a glimmer of recall in her expression before her eyes hardened once more.

"I told you weeks ago," he added, taking another step.

"Of *course*. You *would* tell me that, though, wouldn't you? I think you forget that we've been down this road before, Roy. Alibis. Cover-ups. No fucking singing bones, right?"

"Suze," he said, holding up his right hand, "I swear to God, I don't know what the fuck you're talking about."

Roy took another step toward her. They were close now. Not close enough to touch, but close enough for him to see the artery in her neck pulsing. She was fuming, the way she used to get... before.

A breeze blew across them, capturing strands of Susie's hair to blow them about her face. The trees below swayed and the leaves rustled.

"But, if it's true," he continued, his face darkening, "if that bitch is truly dead, I'm not sorry. I'm glad someone fucking shot her..."

Susie opened her mouth to speak, but stopped. She could see it in his eyes.

Sorrow. Betrayal. The end... of everything.

Oh, God. No.

He knows? Does he know about Joan?

For a long moment, everything went still—as if the air had been sucked out of the world. The only sound was a faint electric buzz from one of the outdoor lights on the terrace. Susie felt dizzy. She reached back and grabbed the metal railing for support.

Roy took another step, closing the gap between them before placing his hands on his wife's shoulders, grabbing her firmly, his feet apart, and looking into her eyes. "I only wish it *had* been me that killed her... for Joan's sake," he said.

Susie's mouth fell open. She gasped for air and her face turned white. She leaned back on the railing and brought her hands up to her face, covering her nose and mouth. Then her chest began to convulse as her body was racked, silently, violently sobbing.

CHAPTER FORTY-TWO

Some time later, over drinks, Roy and I discussed the concept of remorse.

In every life, there are high and low points. Roy's greatest point of pride was his family—not the one he was born into, but the one he chose. So much joy. So much tragedy, as well.

Roy didn't regret anything he'd done. What he regretted was his pride. Thinking that he—that they, he and Susie and Deb and Tom—could somehow become dispensers of justice; that they had the right to mete out punishment, and that there wouldn't be consequences.

We were sitting out on my terrace. And, between sips of scotch, Roy explained it to me like this.

"The problem isn't the things we did. I don't regret, for example, taking out that little fucker Harlan. What I regret is that I was so stupid as to think that there wouldn't be repercussions. Not legal—like jail or whatever—but... karmic. See, the things we do, everything—the universe is watching. Good and bad. And that motherfucker is making a list like a goddammed accountant. And, in the end, all the accounts have to balance.

"And it was right there in front of me that night. I just missed it.

"See, months before this, Susie told me that, when Camilla died, she got Deb to kill Liam Bareto. Hell, she showed me Bareto's hospital ID bracelet." He shook his head. "I couldn't believe she'd kept it... in our house! Then, when Harlan raped Kristy, Deb called in the favor, asking Susie to kill him. And Susie manipulated me into helping her. I could understand all of that. The missing piece for me was always *why?* Why did Deb agree to kill Liam? What was it in her and Susie's past that even made that an option? And if they were so close, why was it that Susie had never mentioned Deb? Why didn't they ever get together?

"Joan. She was the missing puzzle piece.

"And that night on the balcony, just for a moment, I saw a hint, an inkling of karmic action—of how the universe settles accounts. Look at what Deb had done, and what happened to her. Classic karmic equilibrium.

"I should have seen it as a warning. If I'd stopped to think about it, I would have known that there was more to come. And I'd have been more cautious. Vigilant. But I was too wrapped up in the moment. You know, 'where do we go from here?' My only worry was how I—how *we*—could get past it. Past Joan. I mean, it was *huge.* And *that* was all I cared about. Now what?

"Then, like magic, it seemed like the universe provided a solution. And I thought—okay, this is how. This will work. There's hope—light at the end of the tunnel. A silver lining, you know?" Roy shook his head. "Fuck. I was so stupid. I was too proud to realize that there was no way it could ever happen. That there couldn't be a happy ending for us. It was just a set-up. You see, the universe still had accounts to settle. And Susie and I, we were way overdrawn."

CHAPTER FORTY-THREE

Roy held Susie as she sobbed uncontrollably. When there were no more tears, she began. She explained everything, profusely and in detail.

Then, she asked for forgiveness.

Repeatedly.

They sat there on the cold tiles of the terrace—him holding her close for what must have been minutes, but seemed like hours.

Eventually, Susie regained some semblance of composure. While she took a hot shower, Roy had another drink on the terrace. The alcohol had no effect on him. He was numb. Not long after he heard the shower stop, he went inside to find Susie quietly weeping in bed. He turned out the lights, sliding into bed next to her and pulling her into an embrace. As they lay together, he mentally ran through everything she'd told him. He believed her.

She had met Deb at camp. They'd become friends. Joan's death had been unintended. Deb's fault. They'd been two thirteen-year-old girls who were scared to death, not knowing what to do. Although, something told him that Deb had known exactly what she was doing. She was evil.

Either way, they'd tried to make Joan's death look like an accident. And they'd gotten away with it.

It had haunted Susie—all of it. So much so that, years later, she had sought Roy out, wanting to meet him and to find some way to make amends. She hadn't planned on falling in love with him. It had just happened. And then it had been too late to tell him because she hadn't wanted to risk losing him over the ugly truth.

It all made sense. Deep down, he wanted to believe it was true, to believe that she loved him.

We'll be working through this one for a while. Fucking therapy.

Roy thought Susie had fallen asleep, when she interrupted his ruminations. "Do you still love me?" she asked.

"Of course, I do. I just... we have to see how we move forward from here."

Susie cleared her throat. "Then, there's something else you should know."

Roy's heart sank. *Oh fuck. What now?*

Susie wiggled herself free from his embrace, sat up in bed, and turned on the light. Roy propped himself up on his elbow. She looked like shit. Her eyes were puffy and she had a red rash under her nose.

She sniffled, then said two words to him—if anyone had asked him, he'd have said they were the two words he'd least expected to hear.

Hope—the light at the end of the tunnel. A silver lining.

"I'm pregnant."

From misery and tragedy to overwhelming joy. Roy kissed her as she explained. The doctor. The Clomid pills—her 2.5 milligrams of salvation in a tablet. She'd wanted to tell him sooner, but was so worried that she might miscarry.

"How far along are you?"

Susie smiled, "Eleven weeks."

She was ecstatic. Roy was thrilled, as well. He was beside himself.

Once they were over the excitement, she curled back up next to him and he held her until she drifted off to sleep.

He crawled out of bed, being careful not to wake her, and returned to the terrace, where he poured himself another drink.

Fucking crazy life.

A baby!

Roy raised a glass to the universe. A premature and ill-advised gesture.

Then he sat thinking about the other part of the equation,

forgotten for now—how the whole evening had gotten started. He wondered if Susie had believed him when he'd said that he hadn't killed Deb. He had promised to show her the Glock when they got home.

Susie was hard to read sometimes. But he had gotten pretty good at it over the years. He was pretty sure she'd believed him. Though, he was also sure that she was letting the issue slide for now because he knew about Joan. It was difficult for her to accuse him of lying about Deb when she had been hiding the truth about Joan for over twenty years.

CHAPTER FORTY-FOUR

Thursday
October 24, 2019
Austin, Texas

Senator Harlan was working from his law office in downtown Austin. It was meant to be a relatively slow day. Not much on the calendar besides coffee with the Bareto woman late in the afternoon.

That was before he received three peculiar phone calls.

The first came in at around 10:30 a.m., Texas time—11:30 a.m. Eastern. It was from John Cornyn, one of the two U.S. Senators from Texas. Harlan had known him for a long time. They exchanged Christmas cards and chatted at political events, but rarely talked on the phone. More acquaintances than friends.

And yet, the call lasted almost twenty minutes and focused on nothing in particular. Cornyn just wanted to "touch base."

The second call came at 1:15 p.m. from Congressman Will Hurd. Hurd was a Texas member of the U.S House of Representatives. This call lasted around thirty minutes and focused briefly on the upcoming elections before moving on to gossip about recent political scandals as well as general chit-chat.

After the second call, Harlan began pacing. His political instincts were on fire. He sat down at his computer to do some research in an effort to narrow the possibilities. He knew that Cornyn was on the Senate Intelligence Committee. He discovered that Hurd was also on the House Intelligence Committee.

Something was up.

The third call clinched it. It came in at 3:00 p.m.

It had been years since Harlan had spoken to General Ari Gordon. Gordon had been a Major back when Harlan had served in El Salvador. He was obviously a career-man, even back then, and he'd done well for himself.

But the two men had not spoken in over a decade. And, as if to make sure that Harlan understood that something was up, Gordon called Harlan on his mobile phone rather than at his office number. How did he even have that number?

Harlan was being vetted for something. Of that he was certain. And people in the know were making contact so that he would know that they knew, and that they had played a role in getting him there. They wanted him to owe them one, or at least for him to think he did.

Harlan considered calling Congresswoman Hertig. It was possible that she might know something. But that felt like jumping the gun. If she didn't know anything, he'd be tipping her off, potentially triggering her own inquiry that could end up upsetting the apple cart.

No. He decided it was best to wait it out. If something was in the works, he would know sooner rather than later.

As he considered his options, his cellphone vibrated. The burner.

Slipknot.

"Hello."

"Hey, Joe. You got a few seconds to chat?"

"Sure," Harlan said, injecting a smile into his tone. He was suddenly regretting getting involved with Slipknot, as his *activities* could potentially derail whatever might be in the works.

"So, quick update," Slipknot continued. In the background, Harlan could hear a female voice speaking over a PA system. It sounded as if the man was at an airport. "Cruise is traveling. Out of country. I paid his associate a visit, although he doesn't seem to know anything. And that was with me being my usual persuasive self."

Harlan's gut fluttered. How persuasive? He didn't even want

to imagine. It worried him that Slipknot may have gone too far. They weren't in the military anymore. There might be blowback. And given that morning's developments, he didn't want any complications.

"If he'd known something, I am sure he would have told me," Slipknot continued, bringing Harlan back to the conversation. "But there was nothing there. I think it's safe to say that the guy wasn't involved. At least not knowingly."

"Is he...?" Harlan was suddenly worried that he might be overheard. Maybe the call was being monitored. Maybe Slipknot was recording it. He cleared his voice and asked casually, "How is he doing?"

"Fine. Fine. Nothing a few weeks and some stitches won't cure." Slipknot chuckled. "Next stop, down in your neck of the woods."

"That all sounds great, but maybe we should take it easy? Slow things down a bit. Wait for his friend to get back in town. He seems like the next logical step, doesn't he?"

"Don't worry, Joe. I got this. I know what I'm doing. Just wanted to give you a quick update. Catching a flight now. Trust me. More soon. Gotta go."

Before Harlan could say anything else, the connection went dead.

Shit!

As he sat mulling over potential repercussions, an alert sounded on his computer. It was a reminder of his afternoon appointment with Liza Bareto. He rose, put on his suit jacket, and headed out.

CHAPTER FORTY-FIVE

His meeting was at the Starbucks on Fifth Street. A safe public setting in case she turned out to be problematic. As Harlan walked up Congress Avenue, he played out different scenarios, different ways that Slipknot could fuck things up. He considered how to best distance himself if necessary—and, of course, how to do damage control. Plausible deniability. It was something he was skilled at.

As far as he could tell, right there and then, the only thing tying him to Slipknot was their chance encounter on the airplane and their recent communications, which had all taken place via the burner phone. He had personally copied Joe's file before sending it to Slipknot, and he'd been sure to wear latex gloves. Paranoid, perhaps, but he had been in politics long enough to know that it never hurt to take precautions, and he didn't want anything in that file to be tied back to him.

If Slipknot was somehow caught or questioned, Harlan would simply deny any connection. He would throw him under the bus in a heartbeat.

Sure, they had known each other once upon a time, but they hadn't spoken in decades until that chance encounter on the plane. Then the guy had deluded himself into thinking that they had forged a connection. It wasn't unusual. He wasn't the first and he wouldn't be the last to presume an intimacy that did not exist.

Deny. Deny. Deny.

That said, it was unlikely that Slipknot would screw up and get caught. He had been through a lot worse and had always proven to be capable and resourceful. Self-preservation being what it was, Harlan felt relatively sure Slipknot would not take undue risks.

A new concern was whether the man was recording their conversations. The guy he'd known in El Salvador had seemed honorable enough. But that had been years ago. People change. Circumstances change. This could all be a set-up for blackmail.

Maybe the meeting on the flight wasn't a coincidence.

The calls he'd received earlier, the possibility that something was afoot, had raised the stakes and made him look at the situation with Slipknot with fresh eyes. He had been careless. Blinded by grief.

He could cease all communication. Then again, it might already be too late.

Fuck.

Harlan put on his best politician's smile and entered the coffee shop.

He was looking for a woman. A mother. She'd told him she'd be wearing a white silk blouse and a lavender skirt. The place wasn't too busy, which meant that it was easy to spot the woman waving at him from the back corner of the room. He made his way toward her while she appeared to be finishing up on a phone call. He noticed that she turned away from him as she did. He also noticed her slender figure and perfect ass.

Harlan's smile turned to one of appreciation.

From what he could see, she was tanned. Fit. Well-built. Although she must be in her mid-to-late-forties, she carried it well. He wondered whether her breasts were real or fake. They seemed too large for her frame. He hoped they were real. Her blouse was unbuttoned just enough to showcase them. He decided that, after their greeting, he would let her sit first, in the hopes that he might get a better look.

He extended his hand and gave her his best campaign smile. "You must be Liz. I am so pleased we could meet. I'm Joe Harlan."

CHAPTER FORTY-SIX

Kristy Wise was about to meet "the devil she didn't know."

After her meeting with Detective Travers, she'd swung by his office and picked up a copy of her father's interview regarding Harlan's disappearance. It was short, but revealing.

Throughout the interview, her father had repeatedly denied knowing or ever having met Roy Cruise. Kristy knew that was false. And, she could tell from the interview transcript that her father had made several missteps in covering that up. Kristy had actually cringed as she'd read through it.

Tom Wise was clearly hiding something—and lying to the police about it. At one point, Detective Travers had even accused him of it.

Kristy was determined to find out what he was hiding. She used the number she'd taken from her father's phone to call the Bareto woman. Their conversation had been short. It turned out that Liz Bareto was already in Austin *on business*, and they'd agreed to meet face-to-face.

When Kristy entered the coffee shop, she was waved down by a woman in a white silk blouse and a lavender skirt. They shook hands briefly, and as she sat down opposite the woman and they made eye contact, Kristy's stomach clenched.

It had been a while since she had seen that look, and it was painted all over this woman's face. The cow-eyes of pity. The face of a stranger who knew everything about her, or at least about what had been done to her. She felt herself assuming a defensive posture, shutting herself off from the woman, and she fought it, sitting up straight and raising her chin.

I'm not a fucking victim!

It was always worse with women, for some reason. At least men generally had the decency to look awkward, embarrassed, and uncomfortable, with shifty eyes and fake smiles, as if they felt guilty that one of "them"—one of their "brothers"—had raped her. Those looks, she could handle.

She also didn't mind the women who looked at her with judgment, eyeing her up and down and speaking with their eyes— *What did you do to deserve it?* She could handle those, as well, responding to their smugness with antagonism. It was easy to hate the ones who looked at her like that.

But not this woman. Kristy couldn't hate her for sympathizing, but she didn't have to like it.

"Like I said on the phone, I overheard your call with my father, Ms. Bareto. It's been hard for him since Mom passed, as you can imagine. And, well, I'm looking for answers," she said matter-of-factly, pursing her lips together when she finished. Kristy wanted information. The problem was that she didn't know what she needed to know or how to go about getting it.

"Please, call me Liz." The woman smiled. "How did you get my number?"

"My dad. Well, not exactly from him. From his phone."

"Ah. Resourceful. I like that. Do you want to get something to drink?"

"No, I'm good."

"Well," Liz began, "I called your father…. Actually, I was very sorry to hear about your mother. I should have started there, really." She blushed, looking at her hands for a moment.

Kristy took the opportunity to study her closely, and she could see that, despite her tanned skin, the woman's neck and chest had flushed pink, and she was fidgeting with her left ring finger even though she wasn't wearing a wedding band. She was obviously feeling awkward, maybe even guilty about meeting with Kristy after her father had turned her away.

"It's okay, Liz. In the scheme of things, it's terrible, but it's life." Kristy was oddly grateful that she'd skipped the condolences.

She had heard enough of those and just wanted to get down to business. "From what I heard of your call with my dad, I, um, I got the impression that you might have had some information for him. About my mom, maybe?" Kristy had used "dad" and "mom" intentionally. She felt she might get more out of Liz if the woman saw Kristy as a young, motherless child.

"My God. Where to begin? There's so much you don't know," Liz said.

Kristy placed trembling hands on the table and said, "That's exactly why I'm here."

And so, Liz Bareto laid it all out for her. Liam's crash. Camilla Cruise's death, followed by her son Liam's, months later. The autopsy. Roy and Susie's alibi. She showed Kristy the 'ladyfinger photos' on her phone, although the images were grainy.

As the story unfolded before her, Kristy's sense of unease increased. Her ears burned, her neck became tight, and she felt like she was on the verge of breaking out in a sweat. She breathed slowly, trying to remain calm—to look calm, at least.

Liz told the whole tale succinctly and effectively. Yet, Kristy could tell from the occasional moisture in her eyes and cracks in her voice that, despite the number of times she must have told the story, her frustration at the lack of progress with her son's case remained raw. Visceral—not unlike Kristy's own pain.

Kristy felt overwhelmed. It was all she could do to keep from crying. What had happened to Liz Bareto was not right. Kristy hoped that she herself was not looking back at Liz with cow-eyes of pity now.

When Liz stopped talking, Kristy took a few seconds before responding. Her mouth was dry.

"Liz. It's a terrible story. I am truly sorry for your loss. But, if I'm honest, I'm not quite sure what any of this has to do with me. Or with our family." Liz nibbled on her bottom lip, her shoulders tense. It was clear to Kristy that she had more to say, but was trying to decide just what, or how to share it. So, Kristy tried to encourage her. "I know that Roy Cruise was questioned in connection with Joe Harlan's disappearance," she offered, "but he had an alibi. Do you think he was involved in Liam's case? And my mom's, too?"

Instinctively, Liz reached out and touched the young lady's hand before looking her in the eyes and saying, "That's what I'm trying to find out. There's a lot about Mr. Cruise and his wife that seems fishy. It's not any one thing, but when you add everything up and look at the big picture, it feels like there's more going on than meets the eye.

"Kristy, someday you'll have children—if you decide that's for you. And when you do, you'll understand a mother's love. You'll understand what sacrifice means. Because you'll be willing— happy—to give your life for your child's."

Those words hit home. Kristy thought of her own mother and what she may have done for her. And what it had cost her.

"I will not rest until I know what happened to Liam. I called your father because I was hoping he could help... maybe clear some things up."

"Tell me, Liz. I'll try to find out. What happened to Liam is wrong. And I know what it's like to be wronged. If there is anything I can do, any information I can get from Dad for you, I will. What are you trying to find out?"

Liz's smile faded, her lips pursed, and she slowly released Kristy's hand. "Honey, it's like I said, when you add it all up...." She paused, and then added, "One of the detectives in Miami told me that the odds of a person being connected to one violent crime in their lifetime are low. Just one. Roy Cruise has been connected to Liam, Joe Harlan, and..." she looked around them, and lowered her voice conspiratorially, "your mother."

Kristy's eyes widened. "My mom's? How?"

"He was in Austin when it happened. That might be a coincidence, but maybe not."

"Are you sure?" Kristy asked. Cruise being in Austin made the possibility of his and Susie's involvement in her mother's death real.

Liz nodded. "Positive. I have an investigator that I am

working with. I'm looking into it myself since, between you and me, I really don't have much faith in the police. I'm actually starting to lose faith not just in them, but in the whole system."

Kristy nodded, agreeing wholeheartedly. *Who is this amazing woman? This fighter!*

"And there's more. Cruise, his twin sister—she died in an accident when he was young. Around eleven years old."

"He had a twin? What kind of accident?"

"At camp. Best information I've found is that the police concluded that she fell off a cliff."

Kristy drew in a breath. "So, you think he killed my mom *and* his sister, too?"

"I don't know for sure. But that's one of the reasons I'm here. I'm trying to get answers. Death seems to follow this guy around. That, or a whole bunch of strange coincidences."

"But you're saying he was in town, in Austin, when my mom died. That's not consistent with what you told me... I mean, about him being out of town—his alibi when Liam and Harlan... you know."

Liz pulled a face. Clearly, she did not like being contradicted. Kristy made a mental note of it.

"It's a question of probabilities," she said. "He's just connected to too many deaths. Where there's smoke, there's fire. And then there's this... his real name isn't even Cruise. It's Diaz. Roy Diaz. He changed his name. I think he did it to put distance between him and what happened to his sister."

Kristy said nothing.

"Look, I know this is a lot to take in all at once. And you wouldn't be the first person to think I'm paranoid. Obsessed. That's fine. I'm used to it. But I know there's something behind all this. And I know I'm getting closer."

"So, how can I help?"

"I wanted to ask your father if he knows Cruise or Font. I wanted to see if there was some reason why they would want to hurt your mom. Maybe something way back? Maybe he never met Roy Cruise, but the name Roy Diaz might ring a bell."

Liz looked long and hard at Kristy. She cocked her head in anticipation.

Kristy made a show of processing what she had just heard. "Dad's been having a hard time since Mom passed," she said. She couldn't bring herself to outright lie—like Tom had to the police—and tell Liz that Tom had never heard of Roy or Susie. "But, I'll talk to him. If he knows anything, I'll find out. But this is a lot to take in, Liz. Is it okay if I take some notes?"

"Of course," she responded eagerly.

Kristy typed notes into her iPhone. Liz then offered to text Kristy the "ladyfinger" images and to email her the short security video clip from which the photos had been taken.

As they rose to say goodbye, they embraced. Kristy breathed in and almost melted into Liz's arms; she felt herself on the verge of tears and fought to keep herself together.

"Thanks so much, Kristy. Do what you can. If I find out anything related to your mom, I'll let you know. And I will keep looking." She stepped closer and placed her hands on Kristy's arms. "I will not rest until I know that Liam's killer has been brought to justice," she said, her eyes bright with determination.

CHAPTER FORTY-SEVEN

Back at her car, Kristy strapped in, locked the doors, and started the engine.

She then took a few moments to try to compose herself. Tears were running down her cheeks.

In many ways, Kristy saw parallels between Liz Bareto and her mother. Two women who would do anything for their children. She felt a connection to Liz, and because of that connection, her heart had fallen after hearing everything she had been through. Maybe it was just pent up emotion, but Kristy broke down sobbing now—for Liz and for her mother.

She cried for almost five minutes. Once the worst was over, Kristy opened her backpack and took out her laptop. She cranked it up. As it booted, she took a few moments to consider what she had just learned. Roy Cruise being in Austin, his dead sister, his name change—all new information.

As she thought through what Liz had told her and sliced it and diced it, she was able to distill everything into three key questions.

First, what had Roy Cruise/Diaz been doing in Austin on the day her mother had been shot? She knew from her research that he had investments in town. Was that it? Or was there something more?

Second, what did the death of Roy's sister have to do with all of this?

Third, the 'ladyfinger' pictures and the video...

Kristy's laptop beeped, signaling that it was up and running. She downloaded her email via hotspot, then opened Liz's email and played the video clip. Then she played it again, and again. Six, seven, ten times.

Kristy knew her mother. She knew her body. She knew her posture, the way she moved. She also knew the way she put her hair up to get it out of her way when she needed to.

She wasn't positive, but she was pretty sure.

Her mother was "the ladyfinger."

CHAPTER FORTY-EIGHT

What a night!

Frank Stern was finally home. It was almost midnight. He'd planned to make an early night of it, as he'd only had three deliveries to make that evening. On a whim, though, he'd decided to ping Angela—the hot mom in the Hills—to see if she'd be up for a booty call. That had been at eight.

What a great lay!

Older women... wow!

It had been about five months since Frank had seen Angela. He'd been avoiding her because he'd been worried about surveillance. In early August, he'd come home from work to find Pippa sitting in his living room. There was nothing unusual in that—she had a key. The problem was what had been lying on the coffee table. Pictures of him and Angela. In Angela's house. In her jacuzzi. On her kitchen table.

Fuck.

Frank assumed that the photos were the result of Judge Warren, Pippa's father, inserting himself into their relationship.

Watching out for his little girl.

Pippa had been livid. She'd screamed. She'd cried. She'd broken a lamp and a mirror by throwing one into the other. She'd tried to punch him, but he'd dodged and she'd missed, falling and banging her knee on the coffee table. He'd fought hard not to laugh as she'd limped around the room cursing at him. No point in making things worse.

"Dad was right about you!

"You piece of shit, cheating motherfucker!

"You better watch your fuckin' back, asshole!

"This doesn't end here!

"You... are... soooo... fucked!"

In the end, she'd limped out of his apartment, vowing never to see him again. She'd slammed the door on her way out. Then opened it and slammed it again.

That same night, Frank had gone into stealth mode. He'd set up a Plan B long ago, in case something like this happened—something that put his business at risk. He had rented a storage unit and put a small safe in it—large enough to hold his cash and drugs. He knew it was "a little belt and suspenders," but he liked to be careful.

After Pippa's grand exit, he'd moved everything into the safe in the storage unit—including the pictures of him and Angela. There were a couple of good shots of him going at her from behind.

Using the storage unit meant one extra stop on delivery nights, but it was a small price to pay for security. He figured he'd give it another couple of weeks, and if nothing unusual happened, he'd assume Pippa's threats had been just that and go back to business as usual.

Frank entered his apartment and headed to the kitchen. He needed to catch up on email from his day job, but he'd done a few lines of coke with Angela earlier and wanted just a little more. He always kept a little somethin' somethin' around the house, just in case. He set up the line on the kitchen counter and bent over with a small straw to his right nostril.

Suddenly, Frank's right cheek felt cold and his neck ached. His vision was blurry. As it cleared up, it seemed to him that he was leaning against a strange, white tile wall. It was cold—and he realized his face was pressed against it. There appeared to be metal bars protruding from it. He tried to turn to get a better look at it, but searing pain shot through his head.

"You awake, princess?" a distorted voice asked from somewhere to his left.

He turned his head toward the voice, and there was that shooting pain again.

The metal bars moved toward him, making a loud noise that pierced Frank's skull as they scraped against the wall.

Frank saw boots.

What the fuck? Someone's standing on the wall. Sideways?

Suddenly, a face came into view. Right up against his. It was that of a pale, bald man with small, dark eyes and pockmarked cheeks.

"Wakey! Wakey!"

A hand roughly slapped his cheek. Again, the pain!

Frank blinked, then slowly understood. *His world* had turned sideways. That wasn't a white tile wall. It was the floor. He was lying on the floor in his kitchen. The metal bars were the legs of a kitchen chair.

He felt strong wiry hands grip his upper arms and pull him upright. His head spun as he changed position, and he felt nauseous.

The man scraped the metal chair across the floor, setting it in front of Frank, and sat down. He casually held a gun in one hand.

Frank stammered, in fear for his life. "Look, man. We had a deal. Ten thousand a month. I've been paying on time. Please. Let me talk to Jerry."

"I... do not know... *what* the *fuck*... you are talking about."

"I'll pay more. I can do fifteen a month. I just need a little more time to get caught up. If only—"

"Shut the fuck up!" shouted the man. "I don't give a shit about your money problems."

Frank's eyes raced from the man's face to the floor to the ceiling, as though the answer to his confusion was hiding somewhere in the room. "Wait, Jerry didn't send you?"

"You got bigger problems than Jerry, princess." The man leaned forward, pointing the gun at Frank's right eye. "Now, from the top, you're gonna tell me everything there is to tell about your buddy Joe Harlan."

CHAPTER FORTY-NINE

Susie awoke to an empty room, and as she looked around her, the memory of the previous night's revelations came rushing back to her. She felt lightheaded. Her heart pounded in her chest and ears, her face and neck flushed, and her hands trembled slightly. Adrenaline.

She looked around the room. Roy's suitcase was still there. The shirt he'd worn yesterday was reassuringly slung over the back of a chair.

Thank God!

"Hello?"

Silence.

"Roy?"

Nothing.

Out for a run?

Susie slid out of bed and padded to the bathroom, where she found a note from her husband on hotel stationery, lying on the floor in the doorway.

Running some errands. Coffee and toast in living room. Back soon. Love you!

She sighed with relief and went into the bathroom, where she looked at her reflection in the mirror.

Oh my God, girl, you look like warmed over shit.

Her hair was matted on one side. She had puffy dark bags under her eyes from all the crying.

Yet, for the first time in a long time, she felt at peace. Having the "Joan issue" out in the light of day felt good. She hadn't realized how much of a burden it had been to carry the secret and hide it from Roy. She felt like a massive weight had been lifted.

"Joan" also explained why Roy had been behaving out of character. Subdued. Preoccupied. He had known for over a month now.

In any relationship, secrets are cancer. Susie knew that.

Until the previous night, Susie had been the only person in the world who knew that she had been involved in Joan's death and had then married her brother. Even Deb hadn't known about that connection. Deb had never cared who Joan was. Susie had hinted about the connection several times over the years, talking about looking into Joan, into whose family they had forever changed, but Deb's response had always been the same.

Water under the bridge.

At first, Susie had thought maybe it was because Deb didn't want to deal with the guilt. But, as she'd gotten to know Deb better, she'd concluded that the truth was simply that Deb Wise did not give a shit. She lived in the "now." Susie had often envied that about her. Wished that she could be as carefree.

No fear. No guilt.

Susie was more like Roy in that respect. She thought about the consequences of her actions. They weighed on her. She believed Roy was the same. At least, she wanted to believe that.

And she wanted to believe him.

She recalled what he'd said about Deb: *"I only wish it had been me that killed her... for Joan's sake."*

Are you lying to me, Roy Cruise? There's no denying that you were in Austin, and you admit that you met with her the night she was killed.

Roy claimed that he had simply told Deb to stay away from them, after which she'd berated him and spilled the beans about Joan. And then he'd walked away.

Was it true? Susie hoped it was. And, for now, that would have to be good enough.

Not the best time to be stirring up shit, Susie Q!

Susie stared at herself in the mirror. She frowned, and sighed.

So. Many. Fucking. Wrinkles. When did you become your mother?

She put her hands on either side of her eyes and pulled her skin taut. It smoothed out, but it also gave her that overdone-plastic-surgery-cat-face look.

Ugh. You're getting old. Can't even have a good cry and wake up looking human anymore.

She took a long shower, still feeling a little jetlagged. The time difference plus the confrontation with Roy had left her exhausted. Her nerves were fried.

As she primped and dressed, she recognized that this alone time was good. It gave her an opportunity to reflect. Recharge.

She suspected that Roy knew that and had made himself absent for this very reason. He knew her like no one else living. And she loved him for it. He was amazing that way. He always seemed to know what she needed, although she'd never admit to it. Not to him, anyway.

To admit that to him would give him too much power over her.

CHAPTER FIFTY

Roy's early morning excursion away from Susie had nothing to do with giving her alone time. He was on a mission. You will recall that he had spent months doing research and planning for getting away with murder in Mallorca. If everything worked out that morning, he would make first contact with his victim.

From an investigator's perspective, there are three elements to a homicide: motive, means, and opportunity.

Roy had a motive.

What he was out to find that morning was opportunity, which in his mind would then define the means. His plan was to surveil his victim in order to identify patterns and routines.

We are all creatures of habit. And while people deviate from routines based on daily circumstances, we all tend to follow patterns. Roy wanted to identify those patterns. His objective was not to predict all of the target's activities. All he needed was to identify a single routine that he could exploit to his advantage. He would then build the kill around that.

Roy drove the Fiat to a village called Port de Pollença and parked at the corner of Avinguda de Llenaira and Carrer de Magraner. The spot was about half a block from his victim's home. It was 7:30 a.m.—about fifteen minutes before sunrise. The sky was already a beautiful orange-blue color.

Roy wore a dark blue swimsuit, a non-descript grey t-shirt, and Converse tennis shoes. Beachwear, to fit in. Shoes for running, if needed. Bland colors, less likely to stand out.

Roy had studied pictures of his target in order to memorize his face, but the most recent images he'd been able to locate were about five years old. He'd also tried to imagine the man with shorter hair, with longer hair, with a moustache or beard, and a bit thinner, a bit heavier. He'd even printed photos and sketched different lengths of hair and different forms of facial hair onto him.

He needn't have worried.

As Roy was parallel parking, he saw a man exiting the house he'd come to scope out. He was wearing flip-flops, black shorts, and a white t-shirt, and carrying a small wicker bag. He also seemed to have something tied around his waist.

It was him. The man had not changed relative to his photos, with the exception of a glowing tan and a thinning hairline. As the man passed the Fiat, Roy turned away and rummaged through the car's empty glove box. Then, after a few moments, he exited the vehicle and began following, being sure to keep a safe distance.

Day still hadn't broken. The sun lingered lazily on the horizon.

Roy followed, walking along Avinguda de Llenaira until he reached a small roundabout where the street dead-ended into Via Alemanya, a road that ran along the coast of the Port of Pollença. The man crossed over and began to walk along the boardwalk until he reached a small wooden pathway that led to the beach. He continued toward the bay and stopped about twenty feet from shore.

The man dropped his bag on the sand and then stepped out of his flip-flops while removing his t-shirt. It was then that Roy realized that the man didn't have anything hanging around his waist at all. He was wearing a full-body wetsuit, but had only put on the bottoms. The top hung down from his waist, mostly behind him.

As Roy watched from a distance, the man placed his shirt in the bag, then wiggled his way into the wetsuit top. Roy couldn't help but notice that the man was in good shape. He had a small paunch, but his back and shoulders were well defined.

The man walked toward the shore and put on a pair of swim goggles and what looked like ear plugs in both ears. He stopped by the water's edge and began twisting and stretching, then paused a few moments and seemed to admire the sunrise, which he was facing—due east. Then, he sloshed into the sea before diving and breaking into a swim.

When the man hit the water, Roy hit the start button on his Panerai Chronograph. He wanted to time the swim.

So as not to stand out, Roy kept walking and turned north up Via Alemnaya. He reached the first cross street, Carrer de Llimonera, and turned, stopping to light a cigarette and look at his phone. Then, he positioned himself so that he could comfortably see when the man came out of the water.

It was still early, and there was little activity on the street. A few cars driving by. Some pedestrians. But, standing, smoking, and checking his phone, Roy seemed inconspicuous. A guy waiting for someone or simply admiring the view.

The ocean was choppy, but Roy managed to see the man swim out in a straight line from shore before he lost him in the waves.

About thirty minutes passed before Roy saw movement in the water that appeared to be arms swimming strokes. Someone reappeared, and when he emerged from the water, Roy saw it was his target and stopped the Chronograph. It had been thirty-five minutes. He watched as the man toweled off, put away his goggles and earplugs, picked up his bag, and headed back towards his house.

It was Thursday. Roy had no idea if the man swam daily or with what regularity. He could tell, though, given his gear and the man's fitness, that this was not a one-off event.

The swim presented a very interesting opportunity. As Roy watched the man disappear up the street, he was already putting the pieces in place for a very simple plan.

A plan to kill former Congressman Jeff Getz.

There was only one issue. It was one that he'd anticipated as he'd planned everything in Miami, but had wanted to wait to confirm once he was on the ground in Mallorca.

Now, he was sure. He couldn't do this alone.

CHAPTER FIFTY-ONE

"Getz is a very bad guy, Susie. He twisted the system to his benefit and hurt thousands of people." Roy had prepared well. He had data on Getz, on his political machinations, and on his corruption. And he was now making his case to Susie.

"You know me too well, Roy." She half-smiled, and nodded. "It's appalling that no one was held accountable for the disaster in 2008. Wall Street made a fortune peddling CLOs before the crash. Then they were bonusing themselves again in 2009, as if nothing had happened. Meanwhile, a lot of Main Street folks lost everything. Everything. And there wasn't a single Wall Street prosecution. Not one. The government, the DOJ.... The Democrats completely sold out on that one, Roy. I just didn't realize how bad it was." She was looking at a fact sheet Roy had prepared and shaking her head. "I mean, sure, you expect that people are going to be stressed—pushed to extremes—when they lose their homes. But fifty suicides? Thirty-five thousand families displaced..." Susie sighed in disbelief.

They were having lunch at Anthony's Restaurant in a town called Inca. It was an odd spot. Half the place was dedicated to dining. The other half sold leather goods—jackets, purses, shirts, and some shoes.

Quirky.

Roy had ordered lamb chops and Susie had gotten a typical Mallorcan fish, a Cap Roix—grilled. For dessert, they'd had a very special treat—a *Cardenal* that consisted of a base of merengue topped with more merengue and cream.

The restaurant had been recommended to Roy by his lawyer, Mark Moran, who had explained to him that the *Cardenales* at Anthony's were made by nuns at a nearby convent. When the restaurant ran out, it was often several days before they could replenish their inventory. Moran had dined there several times, but never managed to have the *Cardenal* dessert. Roy had texted Moran a selfie of him and Susie with two *Cardenales* on the table.

They were sitting next to each other at a small table for four—huddled close, touching one another often, and speaking in hushed tones. Anyone observing them would have assumed they were newlyweds madly in love. Had that same person come in closer, they would have been shocked by the content of their conversation.

"But, after everything we went through with Harlan, and Deb..." Susie continued, "I mean, we're still experiencing fallout from that." She was referring to the events of the night before. "Is this something we really want to do?"

"I hear you. I hear you." Roy nodded.

Susie studied him. "You're not telling me everything, are you? I know you, Roy Cruise." Susie took his hand. "Mr. Diaz."

He smiled. "He is a very bad man, Susie. But, there... there is something else. Something that clinched it for me."

Roy leaned in and, as Paul Harvey used to say, told her *the rest of the story.*

Once he had explained his other, more personal motivation for revenge against Getz, Susie was stunned. She didn't speak for almost a minute, staring off into the middle distance.

"You understand what this means? The... implications?"

Susie nodded. She was also calculating. Roy was proposing a murder. He wasn't manipulating her into it. He was simply laying the facts on the table, making the case, and giving her a choice. But, he had made clear that this was something he believed they needed to do. And, given what had just transpired between them—him finding out about Joan—and the reasons behind Susie manipulating him into killing Harlan, she felt hard-pressed to say no.

When she finally spoke, she said simply, "Let's do it."

After that, talk turned from the question of *if we do it* to the issue of *how.*

From the restaurant, Susie and Roy headed back to the

marina at the port of Alcúdia. Although Roy had called the marina repeatedly to confirm that everything was being finalized on *Altamira*, he wanted to go in person and make sure that all of the preparations were being made.

While they drove, Roy updated her on his surveillance of Getz from that morning. He also shared what he had learned online about killing overseas. One thing that Roy had come to believe was the simpler the better. Roy explained his plan for ending Getz to Susie.

She had to admit, it was simple. Elegant. Clever.

When they arrived, they found the broker on board checking systems. They performed their own rudimentary check and, after asking permission, unloaded a small duffle bag they'd brought with them and stowed it in the main cabin. They then headed to a small scuba shop near the Bon Aire Marina. Roy had called the shop earlier and spoken to a guy named Felix about renting gear. It was here that a minor change to their plans needed to be made. Their plan had been to dive various locations in the Bay of Pollença. With Susie pregnant, that needed to change. Her solution, however, was simple.

"I'll snorkel," she said, smiling.

When they arrived, they met Felix face to face. He was a German transplant who was also fluent in English and Spanish, and someone for whom nothing was ever too much trouble. Roy bought a map of nearby scuba diving sites and then spent some time getting tips from Felix on the best diving spots in the area.

They rented two wetsuits, along with a BDC, regulator, and two twelve-liter oxygen tanks for Roy, who always believed in having a spare. Susie got a mask and snorkeling equipment instead of the standard scuba kit. The pregnancy meant she couldn't do any deep dives, but many of the sites that Felix recommended would still be fun from the surface.

It was a bit of a struggle getting the gear into the Fiat, but between the trunk and the back seats, they made it work. They drove back to the marina in the Port of Alcúdia and unloaded everything onto the boat. They would spend one last night at Son Brüll before starting the nautical part of their trip.

CHAPTER FIFTY-TWO

"Come on, Rosa. I feel fine."

"You may feel fine, but you look like shit. You look like you got run over by a truck. You need to rest, end of story."

Four days had passed since David had woken up in the hospital. The pain was much better now. Bearable. The swelling was down, and he could see out of both eyes again. He had even started eating a little. But he was also still on painkillers, which had two side effects: They made him sleep all the time and he was constipated. The former was okay. The latter sucked. Particularly with his banged-up ribs.

He'd tried contacting Roy when he'd first awoken. His call had gone straight to voicemail, though, which hadn't surprised him. He knew that, when Roy traveled internationally, he set his phone to "do not disturb" at night. He knew this because Roy had complained to him about receiving calls from clients and telemarketers on his mobile when he was in other time zones, and David had showed him how to use the DND function. Although he and Roy had traded voicemails, they'd still not spoken.

David's second call had been to his girlfriend, Rosa Pérez. She was the closest thing to family he had, after Roy and Susie. David had moved to Miami from the West Coast. He was an only child and his parents were both deceased.

Today was the first day that David was feeling somewhat normal. He'd woken a bit late, around 11:00 a.m., and had breakfast.

He'd been about to try calling Roy again when Rosa had surprised him with a visit, followed by his doctor.

David had been pushing to be released early. He *hated* hospitals.

Having lost his mother to cancer when he'd still been in his teens, he'd had more than his fill of hospitals and hospices and their smell of disinfectant and sickness. Hospitals and David's generalized paranoia did not mix well. Too many germs.

There's just something illogical about healing in a building full of sick people. It's like holding AA meetings at a bar.

After much argument, his doctor had intimated that he might be able to leave the next day. Of course, that didn't stop David from trying to cajole Rosa into helping him out of bed to escape earlier. Rosa, ever practical, pointed out that he might want to consider that, if he needed her help to get out of bed and leave, then he probably wasn't ready to go.

It was good to have Rosa there. She lifted his spirits.

They'd met when David had been questioned by the police regarding Harlan's disappearance. He'd been smitten from the moment he'd seen her, but it had taken a long time to secure a date.

It's a conflict of interest.

It's against department policy.

You're not my type.

He'd overcome all of her objections.

For their first date, he'd taken her to El Cielo by José Manuel Barrientos, on the Miami River—in style. David hadn't told her where they were going, but had gotten her to meet him for a drink at the Monty's by Dinner Key Marina. It's a fried shrimp and beer kind of place.

After drinks, he'd walked her over to the marina, where they'd boarded his Boston Whaler and he'd navigated a scenic route through the bay and up the Miami River. They'd tied up at the dock at El Cielo for dinner.

As the evening had progressed, David could tell she was getting into the date, but that her police brain was still working. After all, there had been some strange nautical connections to Harlan's disappearance. He'd bought boat shoes, there'd been the whole "Cruise Captain" contact thing, and he'd asked an Uber driver for directions to Bayfront Marina.

David had organized the date as a way to erase any doubts in her mind about whether or not he was involved. He'd thought the best way to accomplish that would be for her to see all possible connections right up front. After dinner, as they'd headed back to the marina, David had said, as if the thought had just occurred to him, "Hey, I know. This'll be fun. How about I show you where we dumped the body?" He'd followed that up with a wide grin.

Rosa had paused, then replied, "Nice try. I'm afraid your whereabouts are fully accounted for between the time Harlan disappeared and the time he was discovered missing. And, you bought this boat almost six months after he disappeared. But, most importantly, I know people." She'd looked him in the eye. "And I've been studying you," she'd said coyly. "You're just not the type."

That had been the first time they'd kissed, although David would say that he wasn't sure who'd kissed who first.

Presently, he was enjoying playing the unreasonable sick boyfriend. It was a nice distraction from what was really weighing on his mind—the little guy in the green leather jacket.

David hadn't told Rosa what really happened. Not yet.

No police.

He wanted to try calling Roy again while it was still early in Spain, but he couldn't with Rosa there. He had sent Roy a WhatsApp message at some point—though, through the fog of pain meds he couldn't remember exactly when—stating simply: *Call me when you can. Important.*

Roy had called back—but David hadn't heard the phone ring.

David wasn't too concerned, as he doubted green leather jacket guy was going to travel overseas and track his partner down, but he felt that he needed to warn Roy before he returned to the States.

"Where are you right now, Mr. Kim?"

"I'm here, Rosa. Just thinking."

"Thinking what?" she asked, raising an eyebrow.

"How much I need you."

"Hah!" She leaned over and kissed him, and as she did, she ran her hand gently under his hospital gown. The surprise of it caused him to jerk up, killing his ribs and banging his teeth into hers. They pulled apart, smarting from the pain and laughing.

Rosa went over to the mirror, mock-checking herself for dental damage. "You're trying to get rid of me, aren't you?" she asked.

"Not a chance. Though, seriously, don't you have to work?"

Rosa checked her watch and frowned. "Yeah. I have a two o'clock I still haven't prepared for." She sighed. "I'd best get to it." She pulled her jacket on and gathered her purse, then leaned over her boyfriend and kissed him on the forehead. She only did that when she was serious. "At some point," she said, looking him in the eye, "you're going to have to tell me what really happened to you. young man. You know that, right?"

David half-smiled and took her hand. "I know. I will."

She smiled at him and left.

CHAPTER FIFTY-THREE

David waited several seconds after the door closed before grabbing his phone and dialing Roy again. His partner picked up on the third ring.

"Hey, David! How's it going? Is everything okay?" The office only bothered Roy on vacation if there was a problem.

"Hi. Yeah. No, actually not."

"Talk to me. I'm driving, but I've got AirPods," Roy said. Roy and Susie were driving back from the Port of Alcúdia to Son Brüll.

"Okay… so, you should know that some guy beat the shit out of me. And I'm in the hospital."

"What? Are you okay? What happened?"

"I got to my building late on Friday. A guy came up to me after I got out of my car and, um, well," David lowered his voice, "he pulled out a fucking gun." His voice faltered, and he swallowed hard. The words had brought on unexpected flashbacks.

"Fuck!"

"Yeah, fuck is right! I thought he was gonna mug me, you know? So, I tried to give him my car keys, wallet…" he paused, "but instead, he started asking about the Harlan kid. Wanted to know if I had anything to do with his disappearance. If I killed him. If *we* killed him! You and me…. When I told him that I didn't know what he was talking about, he beat the fuck out of me and then put the gun in my mouth. And he kept asking over and over." David barely managed to get the next words out as he fought back bile in his throat. "I thought I was dead, man."

"Holy shit, David! That's fucked up. I'm really sorry,

man. What did the cops say? Is there any security video or anything?"

"No!" David caught himself and lowered his voice. "No cops, Roy. He swore that if I went to the cops, he'd come back and kill me. And no, no video. Nothing. He knew what he was doing. No cameras where he stopped me. I've just told everyone, including Rosa, that I don't remember anything. Hit and run."

"Shit, David. I don't know what to say. Are you okay?"

"I'll survive. Nothing permanent. But I've been doped up most of the time since. Missed your call. Sorry about that."

"No, no, no. Hey, you rest up. Take care of yourself. When do you get out? How long are you in for?"

"Hopefully soon. I need to be able to go to and from the toilet by myself before they let me out."

"By yourself...? Jesus, man, how bad are you?"

"It's okay. My ribs are the worst. I'll be fine. I just wanted to tell you 'cuz he asked about you. Don't worry, I didn't say where you are. But he did ask about you and Harlan, so I wanted to warn you. I mean, I don't think he's gonna come to Europe or anything, but you never know what this psycho might be capable of, right? Especially when you get back."

"Right. Yeah. No, I agree. Thanks, man. I appreciate the heads-up, but it is a long trip to make. And we'd be pretty hard to find." Roy paused. "This has got to be coming from the dad—the senator. I mean, he's the only family the kid had, right?"

"I hadn't really thought about it, Roy."

"No. Of course not. Anyway. Okay, well listen, you rest up. Take care of yourself. Heal."

"I will."

"And thanks for the warning. 'ppreciate it."

* * *

"Shit, Roy," Susie breathed out. She had listened to Roy's side of the call. He filled her in on the rest. "It's gotta be coming from Harlan, right? Where else?"

"I agree," he said.

"Good thing we're out of the country."

"Yeah. No shit! But we can't stay here forever."

"What are you thinking?" she asked.

"We need to figure out how to head this off."

CHAPTER FIFTY-FOUR

Liz Bareto was walking on air. The meeting with Kristy Wise could not have gone any better. And, she was even more pleased with her meeting with Senator Harlan. She knew in her heart that she had succeeded in connecting with both.

Kristy seemed sharp. Resourceful. She was out there now, digging for more information. Liz felt confident that Debra Wise's daughter would come back to her with something useful.

And then there was the senator. Well, she knew she had gotten through to him. When she'd explained that she still wanted justice for Liam, that the record needed to be set right, she'd seen something in his eyes. A spark. He'd still retained his professional and stoic public demeanor, but there'd been something there. She'd gotten the impression that he knew more than he was letting on as he'd actively listened to her. Nodding in the right places and at times smiling, looking sympathetic at others. Liz knew that she was getting close and was ecstatic that she'd managed to share her theories with a man who was in public office, and who appeared to be as motivated as she was to get to the truth.

Her intuition told her that Roy Cruise was the key to resolving what had happened to Liam. And possibly even to Joe Harlan and Deb Wise.

Heartbreak had driven her through the last four years. It had motivated her when all she'd wanted to do was curl up in a ball in a closet and never wake up. Her quest to uncover what exactly had happened to her baby boy was what kept her going, day by day, week by week, and sometimes hour by hour. Her life had changed because of what had happened. She had been to places she would otherwise never have been and met people she would otherwise not have had the time nor inclination to meet. She'd been surprised to discover that many of them were carrying their own burden of tragedy.

She felt a lot of empathy for the senator. He'd had his fair share of heartache. And he was a charming man. Not at all what she'd expected. A bit older than Liz, to be sure. But so gracious. And elegant, in a southern gentleman kind of way.

That was why she found herself dressing up for dinner. The senator—or Joe, as he insisted she call him that—was picking her up at seven.

Of course, she did find herself questioning what exactly the southern gentlemen's motives were. How much of the dinner invitation was based on shared tragedies and kindred heartache, and how much was based on something else? Yes, she had noticed the way he'd looked at her, with those intelligent, hungry eyes of his roving all over her as she spoke.

As she put on her pearls, the choker her grandmother had given her, her cell phone vibrated. She realized she'd had it on silent mode since her meetings earlier in the day. She glanced at the illuminated screen. It was Eddie. He might have more information for her.

She snatched up the device and put it to her ear. "Hello, Eddie!" she said with a beaming smile—before realizing her tone and to whom she was speaking.

Oh shit.

"Hi Liz," Eddie replied enthusiastically. "Great to hear your voice. You okay to talk? Sorry to call so late in the evening."

It was almost 8:00 p.m. in Miami.

"Not at all, Detective," she said, using his title to try to counterbalance her overly personal greeting. "I can talk."

"Great. Well, I just wanted to give you a quick update on things. Roy Cruise is out of the country—"

"You don't say? Out of the country again? Has anyone died?" Liz's sarcasm was sharp, and came across as though it were aimed at Eddie.

"Not exactly," he said, sounding less enthused. "But I did

pay David Kim a visit. He was actually in the hospital after an apparent hit and run."

Liz's heart raced. Another development. She needed to keep Eddie talking, and changed her tack. "Oh my God, Eddie!" she said too cheerfully. "And Mr. Cruise has an alibi, again! I know you don't think that's normal, Eddie! Deb Wise dead. Kim in a hit and run. And Cruise out of town."

"I know, Liz. Kim claims Cruise was already out of the country when it happened. In fact, he says that Cruise hasn't contacted him since. He said that Cruise doesn't even know."

"What do your instincts tell you, Eddie? You're so intuitive. That's what makes you such a great detective," Liz poured it on.

When Eddie spoke, the cheer was back in his voice. "I'm pursuing multiple avenues of investigation."

"Oh, Eddie. That sounds so... for the media. It's me you're talking to, Liz."

There was a pause.

"There's been another development," Eddie said. "I really can't go into details, but I think I'm close to setting up surveillance on Cruise and Font."

Now it was Liz's turn to pause as her mouth dropped open. "Are you serious? Oh my... what have you found?"

"Honest, Liz, I really can't get into it. I just want you to know that you're my... I mean, your case... is a high priority for me. I am all over it. And we are making progress. But I just can't give you details. That could damage what we're trying to accomplish."

Liz knew a brick wall when she saw one, but she was ecstatic at the news Eddie had shared. "I really appreciate everything you have done for me—for us, Eddie. You're a wonderful man. A great human being." Liz felt she should share more with him, to make him feel even more like her co-conspirator. "I'm doing some investigating of my own. You'll never guess who I am having dinner with tonight."

Eddie said nothing.

"Eddie?"

"Yeah, Liz. I'm listening. Who?"

"Senator Joe Harlan."

"What's he doing in Miami?"

"No, silly, I'm in Texas. In Austin. It makes sense. We've both been through a terrible tragedy, and in each of our cases, the same person seems to be somehow involved. I felt that if we joined forces, so to speak, we might make more progress."

Eddie had his own thoughts about where this might lead, but tried not to show it. He was slow to respond, and then said, "Okay. It can't hurt, I suppose. Just be careful, Liz. You're just getting through the divorce and all. He's got a bit of a reputation."

"Um, excuse me?" The comment had hit Liz in a weak spot.

"Wait, Liz, I didn't mean that—"

"I'll have you know that he's been nothing but the perfect gentleman. And, Detective, I'm not sure how appropriate it is for you to comment on—"

"Liz, I'm sorry. That came out wrong. I didn't mean anything.... I just mean... be careful, is all. Texas is different. I just don't want you getting your hopes up or getting hurt."

She didn't respond immediately. She wanted him to appreciate that there was a line between friendly and intimate, and exactly where on the spectrum he belonged. But she still needed his help, and he'd just given her great news. "I know, Eddie, and I appreciate it," she said. "I appreciate you. I'm going to chase down some leads here. As soon as I have more information, we can compare notes. Is that fair?"

"Within reason, I hope. Liz, you know that you should really report anything you find to us and let us look into it," Eddie said, apparently trying to sound detached and professional.

Liz responded earnestly, though she didn't feel that way at all—the police had had their chance, and they had jack to show for it. "Of course. Will do. Thanks for the update. It really feels like we're finally getting close to finding out what happened to my boy. Anyway. Gotta go!"

"Bye, Liz, and hope you have a great evening."

Liz Bareto didn't hear Eddie because she'd already disconnected the call.

CHAPTER FIFTY-FIVE

While Liz Bareto dined with the senator, Slipknot was only a few miles away picking at a scab on his neck. His skin had begun giving him issues when he'd arrived in Austin.

It's so goddammed dry here.

When he landed at the airport, he had rented a white cargo van—inconspicuous, if properly handled—and canvassed the neighborhood near the Wise home. The area was called Tarrytown. Nice houses. Older construction, with some new rebuilds interspersed. Eventually, he'd found what he was looking for: a vacant house one block up from the Wise's residence. There was a 'for sale' sign outside and the house was in need of repair. A fixer-upper. He'd checked Zillow—a seven-hundred-thousand-dollar fixer-upper.

Fucking crazy Austin property market.

He'd parked the car in front of the house in a way that gave him a good view of the traffic to and from the Wises'. If anybody entered or left the property, he'd know about it.

Now, as the sun sank low in a clear sky, he had completed day one of surveillance on Tom Wise. Though, that wasn't entirely accurate, as he still hadn't seen the man.

The daughter, on the other hand, had come and gone a few times in a red Mini.

What a fine piece of woman.

He'd followed her the second time to a Starbucks. She didn't seem to work there. She'd had coffee with a woman. In and out in just under forty-five minutes. And then she'd gone back to the house, where there was still no sign of the father. Just to be sure, he called the guy's office again and was told, this time by a different receptionist, that Tom Wise was on a sabbatical.

Interesting word. No doubt evolved from the Hebrew shabbāth—the day of rest. That's an old one.

Slipknot was tempted to do some digging on his smart phone, but he knew how engrossed he could get when researching words and he didn't need any distractions. Instead, he added sabbatical to his list of words for future research. There would be time enough later, once he'd dealt with business.

He didn't need much. A small window of opportunity. An hour would be plenty.

He finally managed to get the scab off and, without thinking, slipped it into his mouth and chewed.

CHAPTER FIFTY-SIX

Kristy spent the better part of the night awake.

What was most disturbing to her was coming to grips with the "ladyfinger video." She had watched it repeatedly. The more she did, the more certain she was that it was her mother, which meant that, as much as she didn't want to believe it, her mother had most likely murdered Liam Bareto.

And every time she thought about that, it sent a shiver down her spine. Kristy knew her mother had been prone to extremes. She'd grown up on a ranch, and she'd always told stories about East Texas justice. Fence disputes, dead chickens, dead dogs. Nothing involving murder, exactly. Yet she'd left no doubt that she'd had a rugged upbringing with a weird mix of religion and frontier values. But this…

Killing a comatose guy in Miami?

Why?

What did Susie Font have over you to justify killing someone?

And what about Harlan? How did his death fit into all of this?

And what about you, Mom? Who killed you?

She was at a loss. She didn't even feel comfortable sharing this with Bethany—not until she was more certain.

She thought about Liz and everything the woman had been through. She was still fighting to avenge her son. Liz said she wanted the killer "brought to justice," which was just code for her wanting payback. Kristy understood that. She admired Bareto. She had been at it for almost four years now, and she was still fighting. Still keeping the faith.

Plus, Kristy was grateful to her. Liz had helped with information Kristy would otherwise never have known. Kristy even felt obligated to somehow return the favor. Although, she had no idea how.

She couldn't help but wonder if the woman had somehow discovered that it had been her mother at the hospital who'd exacted Susie Font's revenge. But if that were true, then why would Liz have made contact with Tom? Why make a show of meeting with her, of sharing all this information? It didn't make sense.

Liz's focus was clearly on Roy Cruise, not Susie.

As Kristy thought through their meeting, she realized that Liz had been very clear about what she knew regarding what had happened and where there were gaps in her information. She'd even inspired Kristy to try to put together everything she knew to see if she could come any closer to figuring out who'd killed her mom.

But as hard as she tried, she couldn't organize it all in her head. At about two in the morning she gave up on sleep. She slid out of bed and grabbed a stack of index cards.

She sat down at her desk and began to write down all of the things she did and did not know on separate index cards, then tried to organize them into a logical sequence that, at least in some way, told a story.

1. Camilla Cruise was killed in accident caused by Liam Bareto.

2. Liam had strange needle mark in his arm when he died.

3. Mom is the ladyfinger? Killed Liam Bareto?

4. Mom wrote about "not being there for me" to Dad, not "like Susie" was.

5. Joe disappeared in Miami—where Susie and husband live.

6. Mom knew Font and trusted her. (Doesn't say the same for Cruise. Does this mean Cruise is questionable?)

7. Lots of people have died around Cruise—but does that matter? Or does it make him a suspect?
    Joan Díaz (?)
    Camilla Cruise (Accident probably)
    Liam Bareto (Mom killed him?)
    Joe Harlan (Maybe Font did it? With Cruise?)
    Mom (Did Bareto kill her? What about Cruise? If so, why?)
8. Cruise was in town day Mom was shot. (Need to verify—but assume true for now.)
9. Cruise changed his name from Díaz. (Why?)
10. Cruise's sister died at Camp Willow.

The largest gap in Kristy's knowledge centered around her most recently acquired piece of information.

What can I find out about Joan Diaz?

CHAPTER FIFTY-SEVEN

When they'd met, Liz Bareto had told Kristy about a news article that her private investigator had found regarding Joan's death. It took Kristy about fifteen minutes to find it online.

June 26, 1988

Tragedy Strikes Local Camper
Last Thursday, June 24, the body of an eleven-year-old girl was found dead on the banks of the Brazos River. Joan Diaz had been attending camp at nearby Camp Willow when police say she became lost at night and fell to her death. The tragic accident...***more***

The article went on to speculate how Joan might have gotten lost, along with offering the typical niceties about the little girl from camp officials. It ended by stating that Joan had left behind a mother, father, and twin brother.

Kristy continued her online search to see if she could learn more about the camp itself. She searched local newspaper archives in the surrounding area for more information. There, she found an article discussing the camp, which had been written only weeks before Joan had died, but nothing further regarding the incident. No obituary.

Kristy then focused on Camp Willow. It was located on the Brazos River. She found it on Google Maps and saw that the closest large city was Fort Worth, Texas, which was just north of it.

Camp Willow had a website showcasing photos of last year's campers. It was a large group—she estimated two hundred boys and girls. She looked for an archive section for prior years' photos, but there wasn't one.

Maybe there aren't any online, but what about at the camp itself? Could there be something there? They normally frame that stuff and put it up on a wall.

She went back to Google Maps. The camp was two and a half hours away from Austin. It was definitely worth a road trip. The more she thought about it, the more she was sure she'd find answers there.

She called Bethany.

A groggy voice answered. "What the fuck, Kris? It's like three in the fucking a.m., man."

"I know, Beth, sorry, but listen. I've been researching Cruise, based on what Liz had to say. I think it makes sense to check out the camp where his sister died. It's up near Fort Worth. You think we could stay at your parents' house?"

"Camp what? When?"

"Tomorrow. We'll drive up, check it out, then crash at your folks' place with you if that's okay?"

"Whatever. Fine. They love you. Just text my mom and let her know you're coming."

"Me? Why don't you tell her?"

"'Cause I'm fucking going back to sleep."

The line went dead.

Shit.

Kristy searched for Bethany's mom's number in her contacts and drafted a text. She thought better of it before hitting send and decided to wait until the morning.

Kristy plugged the phone into its charger. She was about to tuck in, but decided to first go downstairs and run all of the index cards through the shredder in her father's office. Then, she grabbed a bottle of water and made her way back up to bed.

She would pack an overnight bag in the morning.

CHAPTER FIFTY-EIGHT

Friday
October 25, 2019
Austin, Texas

Kristy woke early and sent Bethany's mom a quick text.

Hi Mrs. Rosen. Sorry to bother you. I'm going to be in the area and was wondering if staying the night tomorrow was okay?

Once that was done, she packed a bag for the weekend. She wanted to get up to Camp Willow by 11:30 a.m. The website indicated that off-season office hours were from 10:00 a.m. to 1:00 p.m.

At 8:00am, she received a reply text message from Bethany's mom.

Hi Kristy. ¡Mi casa es su casa! Ha! Ha! Stay as long as you want!

When she came downstairs, she could hear a news bulletin coming from the TV in her father's office. She was surprised. It was usually much later that he crawled out of his room, hungover and searching for his first drink of the day. She was also happily surprised to smell coffee. Her father loved coffee, but not when he was drinking heavily, which he had been since his wife's death.

She knocked lightly, then opened the door. Tom Wise was sitting at his desk writing. Next to him was the lockbox he normally kept in the safe. It was closed, but the key, which had a small red disk hanging from it, was still in the lock.

So that's what it looks like. But where does he keep it?

She scanned the office for clues—an open drawer, anything, as she greeted him. "Good morning."

He looked up and smiled.

"Good morning, sweet pea." He paused and put his pen down. "There's coffee in the kitchen. Want some?"

"Sure."

Tom rose, picked up his coffee cup, and followed his daughter into the kitchen. He watched her pour the black liquid into a mug and held out his own for a top-off. That's when he noticed the bag on the island. "Going somewhere?"

"M-hmm," Kristy said while sipping the hot coffee. "Fort Worth. Just want to get away from everything for a bit. Staying at Beth's."

Tom bit his lip, pondering. There was an awkward pause that Kristy filled in by sipping on her coffee.

"Look, Kristy. Um, I want to apologize," Tom began, not knowing where to look.

"It's okay, Dad."

"No, I... I know I haven't been of much use to you lately."

"Dad, it's fine," she reassured him.

"No. It isn't fine. This has been a terrible time for us and... you've needed me and... well, I've been selfish. And, I just wanted to say that, um, well...." Tom's eyes watered. "I'm sorry, and things... they're going to change." He held his cup aloft toward her as proof.

Kristy smiled encouragingly. She clinked her cup against his. "Okay," she said. "But you can't do this alone. You shouldn't. And Mom..."

"We have to learn to survive, no—to thrive—without her. That's the bottom line. That's exactly how she'd want it, too. So, I'm going back to AA. Again... tonight. Already called my sponsor. The whole nine yards." Tom held his daughter's gaze. "Sweetie, listen to me. This is important. Something you'll understand when you're a parent..."

"So I keep hearing."

"Huh?"

"Never mind, go ahead..."

"Um... well, I've lived half my life without your mom. And if I've done it before, I can do it again. But you, Kristy, I cannot imagine my life without you. And, um, I, well, I promise you. I am going to get through this. I am going to get sober, get back to work, and we are going to be great." Tom Wise swallowed hard several times, his eyes blinking away tears.

Kristy wiped her eyes with the back of her hand. The speech wasn't exactly alien to her, but there was something about this one. Her father seemed determined. This could finally be the turning point that she had hoped for.

"You can't be a victim, Dad. You have to take control. You choose what happens. You choose who you are."

Tom Wise suppressed tears and chuckled. "You sound just like her now. Come here," he said, setting down his cup and holding out his arms. Kristy put her arms around him, he folded her into an enveloping hug, and she cried. At first just a few tears, but when she found herself warm and safe in his embrace, the dam broke and she was soon sobbing in his arms.

They separated minutes later, Kristy still sniffling. "Shit, Dad. Now I gotta go redo my face," she said with a sniff and a laugh.

"Like you need to. You're beautiful, honey, and I love you so much."

Kristy left the house at 8:56 a.m., a little later than she'd planned. Tom had told her to take his Audi, as she was going to be on the road for a while, then he'd helped her to the car, carrying her duffle bag and putting it in the passenger's seat.

Tom Wise waved and smiled at his daughter until the Audi disappeared around the corner, oblivious of the pair of eyes watching them both from a white van parked down the street.

CHAPTER FIFTY-NINE

The door closed behind Tom, but Slipknot was already analyzing everything he had just seen and started the van.

Early morning departure. Dad comes out to say goodbye. Carries daughter's overnight bag to the car. Road trip—probably overnight.

He eased the cargo van down the street, following the Audi at a safe distance.

They headed down Enfield Road, then got onto MoPac Highway heading north. Slipknot continued to follow at a distance.

After several miles, the Audi exited MoPac and got onto I-35, still heading north.

Slipknot followed.

He loved the feeling of stalking prey. Unseen. Hidden. He felt himself becoming aroused.

Where are you taking me, princess?

CHAPTER SIXTY

Camp Willow is set on 725 acres of Texas land and is located near the town of Smith's Bend on the Brazos River. The land in that part of Texas is surprisingly piney. Those who've never been and expect to see tumbleweeds and dust simply don't know Texas. The state is enormous. There is room for every type of geography. And the area around Camp Willow is the perfect location for a summer camp.

A winding road leads from the highway to the main cabin, and near that cabin is the business office. Not unlike one of those quaint old grocery stores, a clutch of bells was attached to the interior of the door frame to the office and announced visitors by jangling every time the door was opened.

Etta Mae Nunley was sitting behind a desk stuffing envelopes with progress reports.

At the end of every camp session, the counselors wrote up reports on each camper's best qualities and areas for improvement. These were collected over the course of the summer and then sent out all at once, bulk mail pricing. It was always a chore to get them finalized and sent out before the first of October.

Etta Mae was behind schedule.

The envelopes were self-sealing, thank God, but the progress reports still had to be folded and stuffed into the correct envelopes. Etta Mae had just bent down to pick up her glasses, which she'd accidentally dropped, when she heard the clutch of bells jingle.

She looked up and was greeted by an attractive young lady with a wide smile.

"Hello. I was looking for the business office."

"You found it, dear. What there is of it," Etta Mae said, looking around her humble digs. "How can I help you?" It was odd to receive visitors this time of year, but a welcome distraction.

"I'm a bridesmaid," the woman explained, then paused, rolling her eyes and laughing to herself. Etta Mae thought she seemed nervous. "Okay, that came out wrong. I'm helping to plan a wedding. And I'm supposed to find material for a video about the bride, for the rehearsal dinner."

"Was she a camper here?" Etta Mae asked.

"Exactly! She loves this place. She always raves about what a great experience being here was. How much fun she had, how much she learned and grew, and the friends she made."

Alright. Easy girl. Dial it down.

Kristy cleared her throat and took a breath. "So, the girls and I, we all thought it would be fun if we could include something about Camp Willow in the video. I mean, I've already taken some pictures outside—the entrance sign to camp, the main house, and all that. I thought that would be cute. I hope that's okay. Anyway, when I saw the office was open, I thought that maybe you guys might have some kind of archive here. You know, files, photo albums and stuff. Anything you have from that time would be really cool."

"Well, bless your heart. That is the sweetest idea. That bride is a lucky lady, havin' friends like you!"

Southern hospitality being what it was, and Etta Mae's workload being what it was, she was happy to take a break and show her guest to the camp's photo archives. The albums neatly lined a shelf to the right of Etta Mae's desk. They were identified by handwritten labels noting the year on the spines and across each book's front cover. The earliest album was dated 1926. Etta Mae carefully opened it and showed her guest the three pictures it contained. Etta Mae explained that the first camp class had been very small—only fourteen girls.

"There are some years with no group photos, earlier on. It wasn't always easy to get a photographer. Not like these days, with cameras on your phone and what not. In the fifties, they started making it a tradition, taking a group photo the day before camp ended. Even then, it was still only forty or so girls.

"But, oh, how it's grown. I look through these once in a while—to see how the styles changed—the hair and the clothes. But the girls' faces—why, they could be from any time."

"When did it change to co-ed? I mean, I know it was all girls at the start, but...?"

"Oh, yes. They went co-ed back in 1990. Big mistake if you ask me, but they had to compete with all of the other camps, I suppose."

So, Cruise and his sister did not attend together. That makes it kind of hard for him to have killed her...

"Did you attend?" Kristy asked.

"Who, me? Lord no! Couldn't afford anything this fancy. But I been workin' here for going on twelve years now. Most of the kids—not all, mind you, but most—are little darlin's. Just as sweet and polite as can be. Speaking of polite. Where *are* my manners? Could I get you water, coffee, anything?"

"Coffee would be great, if it's not too much trouble."

"One cup, comin' right up. You go on and look through these—see if you can find your friend..." Etta Mae said as she shuffled through a doorway into another room.

As she poured coffee, Etta Mae watched her guest through the doorway.

The older albums contained actual photographs—developed from negatives onto photo paper. The more modern albums—from the 1960s forward—were the type that had the photos held in place by little white, triangular, adhesive photo corners.

"What year did she attend?" Etta May asked loudly.

Her guest hesitated, then answered, "In the eighties, I think."

Etta Mae made a face—calculating.

"Second marriage," her guest added.

"Why, I guess it's never too late to find Mr. Right," the old lady said, returning with a cup of coffee on a saucer.

Kristy forced a smile, but said nothing. She was too busy trying to find a needle in the haystack of faces.

"Any luck, dear?" Etta May asked.

"I found one of the years she was here. There's a group photo. But it's been so long, it's hard to tell."

"Do you know which session she attended?"

"Session? No, I'm afraid not."

"What year is it you're looking at?"

"Umm... 1988."

"Oh. Long before my time. All those files are in the back. I can have a look for you, if you like?"

"You keep files?"

"Sure, honey. They're confidential, but I think we can make an exception, just to see if we can find a picture of your friend."

"That would be great. Thank you so much!"

"Don't you mention it," said Etta Mae, heading into a small office behind the reception area. At the back was a small filing cabinet. "It's been a slow day," she added, raising her voice again. "So, I'm glad for the company."

"Oh, really?"

"Yeah. Been stuffing envelopes all day. Nice to get a break," she said distractedly as she rummaged through the drawers. "There you are," she said under her breath, grabbing two Redweld folders. "What was your friend's name?" she called out. "I don't think you said."

Her only reply was the sound of the jingling bells.

When Etta Mae returned to the front office, still clutching the two folders, she found that it was empty. Her guest was gone.

As she scanned the office, she saw that everything was in order and that all of the albums were on their shelf—all except for 1988, which lay on her desk. She idly flipped through it until she came to one page where there were two large photos on the left-hand page, and four smaller ones on the right-hand page. At least, there had been. One of the photos on the right-hand page was missing, four little white triangular photo corners testifying to its absence.

But then, many of the albums were missing photos. Etta Mae shrugged, then carefully closed the album, returned it to the shelf, and went back to her envelopes.

CHAPTER SIXTY-ONE

Slipknot loved Dairy Queen. There'd always been Dairy Queens near his family home growing up. Eating there reminded him of family road trips as a child, the one fond memory he held of his childhood.

He'd been to Texas a number of times, and loved the Lone Star State. And one of the reasons for that was Dairy Queen. There were more Dairy Queens in Texas than in any other state in the Union.

It had been a long day. A lot of driving. Slipknot had followed Kristy all the way up from Austin to Camp Willow. He'd not driven onto the camp premises as that would have been too obvious. He'd just parked down the highway and waited. She hadn't been there long.

He'd followed her when she'd left the camp, continuing north on I-35. Just before reaching Fort Worth, Kristy had exited the interstate and, after taking a few turns, entered a subdivision and finally pulled into the driveway of a nice home near the Southern Oaks Golf and Tennis Club.

When she'd exited the Audi, she'd been greeted enthusiastically by a girl about her age. The two had hugged and chatted animatedly for a short while before Kristy returned to her car to retrieve the overnight bag from the front seat before following the girl inside.

Goodbye, princess. And thanks for making this so easy. We'll see each other again soon.

Slipknot had turned around and headed back to Austin, but he'd made sure to stop at the Dairy Queen just past the town of Troy.

He was starving. He ordered a Crispy Chicken Sandwich, Onion Rings, and an Oreo Cookie Blizzard.

Fuck it. You only live once.

The pimple-faced kid at the counter did right by him, and flipped the Blizzard upside down for a few seconds, before placing it on Slipknot's tray. Slipknot smiled and let him keep the change.

He'd been working since early that morning. No chance for food. And, he'd made the mistake of not bringing any with him. An amateur move, especially when working surveillance, as you never knew where a target would take you. But the DQ made up for it.

He felt a little guilty having the Blizzard. A Coke would have sufficed. He liked that word—*sufficed.*

Slipknot knew he still had a long day ahead of him. He needed his sustenance. He checked his watch. If he left now, he'd be back at the Wise house by 6:00 p.m. easy. Maybe even a little earlier, depending on traffic.

He had two stops left to make before he headed home.

First, a visit to see Tom Wise. Then, if everything went according to plan, he'd swing by Allen's. He needed a new pair of Lucchese boots.

Work first, then play.

Lucchese—another Texas treat. Just like Dairy Queen.

CHAPTER SIXTY-TWO

Susie and Roy loaded their luggage onto the *Altamira* Friday afternoon. They'd checked out of their hotel room, though they left one medium-sized suitcase containing land-clothes and shoes at the hotel for pick-up after the marine portion of their vacation.

That night, they went out for dinner in the Port of Alcúdia. They left the marina and walked west to the Restaurante Miramar. They dined on seafood and admired the view before heading back to the boat, where they sat in the saloon and reviewed Roy's plan.

As it stood, the plan was relatively low risk. Minimal touch. Minimal exposure.

Over the course of his planning, Roy had resurrected and refined his rules for murder. They were still the initial six that he'd identified when planning Joe Harlan's death, but he had eliminated the fluff.

Roy's Rules for Murder

1. The killer should have no discernible motive for killing the victim.
2. The killer should minimize or eliminate forensic residue.
3. The killer should leave no body.
4. The killer should leave no witnesses.
5. The killer should have a verifiable alibi.
6. The killer should implicate others in the killing.

He did not have these written down anywhere because, as he put it, "That would be pretty fucking stupid."

He summarized them simply as:

1. no **M**otive
2. no **F**orensic residue
3. no **B**ody
4. no **W**itnesses
5. **A**libi
6. **I**mplicate **O**thers

His mnemonic device for remembering his Rules for Murder was divorce-based, oddly:

Mother **F**ucking **B**itch **W**ants **A**ll **I** **O**wn

Susie did not find it amusing, but she agreed it was hard to forget. Her attempt wasn't as catchy.

Madonna's **F**lat **B**utt **W**ill **A**lways **I**mpress **O**thers

Harlan's murder had followed each and every one of these rules.

They'd had no discernible reason to want Harlan dead—no motive. They had lured him onto a boat where they could kill him with minimum "forensic residue," as Roy liked to call it. "Forensic residue" simply meant forensic evidence—traces of them left behind. "Leave no trace" captured the gist of this rule well, and they were meticulous in following it. They had then disposed of Harlan in a body of water and weighed him down well. This was effective, as nature—salt and sea creatures—worked with you to destroy the corpse quickly.

They had been as careful as they could be about witnesses, and beyond that, they had concocted an alibi—Bimini. Just like Susie had planned a family trip to see her mother when Deb had come to Miami to kill Liam Bareto. Liz Bareto was right to claim that they always seemed to be conveniently away when bad things happened. While she was overly fixated on the issue—I think Eddie got to her with his statistical mumbo jumbo—there was something to it. It was true that a rock-solid alibi was part of their planning.

Lastly, as it was impossible to leave absolutely no evidence, they had ensured that any trace evidence misdirected the authorities. The Seattle burner phone, for example—it didn't frame anyone else for their crime, but it pointed away from them.

This plan of theirs in Mallorca did not comply with all of Roy's Rules, however. Specifically, rule three. They were not going to get rid of the body.

This concerned Susie.

"Do what you know, Roy. Do what works. That's what you always say in business. Why should this be any different?"

Roy sighed. He hated it when his business axioms were used against him. Roy acknowledged that the plan complied with all of his Rules for Murder except for number three, but he claimed that that this was out of necessity. He wanted this death to look like an accident.

Eventually, he managed to convince Susie to go along with the new approach.

That night was their first night on the *Altamira,* and they decided to go to bed early, given that the plan called for them to leave the marina at 6:00 a.m. the next morning. Although that didn't stop Roy running through another series of checks on the boat's systems along with their gear. He had already charted out their first day's navigation, which would begin well before sunrise to give them enough time to navigate north around the Cap des Pinar and be in the Bay of Pollença well before Getz began his morning swim.

CHAPTER SiXTY-THREE

It had been a while since Kristy had actually taken time out to relax. She'd been so absorbed by her mother's death, all the revelations that had come with it, and her father's drinking that she hadn't realized how on edge she'd been. How stressed.

Hanging with the Rosens was like going back to life as it used to be.

Bethany's family was Texan, through and through. Her dad was an oil and gas engineer, and had worked for years for PEMEX before returning to the States to take an executive position with Texaco. As a result, Bethany and her sister Sophia had been born and raised in Mexico City, where they'd learned Spanish. Kristy, on the other hand, had studied Spanish throughout school and college. On this visit, the girls lounged in their sweats and stayed up most of the night, eating popcorn and ice cream and binge-watching *The House of Flowers* on Netflix in Spanish.

Once Sophia and the parents had gone to bed, Kristy paused the show and handed Bethany the photo she'd stolen from Camp Willow.

"Okay, that little girl on the right... that's definitely your mom. Hell, she could be you. Is this other girl Cruise's sister?" Bethany asked.

Kristy shook her head. "Check this out," she said, showing Bethany her iPhone, on which was displayed a photo of a thirty-ish looking woman.

"Mm-hmm. Yep. I give up." Bethany shrugged.

"Doesn't this look like an older version of the girl with my mom?"

There was a light knock on the door, and Bethany's mother poked her head in. Kristy instinctively hid the phone.

"Everything okay in here?"

"Fine."

Mrs. Rosen looked at Kristy with sad eyes. She'd been at Deb's funeral and was a very nice lady. Kristy always felt at home with her.

"Well, don't stay up too late. Light on or off?"

"Off is good."

"And door closed."

After the lights clicked off and the door pulled shut, Bethany asked, "So, who's the woman?"

"Susie Font."

"Lemme see." Bethany took the phone from Kristy and compared it to the photo. "Could be her. Same shape eyes. Yep. Definitely could be her. So, what—your mom and Susie were friends at camp?"

Kristy stared up at the dark ceiling and whispered, "I don't know for sure. But I'm gonna find out."

Bethany propped herself up on an elbow and returned the phone. "I think you're running out of angles, girl. You gotta go see her. Susie. Confront her, you know?"

Kristy sighed. "I think you're right."

When they woke the next day, Bethany's mom had breakfast waiting: pancakes with a side order of reminiscing and laughter. Kristy's plan had been to leave for Austin early the following morning, Sunday, but she let herself be convinced to stay an extra day and return Monday morning.

She called Tom to let him know, but got voicemail. Kristy felt that familiar knot of worry in her belly at the thought that he might be drinking again.

He seemed so adamant yesterday that he was done....

Kristy so desperately wanted to believe him that she pushed the worry away and texted him.

Kristy: Dad. Staying one more night. Everyone says hello. See you Monday instead... Love you!

He replied immediately.

Dad: No worries, princess. At AA meeting. Love you too!

CHAPTER SIXTY-FOUR

Saturday
October 26, 2019
Bay of Pollença, Spain

Susie and Roy woke early.

It was still dark when they left Alcúdia Marina at just past 6:00 a.m. They ran the *Altamira* at about twelve knots to be sure they'd make good time. The Rodman 41 headed north along the coast at a nice clip, following a route that would circumnavigate the Cap des Pinar.

Some have described the shape of the island of Mallorca as a horse's head facing west. If that is the case, then the Cap des Pinar is the little peninsula on Mallorca's northeast coast that forms the tip of the horse's lower ear. And, in between the tip of that ear and the one to the north—Cap de Formentor—is the Bay of Pollença, which was their destination that morning.

As they reached the Cap des Pinar, the sky was grey and the seas were relatively calm. Once they entered the Bay of Pollença, Susie set the autopilot to 270°, which would take them straight into the port.

While she kept watch above, Roy was getting into scuba gear below. He wore a full wetsuit with boots and gloves. Based on his surface air consumption rate, the twelve-liter tank should last him at least an hour. He had a snorkel attached to his mask, both of which were all black. The only other tools he needed for the job were a dive knife and a ten-foot, black nylon boat line.

The morning he'd surveilled Getz, Roy had observed the

man swimming in the ocean for approximately thirty-five minutes. Getz's gear and the way he had prepared for the swim pointed to him being a habitual swimmer, although this was not verified. It was more intuition, a feeling, but something Roy felt sure enough of to build a plan around. Roy also assumed, from his age and physique, that Getz was a swimmer of average abilities. That would put his average swim speed at about 160 feet/minute. That speed multiplied by thirty-five minutes meant that Getz swam approximately 1,700 meters.

Using Navionics software, Roy had pulled up a chart of the Bay of Pollença and studied the sea depth in the area. The water was relatively shallow—with maximum depth of about eleven feet. He'd tried to guess where Getz's swim route would take him and plan accordingly.

When the *Altamira* was about one-and-a half kilometers from the Port of Pollença, Susie adjusted the heading on the autopilot to 252°. This heading would take them to a public pier that was about 120 feet south of the wooden boardwalk that Getz had used to access the beach.

Because of the pier's proximity to Getz's swim path, Roy had first thought that maybe Getz was swimming the length of the pier and back. The end of the pier would make for a simple, logical landmark for a swimmer. But, when he'd measured the pier on Navionics, it had turned out that it was much too short for that to be the case—only 480 feet.

Susie slowed the *Altamira* to five knots when she saw that they were half a kilometer from the end of the pier. She turned off the autopilot and began to make what looked like haphazard maneuvers—turning slowly, changing directions, and circling. The idea was to make it appear that the yacht was looking for a good spot to anchor. As she made her maneuvers, she was also checking to see if there were any nearby boats that might witness their activities.

There were none.

In the meantime, Roy waited in the back of the boat near the transom. He was ready but still inside, hidden from view.

When Susie felt satisfied that they weren't being watched,

she piloted the boat so that it was heading straight toward the pier. When they reached coordinates 39° 53.532' N, 3° 4.994' E, Susie gently put the craft in reverse before coming to a stop and setting the engines to neutral.

Below, Roy began a slow count to twenty. When he reached five, he carefully exited the saloon, crossed the transom, and slipped into the water. He was visible for all of three seconds. But, as the boat was facing shore and there were no other boats around, there was no one to see him.

It was just past 7:15 a.m.

When he hit the water, the chill immediately pushed its way through the gaps in his wetsuit. Roy kept counting. He released a little air from his Buoyancy Control Device (BCD) to descend below the surface and kicked slowly to distance himself from the boat, moving to the south. He didn't want to be anywhere near the boat when Susie engaged the engines and headed north. He let himself sink just a few feet to get underwater and be able to swim comfortably. He was only in about eleven feet of water.

On deck, Susie was also counting to twenty.

When Roy reached twenty, he listened for the sound of the engines, but continued counting and swimming away from the boat. There was nothing.

It's just Susie being extra careful.

When he reached twenty-seven, he heard the engines rev up.

Susie piloted the boat north, slowly taking the engines to eight knots. Then, she set course for an anchorage about one kilometer southeast of the Pollença Marina and the same distance northeast of the pier.

Meanwhile, Roy swam for about two minutes, then slowly inflated his BCD. He was approximately 300 feet from the end of the pier, though he had veered a bit to the south. He adjusted his direction, submerged, and continued to swim.

He reached the end of the pier at 7:25 a.m.—about half an hour before sunrise.

Still in roughly ten feet of water, he surfaced. The sun was lighting up the horizon, and the sky was a lighter grey than when he had hit the water off the boat. But it was still dark out. He positioned himself about twenty feet from the end of the pier, using the BCD to stay afloat and kicking to stay in place. From there, he had a decent view of the shore, the wooden boardwalk, and the end of the street down which Getz should come.

Roy was satisfied that he wouldn't be seen from shore. Certainly not with the naked eye. He was backlit, and there were enough waves to break up an observer's line of sight.

He removed the scuba mask and snorkel so as to maintain the lowest possible profile in the water.

And he waited.

CHAPTER SiXTY-FiVE

As luck would have it, Getz did not swim every day.

At 8:15 a.m., Susie headed back toward the drop-off point. She kept her speed at ten knots. There were more boats in the bay now, though none were near the pier. She approached the position on a path parallel to the shoreline. It took five minutes to reach the spot.

There were no watercraft nearby, so again she brought the boat around to face inland. This positioning was the all-clear signal for Roy to approach. He was floating about one hundred feet away when he saw the signal. He swam underwater and came up at the stern. He removed his BCD in the water.

"Did he show?" she asked. She'd been watching from a distance with binoculars, but hadn't seen anything and wanted to be sure.

"Nothing. Thirty minutes watching and waiting." Roy handed up the BCD.

She quickly put the gear inside and out of sight while Roy climbed up the swim ladder and got himself out of sight, as well. Susie then hurried back up to the flybridge and turned the boat, setting course at 114° to take them to the southern end of the bay while Roy changed.

Their destination was one of the top locations on the list of dive sites that Felix, the young man who had rented them the scuba gear, recommended. It was called *El Quesito*, or in English, "the little cheese." It had the added benefit that it was close to a marina near the scuba shop where they'd rented their gear.

It took them about fifteen minutes to get to the spot. They

pulled in close to shore and dropped anchor. Susie set up breakfast while Roy stayed below working on raising his body temperature.

The plan was to have Roy spend the morning diving to deplete one of his scuba tanks. Susie would snorkel and take pictures of his dive. Then they would return to the scuba shop to refill the tank and take another shot at Getz the following day.

When Roy joined her for breakfast, Susie asked, "How was it out there?"

"Fucking cold!" he responded with an exaggerated shiver. "Wetsuit helps, but this ain't the Bahamas."

"I watched from the boat. I saw a couple of folks walking along the main street. But aside from that, nothing. No one coming down or going up his street," Susie said as she sipped tea.

"Yeah, I guess he doesn't swim every day. Bad luck. Maybe tomorrow," Roy said as he tore a piece of bread in two and slathered it with butter and fig preserves.

They ate in silence punctuated by the sloshing of water against the boat.

Then Susie asked, "What if he doesn't go for another swim before we leave?"

Roy finished chewing before responding. "It's a problem. If he doesn't go swimming again by Wednesday, we have two options. Either we come back for him, or we extend our stay."

"Can we do that? Extend, I mean? The boat and all?"

"It's not ideal. And the change in plans is a red flag of sorts, I guess. But, hey, let's be optimistic. It's only day one. We still have a lot of time."

Susie and Roy hit the water at *El Quesito*. The ocean was crystal clear, though cold. Roy took pictures with his GoPro as he swam around and through the rocks until his tank was low, and Susie snapped a few from her vantage point for good measure. Then they returned to the boat and stowed their gear.

Roy took the helm to give Susie a break and headed for the Bon Aire Marina, which was just to the south. They pulled up to the dock and Roy unloaded his empty tank. Susie debarked and waited for him. She carried a small duffle.

Roy stayed aboard, taking the boat out to an anchorage just outside of the marina in front of a small beach. He dropped anchor and made sure the boat was secure, then dove into the water and made the fifty-meter swim to the beach. Roy carried the tank to the scuba shop, where he handed it over to Felix for a refill.

They would try again the next day.

CHAPTER SIXTY-SIX

Sunday
October 27, 2019
Bay of Pollença, Spain

Their phone alarms woke Susie and Roy at 6:30 a.m.

It didn't take them long to get dressed and organized. Susie put on a bathing suit with shorts and a t-shirt while Roy donned the wetsuit, which was still damp from the day before. Nothing will wake you up in the morning quite like getting into a cold wetsuit.

Unlike the day before, there was some swell, which meant that the boat was rocking more than they would have liked. It wasn't stormy, but it was windy. Not a great day for the sea.

"You think he'll go for a swim in this?" Susie asked, looking out to shore.

They were in the saloon. She was putting her hair up into a ponytail while Roy sat on the sofa trying to get his wet boots on.

"Beats me, Suze. Could be yes, as it's a more challenging swim. Could be no, because it's too choppy." Roy was irritated.

She looked at him. "You're thinking we should have done more surveillance?"

Roy sighed, looking up. "Sort of. I'm thinking it would have been nice to have done more. To know what his swim routine is. But we're not here for that long. We don't have that luxury. What I *should* have done is more surveillance the day I *was* watching him, to see if there was some other opportunity besides the swim. I think I jumped the gun. I started visualizing the plan before getting enough info on the guy."

Susie bit her lower lip, the way she did when she was thinking.

"What?" Roy asked.

"Well, we still have four days before we head home. If we're going to re-think the plan, or maybe look for another angle, now's the time."

"If we do, we lose another day to doing more surveillance—minimum. Then we have to come up with a new plan and get the gear. And *then* we have to execute it. Assuming one day of surveillance and another day to gear up, that only leaves us with two days to get it done."

"Kinda cutting it close."

"Yeah. I think I'd rather stick with the plan we've got," Roy said as Susie pulled her iPhone out of her pocket and began to tap the screen. "At least then we'll have five more shots at him," Roy continued. "We just need him to go for one swim in the next few days."

"Yeah," she replied. "I was just re-checking the weather. The next few days look good as far as wind and rain go."

They looked at each other.

"Your call," Susie said. "I'm not the one freezing his balls off waiting for the guy."

One thing I have noticed in my work with Susie and Roy is that they are rational to an extreme—perhaps sometimes to a fault. One of the reasons I think they get along so well is because their thinking patterns are very similar. I don't know if it's the legal training or something more innate, but I have watched them both—independently—work through problems, decision-making processes, and complex analyses. Even when they are thinking through something alone, they both seem to approach it in a very similar way.

They have a similar level of risk tolerance, as well. And they are prepared, at any given moment, to completely rethink their approach. They don't fear failure, and I don't mean that they don't think they can fail. On the contrary, they view failure as a real *and acceptable* outcome. To them, failure is merely one of a number of possible outcomes in a process. They don't seem to consider it a reflection on their effort. They see it more as a statistical reality.

Roy explained it to me like this.

"Doc, it's impossible to succeed every time you do something, right? True statement? There's always going to be variability. And things are not always going to go your way.

"So, if that's just reality, why do people take failure so personally? I mean, it's got to happen sometime. So, you choose your battles, you make the best plan you can, and you go do your thing. And—of course—you try to minimize the damage if you do fail, but you have to be prepared for it. Failure is nothing personal. It's not a reflection on you or your effort. It's just a fact."

As the two of them sat in silence, contemplating whether to change directions or continue with their current plan, balancing their thoughts between risk tolerance and practicality led them both to the same conclusion.

"Fuck it," Roy said. "I'll get the tank ready."

CHAPTER SIXTY-SEVEN

The weather had not improved, and Getz had not gone swimming.

Roy had barely used any of the air in the tank that second morning as he'd waited for the man to show. They'd followed the same procedure as the day before. The haphazard approach, the turn toward shore. There'd been fewer boats on the bay the second day due to the weather, so they were certain no one had spotted Roy in the water.

Susie picked him up at 8:00 a.m.

They debated over how to spend the rest of the day. Conditions were crappy.

"All the more reason to go for a dive," Susie said.

Their alibi for this murder was not as clear-cut as being in another location when the crime was committed. Their cover for this kill was diving. It would explain what they were doing in the area. They had sold themselves to Felix at the dive shop as underwater enthusiasts, and Susie had played up her disappointment at being relegated to snorkeling. Felix had given them a thumbs up when he took note of the protective hand that Susie placed over her belly, before he winked and said that diving could be even more fun with kids around.

They had also told everyone at the hotel that the main purpose of their trip was to explore the Bay of Pollença. Assuming there were no witnesses to the attack, and given that they had no motive for killing the would-be victim, they expected that their alibi would suffice.

But, they needed it to be as real as possible. That meant

going out even in crappy conditions, as long as it wasn't unsafe. They needed to be seen by others as much as possible and to take enough photos to plausibly establish their whereabouts.

So, they headed to the north end of the bay and the small cove of Cala Engossauba. There's a wonderful dive there known as Pedro's Wall. It was ideal for that day because the cove and the dive site are well sheltered—the perfect place to go on a lousy day. In fact, they came across two other groups of divers that had apparently reached the same conclusion.

They finished well before lunch and headed back to Bon Aire Marina for a refill of Roy's other oxygen tank—he was alternating between the two. Since the bay was still choppy, while they waited for the tank refill, Roy called the Pollença Marina and secured a slip for the night. It would be more comfortable sleeping in a protected slip than in the bay. Neither of them had slept well the night before. The mattresses on the *Altamira* did not compare to the ones on their Sunseeker at home.

Felix overheard Roy on the phone and recommended that they make dinner reservations at Stay, a restaurant at the marina. He also made a point of warning them that—unlike most Spanish restaurants where dinner service began at 9:30 p.m.—Stay actually closed at 10:30 p.m., so they should plan to eat on "American time."

While Roy called to reserve a table, Susie took the opportunity to show Felix their photos from the day. The threesome shared scuba stories until the tank was ready, and then Susie and Roy headed back to Pollença Marina, where they refueled before taking an afternoon siesta.

CHAPTER SiXTY-EiGHT

Once they tied up at Pollença Marina, Susie and Roy were able to relax for the first time in several days.

They were on a strange boat in strange waters. And, when you layer on top of that the fact that they were attempting to commit murder in a foreign country, well, it all added up. Spending the night at the marina and going ashore for good food, good drinks, and good service was a welcome distraction.

They dined out on the terrace at Stay, overlooking the bay. Some garlic shrimp, some tomato bread with Spanish ham, some anchovies in vinegar—simple pleasures.

If you've ever cooked a can of beans over an open flame on a camping trip and been amazed at how much better they taste, this was the same experience. After a few days on the boat, a good meal on *terra firma* tasted amazing.

Though they had another rough day ahead of them, or maybe because of that, Roy was able to convince Susie to have a chamomile tea while he had a gin and tonic after dinner. It was getting a bit chilly out, and the sun had just set over the city. They were chatting about home, law school, and reminiscing a bit about their early days together, when Roy noticed Susie's face change. Her expression froze, and though she appeared to be listening to him, he could tell that she was somewhere else.

"What's up, babe?"

Susie took a sip from her cup nonchalantly, then said through tight lips, "Getz is here. He just went to take a leak."

Now it was Roy who froze. As he took in the information, his mind began a series of calculations, possibilities, likely outcomes, and pitfalls, also factoring in how much alcohol he himself had consumed.

It wasn't that surprising, really. The marina was maybe half a mile from Getz's house. While there were a lot of small restaurants and bars in town, the view here was amazing. It was also a high-end kind of place. Swanky. An international hangout for boaters from all around the world.

"Is he at a table or at the bar?" Roy asked.

"Bar, I think," Susie replied.

Roy pondered for a few moments, drained what remained of his gin and tonic, and called for the check. Once he was sure the waitress had registered his request, he looked back at Susie, smiled mischievously, and asked, "Nightcap? At the bar?"

"Risky," she replied. "We should just get out. Avoid contact. You know? No witnesses. No forensic residue."

To her surprise, he said, "Let's just eavesdrop, if we can. Call it surveillance. I haven't had a Bailey's and coffee in forever."

She frowned, but reluctantly agreed. In her mind, there was always optionality. They could always abandon their plan if anything happened that increased the risk.

While Roy was signing the check, Getz passed again going in the other direction.

"Definitely bar," Susie said.

Roy nodded.

They made their way over to the bar. The counter was full, but there was a nice vacant leather sofa across from it. Susie took a seat while Roy sidled up between a young couple and an older-looking guy and ordered himself a Bailey's and coffee as well as a sparkling water with lime for Susie.

Getz was seated at the bar, about four occupied seats down. Roy waited for the drinks, then returned to the sofa with them. They began to drink and make small talk, feigning deep conversation. There was way too much noise at the bar, though, making eavesdropping at a distance impossible.

Roy raised his eyebrows in disappointment just as Susie flicked her eyes upward and a man's voice said, "Americans?"

Susie smiled and Roy followed her gaze. Getz, the man who he had been trying to kill, was standing just two feet from him.

"Why yes. Do we dress that poorly?" Susie asked.

Getz laughed. It was a rich laugh. He had a deep, sonorous voice.

"I overheard your husband ordering at the bar." He looked at Roy. "Your Spanish is good, but there was a slight accent there. Get a lot of Brits here, but there's no mistaking that American twang." He looked at them both. "Hearing American English is like drinking a tall glass of cool water." He drank from his glass.

Roy stood, as protocol demanded, and offered his hand, "I'm Roy."

They shook hands.

"Susie," she said.

"Pleasure," Getz replied, looking her over appreciatively. "I don't want to bother you. I just wanted to say 'hello.'"

He wasn't drunk, but by the mild slur in his speech, it was obvious that the man had had a few.

This was, of course, a *major* violation of Roy's Rules. Here they were, Susie and Roy, talking in a public place with a target whose life, if things worked out as they hoped, they would be ending the following morning, less than one kilometer from where they were having drinks.

As Roy would later say, *Fucking stupid.*

The bar was full of potential witnesses. Most seemed to be absorbed in their own conversations, but their waitress could testify to their having been there. The bartender would most likely be able to place the three of them together. The smart thing to do was to respond to Getz's tentative retreat with a polite, "Nice to have met you."

But, alcohol being what it is, Roy replied, "Not at all, great to meet a fellow American who'll no doubt be able to give us the inside scoop on Mallorca…?" It was a question to which, of course, Roy already knew the answer.

They began to chat, keeping the conversation light. Susie

snuggled up to Roy on the sofa, making a space for Getz at the other end.

Getz was vague about his reasons for being in Mallorca while Roy and Susie excitedly shared that they were on a diving vacation. Getz was quick to point out that diving was not for him. Claustrophobia—he hated the mask over his nose and the regulator in his mouth—but he did confess to enjoying a swim in the bay. He found the cold water rejuvenating.

"Do you miss the States?" Susie asked.

"I miss the efficiency, things functioning as they should, a reliable internet connection, and good cell coverage. They have all the basics here, but it's always spotty. But, as the Spanish say, *Se vive muy bien.*"

"It *is* a good life. Great food. And a more relaxed pace," added Roy.

All in all, Getz shared that he enjoyed his life in Spain. "I've grown attached to this place. Don't know if I'd ever go back to the States now."

"Do you have any family here? I mean, why Mallorca?" Susie asked.

"Nope, just me. Retired. Wanted to live somewhere with great weather, good food, and great siestas!" Getz looked at his watch. "Speaking of which, I should go. Got an early day tomorrow." He stood, swaying a little on his feet. "It was a pleasure meeting you both," he said. With that, he left.

Roy convinced Susie to stay for one more drink, for post-conversation reconnaissance.

He went up to the bar and ordered another round. The bar crowd was thinning. He asked the bartender, feigning annoyance at the conversation with Getz, *"Quien es ese viejo?"*

"Un americano. Vive aquí desde hace tiempo."

"¿Un poco pesado, no?"

"Pesado, y putón. Tiene fama. Un viejo verde."

Roy returned to the sofa.

"He's been around for a while, according to the bartender,"

Roy said. "Apparently, he's got a reputation as an asshole and a skirt chaser. Likes 'em young."

They finished half of their drinks, then called it a night.

CHAPTER SIXTY-NINE

Tom Wise was conflicted.

He had lost his wife. Since then, he'd been on a six-week bender. Worse, he had failed to be there for his daughter during a terrible time. But then, he'd miserably failed her in many ways. Deb had been sure to remind him of that.

There were a lot of regrets in Tom's life.

The conflict he felt was that he needed to forgive himself for all the bad things he'd done—things he hated himself for—if he was going to be a better person. He knew full well that failure to do this would only lead to depression, which would lead to self-medication with alcohol, which would put him back in bender mode. And he was committed to not letting that happen again.

For Kristy.

After all, everything he had done, good and bad, had been for her.

Yes, he was weak. And yes, he knew it. And, if he ever forgot that, Deb was always there to remind him. Or, she had been.

When Deb had first proposed killing Harlan, he'd been shocked. For him, it had seemed unthinkable. You had to let the system work. He had insisted, and she'd reluctantly agreed.

He had been wrong. The system had failed them.

It had been at that point that the recriminations began, and Deb had insisted that they deliver their own brand of justice. He could still remember the day that Harlan had been acquitted.

"Like Crockett, Tommy," she said with a wry smile. "That's the way this needs to go. You need to be there. You need to be there for our little girl now." She poked him gently in the chest with her

finger. "Don't you let me down." Then she paused and added, "Don't let Kristy down."

Thankfully, she'd had the sense to recognize that they would be prime suspects if anything happened to Harlan. That's when they'd fortuitously overheard a conversation while on vacation in Beaver Creek—a conversation that had been fated to change all their lives.

Of course, what Tom Wise hadn't appreciated at the time is that there's no such thing as coincidence. At least, not if Deb Wise had anything to do with it. He now knew that overhearing Susie and Roy on the balcony that night had been a set-up. Susie and Deb had orchestrated it. He'd been used, and so had Roy. Deb and Susie had been planning it for months.

Months before Beaver Creek, Tom had read an article about a certain Roy Cruise in the UT Alumni Magazine, *The Alcalde.* The article was a feature on Cruise's investment firm and his transition from law to business. It also mentioned the fact that Cruise had lost his daughter in a car accident—the other driver had been texting while driving.

That magazine had been lying around the house for some time. Then, a couple of weeks before their trip to Colorado, Deb had brought the article up in conversation. They'd been having breakfast, and she was flipping through it and asked, "Say, hun, do you know this Cruise guy?"

"Nope," he'd replied. "Impressive, though. I read the article."

"Maybe he'd be a good candidate to invest in some real estate with you?"

"Maybe," he'd replied.

Tom had not thought much of it at the time. Had he, he would have found it odd that Deb, who rarely showed any interest in his work, had suddenly made that suggestion about a complete stranger.

The next time Cruise had been mentioned was when they'd checked into the condo in Colorado, two days before they were to overhear the conversation on the balcony. While they were checking in, Deb tugged on Tom's shirtsleeve and pointed with her head. He looked up to see Roy Cruise and his wife walking past the reception desk.

He'd smiled at Deb, saying, "Small world."

In hindsight… too many coincidences. But, at the time, his wife had convinced him that it was fate. They had stayed up most of the night after they'd overheard Roy and Susie's conversation—debating, disputing, arguing. Her haranguing him. Him trying to dissuade her. All in hushed tones, so that they wouldn't wake Kristy.

In the end, as was often the case, she'd convinced him.

And he'd done it.

He'd asked Roy Cruise to kill Joe Harlan. He still remembered the phrase he'd used, verbatim. He'd rehearsed it, to try to make it sound tough but sympathetic.

For Kristy, and for Camilla. Will you kill this fucker Harlan for us?

What a fool he'd been. Deb had played him like a fiddle. He understood in hindsight that she had set up the whole thing. The trip to Beaver Creek. The drinks on the balcony. Deb had orchestrated it all, with Susie as her accomplice.

She'd admitted to it months later, when she'd showed up with that Ziploc. And then she'd played him again.

He was the one who had asked *them* to do it.

They had taken all of the risk.

He just *had* to do this one final little thing to close the loop.

Deb had been relentless, and he'd caved. Again. He had nailed that kid's dick to his father's front door.

Who the fuck does that?

But that was Deb. Take no prisoners. Cruise and Font? Why they'd taken the risk of sending them the man's penis, he had no idea. He'd only spoken to Cruise that one time in Colorado. He'd never met the wife, Susie.

At least, with that final act, it had been over.

He'd thought.

But with Deb it was never over. There was always one last thing. She'd always wanted more. They say opposites attract, and there was no doubt that she had chosen someone who could be dominated.

It was an ugly, long, and complicated story, and he knew that he owed it to his daughter to tell her the truth—to tell her everything. And, in part, although he knew it was no excuse, part of his drinking over the past six weeks had been due to that.

Avoidance.

He wanted to tell her. He so desperately wanted to share everything with her. But how? How do you go about telling your own daughter that you conspired to end the life of another human being? How do you confess a murder to your little girl?

Deb had given him the answer.

He laughed to himself.

Even from the fuckin' grave, she's telling me what to do.

He'd decided to do what Deb had done: to write Kristy a letter.

At least Kristy would find out everything when he was gone. Maybe sooner, if he got up the nerve. In the meantime, they could heal. They could grow together as a father and daughter. And for now, he could enjoy spending time with his beautiful, talented little girl.

He finished the letter, put it in an envelope—sealed with her name on it—and put the letter in his lockbox. The box also contained other items that would most likely be of interest to her when the time came.

Many years from now, I hope.

He had just put the lockbox back in the safe when the doorbell rang.

It was 7:47 p.m.—a little late for a Sunday visitor.

He walked to the foyer, turned on the porch light, and looked through the glass window at the top of the door.

Outside, on the porch, stood an odd little man in a green leather jacket.

CHAPTER SEVENTY

Monday
October 28, 2019
Austin, Texas

Senator Harlan woke at 4:30 a.m.

He had gotten into the habit early in his political career. Campaigning was a time sink, but very few people got up early in the morning. And there is much that can be done early, when the rest of the world is asleep. It was a routine that had become part of his lifestyle.

Up at 4:30 a.m.

Check email, read news, have coffee until 5:15 a.m.

Leave home for the gym at 5:15 a.m.

Arrive at the Town Lake YMCA at 5:30 a.m.

Swim for 45 minutes. Then shower and head into the office.

This Monday wasn't any different. He was wearing jeans, flip-flops, and a "Keep Austin Weird" t-shirt. He poured himself a cup of coffee and sat down at his laptop.

Once he'd cleared the spam from his inbox, he saw that he had a few emails from colleagues and staff—the usual suspects. One email stood out. It was from Anne Hertig, sent late the night before. The subject line read: *Follow up*. When they'd last spoken, he had called her in response to Liz Bareto's email. There was nothing to follow up on... Harlan's cursor hovered over the email. He considered whether to open it first or save it for last.

He had first met Anne almost seven years back at the Republican National Convention in Tampa. She'd just been starting her first term in Congress, coming out of Ohio. She was fifteen years his junior, but there had been an immediate spark. Just one of those things.

She was married—a condition, not an impediment, as they say—to a doctor who'd then been screwing his secretary. Anne knew, but didn't care. Running for Congress as a doctor's wife with two kids, one in medical school and the other in the Marines, painted a pretty picture. She didn't want to "rock the boat."

But, she had rocked Harlan's. They'd had a nice run of it. Almost two years. It hadn't by any means been a regular thing, but they'd made a point of seeing each other as often as possible. And it had eventually ended on friendly terms.

"It's just too difficult to make time for each other," she had said. Harlan had accepted it, although he was confident that she had simply outgrown him. That hadn't stopped him carrying a flame for her, hoping they might return to their afternoon delights at some point, but he'd been disabused of that notion when he'd noticed that she had started to date men much younger than him.

Normally, he would have saved this email for last, relishing the anticipation. Harlan loved surprises. But, given all of the phone calls he had been receiving, he knew something was up and he guessed that Anne had gotten wind of it.

> Hello there!
> You never called me back after we last spoke. I'm
> still in D.C. And still an early riser...
> Anne

Harlan picked up his mobile phone and called.

"Good morning, Joe!" was her enthusiastic greeting.

"Good morning, Congresswoman."

She laughed on the other end. He'd used to call her that in bed, and it was always good for a giggle. "You obviously got my email."

"Sure did. Just wondering what there is to follow up on."

"You met with Liz?"

"I did." Harlan frowned. Maybe she didn't know anything after all. "Yes. Very nice lady."

"Yes. I thought you'd like her," Ann said coyly. "I know your type, Joe. But, she's more than that. She's inherently a good person. We met in college."

"So she said," Harlan contributed.

"But that isn't want I wanted to talk to you about."

Harlan perked up. "No?"

"No."

"Go on."

"Joe, I wanted you to know that you're being vetted for something. I got a visit—not a call—*a visit* from a couple of guys in dark suits. You know the drill. Spent an hour with me, grilling me on you, your background, us, everything."

"Who were they with?"

"Wouldn't say. 'National security' was all I could get out of them. They asked about your time in the military. In government. Your politics. Your wife. Your son. And about our little fling. They knew everything about you, Joe. It's not everyday spooks get an hour with me and get me to open my kimono. Hell, they're probably listening right now. But, I'm not telling you anything they told me not to, so... "

Still relishing the moment, Harlan conjured his most bewildered tone and said, "Well, Anne, I haven't the slightest. No one's contacted me about anything."

"Well, rest assured that they will. You should hear something soon. Unless, of course," she paused for dramatic effect, "unless they find something they don't like. You don't have any skeletons in your closet, do you, Senator?" she asked, teasing. "Nothing that might be an issue?"

"Not that I know of." Harlan felt a boulder forming in the pit of his belly.

There was another pause. He knew she was toying with him. He used to enjoy it, and normally he would still. But now, while he was on the verge of something potentially life altering, he found it irritating.

"Anyway, I just wanted to give you a heads-up. You know, so you don't forget me when you're running spies and shit."

Harlan laughed. "How could I forget you, Anne? Ever?"

After ending the call with the congresswoman, Senator Harlan called Slipknot on the burner phone. No answer. Though they'd agreed to communicate only by speaking by phone, Harlan violated that agreement and sent him a text message from the burner.

Urgent. We need to talk.

CHAPTER SEVENTY-ONE

Kristy's phone vibrated. It was on the counter next to her, and she heard/felt it at a little past 9:30 a.m.

She was in the Rosens' kitchen digging her way through a grapefruit. Mrs. Rosen was looking in the fridge, already planning lunch. And Bethany was talking nonstop, trying to convince Kristy to go with her on a hunting vacation to Alaska. Bethany loved shooting. She'd grown up spending summers on her grandparents' ranch, the Double H. She loved nature... and wanted Kristy to go with her to Alaska to kill some of it.

The two of them had hunted deer and wild boar on the Double H with their dads. At the time, Kristy had merely been proficient while Bethany had already been an excellent shot. That may have changed as Kristy had started spending time at the gun range, and her accuracy had significantly improved.

"You need to show me your stuff, girl. Bet'cha you still can't out-shoot this momma bear," Bethany laughed, pointing her thumbs at herself.

While Bethany loved being outdoors, if Kristy stopped to think about it, Bethany loved everything. This was one of many things that attracted Kristy to her. She was one of those people who are always one hundred percent on—energetic, positive, optimistic.

Kristy looked down at her phone: **Arthur Travers, Detective**

"Just a sec, I gotta take this."

Bethany stopped mid-sentence, smiling.

Kristy put the phone to her ear and answered, "Hello?"

"Hello, Kristy? This is Detective Travers."

Kristy had no idea why the detective would be calling her, but since it was most likely about something to do with Deb, she wasn't sure she wanted Bethany's mother to hear any of it. So, she stepped away from the kitchen and walked toward the family room for some privacy. "Hi Detective. How are you?"

"I'm good, Kristy, you?"

"I'm fine. But you sound awful, Detective," she said. "Is there something I can help you with?"

"No. Just one of those Mondays, you know. That said, I do need to speak to you again. Sometime today maybe? The sooner the better, really."

"Is this about Mom?"

"Yes, it is," Travers replied. "Are you close? Would that be possible? For you to meet me?"

"Well, I'm up in Fort Worth actually. But I'm heading back to Austin today anyway. So, it'll be a few hours. Is that okay?"

"Um. Yeah. That'd be fine. Can you just come straight to my office? It's important. But I'd rather not discuss it on the phone."

"Is anything wrong?"

He paused for a second before answering. "No. No. We'll talk when you get here."

"Okay." She pulled a face. "But you're making me nervous. Can't you tell me now?"

"It's department policy to talk in person. Best if we wait."

"Okay. Sure. Well, let me get organized and I'll come to you. Assuming traffic's light, I should be there by..." Kristy calculated, "...noon, at the latest."

"Okay, Kristy. Thanks. Drive safe."

"Oh, wait. Should I call Dad and have him come, too?"

"No. That won't be necessary," he said.

"Okay. I'll see you soon. Bye."

"Goodbye."

Kristy pondered for a few seconds.

"Kris?" It was Bethany joining her in the family room. "Is everything okay?"

"Yeah." She forced a smile. "Fine, I just gotta head back."

Bethany frowned, looking back at her mother who was still puttering in the kitchen.

"You should stay," Kristy continued. "Your mom's planning a big lunch."

"You sure?" Bethany asked, then said more quietly, "I'm happy to come with you."

"Definitely," Kristy replied. "We'll catch up later."

It took Kristy just fifteen minutes to get her stuff together. After saying her goodbyes, and as she was making her way to her car, she realized just how much she had missed this. Normal family stuff. The weekend had reminded her that it was still okay to have fun, to enjoy life and not feel shitty about it.

Maybe she would take the Alaska trip with Bethany.

If Dad really is getting his shit together, it'd be nice to get away without having to worry about him.

On the drive back to Austin, she listened to her 80's playlist. She was feeling nostalgic. New wave music brought back memories of her first party at UT. It had been eighties-themed; she'd gone dressed like Cyndi Lauper, and she'd rocked it.

That night, the world still lay open before her, full of promise. That was back when she took her mother's words literally; she really could have anything, all she had to do was reach out and grab it. The naïve Kristy that attended that party was long gone. She'd never see her again, and they'd long since said their "goodbyes."

Kristy spent most of the drive back processing everything she had experienced lately, which made the time fly, though one thing that kept coming to the forefront of her thoughts was Detective Travers. There was something about that call. Something about his tone that unnerved her. Sure, she told herself that he was a cop and that they all talked like that when it was official business. She should know, the guy had called the house enough times.

But why does he want to meet at the station?

At about three quarters of the way back, at 10:45 a.m., she used Siri to call her father.

Voicemail.

Hey Dad. On my way back to Austin. I'm stopping by to see Detective Travers. Should be home around noonish. Maybe we can grab lunch somewhere? I'd really like that. Call me. Love you. Bye.

CHAPTER SEVENTY-TWO

At 11:32 a.m., Kristy pulled up outside the Austin Police Department and killed the engine. She didn't like the place. It was one of those functional government buildings made of beige stone. She entered the building and asked for Detective Travers at the front desk.

Not thirty seconds later, Travers was there to greet her. He walked her back down a hallway that she knew led to his office. But, about three quarters of the way there, they took a right into a small conference room with a round table and four chairs, one of which was occupied by a woman who stood when Kristy walked in.

It was Glo Spoor.

Kristy's heart sank.

She was professionally dressed with a bit of Austin casual, featuring a tiny stud in her nose.

"Kristy, please take a seat. You remember—" Travers began.

"I do. Glo. Victims' advocate. But, we've already been through all that," Kristy said with a sigh as she slid into a plastic chair. "No offense."

Glo smiled, but it was with her mouth. Not her eyes.

"Haven't we?" Kristy prompted them, looking at her two table companions in turn.

"So," Travers began, "Kristy, we wanted to meet with you because 911 received a call this morning from Consuelo. About an incident at your house."

Consuelo was their cleaning lady. She was in the house every weekday.

"Dad?" Kristy asked, looking at Glo, then back at Travers again.

Contrary to his training, Travers averted his gaze and looked down at the scuffed table in front of him before looking up at Glo and then back at Kristy. "Um, Kristy, there's no easy way to say this. I'm sorry to tell you that your father, Tom Wise, is dead."

Kristy squinted at him and then looked at his colleague for confirmation. Lifeless cow-eyes looked back at her. It was exactly the same expression Glo had worn when they had visited the house and told her about her mother.

That's when Kristy lost her breath and her hand fluttered to her mouth as if to stifle a scream. "I... I don't understand," she stammered as tears filled her eyes.

The next hour was a blur. Kristy went into shock.

For a long while, all she heard was a high-pitched whistling. Travers' mouth moved, but made no sound. Or at least she couldn't hear anything he was saying.

Glo was holding her hand, which normally she would have hated. But, while she was aware of it, she was unable—unwilling—to react to or shake that cold clammy thing off of her.

"How?" she heard someone say over and over again, but Travers wasn't responding. His mouth kept moving, but he made no sound. "I want to know how!" someone yelled, and that's when she realized that it was her. It was her who kept asking the question, but her mind kept refusing to hear the answer.

"...alone...."

"...suicide note..."

"All the indications are..."

Kristy scowled at the man sitting opposite her.

"I didn't ask who, Detective, I asked how," she said through gritted teeth, as if the words were made of bitter poison.

"As I said before, it appears to have been an overdose. Pills. Alcohol," Travers said softly.

"Kristy," Glo interjected, "I know this is a shock. My mother committed suicide and it's one of the reasons why I—"

"This doesn't make any sense, Art," Kristy said, ignoring

Glo. "He wasn't in that kind of a place. A couple of weeks ago, maybe, but... we spoke just a few days ago. He was on the mend—"

"Kristy, addiction is one of those things—" began Glo.

"He was getting better," Kristy interrupted her, and spoke to Travers. "He told me he was going to stop drinking! He was going back to AA. He went!"

Travers nodded sympathetically, and then said, "There was alcohol in his system. A lot. Almost double the legal limit."

"And?"

Travers looked at her curiously, not understanding the question.

"And what drugs?" she asked impatiently. "You said he took pills. What pills?"

"Oxycodone. There was over a mil/per in his bloodstream," Travers answered. "I mean, one milligram per liter. That's a lot."

"He never took drugs. Ever," Kristy spat. "Where is—" She was about to ask Travers another question when Glo spoke again, squeezing Kristy's hand.

"People keep secrets, Kristy. There are a lot of things—"

"Listen, you insipid bitch—" Kristy jerked her hand away from Glo and turned to face the woman. She felt like Bethany must have felt on the terrace that day, back at Beaver Creek. "I don't know if you're socially retarded or if it's that you suck at your fuckin' job, but I don't need the emotional bullshit right now. I'm trying to get *the facts*! So, would you please shut your fuckin' mouth and let me talk?"

Glo sat back in her chair, unfazed by the outburst. She'd obviously witnessed this kind of reaction many times before. Kristy took her impassive, empathetic look for smugness, and turned back to Art to avoid slapping the woman.

"So, Art. Just give me the fucking facts, Okay? It's not too much to ask, is it? Where. Is. The. Fucking. Note?"

Travers looked down at a manila folder on the desk and then opened it. He removed a plastic Ziploc bag with an *evidence* sticker on the front and slid it across the table.

There was a note inside. It was in Tom's handwriting, but Kristy barely recognized it. The writing was a messy, uncontrolled scrawl. Not his everyday penmanship. Not even his drunken writing. Worse.

Kristy didn't touch the bag, but read the note from a distance as if the thing might burn her.

> *Kristy,*
> *I can't live the rest of my life without your mom.*
> *I hope you understand.*
> *Love, Dad*

She frowned as she recalled their last conversation and what her father had said.

I've lived half my life without your mom. And if I've done it before, I can do it again. But you, Kristy. I cannot imagine my life without you.

She shook her head. She knew it wasn't suicide. No way. And that handwriting…. Her father had the neatest handwriting she had ever seen. It was certainly neater than hers and that mess inside of that transparent bag.

Her mind raced.

Is it possible?

"What about Cruise?" she demanded.

"I'm sorry," said Travers. "You mean Roy Cruise?"

She nodded her head rapidly.

"As far as I know, he's out of the country. But, Kristy, there are no indications…"

Fucking Liz Bareto is right! But how could they pull it off? I'm gonna kill that motherfucker!

"Where is he?" she asked.

"I don't know. Out of the country, but—"

"Not him, my fucking dad."

"At the morgue," Travers replied.

"So, what? Is my house a crime scene now? Can I go home?"

"Let me make a call real quick." Travers said, rising and

taking out his mobile phone. "Before you go, though, Kristy, I'm just going to need you to—"

"I know the fucking drill, Art," she growled. Then, she took a deep breath. "Sorry. I'm sorry, Art. And, to you, too, Glo," she said, turning to woman who at least this time knew to say nothing. "I know that you're both just doing your jobs. It's not your fault. It's just... as you can imagine, it's been a really shitty couple of months."

CHAPTER SEVENTY-THREE

Kristy sat at the kitchen table alone. It was late afternoon.

She had lost both her parents in the span of about six weeks. Yet, with her having so recently suffered the death of her mother, none of the feelings seemed strange or new. There was a tragic *déjà vu* element to it all.

On the table in front of her was a short list of to-dos. They were all marked "done." It was the list she had put together after her mother had died, listing everything that had to be done—contact the funeral home, the priest, call the lawyers, email family and friends.... A marathon of misery.

It felt as though her mother's death had been some kind of hideous rehearsal.

By 5:00 p.m., she had made all the phone calls. Everyone knew what had happened and what they had to do. She composed a short email and sent it to friends and family, using the same "To" list she had used for her mom's funeral. Then she unplugged the house phone. She knew the calls would start soon, and she was in no frame of mind to deal with them.

She thought about her father. Their last conversation.

He was not suicidal.

That, she knew. He had told her as much before she'd left for her trip. The police's interpretation made no sense. Travers' analysis certainly didn't.

As Kristy looked around the room, the emptiness of the home that was now her house threatened to drown her. She felt completely alone—isolated. Sure, she had extended family, but nobody she was close to. No, the fact was that, at twenty-two years old, Kristy Wise was alone in the world.

She didn't feel like talking to Bethany. When she'd told her the news, Bethany had insisted on coming to the house. Staying with her. Helping where she could. But Kristy had declined. She wanted some time to process everything by herself. She also hadn't texted Alfie. He was still visiting family in Argentina and wouldn't be back until after the funeral. She didn't want him changing plans on her account.

Everything that needed to be done had been taken care of. She could now focus on where she'd left off.

She went into her father's office and opened the safe. Everything was in its proper place. His lockbox was on its shelf. She checked it—locked. She knew there was a little key with a small red disk hanging from it that opened it, but she had no idea where her father kept it. And she had looked.

She picked up the phone and called George Pringle, the estate lawyer who was handling her parents' affairs. He'd given her his direct number and mobile number so that she could reach him after-hours if necessary.

"Hello George, Kristy again."

"Hello Kristy. How can I help you?"

"Sorry, I know it's late and I know we're meeting tomorrow, but I was wondering. Beyond the paperwork and stuff, did my parents leave anything for me in the way of keys?"

"I'm not quite sure, Kristy, but I'm still at the office. Let me just check. Hold on a second."

She heard Pringle put the phone down. Papers shuffling. The klink klunk of a metal filing cabinet sounded, and then he was back on the phone again.

"I have a small envelope here that feels like it may contain keys."

"Could you open it and tell me if it's got a small key with a red disk on it?"

"The envelope is labeled to be opened only by you, Kristy.

I'd... prefer to follow... to honor those wishes. If you'd like, I can have someone bring it by?"

"Sure, George. Yeah. I understand. If you don't mind, that would be great."

"Okay. I'll have it couriered over."

At about 6:30 p.m., the doorbell rang. Kristy checked the peephole and saw George Pringle on her front porch.

"George," she said, opening the door. "You didn't have to come yourself."

"Well, I don't know if there are duplicates somewhere of what's in here, and I didn't want to trust them to a courier."

"Please come in."

They sat at the kitchen table while she opened the envelope and looked inside. George had prepared documents for her to sign, confirming that she had taken possession of one unopened envelope addressed to her.

"Again, I am so very sorry for your loss, Kristy."

His eyes weren't full of pity. The man was methodical. Practical. This pleased her. She could deal with that right now. Nothing else. Just that.

Kristy showed Pringle out and returned to her father's office.

There were two keys in the envelope, both on a small metal loop. One was brass, and the other key was silver. Smaller. The envelope also contained a slip of paper.

On it was written:

1. Wells Fargo, 111 Congress Avenue, Austin, Texas 78701, safe deposit box number 227.
2. Lock box—in home safe.

Kristy inserted the silver key into the lockbox lock and turned it.

Inside were several items.

A small notebook. At the back of the notebook, between

the last page and the back cover, was wedged a plain white envelope with her name on it.

There was also a small manila envelope. Inside was another brass key. She compared it to the safe deposit box key and saw that they matched.

Finally, there were two letters. The letters her mother had written to her father and to Susie Font.

There was nothing else.

Kristy laid everything out on the kitchen table.

She flipped through the pages of the small notebook. It was a journal. Kristy opened it to the first entry.

July 10, 2018

Dear Dr. Genius:

Here it is—my first "unsent letter."

If you want me to articulate what's bothering me so that we can discuss the issues in our sessions—I long for boredom.

Right now, that's what I value most in life.

When life just goes along normally, you don't really appreciate how good "uneventful" and "boring" really is.

These words have negative connotations.

But, when something traumatic happens, it makes you wish that everything could go back to UNEVENTFUL and BORING. Then you realize that BORING is BEAUTIFUL!

The hardest part for me since everything happened has been waking up in the mornings.

Just those first few minutes—when I've forgotten. When I think that everything is still normal and boring.

And then, I remember.

And the reality comes crashing down on me.

Kristy read, skimming some entries, and her heart sank. Journal entry after journal entry, she could feel the desperation, the pain, coming through the pages at her like heat off a stove.

...I feel like my life has run off the rails.

...I've made some choices that I'm proud of. And some I regret. But who hasn't?

...How do I reconcile the path I've chosen with the people I love?

...I think that secrets are relationship killers.

Kristy flipped to the last journal entry.

August 2, 2019

I've put up with lies. I've abandoned my beliefs.
But everyone has a breaking point.
There is a line. I think I'm there.
I play the role; I do my part. But this is eating me up inside. If it was just me, maybe I could go on.
But, it's not just about me. It's never been just about me. That's part of the problem. It's affecting others.
We're hurting others.
I have to find a way out that does the least harm. That minimizes the damage.
And, I think I have.
It's not pretty but, I think it's the only way I can maintain my sanity and protect what I hold most dear.
Oh God. This is not going to end well.

Next, Kristy opened the plain, letter-sized envelope addressed to her. Inside was a two-page, handwritten letter.

My dear angel, Kristy,
If you are reading this, it is because I am gone. First, let me say I love you more than my life. Everything I've done was done intending the best for you. That said, I want to tell you what I can so you don't live with the pain of not knowing. And, I need for you to understand why I did what I did in the hopes that maybe you can forgive me.

Your mother had many great qualities. And I loved her with all my heart. But, she had a dark side to her as well. In the end, that darkness consumed all the good that we had together. After what happened to you—what Harlan did to you and got away with—I have to confess that the same darkness infected me. I wanted with all my heart for your pain to go away. Your mom convinced me that the best thing that we could do was to make Harlan pay. To make him disappear. We made it happen, and we made sure the world knew he was gone. It was me that nailed what was left of Harlan to his father's door.

How did Harlan die? I don't know all the specifics, but what I do know I will tell you. I am leaving out names because I don't want to implicate anyone who may still be living if this falls into the wrong hands.

Your mom told me that a few years back a young man killed a girl, the daughter of an old friend of hers. Your mother told me that she "took care of him." Those same folks—the dead girl's parents—are the ones who helped us out with Harlan. It was wrong. I regret doing it. It has weighed on me terribly. I'm just not cut out for that sort of thing. Your mother was different. Towards the end I was afraid of her. Afraid to leave her. Afraid of what she might do to me, even to you. I came to see her as a disease. I got to the point where even the alcohol couldn't numb the pain or distract me from the truth.

Everything came to a head when she decided that there were too many "loose ends." She told me we had to clean things up by killing the people that killed Harlan. At least that's what she told me—who knows what her plan really was... The day she died, she had agreed to a meeting with one of them. The plan was for her to distract him, and for me to kill him. When the moment came, I couldn't do it. But something came over me. I saw the opportunity. And I took it. Your mother is gone because of me. I killed her. Kristy, my angel. I'm so sorry. Words cannot describe how sorry I am. I tried to live with all of this and with her. But I couldn't. I was living with a monster. I didn't see any other way out.

Please know that I believe with all my heart that you are better off without her. You've grown into a strong, well-balanced young woman—despite having two really fucked up parents. I don't take what I did lightly. Depriving you of your mother was a terrible thing. Probably unforgiveable. But, I am convinced that you are better off without her than with her. The world is a better place without Deb in it. I only hope that in the time between her death and when you read this letter I will have had time to make amends.

> *I'm sorry. Forgive me.*
> *I love you with all my heart.*
> *Dad*

Kristy wept.
For her father.
And for her mother.

This was too much to take alone. She needed someone. She needed to reach out to Bethany. She'd know what to do.

CHAPTER SEVENTY-FOUR

Senator Harlan downed the rest of his scotch.

The last time he'd felt this anxious had been when Art Travers told him that his son's penis had been found nailed to his front door. He got up and poured himself another drink.

Fuck. Fuck. Fuck. Fuck!

He had just finished watching the six o'clock news—the local news, which was a rare thing for him. He usually had a business dinner or some sort of community event to attend. He had, in fact, planned to have dinner that night with some folks coming into town from Apple—two execs and their lobbyist. They'd canceled around lunchtime due to flight delays, which at the time he'd welcomed.

It wasn't often that he got a quiet night at home alone.

And he'd been enjoying it until he'd happened to look up from reading and spotted the segment. At first, he'd thought he had misread the caption, but he damn well hadn't. He really had seen the words *BREAKING NEWS* and *TOM WISE* scroll across the bottom of the screen. Things only got worse when he unmuted the TV. The very last thing he had expected to hear filled the room like the foul stench of a fucking fart in an airplane.

Apparent suicide—father of Harlan rape accuser.

He wondered if Slipknot was involved. It could just be a coincidence.

But what a fucking coincidence.

Should I call him?

He picked up and put down the burner phone so many times that he finally got up and put the thing on the dining room table, far away from him. He considered searching for more details about the story online, but decided against it for fear that he may create unnecessary digital evidence of his interest in the story.

So, he channel-hopped instead in an attempt to get more information. What he found particularly troubling were the words "apparent suicide." "Apparent" was code for the fact that they hadn't ruled out "foul play."

Fuck.

He was also interested in the time of death because he wanted to know where he'd been when it had happened so that he could get his alibi straight—since there was no doubt he'd be on the police's suspect list, if not at the very top of it.

Fuck!

Sunday, he had spent most of the day at home, alone. No alibi. He'd had dinner at Eddie V's with a potential new client and another attorney from his law firm. They'd all been together until almost 9:00 p.m. Good. That was good.

Then, he'd had drinks and "dessert" with Liz Bareto.

Oh God, did I overstep there, too?

He was into her. They had a good time. And she was a step above the women he usually screwed. At first, he had been ready to write her off as some nut obsessed with the whole "dead kid" thing, but then it had turned out that she wasn't that bad at all, that she was actually quite balanced. She could turn it off and be a regular person, too. Fun. He liked fun.

But, last night, he'd had a couple drinks too many. And they *had* talked about the kids. And they had commiserated at the unfairness. The injustice of it. And, after a few too many, he'd held her and told her—no, worse—*promised* her that the injustices which they had suffered would be avenged.

Fuck!

He cringed. He could imagine her testifying in front of a jury to what he'd said: "They will be avenged, Liz. I swear it on my life."

Goddammit, Joe! Always fucking trying to impress.

He hoped to God he didn't have to bring her into this. It was only a matter of time before he got a call. Probably from Travers.

Shit.

He thought back to what he'd done when he'd heard that Deb Wise had been killed. He had called Travers.

Oh man, I've gotta be consistent.

He picked up his mobile phone—the regular one—to make the call, and then put it back down. He needed to think some more.

Don't be hasty. Keep it together.

When he'd called Travers about Deb, he'd been calm, cool, and collected. He'd been surprised that she'd died. He hadn't been involved and had nothing to hide.

Right now, he knew that he was none of those things. He'd already had a scotch, a double, and he looked down to find that his second double was almost gone, too.

Would he give something away if he called? Through his voice? His questions? It might be better to wait; let the adrenaline drain from his body.

Adrenaline? Let the damned scotch drain from your body, you idiot!

He poured himself just a bit more scotch—just a smidgeon. He needed to knock the edge off. He could always pretend he hadn't heard yet. Just go to bed and wait until he saw it in the papers tomorrow. Picking up the remote, he turned off the TV.

He'd had too much to drink already. He was distressed. He needed to rest.

He went to the kitchen and poured his drink down the sink. If only he could pour all this crap down the disposal. Then, he headed upstairs to bed. Halfway there, he stopped and headed back down to the dining room, where he snatched up the burner phone and headed back up again.

As he lay in bed, he began to do some simple relaxation exercises he had learned online—on YouTube. A few years back, he'd told Joe about the fact that he sometimes had trouble winding down, switching off, especially if it was the end of a particularly stressful day. Joe Junior had done some research for him. Nothing fancy... just a couple of videos on relaxation techniques that he found very effective. Harlan had used them since.

Senator Joe Harlan was just dozing off, sinking deeper and deeper into a huge imaginary featherbed, when his phone rang. He jolted upright and snapped on the bedside lamp. He felt better. More centered already. He was ready for Travers.

He picked the phone up and tried to answer, but the damn thing kept on ringing.

That's when he realized he'd grabbed the wrong one. He dropped the phone on the bed and reached for the burner instead. It vibrated and rang in his hand like an angry insect.

CHAPTER SEVENTY-FIVE

"Hello?"

"Hey Joe. You asleep?"

"No. No. I'm good." Harlan paused. Heart pounding in anticipation.

"Well, one down..."

Lead settled at the bottom of Harlan's stomach. All of his fears realized.

"...one or two more to go."

He cleared his throat and asked, "How do you mean?"

"The chickens are coming home to roost, my friend. Your neighbor got very chatty when I explained to him that, if he didn't cooperate, there could be... repercussions. His daughter, specifically."

Harlan winced.

What if someone's listening? If my phone's tapped? Unlikely, but...

"He confessed. All of it, Joe. He personally did the job on your door. Your front door." Slipknot paused, almost as if waiting for fucking applause.

For a moment, Harlan forgot about the risk of getting caught. He lifted the sheets and swung his bare feet over the side of the bed, finding something oddly soothing about the cool wooden floor.

"Well, I'll be goddamned. He did? He confessed? That he did?" Harlan whispered, incredulously. "He admitted it?"

"Yes, sir. And, there's more. He said it was his missus that organized everything. He found out after the fact. At least, that's what he claimed. But the man still did his part. Said she organized it all with the help of the folks in Florida."

Harlan was torn, only half-listening now. He relished the satisfaction of knowing that his son had been avenged, even if only in part. Slipknot had killed Wise. He was under no illusion about that. He must have tried to make it look like a suicide; the question was whether or not he had succeeded. And from the sound of it, before dying, Wise had implicated Cruise and Kim. This was real progress beyond anything he had imagined. After all this time not knowing. The thought brought tears to his eyes.

But then reality kicked in. He had no idea as to the quality of Slipknot's work. How good was he at this stuff? For all Harlan knew, Slipknot could have been so sloppy that it was only a matter of time before the police came knocking on his door. And he couldn't have any of this getting back to him.

He stood and began to pace, the wood creaking in protest in some parts of the room.

"That's great news, Slipknot. Great work," he heard himself say. "But, listen. I've got some stuff going on—kind of high-level stuff—that all of this could impact, you know, negatively. We... you... I need you to be very careful. Discreet. You know. I'm thinking that we need to hold off on the next part for a bit. You know, until things have calmed down."

Slipknot didn't seem to hear. He continued, "That confession was all I needed. Did you see it on the news, Joe? The local news? Poor Tom..." Slipknot mock-cleared his throat, "he killed himself." Slipknot laughed. "Couldn't go on living without his wife, I suspect."

Harlan felt a bit of comfort. Slipknot had used Wise's name. At least there was no way he was recording this. The guy wasn't that dumb.

Then Anne's words came back to him. "*Hell, they're probably listening right now...*"

Harlan feigned surprise, "Oh my. That's terrible news. Poor man." If he was being vetted for something high-level, could they be listening to his calls on the burner? Was that even possible? He walked away from the windows and into the bathroom and closed the door. He knew all about directional microphones.

Fuck, I'm getting paranoid. No, who are you kidding? You've always been that way.

There were a few beats of silence on the line. Harlan sat on the edge of the bathtub and continued, "Like I was saying, maybe we should just press pause for a bit. See exactly how the land lies—"

"You're not wimping out on me now, are you, man? I gotcha covered. Don't worry. It's all gonna go down like we discussed. No need to worry. We'll settle up after."

"I know," Harlan interjected, trying to remain calm. "But, like I said, things are getting complicated. All I'm saying is, we take a breather. Just a short spell. Let things settle down, you know?"

"Look, Joe. That sum-bitch told me his wife arranged for Joe—your son—to be killed in Florida. He said Cruise and his wife were involved."

Harlan's mind reeled. It felt as if a rug had been pulled out from under him. He leaned heavily against the wall. The connection to Cruise wasn't a huge surprise. He'd read the interview. Seen the evidence. He knew Cruise was on the radar.

But the *wives?*

"His wife? And Deb Wise? What did he say about the wife? And Deb? Are you sure? What about David Kim?"

"According to Wise, Kim had nothing to do with it. It was the wives who knew each other, from way back." Slipknot continued, "Crazy as all git-out. It was some sort of a quid pro quo kinda thing. She—Mrs. Wise—apparently killed some kid in Florida that crashed into Cruise's daughter. Joe was them returnin' the favor. I think it's enough to justify a visit to the two of them, don't you?"

Harlan took a few seconds to sift through what he had just heard. He was stunned.

But he quickly recovered and began to calculate—his legal mind in full gear. Was there another angle? Another way to use the information that wouldn't involve Slipknot?

A confession obtained under duress wouldn't mean anything in court. Hell, he couldn't even share the information Slipknot had obtained with the police. And the witness—Tom Wise—was dead at the hand of Slipknot.

No, all legal channels were closed; that was a dead-end.

But still, Slipknot had proof.

He has a confession. Sure, obtained under duress. But why would the man lie? Why blame the husband and wife from Florida?

He now knew who had killed his son. And Liz Bareto's boy, too, from the sound of it. And he had the chance to do something about it. To get justice. To get revenge.

"They will be avenged, Liz. I swear it on my life."

But not now. And if Slipknot wasn't keen on stopping, the only option was to delay him.

"I agree you should pay them a visit. But, give me a few days. I'd like to see if there's any other way to use this information," Harlan said.

"What other way? Use it how? You think I'm gonna sit down with someone and tell them what Wise told me and how it actually went down?" Slipknot laughed. "Don't go getting fucking cold feet on me, Cherry. If I didn't think you had the balls to finish this, I wouldn't have fucking started it. I know the kind of man you are. The kind of men we are. I'm neck-deep now, and I feel morally obligated to complete my mission. It's a question of honor."

The kind of men we are?
Morally obligated?
Cherry???

Harlan closed his eyes. For the first time, he had to question why anyone would agree to do what Slipknot had proposed. Why would anybody of sound mind do so? This guy seemed to have found another war to fight.

Maybe. But at least he got results. At least he managed to do what you and the police have failed to do so far. This is what it takes.

"I'm pretty sure I know where Font and Cruise are," Slipknot continued. "I'll call you when I have further updates. Oh, and if you're worrying right now, don't. I'm on your side. I'm your guy. You're talking to an old pro, Joe. I've got your back. And, once this is done, we'll sit down and discuss our plans for the future. I think you and me can go places together, Mr. Senator... Mr. President."

The line went dead.

Mr. President?

What the fuck?

Harlan put the burner phone on his night table and went back to his relaxation exercises.

It was almost 2:00 a.m. before he finally fell into a welcome slumber.

CHAPTER SEVENTY-SIX

It was a calm day. A great day for a swim. So calm, in fact, that Roy was a bit worried that he might be seen floating near the end of the pier. He had removed the snorkel from his mask, then put on his mask and regulator and deflated his BCD slightly to keep most of his head underwater. Doing this had caused him to deplete air from his scuba tank, but he felt he'd have more than enough left to get the job done—should Getz appear.

8:00 a.m.

He was a little hungover and assumed that Getz would feel the same, which might keep him from his swim.

8:15 a.m.

No sign of Getz. Roy began the slow swim back out to the pick-up point. He stayed low in the water and waited for Susie to make her usual approach, checking for nearby boats. There were quite a few fishing boats heading out of the marina, but they all seemed to be heading east—out to deeper waters.

When Susie made her stop at the pick-up point, Roy kicked vigorously to get there quickly, clambered aboard and, as planned, stayed out of sight while Susie got the boat moving north to the dive spot they'd agreed to visit for the day.

The chat the night before with Getz had been stupid.

Really stupid.

But, to an outsider—to a witness—it could simply be written off as a chance encounter between Americans at a bar.

That morning, sober, they had weighed the pros and cons. They agreed that it had added risk, but they still felt it was safe to move forward with their plan.

After drying off, Roy joined Susie on the flybridge.

Their dive for the day was at a spot just off the Island of Formentor, a tiny island in the Bay of Pollença. After they were done, they headed back to Bon Aire Marina to refill Roy's tank with Felix. He told them that he was taking a group north over the top of the island to a dive called *Los Ojos de Eduardo* the next day, and if they wanted to tag along, they should arrive around 10:00 a.m. for the dive. He pulled up some pictures and emphasized that it was a great spot for both scuba and snorkeling, so Susie wouldn't be disappointed. They told Felix they would love to, and would raise him on the VHF when they were on their way.

After refilling the tank, they went to the grocer across the street and bought some cheese and charcuterie for dinner. Then, they headed back out to the *Altamira* and anchored just east of the Pollença Marina, as they had done two nights before.

"Whatcha thinking?" Susie asked as she finished laying out their meal.

"About David," Roy sighed. "We still have to decide what to do about Harlan."

"You really think he's behind it? I mean, it makes sense. Who else? It just seems really risky for a politician."

"Friends in low places, Suze. If a politician doesn't have them, who would?"

"True. So, what do we do? I mean, besides being careful. You can't very well hide forever. Hire security? We already have it at home. Maybe for the office?" she asked.

"I think our best move is just to call him to the carpet. Tell him that we know what he's up to, and that if anything happens to either of us, we know where he lives."

"You're going to call a Texas State Senator on the phone and threaten him with bodily harm? What if he records the call? That's jail time," Susie said.

"I'm thinking face to face," Roy said.

"Okay. When?"

"As soon as we get back. I think I still have his contact info from when he called me back when his kid *disappeared*." Roy checked the contacts in his iPhone. "Yep. Office phone. Mobile. Email. Got it all."

"I'd set it up now. The sooner the better. That way, he knows you're onto him."

Roy sat with his elbows on the table, composing an email to Senator Harlan using both thumbs.

Subject: Meeting November 5

Hello Senator Harlan,

I hope all is well.

My partner, David Kim, tells me that he ran into a friend of yours.

Small world.

Based on what they discussed, I think it would be mutually beneficial for you and me to sit down and chat. I will see you in your law office at 10:00 a.m. on November 5.

In the meantime, I've shared the topic of our meeting with my lawyer, just in case I can't make it for some reason.

Warmest regards,

Roy Cruise

Sent from my iPhone

CHAPTER SEVENTY-SEVEN

Tuesday
October 29, 2019
Miami, Florida

"Are you sitting down?" Detective Travers asked.

Eddie chuckled. He'd answered the phone only because it was Art Travers. Eddie was in the men's room at the police station.

"Somethin' like that, Tex."

"Well, this time you can't claim you're the last to know. Got the call just twenty-four hours ago. Tom Wise is dead. Apparent suicide."

"You've got to be fucking kidding!" Eddie said.

"Nope. Maid found him. Called 911. Given the address, dispatch called me up. Dead as a doornail," replied Travers.

"And you really think it was suicide?"

"Well, the toxicology points in that direction. The only anomaly is that one of his front teeth was chipped. Just barely. The M.E. picked up on it. They're taking a look up close to see if they can get an idea of what caused it. See if it's recent; waiting on a buccal swab. But, yeah. Bloodwork says alcohol and oxy. Enough to kill a horse. Left a note to his daughter and everything."

"Well, I'll be goddamned. So, here's some news for you. Surprise! Cruise is out of the country—in Spain with his wife. And his partner, David Kim, is *in the hospital*—hit and run. Also happened while Cruise was 'on vacation.' How are you—"

Eddie was interrupted by the sound of a toilet flushing in the next stall.

"Aw fuck, Garza! Are you in the crapper?"

"You know what they say, Art, 'when doodie calls....'" Eddie smirked. "Seriously, though, how are you for alibis? Had time to check?"

"You're disgusting, man." Travers sighed. "So, yeah... the daughter. I contacted her—to let her know. She was up in Fort Worth. Solid alibi.

"Also, I ran the plates on the car she took. An Audi. It ran through a couple of toll booths on the way up to Fort Worth two days before we found the body. Then, I've got the Audi hitting the same toll booths on the way back after I called her.

"Meanwhile, Senator Harlan was at dinner with a lawyer from his firm and a potential client at Eddie V's around the time of death. Still trying to tighten that up, but as of right now, it looks like the senator was having dessert when Tom expired."

"Pretty solid," Eddie muttered, musing. "Well, okay. Let me know if you hear anything interesting on that chipped tooth."

"Will do, but unless there's something really earth-shattering and conclusive, I think this one goes down as a selfie."

CHAPTER SEVENTY-EIGHT

Shaw sighed. He had a meeting scheduled for 11:00 a.m. and he was still waiting.

Although Shaw had been born and raised in Miami, he had gone to college up east, and while there he'd been introduced to the concept of punctuality. He found it so very practical—and loved to explain the concept to anyone in South Florida who would listen.

"The way it works is, two or more people agree to meet at a defined place at a specific time. And then, when that date and—most importantly—*that time* comes, *everyone* shows up!"

He had seen it in action. It was very efficient. Unfortunately, due to some as yet undiscovered natural or cultural phenomenon, the mechanics of punctuality broke down south of Fort Lauderdale.

Shaw was mentally calculating how much productive time was wasted annually on waiting in South Florida—assuming just one meeting per day where someone was 15 minutes late x 1 million workers x 260 work days per year... equals... almost 3 million man-days per year were wasted. Could that be right?

As Shaw redid the math, Detective Garza sauntered up to his desk.

"Hola, Shaw! Como estamos? You busy?"

Shaw looked at his watch and replied, "Nah. Waiting on someone."

"Well, guess who I just talked to?" Eddie asked, flopping down in a chair.

"Tell me."

"Art Travers, Austin PD." Eddie updated Shaw on their conversation.

"Holy shit," said Shaw. "Tom Wise dead..."

"You said you needed more. Well, now you have it." Eddie summarized, ticking off victims on his fingers, "In the last six weeks, Deb Wise—dead while Cruise was in Austin. Then Tom Wise and David Kim—the only two suspects on Joe Harlan Junior besides Cruise—one dies and the other almost. And those, while Cruise is OOC."

"OOC?"

"Out of country."

Shaw shook his head. "It's fucking weird. And I agree with you, it smells... bad. But, it'll be odd—the first time I ask for surveillance on a guy because two crimes were committed when he was *not* around... OOC."

"I thought about that." Eddie leaned forward, smiling. "Look—all these folks are connected to Harlan Junior. Someone killed Deb Wise. Someone ran over David Kim. Now, Tom Wise is dead—*possibly* suicide, maybe murder, but the M.E. is still looking at some stuff. Get the surveillance on Cruise as a precaution. In case he's next on the hit list. *To protect him.*"

Shaw had been listening, fingers steepled and against his mouth. Eddie could see his eyes light up at the idea.

"That," he pointed at Eddie, "I can sell."

* * *

Two hours later, Eddie was having a Cuban coffee at the counter of a little dive café. His mobile phone buzzed. It was Shaw.

"Done deal. By the end of the day today, we'll have cameras in place outside Cruise's house and his office so we can remotely track comings and goings. I've also got authorization to put live eyes on Cruise at our discretion. We'll have to see if and how we implement that once they're back in the country."

"Fantastic," said Eddie.

"I also took the liberty of alerting the CBP so that they'll inform us of any traveling our guy does. Per their records, Cruise and the little missus are due back this Thursday."

"This is great. Thanks, Shaw!" Eddie hung up, then did a discreet fist pump and said in a whisper, "Shock-and-Awe!"

CHAPTER SEVENTY-NINE

Liz had been spending most evenings with the senator.

It had been years since she'd felt so desired and desirable, and she was reluctant to leave Austin, even if it was only for a little while. She'd already rescheduled her return flight twice, just to spend more time with Joe—at his request. They'd really connected, bonded. Two grief-stricken parents with much in common. In fact, they found themselves on the same page on so many things, including the children. For the first time, she felt a small degree of certainty that there would be justice for Liam.

Joe had promised.

Presently, she was set to leave the next day, on Wednesday. She had delayed until now because she had one last loose end to follow-up on. She'd wanted to meet with Kristy Wise one more time and see if she'd managed to get anything out of her father.

And then Joe had called and told her the news.

Tom Wise had committed suicide.

While she was sympathetic, she was at the same time irritated that whatever the man may have known was gone forever. Unless Kristy had managed to extract it from him before he'd offed himself.

Liz wanted—no, she needed—to find out. But as much as she tried, she couldn't bring herself to do it. She remembered how she'd felt when Liam had died. Bereft. Inconsolable. This poor girl had lost both parents in less than a month.

Think about her.

She decided to let a little time pass before making contact.

In the meantime, she sent a large bouquet of flowers.

Dear Kristy,
So sorry for your loss. My deepest condolences. If you ever need to talk, please don't hesitate to reach out.
Liz Bareto

CHAPTER EiGHTY

When Harlan hung up with Liz and turned back to his computer, at the top of his inbox was an email from Roy Cruise. He opened and read it. As he did, his face fell. He felt a chill run down his spine.

Fuck. They're onto me. Goddammit!

Fucking Slipknot!

He pulled the burner phone out of his desk drawer—the drawer with the lock on it—and called Slipknot yet again.

No answer, yet again.

Harlan's stress level regarding the Wise suicide had somewhat diminished. He'd spoken with Travers. Thankfully, Wise's time of death seemed to coincide with Harlan's dinner meeting. He was in the clear as far as an alibi. Travers also hadn't indicated that Wise's death was anything other than a suicide. Nothing different had been reported in the news. Slipknot had apparently made a clean kill.

And yet, Slipknot going after Cruise was different.

On the one hand, given what Wise had confessed, Harlan very much wanted Slipknot to pay Cruise and his wife a visit. But even assuming that it had been them who'd killed Joe, they weren't fools. They had managed to get away with murder before.

People like that should not be underestimated.

And here's proof... son-of-a-bitch told his lawyer about "the topic of our meeting" in case he "can't make it."

"Doesn't make it" is more like it.

Shit. Shit. Shit.

From Cruise's email, it was clear that he had connected the attack on David Kim back to Harlan. Slipknot had dropped the ball there. He should have started at one end or the other. Either with Cruise and Kim or with Wise. Starting with Kim and leaving Cruise hanging out there had been a mistake. The good news was that Cruise's email to Harlan was cautious, discreet. He was coming to see Harlan in person. He didn't want to put anything in writing. No doubt, he would deny any connection to Joe's death. What else could he do?

But, if Slipknot got to him first, all bets were off. It could be a bluff, the thing about the lawyer... but Harlan couldn't run that risk. He had to get through to Slipknot. Get him to stand down.

He called him on the burner again.

No answer, again.

And, once again, Harlan violated their agreement and texted.

URGENT. ABORT.

CHAPTER EIGHTY-ONE

That same morning, Kristy arrived at Wells Fargo just after 9:00 a.m. with the key to safe deposit box number 227 in her pocket. She'd brought a backpack with her, as she had no idea what the box might contain. After a fifteen-minute wait, she was escorted into the vault. On the way there, she was shown three small private rooms where she could take her box and examine the contents.

Box 227 was mid-sized, 12" high x 8" wide x 24" deep. She removed it from the vault and took it into one of the private rooms, locking the door behind her. Then, she carefully opened it.

Inside, she found a handgun. A 9mm Glock. There were also two small plastic bags: one contained a syringe, and the other was empty, but with some sort of residue on the inside. It had contained something at some point—she imagined what, with some disgust. At the very back of the box, there was cash. Bundles of new hundred-dollar bills in ten-thousand-dollar stacks. In total, she counted one hundred thousand dollars.

Seeing the syringe, she was instantly reminded of Liz Bareto—the second autopsy, and the needle mark on her son's arm.

Was this *that* syringe? *Liam Bareto?*

The Glock. *Mom?*

If this was evidence of past crimes, why keep it? Why not destroy it? And who would have put it here? Her father? Her mother? For what purpose?

It could be used to inculpate them.

Or to inculpate others?

Possibly to exonerate others?

She thought for a few moments about the contents and

what to do with it all. Then, she removed the cash, being careful not to touch anything else. There was nothing under it. No note. No letter. No explanation.

She tilted the box gently, causing the other items to slide to the front of the box—and then out and into her backpack.

CHAPTER EIGHTY-TWO

Tuesday marked the fourth day that Susie and Roy headed out with hopes of killing Getz. At this point, the process was becoming routine: early start, dive gear, navigation.

Susie dressed quickly, then checked the weather. The meteorological conditions were the best indicator of how much activity there would be on the bay. Commercial boats were weather agnostic and went out every day through the bay into the Mediterranean. The leisure craft only went out in good weather—and, as they hung around in the bay, they were more likely to unwittingly witness something. It was going to be a cloudy start to the day, followed by lots of sunshine.

From the flybridge, everything looked quiet.

Given the calm, Roy forsook the snorkel. If the water by the pier was anywhere near as smooth as the other day, there was no point having the snorkel sticking up over his head like a flag marking his position.

At 6:30 a.m., they raised anchor and began the slow, haphazard troll over toward the pier. They had a little extra time, so Susie overshot well east of the pier to make the approach from the opposite side today, on the off chance that if someone was watching, they would see that there was no consistency between their early morning movements from day to day. Susie pulled the *Altamira* up to the drop point, making a slow 360° turn. As she did, Roy slipped out the back of the boat and into the water, jumping well away from the props. As soon as he hit the water, he sank. When he felt he had reached the nadir of his plunge, he released air from his BCD in order to maintain himself under water.

Then he began to slowly kick his way to his position at the end of the pier, just as he had every morning for the past few days. Once in position, he unwrapped the ten feet of black line from around his waist and began knotting and unknotting it.

Over the last few days, he'd noticed that, as he floated, waiting, his hands would begin to chill to the point of losing some dexterity. By looping and unlooping the line, he knew he could delay this.

There were small waves rolling through his position, so he felt comfortable coming up to the surface and maintaining watch above water, thus conserving air. In the meantime, Susie circled back toward the south in order to maneuver differently from how they had the previous mornings. Again, in case anyone was watching.

At 7:50 a.m., Roy felt the tension dissolve from his shoulders. The sun was beginning to rise. The window that they had for Getz's swim was ending.

He looked to his left, trying to spot the *Altamira* between the rise and fall of waves, so that he could start to position himself for pick-up. But when he turned back and looked to shore once again, adrenaline fired.

He saw a small figure near the roundabout across the street from the wooden boardwalk. Roy's heart raced. The sun was to his back, which meant the lone pedestrian was well-illuminated.

He watched with anticipation, hoping Susie was watching, as well. The figure made its way around the roundabout, then crossed the street and headed toward the beach. Roy could tell by the odd black skirt-looking-thing hanging from its waist that it was Getz, the top of his wetsuit hanging behind him like it had the first day Roy saw him.

As Roy watched Getz stop at the end of the wooden boardwalk, stretch, and prepare for his swim, he went over the plan in his mind. It was simple, really.

Roy would watch and wait as Getz swam out. After he'd passed by, Roy would swim out behind him and bump into him.

The idea of bumping Getz is something Roy stole from the hunting behavior of bull sharks. The tactic they use is called the "bump and bite." With their heads, they bump what they believe to be prey before attacking. Bull sharks have poor vision, but a keen sense of smell. Scientists speculate that they do the "bump and bite" to ensure that their target is soft, organic, and edible. Like a bull shark, after the bump, Roy would attack.

Before the bump, he would have looped the end of the ten feet of line into a cross constrictor knot. This is a knot known for its tight hold—one that is difficult, if not impossible, to remove once tied.

The plan was to bump Getz to stop and confuse him. Roy would loop one end of this knot around one of Getz's legs; the other would be looped to Roy's dive belt. Then, he would simply dive to the bottom and kick in order to swim rapidly forward.

There was no way Getz would be able keep up with Roy's swim speed—not with one leg tied to the line and Roy having the benefit of scuba fins. In theory, Roy would drag Getz feet-first behind him, making it impossible for Getz to reach him to defend himself. And, as long as Roy stayed near the bottom, Getz would be underwater, too. Between panic and struggle, thirty seconds should be enough for Getz to exhaust himself and drown.

And yet, as he thought through the details, Roy began to second-guess the plan. Could he get the knot around Getz's leg? Would he be able to dive deep enough to drown him? Would he be able to keep Getz far enough away from him to avoid a counterattack?

Roy closed his eyes, took a deep breath, and told himself that the second-thoughts were normal. The byproduct of adrenaline and an overly analytical mind.

Getz was about forty feet north of the pier when he hit the water and began swimming out to sea. Roy glided closer to the pier, watching Getz's strokes.

But then something unexpected happened. The farther Getz swam, the more he seemed to be steering toward the pier. At half the length of the pier, Getz was only twenty feet away from it. At that rate, he was on a trajectory to swim right up to Roy.

Getz would surely see him.

Roy reacted quickly. He began to softly kick himself toward

shore to get out of the way. This had the added benefit of the water being murkier toward shore, lots of sediment kicking up as waves came and went. As morning hadn't yet developed into day, the sun was at a sharp angle to the water. Between that and the murkiness, it would be difficult for Getz to see him coming.

Anyone watching would have seen Getz swimming out on an angle toward the end of the pier and Roy kicking in the opposite direction. They passed one another at about three quarters of the length of the pier—with barely fifteen feet between them.

Once Getz was safely past, Roy turned around and began to follow him, swimming just below the surface. He had the regulator in his mouth and was breathing as slowly as he could in order to consume less air.

When Getz reached the end of the pier, Roy was twenty feet behind him and closing. He raised his head out of the water and looked around to make sure that there were no boats in the area.

Nothing.

He resumed kicking, accelerating to catch up with his quarry. Just past the end of the pier now, Getz made a hard right turn. Roy pulled up, thinking that he'd been spotted, but Getz kept swimming at the same pace, now parallel to shore.

Getz was apparently going to swim out, around the pier, parallel to shore for some distance, and then back. That meant that, in terms of distance, the end of the pier was about as far out as Getz was going. It also meant that, as far as visibility from shore and witnesses were concerned, that was the optimal point for attack.

Roy raised his head one more time. Still no boats nearby.

It was go time.

CHAPTER EIGHTY-THREE

Roy looped the cross-constrictor knot for probably the thousandth time since devising this plan. The loops came easily. He made sure to make them large enough that it would be easy to get them over a foot and onto Getz's leg. The tail end of the line was attached to his dive belt.

The water was dark near shore, and though the sun was rising by the minute, underwater visibility remained poor. This worked to Roy's advantage since it meant he would have the element of surprise, although it also meant he would be working blind, by feel more than sight. He drained more air from his BCD and sank to about eight feet. He lined up with Getz's path, but on a parallel about fifteen feet further out from shore. Once he got up past Getz's slipstream, he could see him relatively clearly.

He ran through the plan one more time in his head, then decided to go for it. He increased the pace of his kicking, accelerating, and simultaneously adjusted his path, setting himself on a collision course with his prey. When he was about three feet away, he extended his right arm about three quarters of full, kicked hard to accelerate even more, and then, just before impact, used his upper body and shoulder to deliver a solid blow with his open palm—just below Getz's left floating ribs.

The contact rattled Roy's arm. Getz made a strange sound that carried underwater.

Immediately after the impact, Roy drained his BCD and exhaled, submerging to the bottom, which was about twelve feet underwater. A bit too far. Getz's feet were about three feet above Roy's head, where he was treading water with a hand on his ribs.

Roy kicked up toward Getz, grasping the loops in the end of the line with both hands and creating a ring into which he had to place one of Getz's feet. As he came up, he saw the man's head come down into the water in an attempt to see what had hit him. Roy exhaled, sending a curtain of bubbles up into Getz's face.

Then, like a predator, Roy rose following the bubbles.

Roy spotted and focused on Getz's left foot. He continued to kick and rise, and grabbed the foot with his left hand. He pulled on it, bringing his chest level with the foot, and twisted his body into Getz, which allowed him to lock Getz's lower leg under his right armpit. He felt the man's fists pummel his back and shoulder, and sensed, or perhaps even imagined, Getz in a panic, trying to understand what was attacking him.

With the man's leg lodged under this arm, Roy was able to slip the loop around his foot and pull tight. Then he released and slipped away, kicking hard. As he did, he felt Getz's hand claw against his head, ripping at his scuba mask.

It came halfway off.

Roy grabbed at it and was just able to keep from losing it entirely as he kicked and swam downward. He finally felt himself separate from his quarry, and then a moment later felt a sharp pull at his waist as the line went taut with Getz at the other end.

Roy began counting.

He kicked harder and felt the weight of the body he was dragging behind him. Roy had his eyes open underwater. He was clutching the scuba mask in his right hand and holding on to the line at his belt with his left. He felt resistance as Getz struggled like a hooked fish against the line. Undeterred, Roy dove and kicked and fought to skim the bottom as best he could, but it was difficult to see without the mask, and he'd become disoriented during the struggle. He thought he was swimming away from the shoreline, but wasn't certain.

Instinct kicked in. To be safe, Roy began to swim in a circle, about thirty feet around if he was right. The last thing he wanted to do was find that he was swimming back to shore and then end up in shallow water with Getz attached to him.

He briefly considered trying to put the mask back on, but at the speed he was kicking, even if he managed it with his one free hand, it would be difficult to clear it enough to be able to see. So, he just kept on swimming.

He'd counted to ten, and Getz continued to struggle against him. He reached fifteen and still the struggling continued. He kicked harder, trying to make it impossible for Getz to snatch a breath.

He was pretty sure that Getz was fully submerged. He wanted to stop to see if Getz had his head above water, but he couldn't, as doing so would release the tension on the line and give the man more room to maneuver. Instead, Roy turned and rolled the line once around his left arm, coiling it and shortening the distance between them while at the same time dragging his victim deeper beneath the surface.

The count had now reached twenty. He was still kicking furiously, but was no longer sure if the resistance he felt was Getz struggling, or simply his body weight.

To be sure, he continued to kick until his count reached thirty-five.

At forty seconds, while still kicking, Roy turned on his side so that he could look up and behind him at Getz as he slightly slowed his pace. Getz's body seemed to be dragging behind him. Roy let go of the line, leaving it to drag only from his belt, and used both his hands to adjust his scuba mask and clear it so he could see better. He continued kicking, just in case.

There was Getz, dragging up and behind Roy, dead. His arms were floating up behind his head—at least two feet under the water's surface, which was now glowing like a liquid mirror in the morning sun.

Roy was about to stop kicking when he heard a sound like the hum of a pipe hitting a metal barrel, and everything went black.

CHAPTER EIGHTY-FOUR

When Roy regained consciousness, his right ear was ringing, his mask was partly filled with sea water, and he was drifting.

Coughing, gagging, he adjusted the mask and cleared it, and then tried to orient himself. He was floating upwards. Getz's corpse was floating nearby, his head and shoulders at the surface of the water.

Roy drained the BCD and sank to the bottom, pulling Getz with him. He landed gently on his knees right next to a shell and barnacle-encrusted piling.

He'd run into the fucking pier, head-first. Thankfully, it was a calm day and the sea hadn't battered him into the pilings. He cleared his head and swam slowly away from the pier. He checked himself. He might have a few cuts. He wasn't sure; his body was numb from the cold water.

Fuck.

Roy spotted a patch of seagrass that appeared to be deeper than the surrounding area and dove down toward it, dragging the body with him. He reached the bottom and turned toward the corpse. Getz had lost his swimming goggles in the struggle. His eyes were wide open. The expression on his face was one of terror.

He was definitely dead.

The depth gauge on Roy's arm read four meters—about twelve feet. This was about as deep a patch underwater as he'd seen in his swims. As good a spot as any. Roy pulled the body down toward him. He took up the slack in the line and wedged it between his knee and the sandy bottom, thus keeping Getz floating upright next to him while freeing both his hands. Then he pulled out his dive knife and carefully cut the top loop on the line that was tied to Getz's leg while holding the other end in his hand. He was careful not to cut into the corpse.

The line came free.

Getz's body floated upright next to Roy, his head now about seven feet underwater. Roy pulled gently, slowly bringing the body into a horizontal floating position next to him, just above the seabed. Drowning had forced all of the air out of Getz's lungs and replaced it with water. There wasn't enough air left inside the corpse to make it float upward.

He examined the spot where the line had been attached. There was some slight bruising. He pulled the body toward him and removed a set of goggles from a small pouch he was carrying. He had anticipated that Getz might lose his goggles in the struggle, so he carefully replaced the missing pair.

He pushed the body to the bottom of the patch of seagrass, then moved slowly away and watched. The body stayed there, swaying gently as it was rocked by the movement of the sea. He counted to sixty. The body did not float upwards. It didn't go anywhere, though a couple of small fish came up to it and began nibbling around Getz's ears and hair.

Roy turned. He could see the end of the pier, so he knew which way to go to rendezvous with Susie. He reached up to touch his head, which stung, and watched a small cloud of red drift in front of his eyes. He was bleeding. Not much, but he'd definitely been cut.

He took one last look at Getz before kicking himself away from the corpse and out to sea. He checked his gauge; he still had over half a tank of air. Plenty. Then he checked his watch: 8:07 a.m. Approximately fifteen minutes had passed since he'd first seen Getz onshore. It felt like an hour, but, thankfully, it was over.

Roy surfaced. The *Altamira* was about two hundred yards to his right. He replaced the mask, dove, and swam.

The plan, once Susie spotted Getz, had called for her to wait about 300 meters southwest of the end of the pier. As they hadn't known exactly where Roy would make contact, it would be simpler for him to come to her than vice versa.

That part of the plan worked perfectly.

About three minutes after spotting the boat, Roy tapped sharply on the bottom of the hull with a dive tool in order to let Susie know he was coming aboard. He clambered up the swim ladder and into the back of the boat, where Susie was ready to help him with his tank.

"What the fuck did you do to your head?"

"How bad is it?"

"It's just all scraped up. Did he get to you?"

"No. I had a head-on with the fucking pier! He knocked my mask off and I almost lost it. So, I was swimming blind. I—"

"Save it," she interrupted him. "We're getting distracted. Let me get us away from here first," she said, leaving him and heading up top.

A moment later, the boat began trolling slowly east away from shore. Roy got out of his gear and checked his head in the mirror. It was a nasty scrape. His hair was matting with blood.

He retrieved the first aid kit and held a bandage against his head to stop the bleeding. They were moving slowly to the east. Susie came back in. "I've got us on autopilot, heading straight out. Seven knots. Let me see your head." She checked it, then poured some peroxide on a piece of gauze and dabbed.

"When was your last tetanus shot?"

Roy laughed. "Fuck if I know."

Susie folded and pressed a piece of gauze against his crown to stop the bleeding, then left him to hold it while she went up top again and altered course, taking them back out to El Quesito. When they arrived, they were the only boat on site. They dove into the water and swam around while they waited for others to arrive.

It was thirty minutes before another boat dropped anchor, carrying four more divers.

Susie and Roy made a big show of getting out of the water and checking Roy's head. Enough of a show that one of the other boat's divers—who said his name was Roberto—shouted across to ask if they needed help.

Susie noted that the boat was called *Victoria*.

She explained—gestured—that Roy had hit his head while swimming under one of the many overhangs that El Quesito was known for, but that it wasn't bad. Roberto laughed knowingly and gave her a thumbs-up.

They finished at El Quesito at 9:30 a.m. and set a course north to meet up with Felix at Los Ojos de Eduardo.

CHAPTER EIGHTY-FIVE

Roy was floating. Weightless. He was seventy feet underwater. He and Susie had reached El Ojo de Eduardo just behind Felix and his crew. They'd greeted each other and then Roy followed Felix into the water. Susie elected to stay on board as this was a deeper dive and there was little to be seen snorkeling.

You can tell a dive pro by their efficiency. Felix used minimal energy to navigate his way around and guide them through the dive zone. He looked like a jellyfish on Xanax—moving slowly, effortlessly.

Roy made sure to maintain the dive enthusiast façade, taking copious amounts of pictures and video with his GoPro even though his head still hurt. As they ascended back to the surface at the end of the dive, he saw Susie diligently swimming around and taking photos of the rock formations and schools of fish.

The dive was completed at 11:15 a.m.

While Felix had one of his assistants help the divers remove and stow their gear on the *Skualo Alcúdia* RIB, he came aboard the *Altamira* to have a look around. Roy and Susie had told him about their charter, but he had yet to see her first-hand.

After a tour of the boat, the three of them sat on the swim platform—Felix and Roy drinking beer—to chat. As they did, Felix told him about another dive site east of Cap de Catalunya. It was a deeper dive, intermediate to advanced level.

Susie was quick to say that Roy needed to take a break, given the dent on his head. As the following day was their last day on the water, Susie and Roy debated back and forth what to do. In the end, they decided to "call it" as far as diving was concerned. That settled, Felix offered to take their gear back with him, so that all they'd need do was stop by after they dropped off their boat to pick up their deposit. They shook on it and helped the young man put their gear on his RIB boat. Then, Felix and company headed off to the southwest, back to Bon Aire Marina.

Meanwhile, Susie and Roy started up the *Altamira* and headed north to the small bay at Cala Sant Vicenç. While they motored north, Roy rehashed the play-by-play of how he had lassoed Getz and drowned him. There'd been no joy in it. As with Harlan, the murder had been clinical. Roy was analyzing the decisions he had made, and changes to the plan that he'd implemented in the fog of murder.

Once they dropped anchor at Cala Sant Vicenç, for the first time since they'd spent the night at the marina, Susie and Roy were able to relax. They took a leisurely swim in to shore and secured a table at the restaurant overlooking the beach.

"Tomorrow, we'll take *Altamira* back to the Port of Alcúdia. Then we need to go by the Skualo Alcúdia—"

"Why don't we leave Felix the deposit as a tip? One less stop?" Susie suggested.

"Good idea. Then we just have to pick up our checked bags at Son Brüll. Tomorrow, we spend the night in Palma so we can get to the airport early. Then, Mallorca to Madrid, Madrid to Miami."

Roy took in the view. Beautiful. The water—because the bay was shallow and sandy—was a bright blue color that reminded him of the Bahamas. He breathed in the salty ocean air.

Spain was nice.

The Mediterranean was great.

But, the Caribbean was paradise.

PART FOUR

Billy Applegate
1989

In the end, Billy had put the gun back in the drawer in his father's desk, where it belonged. But, before he had, he'd sworn an oath—he would make destroying that monster his life's work. Not by killing him—that was too quick, too good for him. Instead, he would expose him for what he was.

Billy slept off the booze and drove up the coast the next day to spend Thanksgiving with his mother and Aunt Brenda.

He was a man on a mission.

And, eight long years later, Billy was on the cusp of his first act of revenge.

Martin's Tavern in Georgetown opened in 1933 on the corner of Wisconsin Avenue and N Street NW. The restaurant has the distinction of having served every U.S. president from Harry Truman to George Bush. They mark this history at Martin's with little bronze plaques in booths where various presidents have sat.

The restaurant was full on this particular night—April 8, 1989—although that was par for the course. It was a popular spot to see and be seen.

Billy Applegate was sitting in a booth—the Richard Nixon booth.

It was almost 7:00 p.m., and his dates were running late.

Both of them, thankfully.

Billy was nursing a club soda with lime when he spotted a man in a navy blue suit, white shirt, and red power tie approaching his booth. His wavy blond hair bobbed as he nodded at Billy. Plain shirt cuffs—no cufflinks—peeked out from under his suit jacket, his left wrist sporting a Timex Ironman watch as he placed his hands on the table to help him slide into the booth across from Billy.

"Evening, Billy."

"How are you, Sam?"

"I'm good. Good."

Billy's guest seemed edgy. There was sweat on his forehead, which seemed odd in April unless the man had jogged there. He watched as Sam loosened his tie, and continued.

"Let's get this done quickly. I don't know why I agreed to this place. I don't need to be seen with you." He looked around the restaurant yet again, confirming that no one he knew was there.

"Relax, man. We went to high school together. Nothing strange about old friends getting a beer and catching up. Anyway, how are things at the Department of Justice?"

Sam pulled a face. "I've got it here, with me. But I have to have your word. One hundred percent anonymous. Deal?"

Billy leaned forward and smiled earnestly. "Sam, come on, you know I would go to jail before revealing a source. I swear it. On my father's grave."

His guest looked him in the eye, and Billy could see the cogs turning.

"You want something to drink? Beer?" Billy asked, looking over his shoulder and raising his arm to get the waitress's attention.

"No. I'm good."

"Come on. It'll look weird if you just pop in and out. What'll you have?"

"Seriously, nothing."

The waitress appeared. Billy looked at his watch, then said to her, "Yeah, could I get another one of these and a glass of champagne, please?"

The waitress cocked her head at Billy's tablemate, then headed off to fetch their order.

"Don't worry. It's not for you," Billy said as he turned back to Sam, who was pulling his hand out of his suit jacket pocket and looking furtively around the restaurant.

"I'm out on a limb here, Billy. There's a solid case here. The guy's a crook. But, it's not going anywhere. The call came down—to kill the investigation. Bury it all. It's bullshit, man. Fuckin' politics. Not what I signed up for."

"Sunlight is a great disinfectant," Billy replied, quoting a Supreme Court Justice.

Sam nodded, and then he carefully slipped an object under the menu in front of him. "It's all there, man. Everything I could get. Look through it. See what you think. This shit is just wrong and I don't know any way to stop it other than—well, you said it, to shine a light on it. But, remember—" he stared Billy in the eyes, his voice quivering slightly, "that's my fucking career on that disc."

Billy nodded. "Okay. Okay. I get it. Dude, relax. I take this stuff very seriously. You have my word. This won't come back to you."

Sam observed him for a few more seconds before nodding. Then, he stood up abruptly. "I need to go. I'll catch you later."

Billy watched Sam leave before turning his attention to the menu. He pushed it aside, revealing a 3.5" floppy disk which he picked up and slipped into his pocket. His heart was racing. He couldn't wait to get back to his computer and review the contents of the disk. He looked at his watch and wondered whether maybe he should cancel his date and head back home.

As he did, he sensed movement behind him and turned to see a woman with shoulder-length dark hair and light brown eyes. She was in an ecru silk blouse tucked into a navy skirt. Her tanned legs ended in navy blue pumps that added two inches to her height, which Billy estimated must be around 5' 7".

She was… amazing.

"William?"

Billy stood quickly. "Hi, uh, yes," he stammered. "That's me. But you can call me Bill. Or Billy, of course. Um, you must be Catherine," he said, offering his hand.

Her skin was soft, her grip solid. She wore her watch on her right wrist; it was a lady's stainless-steel Rolex.

She smiled and, to Billy, the whole room lit up.

"Catherine Jane, actually. Everyone calls me C.J."

"Please, have a seat," Billy indicated.

As they took their seats, his date took in the table, then commented, "Ooh. The Nixon booth. Lisa said you were a journalist. Very *apropos*."

"Oh. Yeah. There's a lot of history in this place. Um, the story is that Kennedy proposed to Jackie in Booth Three." Billy turned, gesturing with his head. "Right over there."

Billy felt himself blush. *Did I really just bring up marriage? Dude, get your shit together!*

His date looked over at Booth Three, her thick lips parted slightly and her eyes wide. Then she turned back to him. Billy was about to say something when the waitress appeared and placed the club soda and flute of champagne on the table.

"A lot cuter than your last date," she quipped, then turned and left with wry smile.

C.J. raised an eyebrow, and asked, "Your last date?"

Billy felt himself sinking into the earth.

CHAPTER EIGHTY-SIX

Wednesday
October 30, 2019
Austin, Texas

Harlan was sleeping late. Well, late for him. It was just past 8:00 a.m. Three-and-a-half hours later than he usually slept.

It was Wednesday, and he hadn't managed to get to sleep before two in the morning. Unusual for a man who was early to bed and early to rise, but then, he hadn't brought a woman home in a while either.

He awoke remembering the night before. He could smell Liz's perfume in the room, on the pillows and on him. He turned to see her slender, naked shoulders peeking out from under the sheets. By the sound of her heavy breathing, she was still sound asleep. She was flying back to Miami later that day, and Harlan was going to miss her.

What a night!

It had been a long time since he'd had sex like that. And he wasn't one to deny himself carnal pleasures, but this woman… she was something different. She was enthusiastic, creative, experienced. The memory of the night before was making him hard again. He began to reposition himself, entertaining the thought of snuggling up to her from behind and giving her a breakfast sausage surprise, when he heard his phone vibrating on the night table.

It was his regular phone.

He picked it up.

UKNOWN

Harlan hated calls from blocked numbers. He didn't usually answer them.

But it was odd, getting one at this time of day. Telemarketers usually called in the evenings.

He decided to take the call, quietly. Besides, it gave him an excuse to get out of bed. He wasn't used to sharing his bed, and his back was killing him. If Liz woke, he would impress her by pretending he was talking to someone important. Harlan always felt the need to impress.

He got up and padded to the bathroom, his semi-hard dick swinging like a divining rod leading the way.

"Hello?"

"Senator Joe Harlan?"

"Speaking."

There was a short pause, then a click.

"Please hold for the President of the United States."

Harlan was standing over his toilet with his dick in his hand, getting ready to pee. He froze, and then he quickly and quietly closed the bathroom door. He stood there, fully naked in front of the mirror. His hair was a matted mess; he had sleep in his eyes and stubble on his face.

He imagined the President sitting at the Resolute Desk in the Oval Office—crisp white shirt, red tie, orange face, signature blond hair.

What a contrast. He reached out for a hand towel and modestly covered his privates.

"Good morning, Joe. I hope I'm not calling too early."

Harlan knew the voice. The cadence. The tone. There was no mistaking it. This was the real deal.

"Not at all, sir," he said in his deepest, most alert voice.

"Good. Listen, Joe. Got a job for you. A big job. Huge job. Huge. Critical. Critical to our national security. You've got the background. You've got the skills. You've been vetted. I think you'll be great for it. The best. I know you won't let me down."

"Sir, I'm honored. However I can be of service."

"I knew I could count on you. It's off-book. Spy stuff.

Top secret. I need someone I can trust to run it. Someone who can deliver. Someone with the background. I'm counting on you, Joe. Can I count on you, Joe?"

"Absolutely, sir."

"Good. Good. You'll have to quit the Senate. Health concerns. Those days are done. I'm going to have someone from the NSA contact you with details." The President's voice dropped in volume as he turned away from the phone and spoke to someone who was with him. "Who's going to contact him? Peters? Alex Peters? Are you sure? I thought it was the other guy? The one with the mole on his face. You're sure? Okay. Okay. Peters." He spoke to Harlan again, "You got that, Joe? Peters. Alex Peters."

"Alex Peters, sir. Got it."

"This is big, Joe. Critical to our success. We're going to make America great again, Joe. I'm glad I can count on you."

"Yes, sir. Thank you, sir."

The line went dead.

Holy shit.

CHAPTER EIGHTY-SEVEN

There had been complaints.

Of course, they hadn't been worded that strongly, given everything Kristy had been through, but she knew that's what they were—complaints. Mainly from her Aunt Charlotte.

Why the rush?

Shouldn't you wait until later in the week?

So that everyone has time to plan?

Having Tom's funeral so soon after he'd died and on such short notice made it difficult for family to attend. That was the point, though, as far as Kristy was concerned. Kristy loved her parents—both of them. But while she tried to see things from her father's perspective, she couldn't. Her mother had apparently arranged for the murder of the man who had raped Kristy. While Kristy herself may not have taken things that far, she could understand her mother doing so. But she simply couldn't understand what her father had done.

She had just been through the whole funereal process with her mother. A second funeral—with the rosary, the mass, the wake, the condolences—she really didn't need. And she didn't want to have to hear again and again what a "good man" her father had been.

Kristy had heeded the adage that *Funerals are for the living.*

She was fed up. She was tired of funerals and wanted to get on with her life. So, she'd condensed the entire process. No rosary. Service at the gravesite, with the wake immediately following.

Now, she was in her father's—in her—home office sitting at her desk, trying to decide if this space made any sense for her. It was a clunky old oak desk. It wasn't ergonomically designed for computer use. Kristy had a small, stand-up desk in her room that was much more comfortable.

She put her feet up on the desk and slowly savored a non-fat yogurt. Bethany was seated across from her in a chair facing the desk. They had hardly spoken at all since Kristy had learned of Tom's death. Kristy had wanted some time alone to grieve and figure things out—and to get everything organized. Now, she finally felt that she was in a place where she could use Bethany's support and advice.

Kristy had just gotten back from meeting with the estate lawyers and was updating Bethany. "So, I thought I was screwed, you know? I mean, the cops say Dad committed suicide. I don't believe it, but..." she shrugged, taking a spoonful of yogurt, "until there's proof to the contrary, that's the deal.

"But apparently, the life insurance wouldn't have paid out for suicide for the first two years after the policy was purchased, but after that, it pays in full. And this policy is like seven years old." She paused. "So, ten million."

"Thank God, Kris! I mean, this is all horrible, but at least you don't have to worry about money for a while, you know?"

Kristy nodded. "No shit. Pringle has it all worked out with the insurance company. There's still taxes to be paid and stuff, but once it's all said and done, I'll own the house free and clear along with some real estate investments, and there should be about six million cash left to go in the bank."

"Fuck, girl."

Kristy stood and went to the kitchen to get another yogurt. She had skipped lunch and she was starving.

On the kitchen island were several bouquets of flowers that had already arrived, including one from the Rosens and one from Liz Bareto.

"What're you gonna do about her?" Bethany asked as she admired the bouquet from Liz and adjusted the position of several of the flowers.

"Dunno. I feel awful for her," Kristy replied as she took another yogurt from the fridge. "What happened to her son isn't right, but there's not much I can do, I guess. Maybe try to give her a little peace of mind?"

Bethany had been standing with her back to the kitchen counter. While Kristy had replied, she'd put both hands behind her and hopped up to sit on the counter facing Kristy, legs dangling. Now, she cocked her head to the side and asked, "Peace of mind how?"

Kristy stood silently for a bit, then said, "I know what happened. Not everything. But bits and pieces."

Kristy told Bethany about the journal. That her mother had probably killed Liam Bareto. That Susie and Roy had probably killed Harlan. That her father had been responsible for the dick on the door. And that her father had confessed to killing her mother. Lastly, she went to the study and came back with a sheet of paper and showed Bethany the letter that Deb had written to Susie.

Bethany read it mostly to herself, though she read some parts aloud.

"...I've been fortunate to have found love, and to have been loved in return. You know what I mean.

"...I will always love you, no matter where I am."

Bethany looked at Kristy and cocked an eyebrow. "Dude. No offense, but... does that sound... platonic to you?"

Kristy shrugged and indicated with her head for Bethany to keep reading, which she did.

After reading several more lines, Bethany paused and said, "Oh shit." Then she read from the letter with emphasis.

"I'm glad that I was able to help you out when you needed it. And I thank you from the bottom of my heart for returning the favor."

"There's more," Kristy said.

Bethany nodded and kept reading. *"If you can, keep an eye on Kristy for me.*

"She's not like us.

"She's fragile.

"What the fuck—fragile? You," Bethany pointed at Kristy with the letter, "are not fragile."

"Apparently that's what my mom thought about me." Kristy curled her lip.

Bethany shook her head, a look of disgust on her face. "That is so unfair."

Kristy nodded in agreement. "Anyway. I'm taking your advice. Bought a ticket. I'm going to Miami. Gonna just… ring the doorbell and surprise her. And get the complete story. Face to face."

"You think she'll talk?"

"All this bullshit cost me my mom. And now my dad. I think she owes it to me to fill in the blanks, don't you?"

CHAPTER EIGHTY-EIGHT

Susie and Roy navigated from Cala Sant Vicenç straight over to the Port of Alcúdia, completely bypassing the Bay of Pollença on their way back. After returning the *Altamira* to the charter agent, they drove their Fiat back to Son Brüll to pick up their remaining luggage, which fit in the Fiat now that they had returned their scuba gear.

They'd decided to pass on picking up the deposit at Skualo Alcúdia. Roy texted Felix, saying that they really appreciated all his help and wanted for him to keep the hundred-euro deposit as a "thank you" for all the great diving advice.

Then they headed back to Palma for a treat. They stayed in town at the best boutique hotel in the city of Palma—Posada Terra Santa. It was within walking distance of everything, had an amazing and attentive staff, was known for hosting celebrities, and was equally well-known for its discretion. Many other hotels in Palma imitated, but none duplicated, the quality of Posada Terra Santa.

Their last full day in Mallorca, Roy checked the local papers and even watched the local news after lunch to see if there was any news regarding Getz.

There was nothing.

Before dinner, Susie and Roy decided to get a drink and take a stroll through the Barrio Gótico of Palma—the old town center. They were walking along a small side street filled with bars and restaurants when Roy stopped, staring.

Susie followed his gaze, and there it was, inside a small bar, on the television. A tarp on a beach—police and civil guards. The caption: *Cuerpo muerto recuperado en playa de Pollença. Dead body found on the beach in Pollença.*

The two walked quickly back to their hotel, where they turned on the TV in their room and scanned channels until they found it.

Getz's body had been found. Neighbors had identified the dead man as former U.S. Congressman Jeff Getz. Initial indications were that the man had drowned, but the police—the civil guards—were not ruling out foul play, pending an autopsy.

"Shit."

CHAPTER EIGHTY-NINE

Thursday
October 31, 2019
Palma de Mallorca, Spain

Roy didn't sleep the night before their departure. He couldn't. Their flight from Mallorca to Madrid was at 9:00 a.m. They'd known it was possible that the body would be recovered, but they had expected it to take longer.

"His fucking lungs were full of water, Suze. Nothing there to make him float."

"Well, something did. The wake from a boat or something," Susie replied. Then she added, "*How* doesn't really matter. The problem is that your 'recognition lag-time' is gone. They've got him, and if they suspect foul play, they're going to be asking questions."

Roy's adrenaline spiked as they made their way through outbound immigration. The officer appeared to have a problem with his passport, and had to "make a call." Eventually and mercifully, he returned the passport and waved them on.

As they sat on the airplane in Mallorca waiting to depart for Madrid, Roy felt an altogether different feeling. One of immense relief. He smiled at Susie, and then kissed her hand and held it during takeoff before falling asleep to the drone of the engines for most of the one-hour flight to Madrid.

The flight to Madrid was uneventful, and as they'd already passed outbound immigration in Mallorca, they were home free. While waiting to board the Miami flight, Roy checked email. His heart skipped when he saw that he'd received a reply from Senator

Harlan about his planned November visit. Just three words: *See you then.*

He was about to show Susie the message when he felt a tap on his shoulder. He turned to see an official of some sort—uniform, badge, the whole nine yards.

Aw, fuck....

"May I please ask you to come with me, sir?" the man asked in very slightly accented English.

Roy stood and the man added, "Is either of these yours?", pointing to two computer bags on the floor next to him and Susie. Roy carried his computer bag and followed the man to a second screening station near their gate. He was asked to put his suitcase through a second scan.

While they watched the bag go through the machine, the officer asked, "How did you enjoy your time in Spain?"

"Very nice. We had a good trip," Roy replied.

"Where were you—in Spain?"

"We went to Madrid, Zaragoza, Barcelona, and then to Mallorca."

"Oh really?" The officer turned toward Roy. "Which part of Mallorca?"

Roy felt his nuts tighten. He fought not to swallow and to appear nonchalant. "We flew into Palma and then we chartered a boat in Alcúdia."

The officer nodded. "May I see your passport, please?"

Roy handed it over, and the man flipped through checking pages. "It is interesting that you were in Mallorca," he said, looking up from the passport. "I am from Manacor."

Roy smiled. "Home of Rafa Nadal, no?"

The man laughed and handed back the passport. "That is correct. You are well-informed, for an American."

"Do you need something further?" asked Roy.

The officer smiled. "No. Just a random check. Thank you for your patience."

The flight from Madrid to Miami took a little over nine hours. They were flying business class. Roy had a bit of a start when one of the male flight attendants offered him champagne while wearing a clown nose. Roy hated clowns. The rubber red nose gave him the creeps. But, it was Halloween, after all. He laughed it off.

They landed ahead of schedule, and after a thirty-minute drive, they finally reached home.

Sanctuary.

The neighborhood was decorated for Halloween: corpses hanging from trees, giant pumpkins in front yards, and ghouls peering out fake candlelit windows. Once they got home, they left their luggage in the foyer and headed into their kitchen for a snack. The food on the plane was miserable and they were famished.

Susie opened the sliding glass door to the terrace to air out the house and set the table on the veranda. Roy put together a light charcuterie plate which they shared while chatting about their trip and enjoying the view.

They were interrupted a couple of times by the doorbell. Trick-or-treaters. Susie, always the planner, had bought candy for the occasion before they'd left for Spain. Roy handed out candies from a large plastic jack-o-lantern bucket.

When bedtime arrived in Miami, their biological clocks were still on Spanish time—5:30 a.m. Almost time to wake up. They decided to watch a little *Killing Eve* in the family room before heading to bed—to unwind. A light breeze blew in from the terrace and through the house, cooling the room.

Roy poured himself a scotch and brought Susie a glass of sparkling water instead of her usual white wine. She pretended to look put out at the difference in drinks, but she couldn't hide the smile spreading across her face.

After all the effort they had gone through to have their first child. After all the pain Camilla's death had brought them.

A new baby. New promise. A new beginning.

The alcohol, the jetlag, the emotional crash after what they'd done in Mallorca—Roy was overwhelmed to the point that tears started rolling down his face before he even had a chance to register them. He reached out and held his wife.

The doorbell rang, yet again. Susie smiled and kissed Roy.

He popped up off the sofa and grabbed the jack-o-lantern, grinning from ear to ear, and almost skipped to the door.

When he pulled the front door open, he found himself face to face with what looked to be some sort of weird albino leprechaun. Small, completely bald, wearing round spectacles and a green leather jacket. Roy looked behind and around him for trick-or-treating children.

That was when he noticed the gun the man was pointing at his chest.

CHAPTER NINETY

Slipknot stepped into Susie and Roy's foyer and closed the door behind him. He gestured with the gun, toward the back of the house where the TV blared. Roy retreated, slowly, hands out away from his body and up at shoulder level, showing that he was defenseless and unarmed.

Susie was still sitting on the couch where Roy had left her, and had just started to speak when the words died in her mouth. "Honey, how many kids..."

Roy remained silent. He had a good sense of who this guy was, and he believed he had nothing to gain by showing his hand. He decided to let him speak first; let him run the show.

With his left hand, the stranger unzipped the fanny pack on his hip and pulled out a handful of zip ties held together with a small rubber band. He tossed them at Roy. They hit him in the chest and fell to the floor.

"Pick 'em up, and have the little lady zip-tie you to that chair over by the wall."

Roy bent slowly, keeping his eyes on the intruder, and did as he was told.

Susie quietly zip-tied Roy's ankles, one to each leg of the chair, and then attached his arms to the arm rests.

"Tighter, honey. I don't want to have to shoot you."

Roy nodded at Susie, and she began to re-tighten all the ties so that they were snug, beginning with his arms and then moving to his legs.

As she finished doing this and before she had a chance to get to her feet and face him, Slipknot took two quick steps forward and cracked her on the back of the head with the butt of his gun.

Roy tried to shout a warning, but it came too late. She crumpled in a heap at his feet.

"You motherfucker! I swear to God, you touch her again and I'll kill you!"

Slipknot grabbed a handful of Susie's hair and dragged her away from where she'd fallen, leaving her a good ten feet in front of her husband's chair.

As he did, Roy shouted, "She's pregnant, you son-of-a-bitch! You hurt her or the baby and you'll wish you'd never been born!"

Slipknot said nothing. Instead, while facing Roy, he quickly zip-tied Susie's hands together, then her feet, effectively immobilizing her in case she should regain consciousness. He repositioned her further from Roy, perpendicular to him. Then, he walked slowly back, taking a seat on the coffee table facing Roy. From this vantage, he could see Susie's unconscious body to his left as he faced the man he had been waiting to interrogate.

Slipknot put his handgun down on the coffee table, right next to Roy. Then he picked up the remote and muted the TV. He slowly, deliberately, removed a pack of Marlboro Reds from his jacket pocket and lit a cigarette.

Roy studied the man as he lit up. He was ugly. His face was pockmarked and craggy. Roy realized that part of what made the man so strange-looking was that he had no eyebrows or eyelashes. He also appeared to have some sort of rash on his neck—it was partially scabbed up and partly raw flesh. The green leather jacket he wore was old and faded. In contrast, he appeared to be wearing brand new, black ostrich skin cowboy boots.

"So, Roy. This can go a couple of ways. We can make it quick and clean. You can tell the truth, and that'll be it. Or, you can lie, make me drag the truth out of you, and her—" he nodded towards Susie, "in which case this gets nasty. Really nasty. And messy. What's it gonna be?"

"Who are you? What do you want? I'll give you the combination to the safe. Take everything."

"Oh, come on, Roy. Cut the bullshit. You know why I'm here. You know who I am. You know who sent me."

Roy stared wide-eyed at the intruder, shaking his head slowly.

"Wise coughed up everything. He's dead, you know? Couldn't live with what he'd done. Suicide," Slipknot laughed. "At least, that's how I made it look. I even dictated his 'goodbye note.' Coward's way out, but then, what kind of man nails a kid's dick to his dad's front door? A kid he didn't even kill...

"A coward.

"At least you had the balls to kill the kid." Slipknot took a drag on his cigarette.

"Unfortunately for you two, you know what else a coward does, Roy? Spills the beans on his crew. That's right. Through all the tears and booze, little Tommy told me all about how you, and the bitch there—" he indicated Susie with his cigarette, "and his wife, killed my friend's son.

"That's problematic, Roy. See, where I come from, we take care of family. And what you did, all of you, that merits punishment."

He cleared his throat. "Retribution, Roy. For you, I'm pretty clear what that means. Eye for eye, tooth for tooth, dick for dick." As Slipknot had said this, he looked down at Roy's crotch and his tongue gently touched his lips, reminding Roy of a snake.

Slipknot laid his cigarette flat on the top of the coffee table. Then he straightened up so that he could access the fanny pack and pulled out a small steak knife with a wooden handle and a short length of rope. He put the rope on the table beside him. Then he raised the knife to his face and pressed it against his cheek as if he was about to shave with it.

"Not too sharp, I'm afraid, but it'll get the job done. Won't be pretty. But then, you'll bleed out. So, you won't be around to clean up the mess.

"What I wasn't so sure about is the little lady." Slipknot looked over to Susie, who had not moved. "What's a fair punishment for her? I was initially thinking I'd maybe take off one of her tits. But that's not really equivalent, is it?

"So, I did a little research. On the worldwide web. And, you know what I discovered? Female circumcision! Now there's an equivalent punishment! Pretty straightforward procedure. Not complicated at all. Amazing what you can learn on YouTube."

Slipknot reached into his fanny pack again and removed a pair of self-locking forceps. Five inches long. He held them in his left hand, opening and closing them like scissors.

"Amazon. Same-day delivery." Then he added, smiling, "I'm a Prime member.

"So... from what I saw on YouTube, all you do is grab the clitoris with this little guy—" he imitated the action with the forceps, "lock it down and pull. Then, just one clean slice at the base," he laughed. "Well, maybe not too clean. This knife could use a little sharpening.

"So, really, the only question is... who to start with?"

He made a show of looking at Roy, then Susie, and then back again as if unable to choose. He picked up his cigarette and took another drag.

"Look," said Roy. "I don't know what you're talking about. I never even met the kid. I never met this Wise guy. You've got the wrong people, man. Why would we get involved in this? We were going to offer the kid a job. That's all I know. I swear!"

Slipknot stared in silence. And then he stared some more. This was closely followed by an impatient sigh. He crushed the cigarette out on the glass-topped coffee table and left it there.

"I guess we'll start with circumcising the little lady first; see if that jogs your memory."

Slipknot moved toward Susie, knife in one hand and forceps in the other. He rolled her onto her back. Then he used his feet to push her knees apart.

"No! Wait! Stop! You've got the wrong people! Call Joe Harlan! Call the senator! Get him on the phone! Let me talk to him!"

"Oh, we're way beyond talking, Roy," Slipknot said over his shoulder. He put the knife between his teeth as he began to pull down on Susie's sweatpants.

"Stop, you stupid motherfucker! Stop! Okay! Okay! It was

me! Me and Tom! I took the kid out! He hung the dick! She had nothing to do with it! Didn't even know about it! Do whatever you want to me, but, please, leave her the fuck out of this!"

Susie stirred, slightly. Slipknot watched to make sure she didn't come to, then moved away from her. He seemed eager to hear Roy's confession.

"Okay. Okay. Now we're getting somewhere... Mr. Diaz." He sat back down on the coffee table. "So, tell me *how* you did it."

"It was easy. Stupid kid. Just offered to buy him dinner. Took him out to the Everglades. Shot him. Dumped the body. Cut off the dick. Mailed it to Austin. Simple as fuck."

"I thought you were in the Bahamas?"

"I came back over on a charter. A little thirty-two-foot job. Paid cash. No paper trail. Two hours to get here. Killed the kid. Then back over the water. Perfect alibi. Told her," Roy indicated to Susie with his head, "I was going fishing."

Slipknot sat on the coffee table nodding his head, pondering. "But why, Roy? Why did you do it?"

Roy glared at the man and spat, "Because the kid was slime. He raped that girl and the little fucker got away with it. He didn't deserve to live."

Slipknot absorbed the information, then nodded. "You know what. You may be right about that." He pointed the knife at Roy. "I've thought about that. Quite a bit. The kid may have had it coming, for stupidity more than anything else. Natural selection, you know? Thinning the herd." Slipknot reached into his fanny pack and pulled out what looked like a small card. He turned it toward Roy, who saw that it was a photo.

Of Kristy Wise.

"A beautiful woman, don't you think?" Slipknot studied the photo. "Have you met her?"

Roy shook his head.

"No? Shame. Photo doesn't do her justice. I can see what Joe Junior saw in her. Him and Stern both."

Roy squinted at Slipknot, slightly shrugging and shaking his head. "What are you talking about?"

"Oh. You wouldn't know that. See, although this here—" Slipknot gestured with his hands to the space they were occupying, "may seem kind of haphazard to you, there is a great deal of thought behind it all. I didn't start out here, or even with Tom Wise.

"First, I interrogated your buddy David—fuckin' little gook held up good, I'll give him that. He didn't know squat. I can tell.

"Then I talked to Joe's buddy Frank—they were business partners, and I figured maybe he'd wanted Joe out of the way. That wasn't the case. But Frank told me everything. Turns out there was a little more to the Kristy story than just Joe Junior. His buddy Frank... see, he's the one that put the roofies in her drink." Slipknot raised the photo toward Roy, indicating that he was talking about Kristy. "Then Joe offered to walk her home. That's what everyone remembered seeing, 'cause Frank ain't no dummy. He was at the party until late.

"But, there was about forty minutes where he wasn't there at all. A gap. He met Joe back at Kristy's place. They'd made a bet, see. And since Frank was the one that got the drugs in her drink, he won. So, Joe let him in through the back stairs, and he got first crack at her while Joe watched.

"But, like I said, Frank ain't no dummy. Once he'd had his fun with her, appears he went down to 'keep an eye out.'" Slipknot had made bunny ears with the cigarette and the knife. "And when he saw her roommate coming, he skedaddled. Didn't warn Joe or nothin'. Just booked it straight back to the party. No one noticed he'd been gone. Pretty solid alibi.

"Joe Junior... not so bright. Caught with his pants down—literally," Slipknot laughed.

"So, you see, Roy. Joe Junior was really only guilty of sloppy seconds." Slipknot shook his head. "You took out the wrong guy. Or, at least, you missed one." Slipknot shrugged. "But, I gotta say, just between us, man to man..." he smiled with admiration, "there's a certain style to how you did it." He nodded, and stood. "You really sent a message!"

Slipknot laughed, standing and shaking his head, "Goddammed dick on the door."

He began to turn toward Susie, then stopped, and continued, "You know the word *panache?*"

Roy stared at him wide-eyed, nodding slightly.

"Well, you done it with *panache*, Roy. You sure did! Did you know that's French?"

Roy shook his head again.

"It's that big plume of feathers on a helmet, you know? First time the word appeared was in 1898—*Cyrano de Bergerac*. It's actually the last word Cyrano says before he dies, and it's the last word in the play. Crazy, huh?" Slipknot struck a pose and dramatically raised his hands as he repeated, "*Panache.*"

He was clearly amused with what he'd just shared, and he watched Roy, who was listening attentively.

"Yep. Your little stunt definitely had *panache*. Unfortunately, that doesn't change what has to happen now. I'm just the angel of death here. My job is revenge. But, let me say with my whole heart, I *do* appreciate your confession. I don't believe it, not a hundred percent. But, I think it's pretty close.

"So, as a gesture of goodwill, what I can do for you is... I promise to shoot you before I cut your dick off. I think that's fair.

"But I still think you need to watch what I'm gonna do to your little lady. More than anything... 'cause it's just fun, you know? Tonight, Roy... it's 'Play first, then work.'"

Slipknot laughed maniacally. Roy couldn't tell if the laugh was real or for effect. Then he reached down and used the remote to turn up the volume on the TV—loud—after which he knelt down on the floor next to Susie and worked to pull her knees apart.

CHAPTER NINETY-ONE

Kristy Wise had hoped to catch Susie at home that night. As it was Halloween, she'd decided to wear a costume to blend in and disguise herself. She'd had her Uber drop her off just down the street, and was walking toward the house when she saw a man walking up the front drive. It seemed odd, as he wasn't in costume and there were no children with him.

As he climbed the front porch steps, she could see that he wore a green leather jacket and black pants. He rang the doorbell. While he stood waiting, it looked to her like he had discreetly pulled a handgun. This was confirmed when the front door opened and he pointed the gun toward whoever had opened the door, and entered the house.

For the briefest moment, she considered calling 911.

How long will it take the police to get here?
How do I explain what I'm doing there?
Will anyone be alive by the time they get here?
Trust the police? Or trust yourself?

Kristy jumped the side wall and made her way up to and across the back terrace, hoping to get a better view of what exactly was going on inside.

Through the window, she'd seen the man knock Susie out. She'd then crept up to the sliding glass door that led from the patio into the house, from where she'd heard most of the discussion once he'd muted the TV.

Kristy had never had occasion to draw her handgun on another human being. But she was so very glad that she had it and knew how to use it.

She took off her shoes and entered the house in her bare feet. The better to approach silently. But, once the man cranked up the TV volume again, it didn't matter.

The man was preoccupied with trying to get Susie's sweat pants down low enough for him to be able to begin his procedure. When Kristy saw that Roy had seen her approaching, she raised an index finger to her lips. Roy kept talking at Slipknot, making more noise and pleading that he leave Susie out of everything.

He later told me that he didn't recognize Kristy at first. He had no idea who she was or what she was doing in his house. To Roy, through the jet lag and adrenaline, Slipknot's presence was already otherworldly. The barefoot young woman in jeans, a green t-shirt, a green baseball cap, and suspenders, wearing a fake moustache and stalking her way across his living room carrying a handgun, seemed surreal.

At that point, things couldn't get much worse.

So, I trusted—hoped—that she was on our side. Hell, at least she wasn't pointing the gun at me.

Kristy fired once at almost point blank range.

The gunshot was barely audible over the noise from the TV.

The bullet entered Slipknot's head just behind his left ear. It would have gone straight into his left ear, but he had seen, or sensed, something just before Kristy had fired, and started to turn his head.

Slipknot fell forward on top of Susie's legs.

Kristy rolled him off of Susie and onto his right side. There was a slow, steady trickle of blood from the entry wound onto the tile floor. Apparently, the bullet remained in his head, as there was no exit splatter.

Susie was slowly coming to, and managed to get herself into a sitting position while tentatively touching the back of her head.

Kristy knelt down and helped her pull up her sweatpants. She then used Slipknot's blunt steak knife to cut the zip ties, after which she crawled over to cut the ties on Roy's arms and handed him the knife so he could get his legs free.

Then, she sat on the sofa and, hands shaking, she picked up Roy's glass of scotch, took a sip, and grimaced.

"You got any beer?" she asked.

Roy pointed her toward the kitchen and then set about helping his wife. She had a nasty lump on her head, but appeared okay otherwise.

As Roy headed out to the hall to fetch Tylenol, Kristy returned with a beer, a towel, and some ice. She wrapped the ice in the towel and handed it to Susie, who was still sitting cross-legged on the floor.

"So, you're Susie," she said more than asked.

Susie looked up at her, and smiled a bit. There was sadness in her eyes.

"You look just like your mom," she replied.

CHAPTER NINETY-TWO

They later told me that, as far as they were concerned, the elephant in the room—oddly—wasn't the dead man on the floor, but rather Senator Joe Harlan. It was clear to them that the man on the floor had killed Tom and attacked David, and that he had been sent by the senator.

There was no point in going to the police. That would only open another can of worms, bringing Roy and Susie under scrutiny yet again for Joe Harlan Junior's murder—and requiring an explanation for the dead body on the floor.

But, they needed to do something.

Roy patted the body down and found a mobile phone. The phone was in airplane mode. Clearly, the dead man knew what he was doing.

From what they saw on the phone, the dead man was communicating with someone with an Austin, Texas area code. Rather than using the phone then and there, they agreed that Roy should do so on the boat, before dumping it with the body, to avoid having the phone triangulate to the house.

"One step at a time," Roy advised.

In the end, the three decided that the best thing to do with Slipknot was a burial at sea. Best to eliminate all traces of him. Roy had long since sold the *Yellowfin* and bought a small *Boston Whaler* to replace it. Between the three of them, they loaded Slipknot's body into a large duffle bag and put his gun, knife, little rope, and zip ties in the bag with him. They loaded the bag into the back of the boat, after which Roy added twenty feet of old anchor chain. He then piloted it out alone. He estimated, all things considered, that it would be a three-hour round trip and that it made sense for the ladies to stay behind and put the house back in order.

While Roy dumped the body, Susie and Kristy cleaned up the family room. Once they were satisfied that they'd eliminated all traces of blood, Susie went into the office and returned with a small bottle of luminol spray.

She spritzed the area, then turned off the lights. After carefully examining the floor and wall around where Slipknot had been shot, she was relieved to find only a couple of stray droplets of blood on the baseboard—about eight feet from where the body had fallen.

She wiped those away. She then cleaned the area again to remove all traces of luminol.

"You guys hunt?" Kristy asked, indicating the luminol with her head.

Susie shook her head. "Left over from Harlan. Coffee? Tea?"

"Tea's good."

Susie went into the kitchen. Kristy followed. While Susie brewed tea, Kristy sat down at the island.

"So," Susie said as an opening for Kristy to speak. She wanted her to lead since she had no idea what the girl did and didn't know.

Kristy reached into her backpack and pulled out the photo she had stolen from Camp Willow. A small photo—4 x 6—of two young girls, Susie and Deb at camp. The same photo Deb had given Susie a few years back, which she had destroyed.

"How about here? I'm guessing this is where everything started? I recognized Mom. I wasn't sure it was you in it with her. Your hair was blonder when you were young," Kristy said.

"Where did you find this?"

"In the camp album. At Willow. I think Liz Bareto is on to you, too, by the way. Or at least getting close, I think."

"I used to have a copy. Your mom gave it to me." Susie smiled, then held the photo up and looked at Kristy, then back at the photo. "You look just like her."

"Is this how you guys met? At camp?"

Susie nodded.

"I saw the letter. From my mom to you." Susie had been pouring out tea, and stopped, looking up at Kristy. "Apparently, you guys were..." Kristy watched Susie's face, weighing her words, and settled on, "...you guys were close."

Susie blushed. She carefully picked up the two cups of tea and brought them to the island. Her hands trembled slightly as she set them down. "Is it true," Susie asked. "What he said about your dad?"

"Yep." Kristy hesitated, then decided to let Susie dodge her question for now. She had a feeling—from Susie's reaction—that she knew the answer. "He's dead, but not suicide. You heard. That fucker—" Kristy gestured at where Slipknot's body had lain, "killed him."

"I'm so sorry... about your parents. We just got back from a trip. I got the letter from Deb, before we left. That's how I found out." Susie looked away, her eyes watering. She busied herself stirring her tea.

"It's all... a mess," said Kristy.

"Do they have any leads? The police?" Roy had not yet shown Susie his Glock. She wanted to believe he hadn't killed Deb, but she wasn't sure. Kristy frowned and shook her head. She had just met this woman. And Susie wasn't being entirely forthcoming with her. Kristy felt no obligation to share with Susie what she had recently learned about her mother's death.

In due time, Kristy thought. She changed the subject. "So, the way I see it, this whole mess really started with your daughter, Camilla?" Kristy noted that Susie unconsciously put her hand on her belly.

Susie hesitated.

How much to tell Kristy? Joan?

She has no right to know about Joan.

Susie was perhaps so accustomed to not speaking of that part of her and Deb's life together that she naturally shied away. Yet, perhaps it was the maternal instinct in Susie—that and having Kristy there before her, a young version of her friend Deb. Or maybe it was the fatigue from the recent trip to Spain, coupled with the mix of emotions she had experienced that evening, which made her weak. But, in that moment, Susie felt Kristy did have a right to know certain things. Not everything, but just enough.

So, despite all the careful planning, and their worries about forensic residue, and the burner laptops, and *Roy's Rules for Murder*, Susie spoke—not wisely, but too well. She did her best to tread the thin line between telling Kristy enough versus too much about what had happened to Harlan.

And why.

It was a terrible mistake.

CHAPTER NINETY-THREE

Roy put the throttle in neutral and let the boat drift to a stop. Per Navionics, the ocean below him was about 1,000 feet deep.

As the boat drifted, he removed the dead man's mobile phone from his jacket pocket. He unzipped the duffle bag and used the man's thumb to unlock the screen. Roy switched the phone off airplane mode and looked through recent calls and messages again. There were several missed calls and two text messages from that Austin phone number. The text messages read:

Urgent. We need to talk.
URGENT. ABORT.

Roy re-dialed the number from recent calls. It was very late. About 1:30 a.m. Miami. Half past midnight in Texas.

He put the phone to his ear and waited.

On the third ring, someone picked up.

"Goddammit Slipknot! Where are the hell have you been? Did you get my message?"

Roy recognized that Texas drawl. "Ha! Slipknot! So that's what he called himself. What a great nickname! Very intimidating! Of course, the downside is... that's a lot of letters to put on a gravestone, Joe."

There was a long pause.

"Who is this?"

"I think you know who this is." Roy paused. "You made a big fucking mistake tonight, Joe. Slipknot paid the price. Now, you better watch your back. You're next."

"Wait. Hold on a second. I don't know what you're talking about."

"Tic-toc, Joey boy. Tic-toc."

Roy disconnected the call. He laughed to himself. He had no specific plans to do anything to the senator. But, as he'd spoken to Harlan, he was reminded of Captain Hook and Peter Pan for some reason, and he just threw it out there. He imagined Harlan would try to decipher some meaning from it, and hopefully lose sleep over it.

Shit!

I should have thought of this before.

He removed his own phone from his pocket, and searched through his contacts until he found what he was looking for—*Senator Joe Harlan-Mobile*. He compared the phone number in his contacts to the one he'd just dialed from Slipknot's phone and he laughed out loud.

You're using a burner Mr. Senator!

Roy sat for a few moments thinking, weighing pros and cons. Then he decided. He opened the Messenger app on Slipknot's phone and entered Senator Harlan's mobile number. Then he typed and sent two words.

Mission accomplished.

Roy chuckled to himself, imagining the look on the Senator's face when the message appeared on his phone, irrefutably connecting him to the dead man. He wiped down the phone once more, then threw it overboard.

It was a bit tricky getting the duffle bag over the gunwale of the boat, mainly because of the weight the anchor chair added to it. But Roy managed it. The *Boston Whaler* was less than 25 feet long, so it was only about three feet from the top of the gunwale to the water. The bag made a small splash as it hit, and sank—1,000 feet to the bottom.

Roy eased the throttle forward and headed back towards the

house. As he headed home, Roy realized had just raised the stakes. He'd just threatened the life of a sitting State Senator. Harlan was now on notice. But what next?

Killing Harlan Junior was a cake walk. He and Susie had made some mistakes, but only small ones. Though, to be fair, the kid had no idea they were after him. In dealing with Getz in in Spain, they had deviate significantly from their protocol and it appeared that they got away with it.

That was sloppy. Reckless.

Well, no more sloppiness.

Roy was going back to ultra-conservative.

As he headed to the house, he started to think through how best to deal with Joe Harlan Senior. The man had just tried to kill him and Susie. This wasn't a question of revenge, or retribution. No, this was simply a case of self-defense. Self-preservation.

His stomach turned. The most obvious solution was that he needed to kill Harlan before he came after them again. He was undecided as to whether to actually do it. But, that decision was for later. First, he would plan it carefully. And then he would decide. And if he did it, he would execute the plan carefully, conservatively, with precision, and...

Fuck, yeah... with panache.

CHAPTER NINETY-FOUR

Susie watched the navigation lights of the *Boston Whaler* as it slowly made its way back to the dock.

Over the last hour, she and Kristy had gotten to know each other. While both held back certain information, regarding other topics they were very forthcoming. They'd chatted about growing up in Texas. Living in Miami. Camilla. Life at UT—before and after the rape. How Susie and Roy had met. Alfie. Bethany. Kristy's plans for the future.

Happily, they'd discovered that they liked each other. When Roy came in the back door, he found the two laughing over Kristy's description of a trip she'd taken with Bethany to Las Vegas, where everything that could have gone wrong did.

It was almost 3:00 a.m.

As they chatted, Roy began to set a small round table in the kitchen. Kristy noticed, but said nothing.

"He always sets the table for breakfast before we go to bed," Susie offered, good-naturedly rolling her eyes, then added, "quirky."

"It's sweet," Kristy replied, watching the man go about his business.

"He's setting it for three." Susie mock whispered, and smiled.

Roy stopped and looked at the two women who were seated about ten feet from him at the kitchen island. "I can hear you. I'm right here."

They all laughed.

It was late. And Susie decided to wrap up the evening, saying to Kristy, "So, how long can you stay with us?"

"Not long. I gotta get back. Bethany and me, we've got some loose ends to tie up, you know."

Susie nodded, understanding. Roy looked up, but said nothing.

"Come on," Susie said. "I'll show you to a guest room."

As they rose to leave the kitchen, Roy told Kristy, "Good night." She replied in kind.

Susie walked Kristy down a long hall and up a flight of stairs into the guest quarters. "Independent—*en suite* bath. You know where the kitchen is. Is that all you brought?" Susie nodded, indicating Kristy's backpack.

Kristy smiled. "It's enough."

"Okay. Well, good night." Susie moved to leave, but paused and then turned to give Kristy a hug, and a light kiss on the forehead. "And thanks."

In her room, Kristy took a shower, washed her hair, brushed and flossed, put on some boxers and a t-shirt, and climbed into bed. She left the light on in the bathroom.

Her wet hair against the pillow felt and smelled nice.

When she was young, she used to leave the bathroom light on all the time. Her mother used to think it was because she was afraid of the dark. Kristy hadn't ever corrected her. She hadn't wanted to explain.

It wasn't because she was afraid of the dark. She just knew that, if someone came for her at night, her odds of survival would be far better if she could see them coming. It wasn't about fear. It was about leveling the playing field. She felt safer, more confident, knowing that she was at least walking into an even match.

She'd had the same feeling earlier that evening when she'd entered the house with the cool heavy weight of the pistol in her right hand. It was about leveling the playing field. And, when she'd walked through the kitchen into the family room to take out the old man, she'd felt good. She'd felt alive.

Truly alive. All her senses engaged.

As she'd approached him, the cool air from the A/C gently

caressed the hairs on her arms. A TV commercial had blared warnings about some pharmaceutical.

May cause internal bleeding. Do not take if pregnant or breastfeeding.

She'd noticed that Roy saw her coming, but he was irrelevant to her at that moment. Just more background noise. A prop. All that existed, all that mattered was her and that old bastard.

She'd felt the hard marble tile against her feet as she stalked her prey. And she'd noticed that her feet were cool and dry.

No sweat.

No fear.

She could have shot sooner. Earlier. She had the sonofabitch sighted in. She wouldn't have missed. But, she knew she could get closer. So, she did. She approached, slowly, seeing just how close she could get. Just before she pulled the trigger, she could actually smell him. She was that close.

She chose not to shoot until she saw him react. Until she knew that he had seen something. Until she was sure that he realized that he was fucked.

She wanted him to know.

Susie had been unconscious. She hadn't heard what the man had said—about Tom; about Frank. But Kristy had heard it. Every word. She killed him—of course—because of what he was going to do to Susie and Roy. But, she also killed him because of what he'd had to say about Frank Stern.

Once again, just as with what Bethany had seen, that old bastard had given Kristy information that she didn't need to know. She could have lived her entire life happily, not knowing.

She hated him for telling her. And for the burden he'd placed on her. Because, now that she knew, she had no choice. Frank Stern had to pay.

CHAPTER NINETY-FIVE

Susie awoke to the sounds of Roy snoring.

Poor thing. All the travel, then the excitement with the intruder last night. Then dumping the body. And Slipknot—what a name—and the senator!

She snuck quietly out of bed and went downstairs.

The kitchen was empty. There was no sign of Kristy.

Susie turned on the coffee maker and sat at the island where the faded photo of two smiling young girls looked up at her. It was a loose end. But there were certainly fewer loose ends now than there had been. Susie knew what Roy would say, that the picture needed to go. But, it really wasn't hers to destroy, was it? It would probably be best if she locked it away somewhere safe—for Kristy, of course. She knew just where to hide it.

Susie put the photo in the pocket of her robe and went to pour herself coffee, but then she remembered. Smiling.

Pregnant.

She opted instead for a cup of herbal tea, which she took with her down to the dock.

It was about 9:20 a.m. A glorious morning. The sun was just coming up over the mangroves and houses on the opposite side of the canal. There was a nice warm breeze playing with her hair. She guessed it to be at around 10-15 knots.

Still a bit of hurricane season left. But not so hot anymore...

As she watched ripples on the water, she thought back to when she'd first married Roy. There'd been so many things that she'd hoped for then. She'd loved him, of course, and she'd hoped that he'd be successful. But she'd also wanted a career of her own. She'd wanted a family, children.

And she'd had it all.

Then fate had snatched it away from her. Fate had taken the one thing that meant everything to her. Camilla. After that, her family, everything had fallen apart. For a time.

Then, what she'd wanted, what she'd needed, had been revenge. Which she had also achieved, in abundance.

Yet, although she'd never given up on the idea of family, she'd never pursued it, either. Never spoken of it. Certainly never planned for it. She had simply ignored it because she'd been too scared. Scared to put herself out there, to open herself up to being hurt again. It was easier to destroy than to create, to hate than to love and lose.

In a strange way, killing— Bareto, Harlan, Getz—had somehow made her appreciate how precious and fragile life was. Theirs, Camilla's, even her own. That recognition had given her the courage to try again. And now, as she stood overlooking the canal, she dared to think—to imagine what it could be like to be a family again. She believed she could make it work. She *could* have it all.

Maybe this was God's way of rewarding her?

She laughed.

Yep. God's giving me a second chance at motherhood as a "thank you" for killing a bunch of scumbags. He's looking down and thinking, "Well done, Susie. You'll make a fine mommy."

Still, Susie felt that there was something to it. After Camilla's death, Susie had stopped wishing and hoping. She'd simply acted. She'd made very specific choices, running real risks, with real life-changing consequences.

She hadn't hoped Liam Bareto would suffer. She hadn't sat and wished for revenge. She'd made it happen. And she'd accepted the consequences: her obligation to eliminate Joe Harlan Junior.

She realized that not everyone would agree with her choices. You could question whether she'd done the right thing. You could debate whether she and Roy had taken too many risks. But, you could not say that they'd failed to act. You could not say that they'd lacked conviction.

Susie took a deep breath. She felt giddy. Elated.

She was going to have a baby.

She already knew, in her heart, that it was a girl. And her daughter was going to be a good, healthy, intelligent, beautiful person.

This was not a wish or a hope. It was a fact. Susie didn't "believe" it. She knew it to be true with conviction—the kind of conviction it takes to commit murder.

CHAPTER NINETY-SIX

Friday
November 1, 2019
Miami, Florida

"There. That's a good image. I think it's the best still we're going to get," said Shaw.

He and Eddie were looking at a computer monitor, reviewing video capturing the front entrance to the Cruise's house. An older man was standing on the porch with his head turned, looking up the street. With the light from the porch, his features were as clear as day.

"We can run facial recognition on him. That's easy. But the database is what it is. We may not get a hit," said Shaw. "The other angle for identification, of course, is how he got there—Uber or his own vehicle. It's odd that there's no parked car visible." Shaw rewound the video. "He just comes walking down the street to the house."

"Trick-or-treater?" Eddie laughed, standing up and stretching his back.

Shaw scrubbed through the remainder of the video. "It seems the guy is still at the house. At least, there's no footage of him coming out the front door," Shaw said, almost to himself.

"Check camera two," Eddie suggested. They had set up two cameras on the public easement near the Cruise property—one on a light pole, the other on a telephone pole. Camera one covered the front of the house. The second surveillance camera covered the side of the Cruise property, which was a corner lot.

"Hold on." Shaw cued up the video from the second camera and scrubbed. Then, he stopped and rewound. "What the fuck? So, still no sign of the old guy coming out, but we've got another visitor. Check this out."

Eddie sat back down next to Shaw in front of the monitor. "Show me."

Shaw scrubbed back to where the second person appeared on the footage from camera two.

"Whoa! What the hell?" Eddie asked to no one.

"You think that's a trick-or-treater? Someone pranking them?"

"Maybe. Zoom it in." Eddie stared, studying the images that played out before him. "What is he dressed as, a chimney cleaner?"

Shaw turned and looked at Eddie with wide eyes. "A what?"

"You know. 'Chim Chimney, Chim Chimney...'" Garza said. "Like in *Mary Poppins*."

Shaw laughed. "You mean a chimney sweep? No. I don't think so, Eddie. *That* is one of the Mario Brothers. It's hard to tell from the light, but I think that's a green shirt and cap. That would be Luigi climbing over the Cruises' fence."

Eddie stared at the screen.

"Looks like a chimney cleaner to me."

* * *

Detective Art Travers was sitting at his desk studying a print-out of a report he had just received from the Medical Examiner. It was a follow-up on the Tom Wise case, specifically looking at the chipped tooth that had been initially identified.

As to the tooth, the results were interesting but not surprising:

```
Sharp edges, showing no sign of
wear. Chipped surface clean, no
evidence of decay. Consistent with
```

```
a recent injury, possibly from a
fall.
```

It was the results of the buccal swab that got Travers' heart rate up.

```
Three compounds were identified in
subject's buccal swab sample:

(1)  Process Oil
(2)  Poly(1-Decene),Hydrogenated
(3)  1-Decene, Polymer with
     1-Octene, Hydrogenated

Poly(1-Decene) is a poly alpha
olefin which is commonly used as a
base in a wide range of industrial
lubricating oil products, both
synthetic and mineral oil based.
However, this combination of
compounds is most consistent with
lubricating oil for firearms. See
e.g. attached Material Safety
Data Sheet for Chem-Pak, Inc. —
Hoppe's Synthetic Lubricating Oil
(aerosol).
```

Travers was familiar with Hoppe's products. He used them for cleaning his guns. He picked up his phone and texted Detective Eddie Garza.

Travers:	*Swab is back. Found gun oil in Tom Wise's mouth.*
Garza:	*No shit... not consistent with suicide by overdose...*
Travers:	*Nope. Not really.*

CHAPTER NINETY-SEVEN

Sunday
November 3, 2019
Coral Gables, Florida

Liz Bareto was back at her home in the Italian Village of Coral Gables, Florida. It was still "comfortable," but she was no longer feeling like a newly single woman. In fact, given her new beau in Austin, she wondered whether Miami was even in her future.

When she'd flown back, Joe had been sweet enough to drive her to the airport. He was considerate. A gentleman. But there had been something odd about him that last morning at breakfast. He had been quieter than usual, though still happy, content.

She didn't know if it had something to do with her, or with "them," or with her leaving, or with something else going on in his life. She had considered asking, but concluded that it was a bit early in their relationship to start prying. The man was a senator. He probably had a lot on his plate.

Interestingly, he had told her that there were some big changes on the horizon for him, and that, all being well, he would like her to be a part of them.

Maybe that was what he had on his mind?

He'd followed that up by saying he wanted to see her again soon.

Liz had already booked the flight—in two weeks. Joe had some meetings in D.C. and he had asked her to meet him there for the weekend.

She was thinking about that upcoming trip when the doorbell rang.

9:00 a.m.

She padded to the front door and opened it. On the porch was an Amazon box.

She looked around. There was nobody in sight. No van. Nothing. She'd been out of town for a little over two weeks. And she didn't recall ordering anything. Not recently.

It was a small box—about the size of an eight-by-ten sheet of paper, and about three inches tall.

She took it back to the kitchen where she'd been having coffee and used a small steak knife to cut the tape along the edges before folding it open.

On top was a sheet of paper folded into thirds. Underneath it was a Ziploc rolled over on itself into the form of a tube. She slipped on her glasses and looked closely. She picked up the plastic bag and unrolled it. It contained a syringe. The needle was still attached.

She delicately unfurled the sheet of paper, careful only to touch the edges.

Dear Liz,

This plastic bag contains a needle that may have been responsible for the mark on your son's arm. I say "may have been" because the person who had it all this time is now dead. I am pretty sure that the same person was responsible for killing your son.

Please have it checked for DNA. If you find a match, then you can rest well knowing that your son's killer is dead.

And, I can assure you, it was not a happy death.

Regards,

A friend

Liz stared at the note, and then at the needle.

Then she thought of Joe, recalling his words, and his promise: "They will be avenged, Liz. I swear it."

CHAPTER NINETY-EIGHT

Friday
December 13, 2019
Austin, Texas

Frank Stern's right cheek felt cold and his neck ached.

His vision was blurry.

As it cleared up, he saw a strange white tile wall next to him with metal bars protruding from it. He tried to turn to get a better look at it, but searing pain shot through his head.

Oh fuck... not again.

Moving only his eyes to avoid the pain, Frank looked around the kitchen for the boots belonging to the strange little man who had interrogated him about Joe. He listened carefully.

Nothing.

How the hell did I end up here?

He lay still, struggling to bring up his most recent memories.

He recalled leaving the office. He remembered going out and making two deliveries—it'd been a slow night for a Friday. It was mid-December and folks were in holiday mode. He'd decided to stop off at MugShots, a little bar on East 7th Street, to get a drink and unwind before coming home.

And that's when he'd started getting text messages again—from Joe. That he was in Austin. That he was fine. That he'd explain what had happened. That he needed to see him. Frank was skeptical, but had texted him that he was at MugShots. Joe had replied that he was on his way. Thirty minutes.

Frank had been so absorbed in texting that he hadn't noticed the guy who'd taken the seat next to him at the bar. He was drinking beer, and claimed to recognize Frank from an entrepreneurship panel he had recently been on. They got to talking start-ups, and Frank had let the guy buy him a Jack and Coke while he waited for Joe.

Then... nothing.

He fought to remember more.

Did Joe show?

Did we have another drink?

Who was that guy?

All he remembered was that he'd been tall. Kind of blond. And he'd had a weird British-y accent.

Nothing else.

Carefully, he moved himself to a sitting position. And that's when the pain really hit him. Not his head. *Between his legs!*

He suddenly realized that he was completely naked. Except... he looked down and saw white. Covering his entire crotch area.

Gauze. A large bandage?

"Oh fuck! Oh no! What the... what the fuck?" he squealed in a high-pitched voice.

There was tape on his belly. Tape on his thighs. The bandage covered his entire groin area.

He felt pain and intense pressure. Between his legs. And there was blood on the bandage.

Frank began to cry.

"No! Dear God, no!" he sobbed, his chest and belly convulsing. He hugged himself, crying, afraid to touch or even look between his legs.

Once the wave of panic and tears passed, he carefully reached down. Gingerly, slowly, he began to pull at the tape attaching the bandage to his belly. It pulled hairs, but he ignored the little pricks of pain. He needed to know what was underneath... or what wasn't.

He pulled further, separating the tape from his skin. When he was done with the tape on his belly, he began to remove tape from his thighs, slowly, until he could see underneath.

Frank screamed.

"No! Oh my God! Noooo! Fuckin' fucker motherfucker... Ahhhhh!"

Underneath the gauze, it was swollen—bloody and blue...

But, it was still there.

His dick was still there.

But on it, running down the front of the shaft, he could see that someone had tattooed a word in all capital letters:

R
A
P
I
S
T

Frank carefully got himself up from the floor, his penis sticking out like an angry fifth limb. Gauze still hung from his left leg by a bit of tape that hadn't come completely off.

On the table in his kitchen, he saw his phone and keys. His clothes were neatly folded on a chair. And in the center of the table was a manila envelope.

Frank picked up his phone. He opened messenger. The text messages—the whole chain of them from the *Unknown* claiming to be Joe—were gone. Deleted.

Frank picked up the manila envelope and opened it.

"Arrghh! You fuckin' bitch!"

Frank threw the manila envelope at the wall and howled in pain as the effort from throwing the envelope caused a surge of electric agony to shoot from his groin up his spine. As the envelope flew through the air, its contents spilled out onto the floor.

He tried to relax, to control his breathing. As he did, he noticed a yellow post-it note stuck on the table. It had been underneath the envelope.

Someone had taken the time to run it through a printer to leave him the following message:

```
In the event that your erection
persists for longer than four
hours, seek immediate medical
assistance.
```

1:30 a.m.

The time was scrawled in blue ink, handwritten. He looked at his phone. It was just past four in the morning.

Frank stood, staring at the note. Then at the floor where the photos had fallen. They were copies of the fucking pictures of him and Angela.

"Fuckin' Pippa..." But as he'd said it, the words had caught in his throat. He looked at the manila envelope. At the photos on the floor. The photos were bent... the manila envelope looked very familiar.

"Oh no..." he whispered. "No!"

Frank hobbled to his room and carefully pulled on a pair of sweat pants and a t-shirt. His dick stuck out like a flashlight in his pants. He grabbed a backpack that he used to cover his groin as he left his apartment and went down the elevator to the parking garage.

The Austin streets were virtually empty at 4:00 a.m. as Frank screamed down I-35, then exited and parked at 24-Hour Storage. He used his code to access the building and hobbled down to his unit. His storage unit key was still on his fob with his car keys. A good sign.

He opened the unit, went inside, and closed the door behind him. Quickly, he entered the digital combination.

Frank dropped to his knees. He howled from the pain of his penis bending against the front of his sweat pants as he did, but he had bigger problems.

No drugs.

No money.

His safe was empty.

EPILOGUE

I have to admit that it feels good to share this whole mess with someone. To finally get it off my chest.

Now that I've given you all the bits, let me put a bow on it for you.

As I told you, my greatest worry as Susie and Roy's therapist was my role as a holder of their secrets. But, as I explained, it was a decision of mine, a conscious choice that I made, which ended my worries, my angst.

You see, after meeting with my lawyer, I sat down and analyzed the root cause of my problem. I wanted to truly understand the basis of my fears.

My primary worry: Susie or Roy might decide to kill me at some point because I "had the goods" on them.

What I came to realize was that all my fears stemmed from one critical issue… *a misalignment of incentives.* You see, I had no incentive to keep their secrets, other than my ethical obligations. If I revealed what they had told me, it would have devastating consequences for them—while the consequences to me were that, what, I *might* lose my license?

My incentives and theirs were not properly aligned. The downside for them and the downside for me differed by an order of magnitude.

Well, about two months after Susie revealed to me that she and Roy had killed Joe Harlan Junior, I attended a conference that changed everything. The topic was *Criminal Deception: Psychological and Legal Issues,* and over the course of two days, several panels of legal experts, judges, and psychologists presented findings and debated issues. On the first evening of the conference, they held a cocktail party in honor of several of the speakers. It was there that I met an older woman, the Honorable Sandra Bissette-Kraft, a recently retired federal judge.

She and I got to talking, and, as folks do, we started connecting the dots between where she was from and where I'd grown up, who I knew and who she knew, until we discovered that Sandra knew Billy Applegate's parents. She had first met them at Billy's parents' home, years ago, at an election night party. In fact, that same night, she also met the man who was to become her husband, Howard Kraft. We laughed at the coincidence and exchanged the usual *"small world"* clichés.

I thought nothing of this brief encounter, and honestly, after I flew home from the conference, I forgot about it for weeks. Until, one day, conversing with Billy, I recalled the chance meeting with the judge. And I told him all about it.

When I did, his face blanched. I thought he was going to faint. I got him some water. Checked his pulse. His heart was racing. He was short of breath. I thought maybe he was having a heart attack. Slowly, he regained his usual color and composure.

Then—and I was shocked at this—he began to cry.

Through sobs, he told me the story. For the first time. The party. Going to bed. The molestation. We talked through it at length. Little by little, he settled down. I told him it wasn't his fault. I told him that he wasn't to blame.

Then, I gave him a couple of Valium. Billy usually doesn't like taking medication, but I recommended he rest. Dredging up so much pain all at once—well, it's taxing. I stayed with him until he drifted off to sleep. When I was sure he was in deep REM, I went out for a walk.

I was beside myself. I was shocked. I was... I was fucking pissed off, is what I was!

I wanted to take his pain away. To do something to make things right. But what? How?

The next day, I returned to work with a heavy heart. I have to admit I was not at my best—distracted. That afternoon, I had my weekly session with Roy. And, halfway through, I had an epiphany. I frankly don't recall the last half of the session, as I was thinking through what exactly to say. How to explain it all to him.

When we were wrapping up, I asked him if he had a few extra minutes. He made time for me.

And so, I began. I told him the story.

Billy's story.

Our story.

I told him how I'd met Billy in Washington, D.C. and how we'd fallen in love. How he'd proposed to me, at Martin's Tavern in the Kennedy booth. How we'd married. Raised children. How, despite our divorce, we have stayed close. For the children, of course, but also because I understood—better than Billy—that what drove us apart was not a lack of love, but something else. An unnamed demon that haunted him—and that stood between us and kept him from fully giving himself to me and our marriage. I knew it was that same thing that drove him to drink.

And I told Roy that the demon now had a name.

I told him about the election night party on November 5, 1974.

I explained what had happened. The pain Billy had suffered. How it had changed his life. How it haunted him to this day. How I believed it shouldn't happen to anyone else, ever again.

When it happened, Billy didn't know who had done it. He'd seen the man's face in the doorway as he'd left the room and he'd kept the incident to himself. It had haunted him.

He was barely fourteen when he started stealing liquor from his parents. Drinking to numb himself. To cope.

He managed to control the drinking before leaving for college, in part because he felt safe at home and in part because he was drinking behind his parents' backs. But, at Columbia University, he felt exposed, and he had free access to alcohol and no supervision. He drank regularly and heavily until he flunked out and had to return home.

Billy again managed to cope when he came back home. The newspaper job helped, and then, when he lost his father and went back to college, he started to get things back on track thanks to the support of his mother.

But the wheels almost came off again when he discovered who had molested him. I told Roy how Billy had learned who Jeff Getz was. The Democratic Party newsletter he'd found in the mail at his parents' house. How Billy had almost missed that Thanksgiving. How he'd sat in his father's study, with a revolver in his mouth.

But he chose a different path.

He committed himself to ruining Getz. To exposing him for what he was.

After graduating, Billy landed a job at *The Wall Street Journal.* He dedicated himself to building connections, sources. He investigated Getz in his spare time. Digging up all his dirty deals. Pursuing him. And writing articles.

Exposé after exposé.

Destroying his marriage.

Destroying his career.

Dogging him relentlessly until the man was forced to resign from Congress and leave the country.

That was as far as Billy had been willing to go. In my opinion, that wasn't enough punishment.

Not for me.

And that is when I threw my hat in with Susie and Roy, aligning all of our incentives, with one simple question.

I said to Roy, my patient:

Roy, for Billy... and for me... will you kill this fucker Getz for us?

Roy appreciated what a bad guy Getz was. His own research—much of which would begin with articles Billy had written about Getz's corruption—would later confirm the fact.

But there was more. I explained to Roy how this favor, if he chose to do it for me, would level the playing field—me, him, Susie. How it would align our incentives.

I have to say that Roy's face changed when I told him that. He looked at me differently, and for the first time with... affection? Maybe respect? I think he felt, at that moment, that I truly understood what had driven him and Susie to do what they had done.

We connected.

As to my proposal, he didn't say yes or no. He said he needed some time to think about it. I didn't want to press the issue, so I treated our following sessions as if nothing had happened.

Two months later, just when I was beginning to think that my proposal had been refused or forgotten, Susie advised me that they would be missing two weeks of therapy because they were taking a vacation to Spain.

I found out about Getz the way the world did. On the news. Billy and I still haven't discussed it. Which makes me think that he possibly suspects something.

Susie and Roy returned to therapy after their trip. But the tenor of our sessions has changed. Our discussions—particularly those I have with Roy—are less formal, more like friends chatting. I still do what I can therapeutically for them, of course, but a distance has been bridged.

Dare I say that Susie and Roy have become my two favorite patients?

It's hard to believe that all of this happened only a few months ago.

I felt so confident then. I'd avenged Billy and solved my Susie and Roy problem. I felt at peace and had finally been able to sleep well again.

It seemed like *we* had everything under control.

Like *I* finally had everything under control.

I was so fucking wrong.

Turn the page for an exclusive preview!

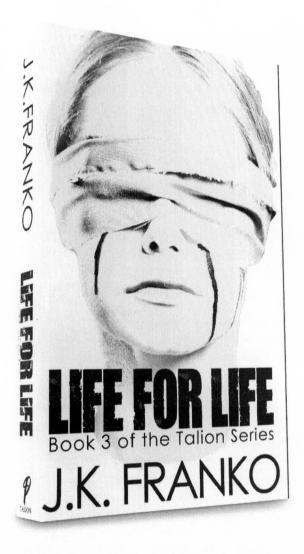

Book 3 in the Talion Series

OUT AUTUMN 2020

That corpse you planted last year in your garden,
Has it begun to sprout? Will it bloom this year?

The Waste Land
T.S. Eliot

PROLOGUE

Death is always several seconds and a few footsteps away. Look around you, wherever you are right now. How many things are there within five feet of you that could kill you? An improperly grounded electrical outlet plugged into your tablet. A slippery, wet bath tile that sends your head smashing into the side of the tub. An invisible virus silently multiplying in your lungs.

From the moment of conception, we fight to cheat death. The majority of what parents do for most of a child's life is simply keep them from dying. And much of what parents teach kids, from avoiding strangers to keeping their fingers out of their mouths, is about staying alive.

Although the odds are stacked against us, we get very good at cheating death. So good that, maybe out of misplaced pride or just to maintain our sanity, we tell ourselves that death is far off.

But it never is. And it comes for us all.

Given my profession, I have always feared death at the hands of a patient. For years, I imagined an unhinged, unmedicated client lashing out at me. Hopefully with a gun, not a knife. When I met Susie and Roy, that changed somewhat. I feared death at their hands not because they were unstable, but because I was expendable.

I must say that after the murder of former Congressman Getz, I believed that I finally had that situation under control. Susie, Roy, and I—and all of our incentives—were finally aligned. We were on the same team, so to speak. I foolishly believed that my life could simply return to normal.

But as I look back on everything now, with twenty-twenty hindsight, I can see that even as Roy was drowning Jeff Getz in the Bay of Pollença in Spain, the rough outlines of our tragic ending had already been sketched—all of the pieces were in place. Death was watching, and planning. .

As you must appreciate by now, my story is inextricably intertwined with the stories of others. This is, of course, fundamental to the human condition. We are all part of a larger whole. Seemingly unrelated people and events, distant in time and location, weave their way in and out of our lives like the threads of a tapestry.

I have told you two stories from the past that directly impacted me, Susie, and Roy. I shared with you the tragic tale of little Joan's death and how she was finally avenged. And, I shared with you the evil done to Billy Applegate and how Jeff Getz paid the ultimate price for that crime.

To complete the circle, for you to understand everything that happened to us, and so that you can take from all this the same cautionary lessons that I have learned, I need to share one final story with you. It is about a woman whose life was irreversibly impacted by our actions.

It is a story about love and death. And, in this case, depending on your point of view, you might even say that her story had a happy ending.

.

PART ONE

Rebecca Forsyth
Turks and Caicos
2020

My work as a therapist requires imagination. To help someone, to really get inside their head, you have to have some sense of what they are going through. If you haven't experienced what your patient is suffering firsthand, you must imagine.

For example, I have never had a panic attack. But then, only five percent of humans will experience a panic attack during their lifetimes. A pretty low number. So, how can I relate?

I must imagine.

From what my patients tell me, a panic attack closely resembles the feeling of claustrophobia. This is something that I have experienced. What gets me there instantly is that scene from *Kill Bill*—the one when the heroine Beatrix is buried under six feet of dirt in a coffin and left to die. Do you know it?

Indulge me.

Imagine that you wake up and open your eyes, but you can't see anything. It's pitch dark. So dark, you're not sure your eyes are even open. You're lying on your back. The air you're breathing feels warm and slightly humid, the way it does when you're sleeping with your head under the sheets.

You don't know where you are, but you don't hear the usual sounds you would hear in your bedroom. No ceiling fan. No A/C blowing. Everything is silent around you. Muffled.

You try to sit up and immediately feel a thump as your

forehead hits something. Your hands automatically react and reach up, discovering that something dry and smooth—heavy, immovable—is laying on top of you, just inches above your body. Right above your face, your torso, your legs.

You try to stretch your arms out to either side, and you feel the same barrier just inches away from your elbows, from your shoulders. You move your legs, spreading them apart and lifting them up. They are able to move only inches before, again, you feel something boxing you in.

Your nose itches, but you can't reach your face to scratch it. You clear your throat and can hear that the sound doesn't travel. It's close to you, stifled by the box you're in. The box is made of wood. There's maybe six inches between you and the box, all around your body. It's so close you can smell it. Damp wood. You can also smell soil.

You're in a box that's been placed in a hole, six feet deep. On top of it, and on top of you, are six feet of dirt. That much dirt weighs over two thousand pounds. One ton.

The weight of the dirt prevents you from opening the box. The lid won't budge. And even if you could break out of the box somehow, the dirt above you would fall into it, suffocating you before you could dig your way up to air.

There is no way out.

No hope.

As you realize this, your heartbeat accelerates—firing more rapidly. Your breathing speeds up. You struggle to take in air. You're not sure if you're already running out of oxygen or simply panicking. You can feel the silent, blind weight of two thousand pounds of earth above you crushing down onto your body. Your legs are tight, anxious. Your body fights for more space... to move, to stretch out, to stand, to run. But on every side you are closed in. You know that out there, everywhere, there is air, freedom. A universe of wide-open space.

But not for you.

You scream. The sound is muffled by the box. The only one who can hear it is you, and you know it. And you remember, as you scream, that there is a very small supply of oxygen in the box. With each breath, you are depleting it, converting it into CO_2.

You're going to suffocate. And there is no way out.

That feeling of being closed in, of paralysis, of heart-racing suffocating hopelessness, is what a panic attack feels like. Just like being trapped in a coffin.

My patients say that this is how you will feel when you're about to die.

When I try to imagine how Rebecca must have felt, 120 feet underwater with an empty scuba tank strapped to her back, I draw on this image.

* * *

Rebecca Forsyth was floating, weightless. Free as a bird. The feeling was otherworldly. And the view was breathtaking. Above her in every direction stretched a majestic canopy of bright blue. Looking heavenward, her eyes traced dancing beams of sunlight up and away until they converged into a round disc of shimmering white firmament. As she gazed downward, the world fell away from her—the bright blue and the light fading, everything becoming darker the further she looked. The only sound she could hear was the too-close, too-loud in-and-out of her own breathing, which she tried to control—relaxing, breathing slowly.

In: *one-two-three-four-five-six-seven-eight-nine-ten.*

Out: *one-two-three-four-five-six-seven-eight-nine-ten.*

She reached up, pinching her nose, and gently blew, equalizing the pressure in her ears—the Valsalva Maneuver.

Scuba diving was something Rebecca enjoyed, to a point. She was no expert, though she was open water certified and dove several times a year. She loved the feeling of weightlessness. And she liked being able to explore the ocean without having to bob up and down for air. She'd never quite mastered using a snorkel—she always had trouble clearing it of water. Scuba was much more convenient. No bobbing up and down. That being said, she had not done many deep dives.

Today was different.

Alan, Rebecca's husband, had talked her into diving a wreck. A sunken ship. It was all perfectly safe. Alan was an extremely experienced diver. A certified instructor. He had spent numerous summers working as an instructor and had logged hundreds of hours. In fact, he was the one who had gotten Rebecca into the sport.

The plan was for Rebecca and Alan to follow standard protocol and stay close to one another, buddy diving in case of an emergency. As Rebecca floated about 40 feet underwater, Alan was signaling for her to follow him down toward the wreck, which at its deepest was 165 feet below the surface. They weren't planning to go down that far. The bow of the ship was at about 110 feet.

Although Rebecca wasn't crazy about diving so deep, she reluctantly followed. They were on vacation, trying to relax. Trying new things to reinvigorate their marriage. After five years married, they'd hit a rough patch. They'd had some issues. Nothing insurmountable, she would have told you.

Part of their problems stemmed from the way they approached things. Rebecca was more conservative in her thinking. Alan was more of a risk-taker. Of course, for her to have chickened out of this dive would only have served to underscore the differences between them.

She checked the air pressure in her tank and noticed that it was dropping a little faster than normal for her, given the amount of time they'd been underwater. But, she knew that she was stressing over the fact that they were going to dive so deep, and she was breathing a little more rapidly than usual. She reached up and slightly reduced the buoyancy of her BCD, then gently frog-kicked her legs to conserve energy and air, following her husband down into the dark blue depths.

Rebecca swam about ten feet behind Alan and a bit to his left. The bow of the wreck still lay another 70 feet below them and hadn't come into view. Rebecca couldn't see it yet. She also couldn't see that, in addition to the bubbles that drifted up and away from her each time she exhaled, a stream of tiny bubbles trailed behind her. Air was escaping from her scuba tank through a small leak in the line to her backup regulator. As she descended into the depths, the water pressure around her grew, increasing the rate at which air was bleeding from her only tank.

Rebecca followed after Alan, taking in the immensity of the ocean floor that lay before her. The vastness of it was almost overwhelming. She tried to focus on keeping pace with her husband, and on breathing slowly.

In: *one-two-three-four-five-six-seven-eight-nine-ten.*

Out: *one-two-three-four-five-six-seven-eight-nine-ten.*

She scanned beyond him, hoping that the wreck would soon come into view as she gently kicked and followed. As they descended, they were following the natural slope of the ocean floor off the coast of the island. The seabed was spotted with seagrass, kelp, small fish, and here and there a lobster. She saw several lionfish as well.

Rebecca enjoyed fish-watching. Although, for her it was always secondary to keeping an eye out for sharks. The Caribbean is home to a great many species—nurse sharks, lemon sharks, reef sharks—which are generally harmless. But now and again, you will see more aggressive bull sharks and hammerheads.

Rebecca followed behind Alan, staying close, but she couldn't help being entertained admiring the seascape. She regularly pinched her nose to clear her ears. After what felt like just a few minutes, a shape began to take form ahead of them. Alan stuck his arm out to his side and gave her a thumbs-up. It was the wreck. A few more kicks, and she could clearly see the silhouette of the freighter sitting on the ocean floor below.

It was a tranquil day and the water was clear. There was still very good visibility as they passed 100 feet, though at that depth the water filtered out most of the reds and yellows in the color spectrum. Everything was draped in shades of blue and green.

Rebecca and Alan were diving just off the coast of Providenciales in the Turks and Caicos Islands. The wreck they were approaching was the W.E. Freighter, a 100-ton ship that was purposely sunken just north of Turtle Cove to create an artificial reef. The plan for the reef had been for the ship to settle in somewhat shallow waters to create an attraction for recreational divers. The ship had unfortunately ended up much deeper than intended and required a bit of expertise to reach.

Once at the bow of the freighter, Alan stopped and gave Rebecca the "okay" sign. She responded in kind, indicating that she was fine. She checked her depth gauge and saw that they were at 110 feet, just what the guidebook had promised. Alan and Rebecca had agreed on the surface not to go inside the vessel. There was always danger of collapse or of getting trapped due to gear catching on something. There was also the risk of getting cut since what remained of the ship was decaying metal that tended to be sharp and jagged. A cut meant blood in the water. And blood in the water attracted sharks.

They hovered for a moment by the bow of the wreck.

As they looked about them, a small school of fish swam out of the boat through a hole in the hull. They were silver with what appeared to be yellow fins and tails, though the color was muted and dull due to the depth. Most were about two feet long. Rebecca recognized them as horse-eye jacks. They shimmered in the water as they swam past the husband and wife, less than three feet away. Alan reached out and touched one of the fish as it went by. It didn't seem to notice or care.

Rebecca watched the school of fish briefly, then her focus shifted. Always scanning for sharks, she'd seen a shadowy movement not far from them—maybe forty feet. Whatever it was had whipped its body and quickly disappeared into the dark, murky distance. She kept scanning as the small school of fish swam away from them.

Suddenly, her peripheral vision registered a rapid movement coming from their left. She focused just in time to see sparkling glints of silver—a large barracuda rocketed in from the murkiness and sank its teeth into one of the jacks as the remainder of the school scattered. Thin wisps of black blood trailed behind the barracuda as it swam off, chomping and chewing on its prey. In the wake of the attack, the remaining jacks re-grouped and continued on as if nothing had happened.

It was not the first time that Rebecca had seen a predator make a meal of another fish. It never ceased to amaze her how an underwater scene could turn from completely tranquil to suddenly violent and bloody, and then return once again to the prior calm as though nothing had happened. She turned to Alan, who was shaking a hand back and forth as if to say, "Holy crap!" She gave him a thumbs-up in reply.

Rebecca continued to scan. Now there was blood in the water. And she was nervous—looking for sharks. As she looked around, Alan drifted a bit deeper examining the wreck. Rebecca was about to follow when a strange shape on the seafloor caught her eye. She felt her belly tighten and reached for her dive knife. She froze and watched carefully. Her patience was rewarded.

A sludgy-looking grey rock, which had apparently been laying low waiting for the barracuda incident to pass, decided that the coast was clear. Rebecca marveled as the rock changed color and texture, turning back into an octopus. The little guy half-swam half-crawled away, in the opposite direction of the barracuda. Rebecca smiled to herself. She loved those smart, creepy, eight-legged mollusks.

The octopus gone, she turned and saw that Alan had drifted about twenty feet away from her, deeper, exploring the hull of the wreck. He looked back at her and waved her towards him. Apparently, he'd found something of interest. Rebecca gave him a thumbs-up, and as she began to move, she looked down at her depth gauge.

Still at 110 feet.

They had agreed not to go below 130 feet, which was the official cut-off for recreational divers. Realizing it had been a while since she'd checked, she also took a look at her air pressure gauge.

Red.

A cold claw of panic squeezed Rebecca's chest when she saw that the needle was in the red zone, between 200 PSI and zero. Almost empty. The gauge had to be wrong. She and Alan had both checked her tank in the boat. It was full then. And they'd not been diving that long—certainly not long enough for her to have used up a full tank of air.

She tapped on the gauge with a gloved finger. The needle didn't move. Still red.

She carefully reached back behind her head with one hand to make sure the tank was fully open. Sometimes a not fully open tank would give a bad reading on a gauge. She turned the air valve in one direction and the flow of air stopped. Then she turned it in the other direction, fully opening the valve, and air flowed. She checked the gauge. Still red.

Rebecca looked up and saw that Alan had swum farther away from her, about thirty feet. And he was still moving. She fought down the panic and breathed out slowly: *one-two-three-four-five-six-seven-eight-nine-ten.*

Then in: *one-two-three-four-five-six-seven-eight-nine-ten.*

She had two choices.

She could try to ascend. If she did, she'd be abandoning Alan—leaving him at risk. She also had no idea if the air in her tank would get her to the surface. If it didn't, she'd have to make a "controlled emergency ascent." She remembered from her training what that meant. Possible decompression sickness. Possible pulmonary barotrauma—essentially her lungs exploding. And, of course, she could drown.

Her other option was to get Alan's attention and return to the surface using his backup regulator—an "alternate air source ascent."

She had to choose quickly. Given her options, Rebecca decided she had to get to Alan. She frog-kicked gently, trying not to accelerate her heart rate or breathing, conserving air, swimming down deeper into the cold sea after her husband. As she swam after him, she removed her dive knife from its sheath and used the metal ball on the end of the hilt to bang on her tank, making a high-pitched metallic *clink clink clink* hoping to get Alan's attention.

Alan continued to descend. He was too far away to hear her. She was still breathing. She still had air.

But her brain began to work against her. Fear gripped her

throat like a noose slowly tightening. As Rebecca swam deeper into the sea, the ocean began to collapse in on her. Tunnel vision. Panic began to rise in her belly. She felt boxed in.

Trapped.

She fought the fear, trying to keep her breathing slow. Kicking gently, trying to get to her husband. He had air. He was only thirty feet away.

Life was only thirty feet away.

She began to feel desperation. To lose hope.

Is this it?

Is this how I die?

Alan didn't hear the continued and more desperately rapid *clinking* of her knife on her tank. He wasn't turning. He was swimming deeper, and she was barely gaining on him. She began to kick harder, knowing that her heart rate would increase. And her breathing as well. She had to get to him. He was still too far away.

Rebecca kicked and breathed.

Kicked and breathed.

Kicked and…

…she breathed in, and three quarters of the way through the breath she hit a wall—it was like she was sucking on a rubber hose that was closed at one end. There was nothing. She was out of air.

She couldn't fight the panic any longer.

Sheer panic.

The feeling of being closed-in, of paralysis, of heart-racing suffocating hopelessness hit Rebecca Forsyth like a brick wall.

The Talion Series

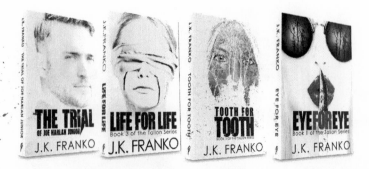

What would YOU do if someone hurt the one you love?

the shocking new book series from J.K. Franko

If you enjoyed

TOOTH FOR TOOTH

Book 2 of the Talion Series

**Please leave an Amazon review
so that others may enjoy it also.**

To find out more about J.K. Franko, the Talion series and
for access to exclusive additional content, register now at
J.K.'s official website.

www.jkfranko.com